·+· THE ·+·
GREAT
ALONE

—+·❈·+—

Also by Kristin Hannah

The Nightingale
Fly Away
Home Front
Night Road
Winter Garden
True Colours
Firefly Lane
Magic Hour
Comfort and Joy
The Things We Do for Love
Between Sisters
Distant Shores
Summer Island
Angel Falls
On Mystic Lake
Home Again
Waiting for the Moon
When Lightning Strikes
If You Believe
Once in Every Life
The Enchantment
A Handful of Heaven

THE
GREAT
ALONE

Kristin Hannah

MACMILLAN

First published 2018 by St Martin's Press, New York

First published in the UK 2018 by Macmillan
an imprint of Pan Macmillan
20 New Wharf Road, London N1 9RR
Associated companies throughout the world
www.panmacmillan.com

ISBN 978-1-4472-8602-8

1 3 5 7 9 8 6 4 2

A CIP catalogue record for this book is available from the British Library.

Printed and bound by CPI Group (UK) Ltd, Croydon, CR0 4YY

Visit **www.panmacmillan.com** to read more about all our books
and to buy them. You will also find features, author interviews and
news of any author events, and you can sign up for e-newsletters
so that you're always first to hear about our new releases.

To the women in my family. All of them are warriors.

Sharon, Debbie, Laura, Julie, Mackenzie, Sara, Kaylee, Toni, Jacquie,

Dana, Leslie, Katie, Joan, Jerrie, Liz, Courtney, and Stephanie.

And to Braden, our newest adventurer.

Nature never deceives us;
it is always we who deceive ourselves.

—Jean-Jacques Rousseau

1974

ONE

That spring, rain fell in great sweeping gusts that rattled the rooftops. Water found its way into the smallest cracks and undermined the sturdiest foundations. Chunks of land that had been steady for generations fell like slag heaps on the roads below, taking houses and cars and swimming pools down with them. Trees fell over, crashed into power lines; electricity was lost. Rivers flooded their banks, washed across yards, ruined homes. People who loved each other snapped and fights erupted as the water rose and the rain continued.

Leni felt edgy, too. She was the new girl at school, just a face in the crowd; a girl with long hair, parted in the middle, who had no friends and walked to school alone.

Now she sat on her bed, with her skinny legs drawn up to her flat chest, a dog-eared paperback copy of *Watership Down* open beside her. Through the thin walls of the rambler, she heard her mother say, *Ernt, baby, please don't. Listen* . . . and her father's angry *leave me the hell alone.*

They were at it again. Arguing. Shouting.

Soon there would be crying.

Weather like this brought out the darkness in her father.

Leni glanced at the clock by her bed. If she didn't leave right now, she was going to be late for school, and the only thing worse than being the new girl in junior high was drawing attention to yourself. She had learned this fact the hard way; in the last four years, she'd gone to five schools. Not once had she found a way to truly fit in, but she remained stubbornly hopeful. She took a deep breath, unfolded, and slid off the twin bed. Moving cautiously through her bare room, she went down the hall, paused at the kitchen doorway.

"Damn it, Cora," Dad said. "You know how hard it is on me."

Mama took a step toward him, reached out. "You need help, baby. It's not your fault. The nightmares—"

Leni cleared her throat to get their attention. "Hey," she said.

Dad saw her and took a step back from Mama. Leni saw how tired he looked, how defeated.

"I—I have to go to school," Leni said.

Mama reached into the breast pocket of her pink waitress uniform and pulled out her cigarettes. She looked tired; she'd worked the late shift last night and had the lunch shift today. "You go on, Leni. You don't want to be late." Her voice was calm and soft, as delicate as she was.

Leni was afraid to stay and afraid to leave. It was strange—stupid, even—but she often felt like the only adult in her family, as if she were the ballast that kept the creaky Allbright boat on an even keel. Mama was engaged in a continual quest to "find" herself. In the past few years, she'd tried EST and the human potential movement, spiritual training, Unitarianism. Even Buddhism. She'd cycled through them all, cherry-picked pieces and bits. Mostly, Leni thought, Mama had come away with T-shirts and sayings. Things like, *What is, is, and what isn't, isn't.* None of it seemed to amount to much.

"Go," Dad said.

Leni grabbed her backpack from the chair by the kitchen table and headed for the front door. As it slammed shut behind her, she heard them start up again.

Damn it, Cora—

Please, Ernt, just listen—

It hadn't always been this way. At least that's what Mama said. Before the war, they'd been happy, back when they'd lived in a trailer park in Kent and Dad had had a good job as a mechanic and Mama had laughed all of the time and danced to "Piece of My Heart" while she made dinner. (Mama dancing was really all Leni remembered about those years.)

Then Dad went off to Vietnam and got shot down and captured. Without him, Mama fell apart; that was when Leni first understood her mother's fragility. They drifted for a while, she and Mama, moved from job to job and town to town until they finally found a home in a commune in Oregon. There, they tended beehives and made lavender sachets to sell at the farmers' market and protested the war. Mama changed her personality just enough to fit in.

When Dad had finally come home, Leni barely recognized him. The handsome, laughing man of her memory had become moody, quick to anger, and distant. He hated everything about the commune, it seemed, and so they moved. Then they moved again. And again. Nothing ever worked out the way he wanted.

He couldn't sleep and couldn't keep a job, even though Mama swore he was the best mechanic ever.

That was what he and Mama were fighting about this morning: Dad getting fired again.

Leni flipped up her hood. On her way to school, she walked through blocks of well-tended homes, bypassed a dark woods (stay away from there), passed the A&W where the high school kids hung out on weekends, and a gas station, where a line of cars waited to fill up for fifty-five cents a gallon. That was something everyone was angry about these days—gas prices.

As far as Leni could tell, adults were edgy in general, and no wonder. The war in Vietnam had divided the country. Newspapers blared bad news daily: bombings by Weatherman or the IRA; planes being hijacked; the kidnapping of Patty Hearst. The massacre at the Munich Olympics had stunned the whole world, as had the Watergate scandal. And recently, college girls in Washington State had begun to disappear without a trace. It was a dangerous world.

She would give anything for a real friend right now. It was all she really wanted: someone to talk to.

On the other hand, it didn't help to talk about her worries. What was the point of confession?

Sure, Dad lost his temper sometimes and he yelled and they never had enough money and they moved all the time to distance themselves from creditors, but that was their way, and they loved each other.

But sometimes, especially on days like today, Leni was afraid. It felt to her as if her family stood poised on the edge of a great precipice that could collapse at any second, crumble away like the houses that crashed down Seattle's unstable, waterlogged hillsides.

✦⟨❁⟩✦

AFTER SCHOOL, Leni walked home in the rain, alone.

Her house sat in the middle of a cul-de-sac, on a yard less tended than the rest: a bark-brown rambler with empty flower boxes and clogged gutters and a garage door that didn't close. Weeds grew in clumps from the decaying gray roof shingles. An empty flagpole pointed accusingly upward, a statement about her father's hatred of where this country was headed. For a man whom Mama called a patriot, he sure hated his government.

She saw Dad in the garage, sitting on a slanted workbench beside Mama's dented-up Mustang with the duct-taped top. Cardboard boxes lined the interior walls, full of stuff they hadn't yet unpacked from the last move.

He was dressed—as usual—in his frayed military jacket and torn Levi's. He sat slouched forward, his elbows resting on his thighs. His long black hair was a tangled mess and his mustache needed trimming. His dirty feet were bare. Even slumped over and tired-looking, he was movie-star handsome. Everyone thought so.

He cocked his head, peered at her through his hair. The smile he gave her was a little worn around the edges, but it still lit up his face. That was the thing about her dad: he might be moody and sharp-tempered, even a little scary sometimes, but that was just because he felt things like love and loss and disappointment so keenly. Love most of all. "Lenora," he said in that scratchy, cigarette-smoker voice of his. "I was waiting for you. I'm sorry. I lost my temper. And my job. You must be disappointed as hell in me."

"No, Dad."

She knew how sorry he was. She could see it on his face. When she was younger, she'd sometimes wondered what good all those sorries were if nothing ever changed, but Mama had explained it to her. The war and captivity had snapped something in him. *It's like his back is broken*, Mama had said, *and you don't stop loving a person when they're hurt. You get stronger so they can lean on you. He needs me. Us.*

Leni sat down beside him. He put an arm around her, pulled her in close. "The world is being run by lunatics. It's not my America anymore. I want . . ." He didn't finish, and Leni didn't say anything. She was used to her dad's sadness, his frustration. He stopped sentences halfway through all the time, as if he were afraid of giving voice to scary or depressing thoughts. Leni knew about that reticence and understood it; lots of times it was better to stay silent.

He reached into his pocket, pulled out a mostly crushed pack of cigarettes. He lit one up and she drew in the acrid, familiar scent.

She knew how much pain he was in. Sometimes she woke up to her dad crying and her mama trying to soothe him, saying stuff like, *Shhh, now, Ernt, it's over now, you're home safe.*

He shook his head, exhaled a stream of blue-gray smoke. "I just want . . . more, I guess. Not a job. A life. I want to walk down the street and not have to worry about being called a baby-killer. I want . . ." He sighed. Smiled. "Don't worry. It'll all be okay. We'll be okay."

"You'll get another job, Dad," she said.

"Sure I will, Red. Tomorrow will be better."

That was what her parents always said.

❖

ON A COLD, BLEAK MORNING in mid-April, Leni got up early and staked out her place on the ratty floral sofa in the living room and turned on the *Today* show. She adjusted the rabbit ears to get a decent picture. When it popped into focus, Barbara Walters was saying ". . . Patricia Hearst, now calling herself Tania, seen here in this photograph holding an M1 carbine at the recent bank robbery in San Francisco. Eyewitnesses report that the nineteen-year-old heiress, who was kidnapped by the Symbionese Liberation Army in February . . ."

Leni was spellbound. She still couldn't believe that an *army* could march in and take a teenager from her apartment. How could anyone be safe anywhere in a world like that? And how did a rich teenager become a revolutionary named Tania?

"Come on, Leni," Mama said from the kitchen. "Get ready for school."

The front door banged open.

Dad came into the house, smiling in a way that made it impossible not to smile back. He looked out of scale, larger than life in the low-ceilinged kitchen, vibrant against the water-marked gray walls. Water dripped from his hair.

Mama stood at the stove, frying bacon for breakfast.

Dad swept into the kitchen and cranked up the transistor radio that sat on the Formica counter. A scratchy rock 'n' roll song came through. Dad laughed and pulled Mama into his arms.

Leni heard his whispered "I'm sorry. Forgive me."

"Always," Mama said, holding him as if she were afraid he'd push her away.

Dad kept his arm around Mama's waist and pulled her over to the kitchen table. He pulled out a chair, said, "Leni, come in here!"

Leni loved it when they included her. She left her spot on the sofa and took a seat beside her mother. Dad smiled down at Leni and handed her a paperback book. *The Call of the Wild.* "You'll love this, Red."

He sat down across from Mama, scooted in close to the table. He was wearing what Leni thought of as his Big Idea smile. She'd seen it before, whenever he had a plan to change their lives. And he'd had a lot of plans: Selling everything and camping for a year as they drove the Big Sur highway. Raising mink (what a horror *that* had been). Selling American Seed packets in Central California.

He reached into his pocket, pulled out a folded-up piece of paper, slapped it triumphantly on the table. "You remember my friend Bo Harlan?"

Mama took a moment to answer. "From 'Nam?"

Dad nodded. To Leni, he said, "Bo Harlan was the crew chief and I was the door gunner. We looked out for each other. We were together when our bird went down and we got captured. We went through hell together."

Leni noticed how he was shaking. His shirtsleeves were rolled up, so she could see the burn scars that ran from his wrist to his elbow in ridges of puckered, disfigured skin that never tanned. Leni didn't know what had caused his scars—he never said and she never asked—but his captors had done it. She had figured out that much. The scars covered his back, too, pulled the skin into swirls and puckers.

"They made me watch him die," he said.

Leni looked worriedly at Mama. Dad had never said this before. To hear the words now unsettled them.

He tapped his foot on the floor, played a beat on the table with fast-moving fingers. He unfolded the letter, smoothed it out, and turned it so they could read the words.

Sergeant Allbright—

You are a hard man to find. I am Earl Harlan.

My son, Bo, wrote many letters home about his friendship with you. I thank you for that.

In his last letter, he told me that if anything happened to him in that piece of shit place, he wanted you to have his land up here in Alaska.

It isn't much. Forty acres with a cabin that needs fixing. But a hardworking man can live off the land up here, away from the crazies and the hippies and the mess in the Lower Forty-eight.

I don't have no phone, but you can write me c/o the Homer Post Office. I'll get the letter sooner or later.

The land is at the end of the road, past the silver gate with a cow skull and just before the burnt tree, at mile marker 13.

Thanks again,

Earl

Mama looked up. She cocked her head, gave a little birdlike tilt as she studied Dad. "This man . . . Bo, has given us a house? A *house?*"

"Think of it," Dad said, lifted out of his seat by enthusiasm. "A house that's *ours*. That we *own*. In a place where we can be self-sufficient, grow our vegetables, hunt our meat, and be free. We've dreamed of it for years, Cora. Living a simpler life away from all the bullshit down here. We could be free. Think of it."

"Wait," Leni said. Even for Dad, this was big. "Alaska? You want to move again? We just moved here."

Mama frowned. "But . . . there's nothing up there, is there? Just bears and Eskimos."

He pulled Mama to her feet with an eagerness that made her stumble, fall into him. Leni saw the desperate edge of his enthusiasm. "I need this, Cora. I need a place where I can breathe again. Sometimes I feel like I'm going to crawl out of my skin. Up there, the flashbacks and shit will stop. I know it. *We* need this. We can go back to the way things were before 'Nam screwed me up."

Mama lifted her face to Dad's, her pallor a sharp contrast to his dark hair and tanned skin.

"Come on, baby," Dad said. "Imagine it . . ."

Leni saw Mama softening, reshaping her needs to match his, imagining this new personality: Alaskan. Maybe she thought it was like EST or yoga or Buddhism. The answer. Where or when or what didn't matter to Mama. All she cared about was him. "Our own house," she said. "But . . . money . . . you could apply for that military disability—"

"Not that discussion again," he said with a sigh. "I'm not doing that. A change is all I need. And I'll be more careful with money from now on, Cora. I swear. I still have a little of the bread I inherited from the old man. And I'll cut back on drinking. I'll go to that veterans' support-group thing you want me to."

Leni had seen all of this before. Ultimately, it didn't matter what she or Mama wanted.

Dad wanted a new beginning. Needed it. And Mama needed him to be happy.

So they would try again in a new place, hoping geography would be the answer. They would go to Alaska in search of this new dream. Leni would do as she was asked and do it with a good attitude. She would be the new girl in school *again*. Because that was what love was.

TWO

The next morning, Leni lay in her bed, listening to rain patter the roof, imagining the emergence of mushrooms beneath her window, their bulbous, poisonous tops pushing up through the mud, glistening temptingly. She had lain awake long past midnight, reading about the vast landscape of Alaska. It had captivated her in an unexpected way. The last frontier was like her dad, it seemed. Larger than life. Expansive. A little dangerous.

She heard music—a tinny, transistor melody. "Hooked on a Feeling." She threw back the covers and got out of bed. In the kitchen, she found her mother standing in front of the stove, smoking a cigarette. She looked ethereal in the lamplight, her shag-cut blond hair still messy from sleep, her face veiled in blue-gray smoke. She was wearing a white tank top that had been washed so often it hung on her slim body, and a pair of hot-pink panties with a sagging elastic waist. A small purple bruise at the base of her throat was strangely beautiful, a starburst almost, highlighting the delicateness of her features.

"You should be sleeping," Mama said. "It's early."

Leni came up beside her mother, rested her head on her shoulder. Mama's skin smelled of rose perfume and cigarettes. "We don't sleep," Leni said.

We don't sleep. It was what Mama always said. You and me. The connection between them a constant, a comfort, as if similarity reinforced the love between them. Certainly it was true that Mama had had trouble sleeping since Dad had come home. Whenever Leni woke in the middle of the night, she invariably found her mother drifting through the house, her diaphanous robe trailing open. In the dark, Mama tended to talk to herself in a whisper, saying words Leni could never quite make out.

"Are we really going?" Leni asked.

Mama stared at the black coffee percolating in the little glass cap at the top of the metal pot. "I guess so."

"When?"

"You know your dad. Soon."

"Will I get to finish the school year?"

Mama shrugged.

"Where is he?"

"He went out before dawn to sell the coin collection he inherited from his dad." Mama poured herself a cup of coffee and took a sip, then set the mug down on the Formica counter. "Alaska. Christ. Why not Siberia?" She took a long drag on her cigarette. Exhaled. "I need a girlfriend to talk to."

"I'm your friend."

"You're thirteen. I'm thirty. I'm supposed to be a *mother* to you. I need to remember that."

Leni heard the despair in her mother's voice and it frightened her. She knew how fragile it all was: her family, her parents. One thing every child of a POW knew was how easily people could be broken. Leni still wore the shiny silver POW bracelet in memory of a captain who hadn't come home to his family.

"He needs a chance. A new start. We all do. Maybe Alaska is the answer."

"Like Oregon was the answer, and Snohomish, and the seed packets that would make us rich. And don't forget the year he thought he could make a fortune in pinball machines. Can we at least wait until the end of the school year?"

Mama sighed. "I don't think so. Now go get dressed for school."

"There's no school today."

Mama was silent for a long time, then said quietly, "You remember the blue dress Dad bought you for your birthday?"

"Yeah."

"Put it on."

"Why?"

"Shoo. Get dressed now. You and I have things to do today."

Although she was irritated and confused, Leni did as she was told. She always did as she was told. It made life easier. She went into her room and burrowed through her closet until she found the dress.

You'll look pretty as a picture in this, Red.

Except that she wouldn't. She knew exactly what she'd look like: a spindly, flat-chested thirteen-year-old in a dowdy dress that revealed her scrawny thighs and made her knees look like doorknobs. A girl who was supposed to be standing on the cusp of womanhood, but clearly wasn't. She was pretty sure she was the only girl in her grade who hadn't started her period or sprouted boobs yet.

She returned to the empty kitchen, which smelled of coffee and cigarette smoke, and flopped into a chair and opened *The Call of the Wild*.

Mama didn't come out of her room for an hour.

Leni hardly recognized her. She had teased and sprayed her blond hair back into a tiny bun; she wore a fitted, buttoned-up, belted avocado-green dress that covered her from throat to wrists to knees. And nylons. And old-lady shoes. "Holy cow."

"Yeah, yeah," Mama said, lighting up a cigarette. "I look like a PTA bake-sale organizer." The blue cream eye shadow she wore had a little sparkle in it. She'd glued her false eyelashes on with a slightly unsteady hand and her eyeliner was thicker than usual. "Are those your only shoes?"

Leni looked down at the spatula-shaped Earth Shoes that lifted her toes the slightest bit above her heels. She had begged and begged for these shoes after Joanne Berkowitz got a pair and everyone in class oohed and aahed. "I have my red tennis shoes, but the laces broke yesterday."

"Okay. Whatever. Let's go."

Leni followed her mother out of the house. They both climbed into the ripped-up red seats of their dented, primer-painted Mustang. The trunk was kept shut by bright yellow bungee cords.

Mama flipped down the visor and checked her makeup in the mirror. (Leni was convinced that the key wouldn't turn in the ignition if her mother didn't check her reflection and light up a cigarette.) She applied fresh lipstick, rolled her lips, and used the triangle tip of her cuff to wipe an invisible imperfection away. When she was finally satisfied, she flipped the visor back up and started the engine. The radio came on, blaring "Midnight at the Oasis."

"Did you know there are a hundred ways to die in Alaska?" Leni asked. "You can fall down a mountainside, or through thin ice. You can freeze or starve. You can even be *eaten*."

"Your father should not have given you that book." Mama popped a tape into the player and Carole King's voice took over. *I feel the earth move . . .*

Mama started singing and Leni joined in. For a beautiful few minutes, they were doing something ordinary, driving down I-5 toward downtown Seattle, Mama changing lanes whenever a car appeared in front of her, a cigarette captured between two fingers of the hand on the steering wheel.

Two blocks later, Mama pulled up in front of the bank. Parked. She checked her makeup again and said, "Stay here," and got out of the car.

Leni leaned over and locked the car door. She watched her mother walk to the front door. Only Mama didn't really walk; she sashayed, her hips moving gently from side to side. She was a beautiful woman and she knew it. That was another thing Mama and Dad fought about. The way men looked at Mama. He hated it, but Leni knew Mama liked the attention (although she was careful never to admit it).

Fifteen minutes later, when Mama came out of the bank, she was not sashaying. She was marching, with her hands balled into fists. She looked mad. Her delicate jaw was clenched tightly. "Son of a *bitch*," she said as she yanked open her door and got into the car. She said it again as she slammed the door shut.

"What?" Leni said.

"Your dad cleared out our savings account. And they won't give me a credit card unless your father or *my* father cosigns." She lit up a cigarette. "Sweet Jesus, it's 1974. I have a job. I make money. And a woman can't get a credit card without a man's signature. It's a man's world, baby girl." She started the car and sped down the street, turning onto the freeway.

Leni had trouble staying in her seat with all of the lane changes; she kept sliding side to side. She was so focused on staying steady that it was another few miles before she realized they had passed the hills of downtown Seattle and were now driving through a quiet, tree-lined neighborhood of stately homes. "Holy moly," Leni said under her breath. Leni hadn't been on this street for years. So many that she'd almost forgotten it.

The houses on this street oozed privilege. Brand-new Cadillacs and Toronados and Lincoln Continentals were parked on cement driveways.

Mama parked in front of a large house made of rough gray stone with diamond-patterned windows. It sat on a small rise of manicured lawn, bordered on all sides by meticulously maintained flower beds. The mailbox read: Golliher.

"Wow. We haven't been here in years," Leni said.

"I know. You stay here."

"No way. Another girl disappeared this month. I'm not staying out here alone."

"Come here," Mama said, pulling a brush and two pink ribbons out of her purse. She yanked Leni close and attacked her long, copper-red hair as if it had offended her. "Ow!" Leni yelped as Mama braided it into pigtails that arced out like spigots from each side of Leni's head.

"You are a listener today, Lenora," Mama said, tying bows at the end of each pigtail.

"I'm too old for pigtails," Leni complained.

"Listener," Mama said again. "Bring your book and sit quietly and let the adults talk." She opened her door and got out of the car. Leni rushed to meet her on the sidewalk.

Mama grabbed Leni's hand and pulled her onto a walkway lined with sculpted hedges and up to a large wooden front door.

Mama glanced at Leni, muttered, "Here goes nothing," and rang the bell. It made a deep clanging sound, like church bells, after which came the sound of muffled footsteps.

Moments later, Leni's grandmother opened the door. In an eggplant-colored dress, with a slim belt at her waist and three strands of pearls around her throat, she looked ready for lunch with the governor. Her chestnut-colored hair was coiled and shellacked like one of those holiday bread loaves. Her heavily made-up eyes widened. "Coraline," she whispered, coming forward, opening her arms.

"Is Dad here?" Mama asked.

Grandmother pulled back, let her arms drop to her sides. "He's in court today."

Mama nodded. "Can we come in?"

Leni saw how the question upset her grandmother; wrinkles settled in waves across her pale, powdered brow. "Of course. And Lenora. How lovely to see you again."

Grandmother stepped back into the shadows. She led them through a foyer, beyond which were rooms and doorways and a staircase that swirled up to a shadowy second floor.

The home smelled like lemon wax and flowers.

She led them into an enclosed back porch with curved glass windows and giant glass doors and plants everywhere. The furniture was all white wicker. Leni was assigned a seat at a small table overlooking the garden outside.

"How I have missed you both," Grandmother said. Then, as if upset by her own admission, she turned and walked away, returning a few moments later, carrying a book. "I remember how much you love to read. Why, even at two, you always had a book in your hands. I bought this for you years ago but . . . I didn't know where to send it. She has red hair, too."

Leni sat down and took the book, which she had read so often she had whole passages memorized. *Pippi Longstocking*. A book for much younger girls. Leni had moved on long ago. "Thank you, ma'am."

"Call me Grandma. Please," she said quietly; there was a tinge of longing in her voice. Then she turned her attention to Mama.

Grandma showed Mama to a white ironwork table over by one window. In a gilded cage nearby, a pair of white birds cooed at each other. Leni thought they must be sad, those birds who couldn't fly.

"I'm surprised you let me in," Mama said, taking a seat.

"Don't be impertinent, Coraline. You're always welcome. Your father and I love you."

"It's my husband you wouldn't allow in."

"He turned you against us. And all of your friends, I might add. He wanted you all to him—"

"I don't want to talk about all of that again. We're moving to Alaska."

Grandma sat down. "Oh, for the love of Pete."

"Ernt has inherited a house and a piece of land. We're going to grow our own vegetables and hunt our meat and live by our own rules. We'll be pure. Pioneers."

"Stop. I can't listen to this nonsense. You're going to follow him to the ends of the earth, where no one will be able to help you. Your father and I tried so hard to protect you from your mistakes, but you refuse to be helped, don't you? You think that life is some game. You just flit—"

"Don't," Mama said sharply. She leaned forward. "Do you know how hard it was for me to come here?"

In the wake of those words, a silence fell, broken only by a bird's cooing.

It felt as if a cold breeze had just come through. Leni would have sworn the expensive transparent curtains fluttered, but there were no open windows.

Leni tried to imagine her mother in this buttoned-down, closed-up world, but she couldn't. The chasm between the girl Mama had been raised to be and the woman she had become seemed impossible to cross. Leni wondered if all those protests she and Mama had marched in while Dad was gone—against nuclear energy, the war—and all those EST seminars and the

different religions Mama had tried on, were really just Mama's way of pro-
testing the woman she'd been raised to be.

"Don't do this crazy, dangerous thing, Coraline. Leave him. Come home.
Be safe."

"I love him, Mother. Can't you understand that?"

"Cora," Grandma said softly. "Listen to me, please. You know he's
dangerous—"

"We're going to Alaska," Mama said firmly. "I came to say goodbye
and . . ." Her voice trailed off. "Are you going to help us or not?"

For a long moment Grandma said nothing, just crossed and uncrossed
her arms. "How much do you need this time?" she finally asked.

✦⟨❀⟩✦

ON THE DRIVE HOME, her mother chain-smoked. She kept the radio volume so high that conversation was impossible. It was just as well, really,
because although Leni had a string of questions, she didn't know where to
begin. Today she had glimpsed a world that lay beneath the surface of her
own. Mama had never said much to Leni about her life before marriage. She
and Dad had run off together; theirs was a beautiful, romantic story of
love against all odds. Mama had quit high school and "lived on love." That
was how she always put it, the fairy tale. Now Leni was old enough to know
that like all fairy tales, theirs was filled with thickets and dark places and
broken dreams, and runaway girls.

Mama was obviously angry with her mother, and yet she'd gone to her
for help and hadn't even had to ask for money to receive it. Leni couldn't
make sense of it, but it unsettled her. How could a mother and daughter fall
so far apart?

Mama turned into their driveway and shut off the engine. The radio
snapped off, leaving them in silence.

"We are not going to tell your father I got money from my mother,"
Mama said. "He's a proud man."

"But—"

"This is not a discussion, Leni. You are not to tell your father." Mama opened her car door and got out, slamming it shut behind her.

Confused by her mother's unexpected edict, Leni followed her across the squishy, muddy grass in the front yard, past the Volkswagen-sized juniper bushes that climbed raggedly over one another, to the front door.

Inside the house, her father sat at the kitchen table with maps and books spread out in front of him. He was drinking Coke from a bottle.

At their entrance, he looked up and smiled broadly. "I've figured out our route. We will drive up through B.C. and the Yukon Territory. It's about twenty-four hundred miles. Mark your calendars, ladies: in four days, our new life begins."

"But school isn't finished—" Leni said.

"Who cares about school? This is a real education, Leni," Dad said. He looked at Mama. "I sold my GTO and my coin collection and my guitar. We have a little cash. We'll trade in your Mustang for a VW bus, but man, we could sure use more bread."

Leni glanced sideways, caught Mama's eye.

Don't tell him.

It didn't feel right. Wasn't lying always wrong? And an omission like this was obviously a lie.

Even so, Leni remained quiet. She never considered defying her mother. In this whole big world—and with the specter of their move to Alaska, it had just tripled in size—Mama was Leni's one true thing.

THREE

L eni, baby, sit up. We're almost there!"

She blinked awake; at first all she saw was her own potato-chip-crumb-dusted lap. Beside her lay an old newspaper, covered in candy wrappers, and her paperback copy of *The Fellowship of the Ring*. It was propped up like a pup tent, yellowed pages splayed out. Her most treasured possession, her Polaroid camera, hung from a strap around her neck.

It had been an amazing trip north on the mostly unpaved ALCAN Highway. Their first true family vacation. Days driving in bright sunlight; nights spent camping beside raging rivers and quiet streams, in the shadows of saw-blade mountain peaks, huddled around a fire, spinning dreams of a future that felt closer every day. They roasted hot dogs for dinner and made s'mores for dessert and shared dreams about what they would discover at the end of the road. Leni had never seen her parents so happy. Her dad most of all. He laughed, he smiled, he told jokes and promised them the moon. He was the dad she remembered from Before.

Usually, on road trips, Leni kept her nose buried in a book, but on this trip the scenery had often demanded her attention, especially through the gorgeous mountains of British Columbia. In the ever-changing landscape, she sat in the backseat of the bus, imagining herself as Frodo or Bilbo, the hero of her own quest.

The VW bus thumped over something—a curb, maybe—and stuff went flying inside, dropped to the floor, rolled into the backpacks and boxes that filled the back of the bus. They screeched to a halt that smelled of burnt rubber and exhaust.

Sunlight streamed through the dirty, mosquito-splattered windows. Leni climbed over the heap of their poorly rolled sleeping bags and opened the side door. Their rainbow-decorated ALASKA OR BUST sign fluttered in the cool breeze, the sides anchored in place by duct tape.

Leni stepped out of the bus.

"We made it, Red." Dad came up beside her, laid a hand on her shoulder. "Land's End. Homer, Alaska. People come here from all over to stock up on supplies. It's kind of the last outpost of civilization. They say it's where the land ends and the sea begins."

"Wow," Mama said.

Even with all the pictures Leni had studied and all the articles and books she'd read, she hadn't been prepared for the wild, spectacular beauty of Alaska. It was otherworldly somehow, magical in its vast expanse, an incomparable landscape of soaring glacier-filled white mountains that ran the length of the horizon, knife-tip points pressed high into a cloudless cornflower-blue sky. Kachemak Bay was a sheet of hammered sterling in the sunlight. Boats dotted the bay. The air smelled briny, deeply of the sea. Shorebirds floated on the wind, dipped and rose effortlessly.

The famous Homer Spit she'd read about was a four-and-a-half-mile-long finger of land that crooked into the bay. A few colorful shacks perched on stilts at the water's edge.

Leni lifted her Polaroid, took pictures as fast as the developer would let her. She peeled one photograph after another out of the camera, watched the images develop in front of her eyes. The buildings sketched themselves onto the shiny white paper line by line.

"Our land is over there," Dad said, pointing across Kachemak Bay to a necklace of lush green humps in the hazy distance. "Our new home. Even though it's on the Kenai Peninsula, there are no roads to it. Massive glaciers and mountains cut Kaneq off from the mainland. So we have to fly or boat in."

Mama moved in beside Leni. In her low-waisted bell-bottom jeans and lace-edged tank top, with her pale face and blond hair, she looked as if she'd been sculpted from the cool colors of this place, an angel alighted on a shore that waited for her. Even her laugh seemed at home here, an echo of the bells that tinkled from wind chimes in front of the shops. A cool breeze molded her top to her braless breasts. "What do you think, baby girl?"

"It's cool," Leni said. She clicked another picture, but no ink and paper could capture the grandeur of that mountain range.

Dad turned to them, smiling so big it crinkled his face. "The ferry to Kaneq is tomorrow. So let's go sightseeing a little and then get a campsite on the beach and walk around. What do you say?"

"Yay!" Leni and Mama said together.

As they drove away from the Spit and up through the town, Leni pressed her nose to the glass and stared out. The homes were an eclectic mix—big houses with shiny windows stood next to lean-tos made livable with plastic and duct tape. There were A-frames and shacks and mobile homes and trailers. Buses parked by the side of the road had curtained windows and chairs set out front. Some yards were manicured and fenced. Others were heaped with rusty junk and abandoned cars and old appliances. Most were unfinished in some way or another. Businesses operated in everything from a rusted old Airstream trailer to a brand-new log building to a roadside shack. The place was a little wild, but didn't feel as foreign and remote as she'd imagined.

Dad cranked up the radio as they turned toward a long gray beach. The tires sank into the sand; it slowed them down. All up and down the beach there were vehicles parked—trucks and vans and cars. People obviously lived on this beach in whatever shelter they could find—tents, broken-down cars, shacks built of driftwood and tarps. "They're called Spit rats," Dad said, looking for a parking place. "They work in the canneries on the Spit and for charter operators."

He maneuvered into a spot between a mud-splattered Econoline van with Nebraska license plates and a lime-green Gremlin with duct-tape-and-cardboard windows. They set up their tent on the sand, tying it to the bus's bumper. The sea-scented wind was insistent down here.

The surf made a quiet shushing sound as it rolled forward and drew back. All around them people were enjoying the day, throwing Frisbees to dogs and building bonfires in the sand and putting boats in the water. The chatter of human voices felt small and transient in the bigness of the world here.

They spent the day as tourists, drifting from place to place. Mama and Dad bought beers at the Salty Dawg Saloon, while Leni bought an ice-cream cone from a shack on the Spit. Then they dug through bins at the Salvation Army until they found rubber boots in all of their sizes. Leni bought fifteen old books (most of them damaged and water-stained in some way) for fifty cents. Dad bought a kite to fly at the beach, while Mama slipped Leni some cash and said, "Get yourself some film, baby girl."

At a little restaurant at the very end of the Spit, they gathered at a picnic table and ate Dungeness crab; Leni fell in love with the sweet, salty taste of the white crabmeat dunked in melted butter. Seagulls cawed to them, floated overhead, eyeing their fries and French bread.

Leni couldn't remember a better day. A bright future had never seemed so close.

The next morning, they drove the bus onto the hulky *Tustamena* ferry (called *Tusty* by the locals) that was a part of the Alaska Marine Highway. The stout old ship serviced remote towns like Homer, Kaneq, Seldovia, Dutch Harbor, Kodiak, and the wild Aleutian Islands. As soon as the bus was parked in its lane, the three of them rushed out onto the deck and headed to the railing. The area was crowded with people, mostly men with long hair and bushy beards, wearing trucker's caps and plaid flannel shirts, puffy down

vests and dirty jeans tucked into brown rubber boots. There were a few
college-aged hippies here, too, recognizable by their backpacks, tie-dyed
shirts, and sandals.

The ferry eased away from the dock, belching smoke. Almost immediately Leni saw that the water in Kachemak Bay wasn't as calm as it had
looked from the safety of the shore. Out here, the sea was wild and white-
tipped. Waves roiled and splashed the sides of the boat. It was beautiful,
magical, wild. She took at least a dozen pictures and tucked them into her
pocket.

A pod of orcas surfaced from the waves; seals peered at them from the
rocks. Otters fed in kelp beds along the rough shores.

Finally, the ferry turned, chugged around an emerald-green mound of
land that protected them from the wind that barreled across the bay. Lush
islands with tree-tossed rocky shores welcomed them into their calm waters.

"Kaneq coming up!" came over the loudspeaker. "Next stop, Seldovia!"

"Come on, Allbrights. Back to the bus!" Dad said, laughing. They maneuvered through the line of cars, found their way back to the bus, and
climbed in.

"I can't wait to see our new home," Mama said.

The ferry docked and they drove off the boat and uphill onto a wide dirt
road that cut through a forest. At the crest of the hill stood a white clapboard
church with a blue-domed steeple topped with a three-slatted Russian cross.
Beside it was a small picket-fenced cemetery studded with wooden crosses.

They crested the hill, came down on the other side, and got their first
look at Kaneq.

"Wait," Leni said, peering out the dirty window. "This can't be it."

She saw trailers parked on grass, with chairs out front, and houses that
would have been called shacks back in Washington. In front of one of the
shacks, three scrawny dogs were chained up; all three stood on top of their
weathered doghouses, barking and yelping furiously. The grassy yard was
pitted with holes where the bored dogs dug.

"It's an old town with a remarkable history," Dad said. "Settled first by

Natives, then by Russian fur traders, and then taken over by adventurers looking for gold. An earthquake in 1964 hit the town so hard that the land dropped five feet in a second. Houses broke apart and fell into the sea."

Leni stared at the few ramshackle, paint-blistered buildings that were connected to one another by an aging boardwalk; the town was perched on pilings above mudflats. Beyond the mud was a harbor full of fishing boats. The main street was less than a block long, and unpaved.

To her left was a saloon called the Kicking Moose. The building was a charred, blackened husk; clearly the victim of a fire. Through the dirty glass window, she saw patrons inside. People drinking at ten A.M. on a Thursday in a burned-out shell of a building.

On the bay side of the street, she saw a closed-up boardinghouse that her dad said had probably been built for Russian fur traders over a hundred years ago. Next to it, a closet-sized diner called Fish On welcomed guests with an open door. Leni could see a few people huddled over a counter inside. A couple of old trucks were parked near the entrance to the harbor.

"Where's the school?" Leni said, feeling a spike of panic.

This was no town. An outpost, maybe. The kind of place one might have found on a wagon train headed west a hundred years ago, the kind of place where no one stayed. Would there be *any* kids her age here?

Dad pulled up in front of a narrow, pointy-roofed Victorian house that appeared to have once been blue and now only showed patches of that color here and there on the faded wood where paint had peeled away. In scrolled, gilt letters on the window were the words ASSAYER'S OFFICE. Someone had duct-taped a hand-lettered TRADING POST/GENERAL STORE sign beneath it. "Let's get directions, Allbrights."

Mama got out of the bus quickly, hurried toward the small civilization this store represented. As she opened the door, a bell tinkled overhead. Leni sidled in behind Mama, put a hand on her hip.

Sunlight came through the windows behind them, illuminating the front quarter of the store; beyond that, only a single shadeless overhead bulb offered light. The back of the store was full of shadows.

The interior smelled of old leather and whiskey and tobacco. The walls were covered in rows of shelving; Leni saw saws, axes, hoes, furry snow boots and rubber fishing boots, heaps of socks, boxes full of headlamps. Steel traps and loops of chain hung from every post. There were at least a dozen taxidermied animals sitting on shelves and counters. A giant king salmon was caught forever on a shiny wooden plaque as were moose heads, antlers, white animal skulls. There was even a stuffed red fox gathering dust in a corner. Off to the left side were food items: bags of potatoes and buckets of onions, stacked cans of salmon and crab and sardines, bags of rice and flour and sugar, canisters of Crisco, and her favorite: the snack aisle, where beautiful multicolored candy wrappers reminded her of home. Potato chips and snack-pack butterscotch puddings and boxes of cereal.

It looked like a store that would have welcomed Laura Ingalls Wilder.

"Customers!"

Leni heard the clapping of hands. A black woman with a large Afro emerged from the shadows. She was tall and broad-shouldered and so wide she had to turn sideways to get out from behind the polished wood counter. Tiny black moles dotted her face.

She came at them fast, bone bracelets clattering on her thick wrists. She was old: at least fifty. She wore a long patchwork denim skirt, mismatched wool socks, open-toed sandals, and a long blue shirt, unbuttoned to reveal a faded T-shirt. A sheathed knife rode the wide leather belt at her waist. "Welcome! I know, it seems disorganized and daunting, but I know where everything is, down to O-rings and triple-A batteries. Folks call me Large Marge, by the way," she said, holding out her hand.

"And you let them?" Mama asked, offering that beautiful smile of hers, the one that pulled people in and made them smile back. She shook the woman's hand.

Large Marge's laughter was loud and barking, like she couldn't get quite enough air. "I love a woman with a sense of humor. So, whom do I have the pleasure of meeting?"

"Cora Allbright," Mama said. "And this is my daughter, Leni."

"Welcome to Kaneq, ladies. We don't get many tourists."

Dad entered the store just in time to say, "We're locals, or about to be. We just arrived."

Large Marge's double chin tripled as she tucked it in. "Locals?"

Dad extended his hand. "Bo Harlan left me his place. We're here to stay."

"Well, hot damn. I'm your neighbor, Marge Birdsall, just a half mile down the road. There's a sign. Most folks around here live off the grid, in the bush, but we're lucky enough to be on a road. So do you have all the supplies you need? You guys can start an account here at the store if you want. Pay me in money or in trade. It's how we do it here."

"That's exactly the kind of life we came looking for," Dad said. "I'll admit, money's a little tight, so trade would be good. I'm a damn good mechanic. I can fix most any motor."

"Good to know. I'll spread the word."

Dad nodded. "Good. We could use some bacon. Maybe a little rice. And some whiskey."

"Over there," Large Marge said, pointing. "Behind the row of axes and hatchets."

Dad followed her direction back into the shadows of the store.

Large Marge turned to Mama, sweeping her from head to toe in a single assessing gaze. "I'm guessing this is your man's dream, Cora Allbright, and that you all came up here without a whole lot of planning."

Mama smiled. "We do everything on impulse, Large Marge. It keeps life exciting."

"Well. You'll need to be tough up here, Cora Allbright. For you and your daughter. You can't just count on your man. You need to be able to save yourself and this beautiful girl of yours."

"That's pretty dramatic," Mama said.

Large Marge bent down for a large cardboard box, dragged it across the floor toward her. She dug through it, her black fingers moving like a piano player's, until she pulled out two whistles on black straps. She placed one around each of their necks. "This is a bear whistle. You'll need it. Lesson number one: no walking quietly—or unarmed—in Alaska. Not this far out, not this time of year."

"Are you trying to scare us?" Mama asked.

"You bet your ass I am. Fear is common sense up here. A lot of folks come up here, Cora, with cameras and dreams of a simpler life. But five out of every one thousand Alaskans go missing every year. Just disappear. And most of the dreamers . . . well, they don't make it past the first winter. They can't wait to get back to the land of drive-in theaters and heat that comes on at the flip of a switch. And sunlight."

"You make it sound dangerous," Mama said uneasily.

"Two kinds of folks come up to Alaska, Cora. People running to something and people running away from something. The second kind—you want to keep your eye out for them. And it isn't just the people you need to watch out for, either. Alaska herself can be Sleeping Beauty one minute and a bitch with a sawed-off shotgun the next. There's a saying: Up here you can make one mistake. The second one will kill you."

Mama lit up a cigarette. Her hand was shaking. "As the welcoming committee, you leave something to be desired, Marge."

Large Marge laughed again. "You're right as rain about that, Cora. My social skills have gone to shit in the bush." She smiled, laid a hand comfortingly on Mama's thin shoulder. "Here's what you want to hear: We are a tight community here in Kaneq. There's less than thirty of us living on this part of the peninsula year-round, but we take care of our own. My land is close to yours. You need anything—anything—just pick up the ham radio. I'll come running."

⋆⟨❀⟩⋆

DAD LAID A SHEET of notebook paper on the steering wheel; on the paper was a map Large Marge had drawn for them. The map showed Kaneq as a big red circle, with a single line shooting out from it. That was the Road (there was only really one, she said) that ran from town to Otter Cove. There were three *x*'s along the straight line. First was Large Marge's homestead, on the left, then Tom Walker's on the right, and lastly Bo Harlan's old place, which was at the very end of the line.

"So," Dad said. "We go two miles past Icicle Creek and we'll see the start of Tom Walker's land, which is marked by a metal gate. Our place is just a little farther on. At the end of the road," Dad said, letting the map fall to the floor as they headed out of town. "Marge said we can't miss it."

They rumbled onto a rickety-looking bridge that arched over a crystalline blue river. They passed soggy marshlands, dusted with yellow and pink flowers, and then an airstrip, where four small, decrepit-looking airplanes were tied down.

Just past the airstrip, the gravel road turned to dirt and rocks. Trees grew thickly on either side. Mud and mosquitoes splattered the windshield. Potholes the size of wading pools made the old bus bump and clatter. "Hot damn," Dad said every time they were thrown out of their seats. There were no houses out here, no signs of civilization, until they came to a driveway littered with rusted junk and rotting vehicles. A hand-lettered sign read BIRDSALL. Large Marge's place.

After that, the road got worse. Bumpier. A combination of rocks and mud puddles. On either side, there was grass that grew wild and sticker bushes and trees tall enough to block the view of anything else.

Now they were *really* in the middle of nowhere.

After another empty patch of road, they came to a bleached-white cow skull on the rusted metal gate that marked the Walker homestead.

"I must say, I'm a little suspicious of neighbors who use dead animals in decorating," Mama said, clinging to the door handle, which came off in her hand when they hit a pothole.

Five minutes later, Dad slammed on the brakes. Two hundred feet farther and they would have careened over a cliff.

"Jesus," Mama said. The road was gone; in its place, scrub brush and a ledge. Land's End. Literally.

"We're here!" Dad jumped out of the bus, slammed the door shut.

Mama looked at Leni. They were both thinking the same thing: there was nothing here but trees and mud and a cliff that could have killed them in the fog. They got out of the bus and huddled together. Not far away—presumably below the cliff in front of them—the waves crashed and roared.

"Will ya look at it?" Dad threw his arms wide, as if he wanted to embrace it all. He seemed to be growing before their eyes, like a tree, spreading branches wide, becoming strong. He *liked* the nothingness he saw, the vast emptiness. It was what he'd come for.

The entrance to their property was a narrow neck of land bordered on either side by cliffs, the bases of which were battered by the ocean. Leni thought that a bolt of lightning or an earthquake could shear this land away from the mainland and set it adrift, a floating fortress of an island.

"That's our driveway," Dad said.

"Driveway?" Mama said, staring at the trail through the trees. It looked like it hadn't been used in years. Thin-trunked alder trees grew in the path.

"Bo's been gone a long time. We'll have to clear the road of new growth, but for now we'll hike in," Dad said.

"Hike?" Mama said.

He set about unpacking the bus. While Leni and Mama stood staring into the trees, Dad divided their necessities into three backpacks and said, "Okay. Here we go."

Leni stared at the packs in disbelief.

"Here, Red," he said, lifting a pack that seemed as big as a Buick.

"You want me to wear that?" she asked.

"I do if you want food and a sleeping bag at the cabin." He grinned. "Come on, Red. You can do this."

She let him fit the backpack on her. She felt like a turtle with an oversized shell. If she fell over, she would never right herself. She moved sideways with exaggerated care as Dad helped Mama put on her pack.

"Okay, Allbrights," Dad said, hefting his own pack on. "Let's go home!"

He took off walking, his arms swinging in time to his steps. Leni could hear his old army boots crunching and squishing in the muddy dirt. He whistled along, like Johnny Appleseed.

Mama glanced longingly back at the bus. Then she turned to Leni and smiled, but it struck Leni as an expression of terror rather than joy. "Okay, then," she said. "Come on."

Leni reached out for Mama's hand.

They walked through a shadow land of trees, following a narrow, winding trail. They could hear the sea crashing all around them. As they continued, the sound of the surf diminished. The land expanded. More trees, more land, more shadow.

"Sweet simple Christ," Mama said after a while. "How much farther is it?" She tripped on a rock, fell, went down hard.

"Mama!" Leni reached for her without thinking and her pack threw her to the ground. Mud filled Leni's mouth, made her sputter.

Dad was beside them in an instant, helping Leni and Mama to stand. "Here, girls, lean on me," he said. And they were off again.

Trees crowded into one another, jostled for space, turned the trail gloomy and dark. Sunlight poked through, changing color and clarity as they walked. The lichen-carpeted ground was springy, like walking on marshmallows. In no time, Leni noticed that she was ankle-deep in shadow. The darkness seemed to be rising rather than the sun falling. As if darkness were the natural order around here.

They got hooked in the face by branches, stumbled atop the spongy ground, until finally they emerged into the light again, into a meadow of knee-high grass and wildflowers. It turned out that their forty acres was a peninsula: a huge thumbprint of grassy land perched above the water on three sides, with a small C-shaped beach in the middle. There, the water was calm, serene.

Leni staggered into the clearing, unhooked her pack, let it crash to the ground. Mama did the same.

And there it was: the home they'd come to claim. A small cabin built of age-blackened logs, with a slanted, moss-furred roof that was studded with dozens of bleached-white animal skulls. A rotting deck jutted out from the front, cluttered with mildewed chairs. Off to the left, between the cabin and the trees, were decrepit animal pens and a dilapidated chicken coop.

There was junk everywhere, lying in the tall grass: a big pile of spokes, oil drums, coils of reddish wire, an old-fashioned wooden washing machine with a hand-cranked wringer.

Dad put his hands on his hips and threw his head back and howled like a wolf. When he stopped, and silence settled in again, he swept Mama into his arms, twirling her around.

When he finally let her go, Mama stumbled back; she was laughing, but there was a kind of horror in her eyes. The cabin looked like something an old, toothless hermit would live in, and it was *small*.

Would they all be crammed into a single room?

"Look at it," Dad said, making a sweeping gesture with his hand. They all turned away from the cabin and looked out to sea. "That's Otter Cove."

At this late afternoon hour, the peninsula and sea seemed to glow from within, like a land enchanted in a fairy tale. The colors were more vibrant than she'd ever seen before. Waves lapping the muddy beach left a sparkling residue. On the opposite shore, the mountains were a lush, deep purple at their bases and stark white at their peaks.

The beach below—their beach—was a curl of gray polished pebbles, washed by an easy white-foam surf. A rickety set of stairs built in the shape of a lightning bolt led from the grassy meadow to the shore. The wood had turned gray from age and was black from mildew; chicken wire covered each step. The stairs looked fragile, as if a good wind could shatter them.

The tide was out; mud coated everything, oozed along the shore, which was draped in seaweed and kelp. Clumps of shiny black mussels lay exposed on the rocks.

Leni remembered her dad telling her that the bore tide in Upper Cook Inlet created waves big enough to surf; only the Bay of Fundy had a higher tide. She hadn't really understood that fact until now, as she saw how far up the stairs the water could get. It would be beautiful at high tide, but now, with the tide ebbed and mud everywhere, she understood what it meant. At low tide, the property was inaccessible by boat.

"Come on," Dad said. "Let's check out the house."

He took Leni by the hand and led them through the grass and wildflowers, past the junk—barrels overturned, stacks of wooden pallets, old coolers, and broken crab pots. Mosquitoes nipped at her skin, drew blood, made a droning sound.

At the porch steps, Mama hesitated. Dad let go of Leni's hand and bounded up the sagging steps and opened the front door and disappeared inside.

Mama stood there a moment, breathing deeply. She slapped hard at her neck, left a smear of blood behind. "Well," she said. "This isn't what I expected."

"Me, either," Leni said.

There was another long silence. Then, quietly, Mama said, "Let's go."

She took Leni's hand as they walked up the rickety steps and entered the dark cabin.

The first thing Leni noticed was the smell.

Poop. Some animal (she *hoped* it was an animal) had pooped everywhere. She pressed a hand over her mouth and nose.

The place was full of shadows, dark shapes and forms. Cobwebs hung in ropy skeins from the rafters. Dust made it hard to breathe. The floor was covered in dead insects, so that each step produced a crunch.

"Yuck," Leni said.

Mama flung open the dirty curtains and sunlight poured in, thick with dust motes.

The interior was bigger than it looked from outside. The floors had been crafted of rough, mismatched plywood nailed into place in a patchwork quilt pattern. Skinned log walls displayed animal traps, fishing poles, baskets, frying pans, water buckets, nets. The kitchen—such as it was—took up one corner of the main room. Leni saw an old camp stove and a sink with no fixtures; beneath it was a curtained-off space. On the counter sat an old ham radio, probably from World War II, cloaked in dust. In the center of the room, a black woodstove held court, its metal pipe rising up to the ceiling like a jointed tin finger pointed at heaven. A ragged sofa, an overturned wooden crate that read BLAZO on the side, and a card table with four metal chairs comprised the cabin's furnishings. A narrow, steeply pitched log ladder led to a skylit loft space, and off to the left a curtain of psychedelic-colored beads hung from a narrow doorway.

Leni pushed through the dusty beaded curtain and went into the bedroom beyond, which was barely bigger than the stained, lumpy mattress on the floor. Here there was more junk hanging from hooks on the walls. It smelled vaguely of animal excrement and settled dust.

Leni kept a hand over her mouth, afraid she'd gag as she returned to the living room (*crunch, crunch* on the dead bugs). "Where's the bathroom?"

Mama gasped, headed for the front door, flung it open, and ran out.

Leni followed her out onto the sagging deck and down the half-broken steps.

"Over there," Mama said and pointed at a small wooden building surrounded by trees. A half-moon cutout on the door identified it.

An outhouse.

An *outhouse*.

"Holy shit," Mama whispered.

"No pun intended," Leni said. She leaned against her mother. She knew what Mama was feeling right now, so Leni had to be strong. That was how they did it, she and Mama. They took turns being strong. It was how they'd gotten through the war years.

"Thanks, baby girl. I needed that." Mama put an arm around Leni, drew her close. "We'll be okay, won't we? We don't need a TV. Or running water. Or electricity." Her voice ended on a high, shrill note that sounded desperate.

"We'll make the best of it," Leni said, trying to sound certain instead of worried. "And he'll be happy this time."

"You think so?"

"I know so."

FOUR

————————— ⊰•❀•⊱ —————————

The next morning, they rolled up their sleeves and got to work. Leni and Mama cleaned the cabin. They swept and scrubbed and washed. It turned out that the sink in the cabin was "dry" (there was no running water inside), so water had to be carried in by the bucketful from a stream not far away and boiled before they could drink it, cook with it, or bathe in it. There was no electricity. Propane-fueled lights swung from the rafters and sat on the plywood countertops. Beneath the house was a root cellar that was at least eight feet by ten feet, layered with sagging, dusty shelving and filled with empty, filthy mason jars and mildewed baskets. So they cleaned all of that, too, while Dad worked on clearing the driveway so they could drive the rest of their supplies onto the homestead.

By the end of the second day (which, by the way, lasted forever; the sun just kept shining and shining), it was ten P.M. before they quit work.

Dad built a bonfire on the beach—their beach—and they sat on fallen logs around it, eating tuna fish sandwiches and drinking warm Coca-Colas. Dad found mussels and butter clams and showed them how to crack them open. They ate each of the slimy mollusks in a single gulp.

Night didn't fall. Instead, the sky became a deep lavender-pink; there were no stars. Leni glanced across the dancing orange firelight, sparks spraying skyward, snapping like music, and saw her parents coiled together, Mama's head on Dad's shoulder, Dad's hand laid lovingly on her thigh, a woolen blanket wrapped around them. Leni took a picture.

At the flash and the *snap-whiz* of the Polaroid, Dad looked up at her and smiled. "We're going to be happy here, Red. Can't you feel it?"

"Yeah," she said, and for the first time ever, she really believed it.

--⊹⟨֍⟩⊹--

LENI WOKE TO THE SOUND of someone—or some*thing*—pounding on the cabin door. She scrambled out of her sleeping bag, shoved it aside, toppling her stack of books in her haste. Downstairs, she heard the rustle of beads and the pounding of footsteps as Mama and Dad ran for the door. Leni dressed quickly, grabbed her camera, and hurried down the ladder.

Large Marge stood in the yard with two other women; behind them, a rusted dirt bike lay on its side in the grass, and beside that was an all-terrain vehicle, loaded down with coiled chicken wire.

"Hullo, Allbrights!" Large Marge said brightly, waving her saucer-sized hand in greeting. "I brought some friends," she said, indicating the two women she'd brought with her. One was a wood sprite, small enough to be a kid, with long gray Silly-String-like hair; the other was tall and thin. All three of them were dressed in flannel shirts and stained jeans that were tucked into brown rubber knee-high boots. Each carried a tool—a chain saw, an ax, a hatchet.

"We've come to offer some help getting started," Large Marge said. "And we brought you a few things you'll need."

Leni saw her father frown. "You think we're incompetent?"

"This is how we do it up here, Ernt," Large Marge said. "Believe me, no matter how much you've read and studied, you can never quite prepare for your first Alaskan winter."

The wood sprite came forward. She was thin and small, with a nose sharp enough to slice bread. Leather gloves stuck out of her shirt pocket. For as slight as she was, she exuded an air of competence. "I'm Natalie Watkins. Large Marge told me ya'all don't know much about life up here. I was the same way ten years ago. I followed a man up here. Classic story. I lost the man and found a life. Got my own fishing boat now. So I get the dream that brings you here, but that's not enough. You're going to have to learn fast." Natalie put on her yellow gloves. "I never found another man worth having. You know what they say about finding a man in Alaska—the odds are good, but the goods are odd."

The taller woman had a beige braid that fell almost to her waist, and eyes so pale they seemed to take their color from the faded sky. "Welcome to Kaneq. I'm Geneva Walker. Gen. Genny. The Generator. I'll answer to almost anything." She smiled, revealing dimples. "My family is from Fairbanks, but I fell in love with my husband's land, so here is where I've stayed. I've been here for twenty years."

"You need a greenhouse and a cache at the very least," Large Marge said. "Old Bo had big plans for this place when he bought it. But Bo went off to war . . . and he was a great one for getting a job half done."

"A cash?" Dad said.

Large Marge nodded brusquely. "A cache is a small building on stilts. Your meat goes there, so the bears can't get at it. This time of year, the bears are hungry."

"Come on, Ernt," Natalie said, reaching down for the chain saw at her feet. "I brought a portable mill. You cut down the trees and I'll saw 'em into planks. First things first, righto?"

Dad went back into the cabin, put on his down vest, and headed into the forest with Natalie. Soon, Leni heard the whir of a chain saw and the thunking of an ax into wood.

"I'll get started on the greenhouse," Geneva said. "I imagine Bo left a tangle of PVC pipe somewhere . . ."

Large Marge walked up to Leni and Mama.

A breeze picked up; it turned cold in the blink of an eye. Mama crossed her arms. She had to be cold, standing there in a Grateful Dead T-shirt and bell-bottom jeans. A mosquito landed on her cheek. She slapped it away in a smear of blood.

"Our mosquitoes are bad," Large Marge said. "I'll bring you some repellant next time I come to visit."

"How long have you lived here?" Mama asked.

"Ten of the best years of my life," Large Marge answered. "Life in the bush is hard work, but you can't beat the taste of salmon you caught in the morning, drizzled with butter you churned from your own fresh cream. Up here, there's no one to tell you what to do or how to do it. We each survive our own way. If you're tough enough, it's heaven on earth."

Leni stared up at the big, rough-looking woman in a kind of awe. She'd never seen a woman so tall or strong-looking. Large Marge looked like she could fell a full-grown cedar tree and sling it over her shoulder and keep going.

"We needed a fresh start," Mama said, surprising Leni. It was the kind of rock-bottom truth Mama tended to avoid.

"He was in 'Nam?"

"POW. How did you know?"

"He has the look. And, well . . . Bo left you this place." Large Marge glanced left, to where Dad and Natalie were cutting down trees. "Is he mean?"

"N-no," Mama said. "Of course not."

"Flashbacks? Nightmares?"

"He hasn't had one since we headed north."

"You're an optimist," Large Marge said. "That'll be good for a start. Well. You'd best change your shirt, Cora. The bugs are going to go mad for all that bare white skin."

Mama nodded and turned back for the cabin.

"And you," Large Marge said. "What's your story, missy?"

"I don't have a story."

"Everyone has a story. Maybe yours just starts up here."

"Maybe."

"What can you do?"

Leni shrugged. "I read and take pictures." She indicated the camera that hung around her neck. "Not much that will do us any good."

"Then you'll learn," Large Marge said. She moved closer, leaned down to whisper conspiratorially into Leni's ear. "This place is magic, kiddo. You just have to open yourself up to it. You'll see what I mean. But it's treacherous, too, and don't you forget that. I think it was Jack London who said there were a thousand ways to die in Alaska. Be on the alert."

"For what?"

"Danger."

"Where will it come from? The weather? Bears? Wolves? What else?"

Large Marge glanced across the yard again to where Dad and Natalie were felling trees. "It can come from anywhere. The weather and the isolation makes some people crazy."

Before Leni could ask another question, Mama came back, dressed for work in jeans and a sweatshirt.

"Cora, can you make coffee?" Large Marge asked.

Mama laughed and hip-bumped Leni. "Well, now, Large Marge, it seems you've found the one thing I *can* do."

❖

LARGE MARGE AND NATALIE and Geneva worked all day alongside Leni and her parents. The Alaskans labored in silence, communicating with grunts and nods and pointed fingers. Natalie put a chain saw in a cage thing and milled the big logs Dad had cut down into boards all by herself. Each fallen tree revealed another slice of sunlight.

Geneva taught Leni how to saw wood and hammer nails and build raised vegetable beds. Together they started the PVC pipe-and-plank structure that would become a greenhouse. Leni helped Geneva carry a huge, heavy roll of plastic sheeting that they found in the broken-down chicken coop. They dropped it onto the ground.

"Sheesh," Leni said. She was breathing hard. Sweat sheened her forehead and made her frizzy hair hang limply on either side of her flushed face. But the skeleton of a garden gave her a sense of pride, of purpose. She actually looked forward to planting the vegetables that would be their food.

As they worked, Geneva talked about what vegetables to grow and how to harvest them and how important they would be when winter came.

Winter was a word these Alaskans said a lot. It might be only May, almost summer, but the Alaskans were already focused on winter.

"Take a break, kiddo," Geneva finally said, pushing to her feet. "I need to use the outhouse."

Leni staggered out of the greenhouse shell and found her mother standing alone, a cigarette in one hand, a cup of coffee in the other.

"I feel like we've fallen down the rabbit hole," Mama said. Beside her, the unsteady card table from the cabin held the remnants of lunch—Mama had made a stack of pan biscuits and fried up some bologna.

The air smelled of wood smoke and cigarette smoke and fresh-cut wood. It sounded of chain saws whirring, boards thumping onto piles, nails being hammered.

Leni saw Large Marge walking toward them. She looked tired and sweaty, but was smiling. "I don't suppose I could have a sip of that coffee?"

Mama handed Large Marge her cup.

The three of them stood there, gazing out at the homestead that was changing before their eyes.

"Your Ernt is a good worker," Large Marge said. "He's got some skills. Said his dad was a rancher."

"Uh-huh," Mama said. "Montana."

"That's good news. I can sell you a breeding pair of goats as soon as you get the pens repaired. I'll give you a good price. They'll be good for milk and cheese. And you can learn a shitload from *Mother Earth News* magazine. I'll bring you over a stack."

"Thank you," Mama said.

"Geneva said Leni was a joy to work with. That's good." She patted Leni so hard she stumbled forward. "But, Cora, I've looked through your supplies. I hope you don't mind. You don't have nearly enough. How are your finances?"

"Things are tight."

Large Marge nodded. Her face settled into grim lines. "Can you shoot?"

Mama laughed.

Large Marge didn't smile. "I mean it, Cora. Can you shoot?"

"A *gun*?" Mama asked.

"Yeah. A gun," Large Marge said.

Mama's laughter died. "No." She stubbed out her cigarette on a rock.

"Well. You aren't the first cheechakos to come up here with a dream and a poor plan."

"Cheechako?" Leni asked.

"Tenderfoot. Alaska isn't about who you were when you headed this way. It's about who you become. You are out here in the wild, girls. That isn't some fable or fairy tale. It's real. Hard. Winter will be here soon, and believe me, it's not like any winter you've ever experienced. It will cull the herd, and fast. You need to know how to survive. You need to know how to shoot and kill to feed yourselves and keep yourselves safe. You are not the top of the food chain here."

Natalie and Dad walked toward them. Natalie was carrying the chain saw and wiping her sweaty forehead with a bunched-up bandanna. She was such a small woman, barely taller than Leni; it seemed impossible that she could carry that heavy chain saw around.

At Mama's side, she stopped, rested the rounded tip of the chain saw on the toe of her rubber boot. "Well. I got to feed my animals. I gave Ernt a good drawing for the cache."

Geneva strode toward them. Black dirt colored her hair, her face, splattered across her shirtfront. "Leni has the right work attitude. Good for you, parents."

Dad laid an arm along Mama's shoulders. "I can't thank you ladies enough," he said.

"Yes. Your help means the world to us," Mama said.

Natalie's smile gave her an elfin look. "Our pleasure, Cora. You remember. Tonight you lock your door when you go to bed. Don't come out till morning. If you need a chamber pot, get one from Large Marge at the Trading Post."

Leni knew her mouth gaped just a little. They wanted her to pee in a *bucket*?

"Bears are dangerous this time of year. Black bears especially. They'll attack sometimes just 'cause they can," Large Marge said. "And there are wolves and moose and God knows what else." She took the chain saw from Natalie and slung it over her shoulder as if it were a stick of balsam wood. "There's no police up here and no telephone except in town, so Ernt, you teach your women to shoot, and do it fast. I'll give you a list of the minimum supplies you'll need before September. You'll need to bag a moose for sure this fall. It's better to shoot 'em in season, but . . . you know, what matters is meat in the freezer."

"We don't have a freezer," Leni pointed out.

The women laughed at that, for some reason.

Dad nodded solemnly. "Gotcha."

"Okay. See you later," the women said in unison. Waving, they walked toward their vehicles and mounted up, and then drove down the trail that led out to the main road. In moments they were gone.

In the silence that followed, a cold breeze ruffled the treetops above them. An eagle flew overhead, a huge silver fish struggling in its talons' grip. Leni saw a dog collar hanging from the top branches of an evergreen. An eagle must have picked up a small dog and carried it away. Could an eagle carry off a girl who was skinny as a beanpole?

Be careful. Learn to shoot a gun.

They lived on a piece of land that couldn't be accessed by water at low tide, on a peninsula with only a handful of people and hundreds of wild animals, in a climate harsh enough to kill you. There was no police station, no telephone service, no one to hear you scream.

For the first time, she really understood what her dad had been saying. *Remote.*

❖

LENI WOKE TO THE SMELL of frying bacon. When she sat up, pain radiated down her arms and up her legs.

She hurt everywhere. Mosquito bites made her skin itch. Five days (and up here the days were *endless*, sunlight lasted until almost midnight) of hard labor had revealed muscles she'd never known she had before.

She climbed out of her sleeping bag and pulled on her hip-hugger jeans. (She'd slept in her sweatshirt and socks.) The inside of her mouth tasted terrible. She'd forgotten to brush her teeth last night. Already she was beginning to conserve water that didn't flow through faucets but had to be hauled inside by the bucketful.

She climbed down the ladder.

Mama was in the kitchen alcove, at the camp stove, pouring oatmeal into a pot of boiling water. Bacon sizzled and snapped in one of the black cast-iron skillets they'd found hanging from a hook.

Leni heard the distant pounding of a hammer. Already that rhythmic beat had become the soundtrack of their lives. Dad worked from sunup to sundown, which was a long day. He'd already repaired the chicken coop and fixed the goat pens.

"I have to go to the bathroom," she said.

"Fun," Mama said.

Leni put on her wafflestompers, and stepped outside into a blue-skied day. The colors were so vibrant, the world hardly looked real: green, swaying grass in the clearing, purple wildflowers, the gray zigzag steps leading to a blue sea that breathed in and out along the pebbled shore. Beyond it all, a fjord of impossible grandeur, sculpted eons ago by glaciers. She wanted to go back for her Polaroid and take pictures of the yard—again—but already she was learning that she needed to conserve her film. Getting more would not be an easy thing up here.

The outhouse was positioned on the bluff, in a stand of thin-trunked spruce, overlooking the rocky coastline. On the toilet lid, someone had painted *I never promised you a rose garden*, and applied flower decals.

She lifted the lid, using her sleeve to protect her fingers, and carefully averted her gaze from the hole as she sat down.

When she finished, Leni headed back to the cabin. A bald eagle soared overhead, gliding in a circle and then swooping up, flying away. She saw a fish carcass hanging high in one of the trees, catching the sunlight like a Christmas ornament. An eagle must have dropped it there, after picking all the meat off the bones. Off to her right, the cache was half finished— four skinned log braces that led to a three-foot-by-three-foot wooden platform twelve feet in the air. Below it were six empty raised beds covered by a hoop-skirt-like structure of pipe and wood that awaited plastic covering to become a greenhouse.

"Leni!" her dad shouted, coming toward her in that exuberant, ground-covering walk of his. His hair was a dirty, dusty mess and his clothes were covered with oil spots and his hands were grubby. Pink sawdust peppered his face and hair. He waved at her, smiling.

The joy on his face brought her to a complete stop. She couldn't remember the last time she'd seen him so happy. "By God, it's beautiful here," he said.

Wiping his hands on a red bandanna he kept wadded up in his jeans pocket, he looped an arm around her shoulder and walked with her into the cabin.

Mama was just serving breakfast.

The card table was rickety as heck, so they stood in the living room, eating oatmeal from their metal camp bowls. Dad shoveled a spoonful of oatmeal in his mouth at the same time he was chewing bacon. Lately, eating seemed to Dad to be a waste of time. There was so much to do outside.

Immediately after breakfast, Leni and Mama returned to cleaning the cabin. Already they had removed layers of dust and dirt and dead bugs. Each of the rugs had been hung over the deck rails and beaten with brooms that looked as dirty as the rugs themselves. Mama took down the curtains and carried them out to one of the big oil drums in the yard. After Leni hauled water up from the river, they filled the antique washing machine with water and laundry soap and Leni stood there for an hour, sweating in the sunshine, stirring the curtains in the soapy water. Then she carried the heavy, dripping mass of fabric to a barrel full of clean water for rinsing.

Now she was feeding the soaking wet curtains through the old-fashioned wringer. The work was hard, backbreaking, exhausting.

She could hear Mama in the yard not far away, singing as she washed another load of clothes in the sudsy water.

Leni heard an engine. She stood up, rubbing an ache out of her lower back. She heard the crunch of rocks, the splash of mud . . . and the old VW bus emerged from the trees and stopped in the yard. The road was finally cleared!

Dad honked the horn. Birds flew up from the trees, squawked in irritation.

Mama stopped stirring the laundry and looked up. The bandanna that covered her blond hair was wet with sweat. Mosquito bites created a red lattice pattern on her pale cheeks. She tented a hand across her eyes. "You did it!" she yelled.

Dad stepped out of the bus and waved them over. "Enough work, Allbrights. Let's go for a drive."

Leni squealed in delight. She was more than ready to take a break from this back-wrenching work. Scooping up the wrung-out fabric, she carried it over to the sagging clothesline Mama had set up between two trees and hung the curtains to dry.

Leni and Mama were both laughing as they climbed into the old bus. They had carried all of their supplies out of the bus already (several trips back and forth, carrying heavy packs); only a few magazines and empty Coke cans were left on the seats.

Dad battled the loose gearshift, shoved it into first gear. The bus made a sound like an old man coughing and shuddered, metal creaking, tires thumping in pits, as it circled the grassy yard.

Leni could now see the driveway Dad had cleared. "It was already there," he said, yelling to be heard over the engine's whine. "A bunch of willows had grown up. I just had to clear it."

It was rough going, a track barely wider than the bus. Branches snapped into the windshield, scraped along the bus's sides. Their banner was ripped off, flew up, stuck in the trees. The driveway was more pits and boulders than dirt; the old bus was constantly rising and thumping down. Tires crunched slowly over exposed roots and rocky outcroppings as they drove into the dark shadows cast by the trees.

At the end of their driveway, they drove into the sunlight and onto a real dirt road.

They rumbled past the Walker metal gate and the Birdsall sign. Leni leaned forward, excited to see the marshes and airfields that signaled the outskirts of Kaneq.

Town! Only a few days ago it had seemed worse than an outpost, but it didn't take much time in the Alaskan bush to reassess one's opinion. Kaneq had a *store*. Leni could get some film and maybe a candy bar.

"Hang on," Dad said as he turned left into the trees.

"Where are we going?" Mama asked.

"To tell Bo Harlan's family thank you. I've brought his father a half gallon of whiskey."

Leni stared out the dirty window. Dust turned the view into a haze. For miles there was nothing but trees and bumps. Every now and then a vehicle was rotting at the side of the road in the tall grass.

There were no houses or mailboxes, just dirt trails here and there that veered off into the trees. If people lived out here, they didn't want you to find them.

The road was rough: two beaten-down tire tracks on rocky, uneven ground. As they climbed in elevation, the trees grew thicker, began to block out more and more of the sun. They saw the first sign about three miles in: NO TRESPASSING. TURN AROUND. YES, WE MEAN YOU. PROPERTY PROTECTED BY DOGS AND GUNS. HIPPIES GO HOME.

The road ended at the crest of a hill with a sign that read, TRESPASSERS WILL BE SHOT. SURVIVORS WILL BE SHOT AGAIN.

"Jesus," Mama said. "Are you sure we're in the right place?"

A man with a rifle appeared in front of them, stood with his legs in a wide stance. He had frizzy brown hair that puffed out from beneath a dirty trucker's cap. "Who are you? What do you want?"

"I think we should turn around," Mama said.

Dad leaned his head out the window. "We're here to see Earl Harlan. I was a friend of Bo's."

The man frowned, then nodded and stepped aside.

"I don't know, Ernt," Mama said. "This doesn't feel right."

Dad worked the gearshift. The old bus grumbled and rolled forward, jouncing over rocks and hillocks.

They drove into a wide, flat patch of muddy ground studded here and there with clumps of yellowing grass. Three houses bordered the field. Well, shacks, really. They looked to have been made of whatever was handy—sheets of plywood, corrugated plastic, skinned logs. A school bus with curtains in the windows sat on tireless rims, hip-deep in the mud. Several scrawny dogs were chained up, straining at their leashes, snarling and barking. Fire barrels belched smoke that had a noxious, rubbery smell.

People dressed in dirty clothes stepped out of the cabins and shacks. Men with ponytails and buzz cuts and women wearing cowboy hats. All wore guns or knives in sheaths at their waists.

Directly in front of them, from a log cabin with a slanted roof, a white-haired man emerged carrying an antique-looking pistol. He was wiry thin, with a long white beard and a toothpick chomped down tight in his mouth. He stepped down into the muddy yard. The dogs went crazy at his appearance, growled and snapped and groveled. A few jumped on top of their houses and kept barking. The old man pointed his gun at their bus.

Dad reached for the door handle.

"Don't get out," Mama said, grabbing his arm.

Dad pulled free of Mama's grasp. He grabbed the half gallon of whiskey he'd brought and opened the door and stepped down into the mud. He left the bus door open behind him.

"Who are you?" the white-haired man yelled, the toothpick bobbing up and down.

"Ernt Allbright, sir."

The man lowered his weapon. "Ernt? It's you? I'm Earl, Bo's daddy."

"It's me, sir."

"Well, slap me silly. Who you got with ya?"

Dad turned and waved at Leni and Mama to get out of the bus.

"Yeah. This seems like a good idea," Mama said as she opened her door.

Leni followed. She stepped down into the mud, heard it squelch up around her wafflestompers.

Around the compound, people were stopped, staring.

Dad pulled them in close. "This is my wife, Cora, and my daughter, Leni. Girls, this is Bo's dad, Earl."

"Folks call me Mad Earl," the old guy said. He shook their hands, then swiped the bottle of whiskey from Dad and led them into his cabin. "Come in. Come in."

Leni had to force herself to enter the small, shadowy interior. It smelled like sweat and mildew. The walls were lined with supplies—food and gallons of water and cases of beer, boxes full of canned goods, heaps of sleeping bags. Along one whole wall: weapons. Guns and knives and boxes of ammunition. Old-fashioned crossbows hung from hooks alongside maces.

Mad Earl plopped onto a chair made of Blazo box slats. He cracked open the whiskey and lifted the bottle to his mouth, drinking deeply. Then he handed the jug to Dad, who drank for a long time before he handed the bottle back to Mad Earl.

Mama bent down, picked an old gas mask up from a box full of them. "Y-you collect war memorabilia?" she said uneasily.

Mad Earl took another drink, draining an amazing amount of whiskey in a single gulp. "Nope. That ain't there for looks. The world's gone mad. A man has to protect himself. I came up here in '62. The Lower Forty-eight was already a mess. Commies everywhere. The Cuban Missile Crisis scarin' the shit outta people. Bomb shelters being built in backyards. I brung my family up here. We had nothing but a gun and a bag of brown rice. Figured we could live in the bush and stay safe and survive the nuclear winter that was comin'." He took another drink, leaned forward. "It ain't getting better down there. It's gettin' worse. What they done to the economy . . . to our poor boys who went off to war. It ain't my America anymore."

"I've been saying that for years," Dad said. There was a look on his face Leni had never seen before. A kind of awe. As if he'd been waiting a long time to hear those words.

"Down there," Mad Earl went on, "Outside, people are standing in line for gas while OPEC laughs all the way to the bank. And you think the good ole USSR forgot about us after Cuba? Think again. We got Negroes calling themselves Black Panthers and raisin' their fists at us, and illegal immigrants stealing our jobs. So what do people do? They protest. They sit down. They throw bombs at empty post office buildings. They carry signs and march down streets. Well. Not me. I got a *plan*."

Dad leaned forward. His eyes were shiny. "What is it?"

"We're prepared up here. We've got guns, gas masks, arrows, ammunition. We're *ready*."

Mama said, "Surely you don't really believe—"

"Oh, I do," Mad Earl said. "The white man is losing out and war is coming." He looked at Dad. "You know what I mean, don't you, Allbright?"

"Of course I know. We all do. How many in your group?" Dad asked.

Mad Earl took a long drink, then wiped the dribble from his spotted lips. His rheumy eyes narrowed, moved from Leni to Mama. "Well. It's just our family, but we take it seriously. And we don't talk about it to strangers. Last thing we want is people knowing where we are when TSHTF."

There was a knock at the door. At Mad Earl's "Come in," the door opened to reveal a small, wiry-looking woman in camo pants and a yellow smiley-face T-shirt. Although she had to be almost forty, she wore her hair in pigtails. The man beside her was big as a house, with a long brown ponytail and bangs that strafed his eyes. She held a stack of Tupperware in her arms and had a pistol holstered at her hip.

"Don't let my daddy scare the bejesus out of you," the woman said, smiling brightly. As she stepped farther into the cabin, a child sidled along beside her, a girl of about four who was barefoot and dirty-faced. "I'm Thelma Schill, Earl's daughter. Bo was my big brother. This is my husband, Ted. This is Marybet. We call her Moppet." Thelma placed a hand on the girl's head.

"I'm Cora," Mama said, extending her hand. "That's Leni."

Leni smiled hesitantly. Thelma's husband, Ted, stared at her through squinty eyes.

Thelma's smile was warm, genuine. "You going to school on Monday, Leni?"

"There's a school?" Leni said.

"'Course. It isn't big, but I think you'll make friends. Kids come from as far away as Bear Cove. I think there's another week of classes. School ends early up here so kids can work."

"Where's the school?" Mama asked.

"On Alpine Street, just behind the saloon, at the base of Church Hill. You can't miss it. Monday morning at nine."

"We'll be there," Mama said, shooting Leni a smile.

"Good. We are so happy to welcome you here, Cora and Ernt and Leni." Thelma faced them, smiling. "Bo wrote us plenty from 'Nam. You meant so much to him. Everyone wants to meet you all." She crossed the room, took Ernt by the arm, and led him out of the cabin.

Leni and Mama followed behind, heard Mad Earl shuffle to his feet, grumbling about Thelma taking over.

Outside, a ragged cluster of people—men, women, children, young adults—stood waiting, each holding something.

"I'm Clyde," said a man with a Santa beard and eyebrows like awnings. "Bo's younger brother." He held out a chain saw, its blade sheathed in bright orange plastic. "I just sharpened the chain." A woman and two young men, each about twenty, stepped forward, along with two dirty-faced girls who were probably seven or eight. "This here's Donna, my wife, and the twins, Darryl and Dave, and our daughters, Agnes and Marthe."

There weren't many of them, but they were friendly and welcoming.

Each person they met gave them a gift: a hacksaw, a coil of rope, sheets of heavy plastic, rolls of duct tape, a bright silver knife called an *ulu* that was shaped like a fan.

There was no one Leni's age. The one teenager—Axle, who was sixteen—barely glanced at Leni. He stood off by himself, throwing knives at a tree trunk. He had long dirty black hair and gray eyes.

"You'll need to get a garden going fast," Thelma said as the men drifted toward one of the burn barrels and began passing the whiskey bottle from man to man. "Weather's unpredictable up here. Some years June is spring, July is summer, August is autumn, and everything else is winter."

Thelma led Leni and Mama to a large garden. A fence made of sagging fishing nets bound to metal stakes kept out animals.

Most of the vegetables were small, clumps of green on the mounds of black earth. Mats of something gross—it looked like kelp—lay drying at the base of the nets, alongside heaps of stinking fish carcasses and eggshells and coffee grounds.

"You know how to garden?" Thelma asked.

"I can tell a ripe melon," Mama said.

"I'd be happy to teach you. Up here the growing season is short, so we have to really work it." She grabbed a dented metal bucket from the dirt beside her. "I have some potatoes and onions I can spare. There's still time for them. I can give you a bunch of carrot starts. And I can spare a few live chickens."

"Oh, really, you shouldn't—"

"Believe me, Cora, you have no idea how long the winter will be and how soon it will be here. It's one thing up here for men—a lot of them are going to leave for work on that new pipeline. You and me—mothers—we stay on the homestead and keep our children alive and well. It's not always easy; the way we do it is together. We help whenever we can. We trade. Tomorrow I'll show you how to can salmon. You need to start filling your root cellar with food for winter now."

"You're scaring me," Mama said.

Thelma touched Mama's arm. "I remember when we first came up here from Kansas City. My mom did nothing but cry. She died the second winter here. I still think she willed herself to die. Just couldn't stand the dark or the cold. A woman has to be tough as steel up here, Cora. You can't count on anyone to save you and your children. You have to be willing to save yourselves. And you have to learn fast. In Alaska you can make one mistake. *One.* The second one will kill you."

"I don't think we're well prepared," Mama said. "Maybe we've already made a mistake by coming here."

"I'll help you," Thelma promised. "We all will."

FIVE

———◇◇◈◇◈◇◇———

The endless daylight rewound Leni's internal clock, made her feel
strangely out of step with the universe, as if even time—the one thing
you could count on—was different in Alaska. It was daylight when she went
to bed and daylight when she woke up.

Now it was Monday morning.

She stood at the window, staring at the newly clean glass, trying to make
out her reflection. A useless effort. There was just too much light.

She could only see a ghost of herself, but she knew she didn't look good,
even for Alaska.

First and always was her hair. Long and untamed and red. And there
was the milky skin that was standard issue with the hair, and freckles like
red-pepper flakes across her nose. The best of her features—her blue-green
eyes—were not enhanced by cinnamon-colored lashes.

Mama came up behind her, placed her hands on Leni's shoulders. "You
are beautiful and you will make friends at this new school."

Leni wanted to take comfort from the familiar words, but how often had
they proven untrue? She'd been the new girl at school a lot of times, and she'd
never yet found a place she fit in. Something was always wrong about her on

the first day—her hair, her clothes, her shoes. First impressions mattered in junior high. She had learned that lesson the hard way. It was hard to recover from a fashion error with thirteen-year-old girls.

"I'm probably the only girl in the whole school," she said with a dramatic sigh. She didn't want to hope for the best; dashed hopes were worse than no hopes at all.

"Certainly you'll be the prettiest," Mama said, tucking the hair behind Leni's ear with a gentleness that reminded Leni that whatever happened, she wasn't ever really alone. She had her mama.

The cabin door opened, bringing in a whoosh of cold air. Dad came in carrying a pair of dead mallards, their broken necks hanging, beaks banging into his thigh. He set his gun in the rack by the door and laid his kill on the wooden counter by the dry sink.

"Ted took me to his blind before dawn. We have duck for dinner." He slipped in beside Mama and kissed the side of her neck.

Mama swatted him away, laughing. "You want coffee?"

When Mama went into the kitchen, Dad turned to Leni. "You look glum for a girl going off to school."

"I'm fine."

"Maybe I know the problem," Dad said.

"I doubt it," she said, sounding as dispirited as she felt.

"Let me see," Dad said, frowning in an exaggerated way. He left her standing there and went into his bedroom. Moments later, he came out carrying a black trash bag, which he set on the table. "Maybe this will help."

Yeah. What she needed was garbage.

"Open it," Dad said.

Leni reluctantly ripped the bag open.

Inside, she found a pair of rust-and-black-striped bell-bottoms and a fuzzy ivory-colored wool fisherman's sweater that looked like it used to be a man's size and someone had shrunk it.

Oh, my God.

Leni might not know much about fashion, but these were definitely boy's pants, and the sweater . . . she didn't think it had been in style in any year of her life.

Leni caught Mama's look. They both knew how hard he had tried. And how profoundly he'd failed. In Seattle, an outfit like this was social suicide.

"Leni?" Dad said, his face falling in disappointment.

She forced a smile. "It's perfect, Dad. Thanks."

He sighed and smiled. "Oh. Good. I spent a long time picking through the bins."

Salvation Army. So he had planned ahead, thought of her the other day when they were in Homer. It made the ugly clothes almost beautiful.

"Put them on," Dad said.

Leni managed a smile. She went into her parents' bedroom and changed her clothes.

The Irish sweater was too small, the wool so thick she could hardly bend her arms.

"You look gorgeous," Mama said.

She tried to smile.

Mama came forward with a metal Winnie the Pooh lunch box. "Thelma thought you'd like this."

And with that, Leni's social fate was sealed, but there was nothing she could do about it.

"Well," she said to her dad, "we better move it. I don't want to be late."

Mama hugged her fiercely, whispered, "Good luck."

Outside, Leni climbed into the passenger seat of the VW bus and they were off, bouncing down the bumpy trail, turning toward town, onto the main road, rumbling past the field that called itself an airstrip. At the bridge, Leni yelled, "Stop!"

Dad hit the brakes and turned to her. "What?"

"Can I walk from here?"

He gave her a disappointed look. "Really?"

She was too nervous to smooth his ruffled feelings. One thing that was true of every school she'd been at was this: once you hit junior high, parents were to be absent. The chances of them embarrassing you were sky-high. "I'm thirteen and this is Alaska, where we're supposed to be tough," Leni said. "Come on, Dad. *Pleeease.*"

"Okay. I'll do it for you."

She got out of the bus and walked alone through town, past a man sitting Indian-style on the side of the road, with a goose in his lap. She heard him say, *No way, Matilda,* to the bird as she hurried past the dirty tent that housed the fishing-charter service.

The one-room schoolhouse sat on a weedy lot behind town. Green and yellow marshes spread out behind it, a river meandering in a sloping S-shape through the tall grass. The school was in an A-frame building made of skinned logs, with a steeply pitched metal roof.

At the open door, Leni paused and peered inside. The room was bigger than it looked from the outside; at least fourteen-by-fourteen. There was a chalkboard on the back wall with the words SEWARD'S FOLLY written in capital letters.

At the front of the room, a Native woman stood behind a big desk, facing the door. She was solid-looking, with broad shoulders and big, capable hands. Long black hair, twined into two sloppy braids, framed a face the color of light coffee. Tattooed black lines ran in vertical stripes from her lower lip to her chin. She wore faded Levi's tucked into rubber boots, a man's flannel shirt, and a fringed suede vest.

She saw Leni and yelled, "Hello! Welcome!"

The kids in the classroom turned in a screeching of chairs.

There were six students. Two younger kids sat in the front row. Girls. She recognized them from Mad Earl's compound: Marthe and Agnes. She also recognized that sour-looking teenage boy, Axle. There were two giggling Native girls who looked to be about eight or nine, sitting at desks pushed together; each was wearing a wilted dandelion crown. On the right side of the room a pair of desks were pushed together, side to side, facing the blackboard. One was empty; at the other sat a scrawny boy about her age with shoulder-length blond hair. He was the only student who seemed interested in her. He had stayed turned around in his seat and was still staring at her.

"I'm Tica Rhodes," the teacher said. "My husband and I live in Bear Cove, so sometimes I can't get here in winter, but I do my best. That's what I expect of my students, too." She smiled. "And you're Lenora Allbright. Thelma told me to expect you."

"Leni."

"You're what, eleven?" Ms. Rhodes said, studying Leni.

"Thirteen," Leni said, feeling her cheeks heat up. If only she would start developing boobs.

Ms. Rhodes nodded. "Perfect. Matthew is thirteen, too. Go take a seat over there." She pointed to the boy with the blond hair. "Go on."

Leni's grip on her stupid Winnie the Pooh lunch box was so tight her fingers hurt. "H-hi," she said to Axle as she passed his desk. He gave her a *who cares?* glance and went back to drawing something that looked like an alien with massive boobs on his Pee-Chee folder.

She slid bumpily into the seat beside the thirteen-year-old boy. "Hey," she mumbled, glancing sideways.

He grinned, showing off a mouth full of crooked teeth. "Thank Christ," he said, shoving the hair out of his face. "I thought I was going to have to sit with Axle for the rest of the year. I think the kid is going to end up in prison."

Leni laughed in spite of herself.

"Where are you from?" he asked.

Leni never knew how to answer that question. It implied a permanence, a Before that had never existed for her. She'd never thought of any place as home. "My last school was near Seattle."

"You must feel like you've fallen into Mordor."

"You read *Lord of the Rings?*"

"I know. Hopelessly uncool. It's Alaska, though. The winters are dark as shit and we don't have TV. Unlike my dad, I can't spend hours listening to old people yammering on the ham radio."

Leni felt the start of an emotion so new she couldn't categorize it. "I love

Tolkien," she said quietly. It felt oddly freeing to be honest with someone. Most of the kids at her last school had cared more about movies and music than books. "And Herbert."

"*Dune* was amazing. 'Fear is the mind-killer.' It's so true, man."

"And *Stranger in a Strange Land*. That's kinda how I feel here."

"You should. Nothing is normal in the last frontier. There's a town up north that has a dog for a mayor."

"No way."

"True. A malamute. They voted him in." Matthew laid a hand to his chest. "You can't make this crap up."

"I saw a man sitting with a goose in his lap on the way here. He was talking to the bird, I think."

"That's Crazy Pete and Matilda. They're married."

Leni laughed out loud.

"You have a weird laugh."

Leni felt her cheeks heat up in embarrassment. No one had ever told her that before. Was it true? What did she sound like? *Oh, God.*

"I—I'm sorry. I don't know why I said that. My social skills blow. You're the first girl my age I've talked to in a while. I mean. You're pretty. That's all. I'm blabbing, aren't I? You're probably going to run away, screaming, and ask to sit next to Axle the soon-to-be murderer and it will be an improvement. Okay. I'm shutting up now."

Leni hadn't heard anything after "pretty."

She tried to tell herself it meant nothing. But when Matthew looked at her, she felt a flutter of possibility. She thought: *We could be friends.* And not ride-the-bus or eat-at-the-same-table friends.

Friends.

The kind who had real things in common. Like Sam and Frodo, Anne and Diana, Ponyboy and Johnny. She closed her eyes for a split second, imagining it. They could laugh and talk and—

"Leni?" he said. "Leni?"

Oh, my God. He'd said her name twice.

"Yeah. I get it. I space out all the time. My mom says it's what happens when you live in your own head with a bunch of made-up people. Then again, she's been reading *Another Roadside Attraction* since Christmas."

"I do that," Leni confessed. "Sometimes I just . . . spaz out."

He shrugged, as if to imply that there was nothing wrong with her. "Hey, have you heard about the barbecue tonight?"

SO WHAT ABOUT THE PARTY? Can you come?

Leni kept replaying it over and over again as she waited for her dad to pick her up from school. She'd wanted to say yes and mean it. She wanted it more than she'd wanted anything in a while.

But her parents weren't community barbecue people. Community anything, really. It wasn't who the Allbrights were. The families in their old neighborhood used to have all kinds of gatherings: backyard barbecues where the dads wore V-necks and drank Scotch and flipped burgers, and the women smoked cigarettes and sipped martinis and carried trays of bacon-wrapped chicken livers while kids screamed and ran around. She knew this because once she'd peered over the neighbors' fence and seen all of it—hula hoops and Slip 'N Slides and sprinklers.

"So, Red, how was school?" Dad asked when Leni climbed into the VW bus and slammed the door. He was the last parent to arrive.

"We learned about the U.S. buying Alaska from Russia. And about Mount Alyeska in the Chugach Mountain Range."

He grunted acceptance of that and put the vehicle in gear.

Leni thought about how to say what she wanted to say. *There's a boy my age in class. He's our neighbor.*

No. Mentioning a boy was the wrong tack.

Our neighbors are hosting a barbecue and invited us.

But Dad hated that kind of thing, or he used to, in all the other places they'd lived.

They rattled down the dirt road, dust billowing up on either side, and turned into their driveway. At home, they discovered a crowd of people in the yard. Most of the Harlan clan was there, working. They moved in wordless harmony, coming together and drifting apart like dancers. Clyde had that cage thing and was milling logs into boards. Ted was finishing the cache, pounding boards to the side stanchions. Donna was stacking firewood.

"Our friends showed up at noon to help us prepare for winter," Dad said. "No. They're better than friends, Red. They're comrades."

Comrades?

Leni frowned. Were they communists now? She was pretty sure her dad hated the commies as much as he hated the Man and hippies.

"This is what the world should be, Red. People helping each other instead of killing their mothers for a little bread."

Leni couldn't help noticing that almost everyone had a gun holstered at his or her waist.

Dad opened the bus door. "We're all going to Sterling this weekend, to fish for salmon at Farmer's Hole on the Kenai River. Apparently these king salmon are a bitch to land." He stepped out into the soggy ground.

Mad Earl waved a gloved hand at her dad, who immediately bounded off in the old man's direction.

Leni walked past a new structure that was about nine feet high by four feet wide, with sides covered in thick black plastic (unspooled garbage bags, Leni was pretty sure). An open door revealed an interior full of sockeye salmon, sliced in half along the spines and hung tented on branches. Thelma was kneeling in the dirt, tending to a fire built in a contained metal box. Smoke puffed up in dark clouds, reached up to the salmon hanging on branches above the fire.

Mama looked up from the salmon she was gutting at a table in the yard. There was a smear of pink guts across her chin. "It's a smokehouse," Mama said, cocking her head toward Thelma. "Thelma is teaching me how to smoke fish. It's quite an art, apparently—too much heat, you cook the fish. It's supposed to smoke and dry at the same time. Yum. How was your first day of school?" A red kerchief kept the hair out of her eyes.

"Cool."

"No social-suicide issues with the clothes or the lunch box? No girls making fun of you?"

Leni couldn't help smiling. "No girls my age at all. But . . . there's a boy . . ."

That got Mama's interest. "A boy?"

Leni felt herself blushing. "A *friend*, Mama. He just happens to be a boy."

"Uh. Huh." Mama was trying not to smile as she lit her cigarette. "Is he cute?"

Leni ignored that. "He says there's a community barbecue tonight, and I want to go."

"Yeah. We're going."

"Really? That's great!"

"Yeah," Mama said, smiling. "I told you it would be different here."

⊹⟨❄⟩⊹

WHEN IT CAME TIME to dress for the barbecue, Leni kind of lost her mind. Honestly, she didn't know what was wrong with her.

She didn't have a lot of clothes to choose from, but that didn't stop her from trying on several different combinations. In the end—mostly because she was exhausted by the desire to look pretty when pretty was impossible—she decided on a pair of plaid polyester bell-bottoms and a ribbed green turtleneck beneath a fringed, fake-suede vest. Try as she might, she couldn't do anything with her hair. She finger-combed it back from her face and twined it into a fuzzy, fist-sized braid.

She found Mama in the kitchen, placing thick squares of cornbread into a Tupperware container. She had brushed her shoulder-length, shag-cut hair until it glimmered in the light. She had definitely dressed to impress in tight bell-bottom jeans and a fitted white sweater with a huge Indian turquoise squash-blossom necklace that she'd bought a few years ago.

Mama seemed distracted as she burped the lid of air from the container. "You're worried, aren't you?"

"Why would you say that?" Mama gave her a quick, bright smile, but the look in her eyes couldn't be so easily transformed. She was wearing makeup for the first time in days and it made her look vibrant and beautiful.

"Remember the fair?"

"That was different. The guy tried to cheat him."

That wasn't how Leni remembered it. They'd been having a good time at the State Fair until her dad started drinking beer. Then some guy had flirted with Mama (and she had flirted back) and Dad had gone ballistic. He shoved the man hard enough to crack his head into the tent pole at the Beer-Haus and started yelling. When the security guys came, Dad was so belligerent that the cops were called. Leni had been mortified to see two of her classmates watching the altercation. They'd seen her dad get dragged over to the cop car.

Dad opened the cabin door and came inside.

"Are my beautiful girls ready to party?"

"You bet," Mama said quickly, smiling.

"Let's go, then," Dad said, herding them into the bus.

In no time—it was less than a quarter of a mile as the crow flew—they drove up to the steel gate with the bleached-white cow head on it. The gate was open in welcome.

The Walker homestead. Their nearest neighbors.

Dad drove slowly forward. The driveway (two ribbons of flattened grass that undulated up and down on lichen-covered ground) unfurled in a lazy *S* through stands of skinny black-trunked spruce trees. Occasionally there was a break in the trees to her left and Leni saw a splash of distant blue, but it wasn't until they came to the clearing that Leni saw the view.

"Wow," Mama said.

They emerged onto a flat ridge situated above a calm blue cove. The huge piece of land had been cleared of all but a few carefully chosen trees and planted in hay.

A large two-story log house sat like a crown at the highest point of land. Its triangular front boasted huge trapezoid windows and a pointed, wrap-around deck. It looked like the prow of some great ship, flung to shore by an angry sea and stuck on land, forever gazing out at the sea upon which it belonged. Mismatched chairs decorated the deck, each one turned toward the spectacular view. On the far side of the house were several animal pens full of cows and goats and chickens and ducks. Coils of barbed wire, wooden crates and pallets, a broken-down tractor and the rusted shovel from an excavator, and the husks of several dead and dying trucks lay scattered in the knee-high grass. Beehives stood clustered together not far from a small wooden structure that puffed smoke. In a break in the trees was the sharp peaked roof of an outhouse.

Down at the water, a gray dock jutted out into the blue sea. At its end, a weathered arch read WALKER COVE. A float plane was tied up to the dock, in addition to two bright silver fishing boats.

"A float plane," Dad muttered. "Must be rich."

They parked the bus and walked past a bright yellow tractor with a black bucket and a shiny red all-terrain vehicle. From the crested rise, Leni saw people gathered down on the beach, at least a dozen of them, around a huge bonfire. Flames shot into the light lavender sky, making a sound like fingers snapping.

Leni followed her parents down the stairs to the beach. From here, she could see everyone at the party. A broad-shouldered man with long blond hair was sitting on a fallen log playing a guitar. Large Marge had turned two white plastic buckets into bongo drums, and Leni's teacher, Ms. Rhodes, was going crazy on a fiddle. Natalie was wicked with a harmonica and Thelma was singing "King of the Road." On *means by no means* everyone joined in.

Clyde and Ted were handling the barbecue, which looked to have been made out of old oil drums. Mad Earl stood nearby, drinking from a crockery jug. The two younger girls from school, Marthe and Agnes, were down at the waterline, bent over, collecting shells with Moppet.

Mama stepped down onto the beach, carrying her Tupperware full of cornbread. Dad was right behind her with a fifth of whiskey.

The big, broad-shouldered man playing the guitar put down his instrument and got to his feet. He was dressed like most of the men here, in a flannel shirt and faded jeans and rubber boots, but even so, he stood out. He looked as if he'd been built for this rugged land, as if he could run all day, hack down an old-growth tree with a hatchet, and skip nimbly along a fallen log over a raging river. Even Leni thought he was handsome—for an old guy. "I'm Tom Walker," he said. "Welcome to my place."

"Ernt Allbright."

Tom shook Dad's hand.

"This is my wife, Cora."

Mama smiled at Tom, shook his hand, then looked back. "This is our daughter, Leni. She's thirteen."

Tom smiled at Leni. "Hey, Leni. My son, Matthew, mentioned you."

"He did?" Leni said. *Don't smile so big. What a dork.*

Geneva Walker slipped in beside her husband. "Hey," she said, smiling at Cora. "I see you've met my husband."

"Ex." Tom Walker put his arm around Geneva, pulled her close. "I love the woman like air, but I can't live with her."

"Can't live without me, either." Geneva smiled, cocked her head to the left. "That's my main squeeze over there. Calhoun Malvey. He doesn't love me as much as Tom does, but he likes me a helluva lot better. And he doesn't snore." She elbowed Mr. Walker in the side playfully.

"I hear you guys aren't too well prepared," Mr. Walker said to Dad. "You're going to have to learn fast. Don't be afraid to ask me for help. I'm always up for it. Anything you need to borrow, I have."

Leni heard something in Dad's "Thanks" that put her on alert. He sounded irritated all of a sudden. Offended. Mama heard it, too; she glanced worriedly at him.

Mad Earl stumbled forward. He was wearing a T-shirt that read I'VE BEEN FISHING SO LONG I'M A MASTER BAITER. He grinned drunkenly, swayed side to side, stumbled. "You offering Ernt help, Big Tom? That's mighty white of you. Sorta like King John offerin' to help his poor serfs. Maybe your friend the governor can help ya out."

"Good Lord, Earl, not again," Geneva said. "Let's play some music. Ernt, can you play an instrument?"

"Guitar," Dad said. "But I sold—"

"Great!" Geneva said, taking him by the arm, pulling him away from Mad Earl and toward Large Marge and the makeshift band gathered at the beach. She handed Dad the guitar Mr. Walker had put down. Mad Earl stumbled over to the fire and retrieved his crockery jug.

Leni wondered if Mama knew how beautiful she looked, standing there in her form-fitting pants, with her blond hair blowing in the sea breeze. Her beauty was as clear as a perfectly sung note and as out of place up here as an orchid.

Yeah. She knew exactly how beautiful she was. And Mr. Walker saw it, too.

"Can I get you something to drink?" he asked Mama. "Is a beer okay?"

"Why, sure, Tom. I'd love a beer," Mama said, letting Mr. Walker lead her toward the food table and the cooler full of Rainier beer.

Mama drifted along beside Mr. Walker. Her hips took up the beat of the music, swaying. She touched his forearm, and Mr. Walker looked down at her and smiled.

"Leni!"

She heard her name being called and turned.

Matthew stood on the point above, not far from the stairs, waving at her to come up.

She climbed the stairs and found him, holding a beer in each hand. "You ever had a beer before?" he asked.

She shook her head.

"Me, either. Come on." He took off into the thicket of trees to his left. They followed a twisting trail that led downward, past rock outcroppings.

He led her to a small clearing, its floor padded by lichen. Through an opening in the black spruce trees, they could see the party. The beach was only fifteen feet away but might have been a different universe. Out there, the adults were laughing and talking and making music. Little kids were pawing through pebbles for unbroken shells. Axle was off by himself, stabbing his knife into a decaying log.

Matthew sat down, stretching his legs out, leaning back against a log. Leni sat down beside him, close but not so close that she was touching him.

He snapped open a beer—*hiss*—and handed it to her. Wrinkling her nose, she took a sip. It fizzed in her throat and tasted bad.

"Gross," Matthew said, and she laughed. Another three sips and she leaned back into the log. A cool breeze came up off the beach, bringing with it the smell of brine and the pungent aroma of roasting meat. The whir and movement of the party was just beyond the trees.

They sat in a companionable silence, which amazed Leni. Usually she was a nervous wreck around kids she wanted to befriend.

Out on the beach, the party was in full swing now. Through a break in the trees, they could see it all. A mason jar was being passed from person to person. Her mother danced in a hip-swaying, hair-tossing way. She was like a woodland fairy, lit from within, dancing for the burly, sodden tree folk.

The beer made Leni feel woozy and light-headed, as if she were full of bubbles.

"What made you guys move up here?" Matthew asked. Before she could answer, he smashed his empty beer can into a rock, crumpling it.

Leni couldn't help laughing. Only a boy would do that. "My dad's kind of . . . an adventurer," she settled on as her answer. (Never tell the truth, never that Dad had trouble keeping a job and staying in one place, and *never* that he drank too much and liked to yell.) "He got tired of Seattle, I guess. What about you guys? When did you move here?"

"My grandpa, Eckhart Walker, came to Alaska during the Great Depression. He said he didn't want to stand in line for watery soup. So he packed up his stuff and hitchhiked to Seattle. He worked his way north from there. Supposedly he walked Alaska from shore to shore and even climbed Mount Alyeska with a ladder strapped to his back so he could cross glacial crevasses. He met my Grandma Lily in Nome. She ran a laundry and diner. They got married and decided to homestead."

"So your grandparents and your dad and you all grew up in that house?"

"Well. The big house was built a lot later, but we all grew up on this land. My mom's family lives in Fairbanks. My sister is living with them while she goes to college. And my folks split up a few years back, so Mom built herself a new house on the homestead and moved into it with her boyfriend, Cal, who is a real douchebag." He grinned. "But we all work together. He and Dad play chess in the winter. It's weird, but it's Alaska."

"Wow. I can't even imagine living in one place my whole life." She heard the edge of longing in her voice and was embarrassed by it. She tilted her beer up, swallowed the last foamy drips.

The makeshift band was going all-out now, hands banging on buckets, the guitar strumming, fiddles playing.

Thelma and Mama and Ms. Rhodes were swishing their hips in time to the music, singing loudly. *Ro-cky Moun-tain high, Color-ado . . .*

Over at the grill, Clyde yelled out, "Moose burgers are ready! Who wants cheese?"

"Come on," Matthew said. "I'm starving." He took her hand (it seemed natural) and led her through the trees and down onto the beach. They came up behind Dad and Mad Earl, who were off by themselves, drinking, and Leni heard Mad Earl clink his mason jar against Dad's, hitting it so hard it made a sturdy *clank*. "Tha' Tom Walker sure thinks his shit don't stink," Dad said.

"When TSHTF, he'll come crawling to me 'cuz I'm prepared," Mad Earl slurred.

Leni froze, mortified. She looked at Matthew. He'd heard it, too.

"Born rich," Dad added, his words slurred and slow in coming. "Thass what you said, right?"

Mad Earl nodded, stumbled into Dad. They held each other up. "He thinks he's better'n us."

Leni pulled away from Matthew; shame made her feel small. Alone.

"Leni?"

"I'm sorry you heard that," she said. And as if her dad's slurred bad-mouthing weren't bad enough, there was Mama over there, standing too close to Mr. Walker, smiling up at him in a way that could start trouble.

Just like all the other times. And Alaska was supposed to be different.

"What's the matter?" Matthew asked.

Leni shook her head, feeling a familiar sadness creep in. She could never tell him how it felt to live with a dad who scared you sometimes and a mother who loved him too much and made him prove how much he loved her in dangerous ways. Like flirting.

These were Leni's secrets. Her burdens. She couldn't share them.

All this time, all these years, she'd dreamed of having a real friend, one who would tell her everything. How had she missed the obvious?

Leni couldn't have a real friend because she couldn't be one. "Sorry," she mumbled. "It's nothing. Come on, let's eat. I'm starving."

SIX

————⋄∘⟫⟩⊗⟨⟪∘⋄————

After the party, back at the cabin, Leni's parents were all over each other, making out like teenagers, banging into walls, pressing their bodies together. The combination of alcohol and music (and maybe Tom Walker's attention) had made them crazy for each other.

Leni hurried up into the loft, where she covered her ears with her pillow and hummed "Come On Get Happy." When the cabin fell silent again, she crawled over to the stack of books she'd bought at the Salvation Army. A book of poetry by someone named Robert Service grabbed her attention. She took it back into bed with her and opened it to a poem called "The Cremation of Sam McGee." She didn't need to light her lantern because it was *still* freaking light outside, even this late.

> *There are strange things done in the midnight sun*
> *By the men who moil for gold;*
> *The Arctic trails have their secret tales*
> *That would make your blood run cold . . .*

Leni found herself falling into the poem's harsh, beautiful world. It captivated her so much that she kept reading, next about Dangerous Dan Mc-Grew and the lady known as Lou, and then "The Law of the Yukon." *This is the law of the Yukon, and ever she makes it plain: / "Send not your foolish and feeble; send me your strong and your sane."* Every line revealed a different side of this strange state they'd come to, but even so, she could never quite get Matthew out of her mind. She kept remembering the embarrassment she'd felt at the party when he overheard her father's ugly words.

Would he still want to be her friend?

The question consumed her, made her so tense she couldn't fall asleep. She would have sworn she didn't sleep at all, except that the next morning she woke to hear, "Come on, sleepyhead. I need your help while Mama cooks us up some grub. You've got time before school starts."

Grub? Had they suddenly become cowboys?

Leni pulled on her jeans and a big sweater and went downstairs for her shoes. Outside she found her dad up on that doghouse-looking thing on stilts. The cache. A skinned log ladder like the one leading up to the loft was propped up against the frame. Her dad stood near the top, hammering planks in place on the roof. "Hand me those penny nails, Red," he said. "A handful."

She grabbed the blue coffee can full of nails and climbed up the ladder behind him.

She fished out a single nail and handed it to him. "Your hand is shaking."

He stared down at the nail in his hand; it bounced in his trembling fist. His face was as pale as a sheet of parchment and his dark eyes looked bruised, the bags were so dark beneath them. "I drank too much last night. Had trouble sleeping."

Leni felt a jab of worry. Lack of sleep wasn't good for Dad; it made him anxious. So far, he'd been sleeping great in Alaska.

"Drinking does all kinds of bad shit to you, Red. I know better, too. Well, that's it," he said, pounding the last nail into the suede work glove that had been used to make the door's hinge. (Large Marge's idea—these Alaskans knew how to make do with anything.)

Leni climbed down and dropped to the ground, the coffee can full of nails rattling at the movement.

Dad rammed his hammer into his belt and started climbing down.

He dropped down beside Leni and tousled her hair. "I guess you're my little carpenter."

"I thought I was your librarian. Or your bookworm."

"Your mama says you can be anything. Some shit about a fish and a bicycle."

Yeah. Leni had heard that. Maybe Gloria Steinem had said it. Who knew? Mama spouted sayings all the time. It made as much sense to Leni as burning a perfectly good bra to make a point. Then again, it made no sense at all that in 1974 a grown woman with a job couldn't get a credit card in her name.

It's a man's world, baby girl.

She followed her dad from the cache to the deck, passing the bones of their new greenhouse and the garbage-bag-wrapped makeshift smokehouse. On the other side of the cabin, their new chickens pecked at the ground in their new enclosure. A rooster preened on the ramp that led to the coop's entrance.

At the water barrel, Dad ladled out a scoopful and splashed his face, which sent brown rivulets running down his cheeks. Then he went to the deck and sat on the bottom step. He looked bad. Like he'd been drunk for days and was sick from it. (Like he used to look, when he had nightmares and lost his temper.)

"Your mama seemed to like Tom Walker."

Leni tensed.

"Did you see the way he shoved our noses in his money? *I can loan you my tractor, Ernt,* or *Do you need a ride to town?* He looked down at me, Red."

"He said to me he thought you were a hero and it was a dang shame what happened to you boys over there," Leni lied.

"He did?" Dad pushed the hair out of his face. A frown creased his sunburned forehead.

"I like this place, Dad," Leni said, realizing suddenly the truth of her words. She already felt more at home in Alaska than she ever had in Seattle. "We're happy here. I see how happy you are. Maybe . . . maybe drinking isn't so good for you."

There was a tense moment of silence; by tacit agreement, Leni and Mama didn't mention his drinking or his temper.

"You're probably right about that, Red." He turned thoughtful. "Come on. Let's get you to school."

✦⟨❀⟩✦

AN HOUR LATER, Leni stared up at the one-room schoolhouse. Slinging her backpack's strap over one shoulder, she made her way to the front door, her lunch box clanging into her right thigh. Lollygagging, Mama would have called it. All Leni knew was that she was in no hurry to get to class.

She was almost to the front door when it banged open and students came out in a laughing, talking clot. Matthew's mom, Geneva, was in the middle, her work-chapped hands raised, telling everyone to calm down.

"Oh. Leni! Great!" Mrs. Walker said. "You're so late, I thought you were going to be absent. Tica couldn't make it in to school today, so I'm teaching. Ha! I barely graduated, let's face it." She laughed at herself. "And since I was more interested in boys than lessons in school, we're going on a field trip. I hate being inside on such a beautiful day."

Leni fell into step beside Mrs. Walker, who put an arm around her and drew her close. "I'm so glad you moved here."

"Me, too."

"Before you, Matthew had a religious aversion to deodorant. Now he wears clean clothes. It's a dream come true for those of us who live with him."

Leni had no idea what to say to that.

They marched down to the harbor in a herd, like the elephants in the *Jungle Book* movie. Leni felt Matthew's gaze on her. Twice she caught him staring at her with a confused expression on his face.

When they reached the guest dock in the harbor, with fishing boats creaking and bobbing all around them, Mrs. Walker paired the students up and assigned them to the canoes. "Matthew. Leni. The green one is yours. Put on your life vests. Matthew, make sure Leni is safe."

Leni did as she was told and climbed down into the back end of the canoe, facing the bow.

Matthew stepped down after her. The canoe rattled and creaked as he dropped into it.

He sat down facing her.

Leni didn't know much about canoeing, but she knew that was wrong. "You're supposed to face the other way."

"Matthew Denali Walker. What in the hell are you doing?" his mother said, gliding past him, with Moppet in her canoe. "Have you had a seizure or something? What's my name?"

"I wanted to talk to Leni for a sec, Mom. We'll catch up."

Mrs. Walker gave her son a knowing look. "Don't be long. It's school, not your first date."

Matthew groaned. "Oh, my God. You are so weird."

"I love you, too," Mrs. Walker said. Laughing, she paddled away. "Come on, kids," she yelled to the other canoes. "Head for Eaglet Cove."

"You're staring at me," Leni said to Matthew when they were alone.

Matthew laid his paddle across his lap. Waves slapped at their canoe, made a hollow, thunking sound as they drifted away from the dock.

She knew he was waiting for her to say something. There was only one thing to say. Wind combed through her hair, pulled corkscrew curls free of the elastic band that bound them. Red strands fluttered across her face. "I'm sorry about last night."

"Sorry for what?"

"Come on, Matthew. You don't have to be so nice."

"I have no idea what you're talking about."

"My dad was drunk," she said cautiously. The admission was more than she'd ever said aloud before and it felt disloyal. Maybe even dangerous. She'd seen some *ABC Afterschool Specials*. She knew that kids sometimes got taken away from unstable parents. The Man could break up any family for anything. She would never want to make waves or get her dad in trouble.

Matthew laughed. "They all were. Big whoop. Last year Mad Earl was so drunk he peed in the smokehouse."

"My dad gets . . . drunk sometimes . . . and mad. He says stuff he doesn't mean. I know you heard what he said about your dad."

"I hear that all the time. Especially from Mad Earl. Crazy Pete isn't too fond of Dad, either, and Billy Horchow tried to kill him once. No one ever found out why. Alaska's like that. Long winters and too much drinking can make a man do weird things. I didn't take it personally. My dad wouldn't, either."

"Wait. You mean you don't care?"

"This is Alaska. We live and let live. I don't care if your dad hates my dad. You're the one who matters, Leni."

"I matter?"

"To me you do."

Leni felt light enough to float right out of the canoe. She had told him one of her darkest, most terrible secrets, and he liked her anyway. "You're crazy."

"You bet your ass I am."

"Matthew Walker, quit yapping and start paddling," Mrs. Walker yelled at them.

"So we're friends, right?" Matthew said. "No matter what?"

Leni nodded. "No matter what."

"Groovy." Matthew turned around and faced the bow and started paddling. "I've got a cool thing to show you when we get where we are going," he said over his shoulder.

"What?"

"The bogs will be full of frogs' eggs. They're completely slimy and gross. Maybe I can get Axle to eat some. That kid is pure crazy."

Leni picked up her paddle.

She was glad he couldn't see how big her smile was.

❖

When Leni stepped out of the schoolhouse, laughing at something Matthew had said, she saw her parents waiting for her in the VW bus. Both of them. Mama leaned out of the window and waved like she was trying out for a spot on *The Price is Right.*

"Jeez. You really get the royal treatment."

Leni laughed and parted ways with him and climbed into the back of the bus.

"So, my little bookworm," Dad said as they rattled along on the dirt road out of town. "What useful thing did you learn today?"

"Well. We went on a field trip to Eaglet Cove and collected leaves for a biology project. Did you know that baneberries will make you have a heart attack if you eat them? And arrowgrass will cause respiratory failure?"

"Great," Mama said. "Now the plants can kill us, too."

Dad laughed. "That's *great*, Leni. Finally, a teacher who is teaching what matters."

"I also learned about the Klondike Gold Rush. The RCMP wouldn't let anyone cross the Chilkoot Trail unless they carried a stove with them. Carried. On their backs. But most of the miners who came up paid Indians to carry their supplies."

Dad nodded. "The rich, riding the backs of better men. It's the history of civilization itself. It's what's destroying America. Men who take, take, take."

Leni had noticed her dad saying more and more things like this since meeting Mad Earl.

Dad turned into their driveway and rumbled bumpily along. When they reached the homestead, he parked hard and said, "Okay, Allbrights, today my girls learn how to shoot."

He jumped out of the bus and dragged a bale of blackened, mildewed hay out from behind the chicken coop.

Mama lit up a cigarette. The smoke formed a gray corona above her blond hair. "This should be fun," she said without joy.

"We have to learn how. Large Marge and Thelma both said so," Leni said.

Mama nodded.

Leni moved to the driver's seat. "Uh. Mama? You noticed that Dad is sorta . . . prickly about Mr. Walker, right?"

Mama turned. Their eyes met. "Is he?" she said coolly.

"You know he is. So. I mean. You know how he can get if you . . . you know. Flirt."

Dad thumped on the front of the bus so hard Mama flinched and made a little sound, like a bitten-off scream. She dropped her cigarette and scrambled down to find it.

Leni knew her mama wouldn't respond anyway; that was another facet of their family weirdness. Dad blew his temper and Mama somehow encouraged it. Like maybe she needed to know how much he loved her all the time.

Dad herded Leni and Mama out of the bus and over the bumpy terrain to where he'd set up the bale of hay with a target on it.

He lifted his rifle from its leather scabbard, aimed, and shot, hitting the target dead center in the head he'd drawn on a piece of paper with a Magic Marker. A bunch of birds flew up from the trees, scattered through the blue sky, cawing angrily at Dad for disturbing them. A giant bald eagle, with a wingspan of at least six feet, glided in to take their place. It perched on an uppermost branch of a tree, pointed its yellow beak down at them. "That's what I expect of you two," Dad said.

Mama exhaled smoke. "We're going to be here awhile, baby girl."

Dad handed Leni the rifle. "Okay, Red. Let's see what you've got naturally. Look through the scope—don't get too close—and when you have the target in your sight, squeeze the trigger. Slow and steady. Breathe evenly. Okay, aim. I'll tell you when to shoot. Watch out for—"

She lifted the rifle, aimed, thought, *Wow, Matthew, I can't wait to tell you*, and accidently pulled the trigger.

The rifle hit her shoulder hard enough to knock her off her feet and the sight slammed into her eye area with a crack that sounded like breaking bone.

Leni screamed in pain, dropped the rifle, and collapsed to her knees in the mud, clamping a hand over her throbbing eye. It hurt so badly she felt sick to her stomach, almost puked.

She was still screaming and crying when she felt someone drop in place beside her, felt a hand rubbing her back. "Shit, Red," Dad said. "I didn't tell you to shoot. You're okay. Just breathe. It's a normal rookie mistake. You'll be fine."

"Is she okay?" Mama screamed. "Is she?"

Dad pulled Leni to her feet. "No crying, Leni," he said. "This isn't some beauty-pageant training where you learn to sing for a college scholarship. You have to listen to me. This is your *life* I'm trying to save."

"But . . ." It hurt so badly. A headache burst into pounding life behind her eyes. She couldn't see well out of her injured eye. Half the world was blurry. It hurt even more that he didn't care about how much it hurt. She couldn't help feeling sorry for herself. She would bet Tom Walker never treated Matthew this way.

"Stop it, Lenora," Dad said, giving her shoulder a little shake. "You said you liked Alaska and wanted to belong here."

"Ernt, please, she's not a soldier," Mama said.

Dad spun Leni around, gripped her shoulders, shook her hard. "How many girls were abducted in Seattle before we left?"

"L-lots. One every month. Sometimes more."

"Who were they?"

"Just girls. Teenagers, mostly?"

"And Patty Hearst was taken from her apartment, with her boyfriend right there, right?"

Leni wiped her eyes, nodded.

"You want to be a victim or a survivor, Lenora?"

Leni had such a headache she couldn't think. "S-survivor?"

"We have to be ready for anything up here. I want you able to protect yourself." His voice broke on that. She saw the emotion he was trying so hard to hide. He loved her. That was why he wanted her to be able to take care of herself. "What if I'm not here when something happens? When a bear breaks down the door or a pack of wolves surrounds you? I need to know you can protect your mom and save yourself."

Leni sniffled hard, struggled for control. He was right. She needed to be strong. "I know."

"Okay. Pick up the rifle," Dad said. "Try again."

Leni picked up the mud-splattered rifle. Aimed.

"Don't hold the sight so close to your eye. The recoil is a mother on this. There. Hold it like that." Dad gently repositioned the weapon. "Put your finger on the trigger. Lightly."

She couldn't do it. She was too scared of getting cracked in the eye again.

"Do it," Dad said.

She took a deep breath and slid her forefinger along the trigger, feeling the cold steel curve.

She ducked her chin, drew back farther from the sight.

She forced herself to concentrate. The sounds faded away: the cawing of the crows and the wind clattering through the trees diminished until all she heard was the beating of her own heart.

She closed her left eye. Tried to calm down.

The world spiraled down to a single circle. Blurry at first, a double image.

Focus.

She saw the bale of hay, the white paper attached to it, the outline of a man's head and shoulders. She was amazed by the clarity of the image. She adjusted the position of the rifle, took aim at the very center of the head.

Slowly, she squeezed the trigger.

The rifle cracked in recoil, hit her hard in the shoulder again, so hard she stumbled, but the sight didn't hit her eye.

The bullet hit the bale of hay. Not the target, not even the white paper around the target, but the bale. She felt a surprising pride in that small achievement.

"I knew you could do it, Red. By the time we're done, you'll be sniper-good."

SEVEN

M s. Rhodes was at the chalkboard writing assignment pages when Leni got to school. "Ah," the teacher said. "It looks like someone put the scope too close to her eye. Do you need an aspirin?"

"Rookie mistake," Leni said, almost proud of her injury. It meant she was becoming an Alaskan. "I'm fine."

Ms. Rhodes nodded. "Take your seat and open your history book."

Leni and Matthew stared at each other as she entered the classroom. His smile was so big she saw his mouthful of crooked teeth.

She sidled into her desk, which clanked against his.

"Almost everyone gets popped in the eye the first time. I had a black eye for, like, a week. Does it hurt?"

"It did. But learning to shoot was so cool, I didn't—"

"Moose!" Axle yelled, popping up from his seat and running to the window.

Leni and Matthew followed him. All of the kids crowded together at the window, watching a giant bull moose amble through the grassy area behind the schoolhouse. He knocked over the picnic table and began eating the bushes.

Matthew leaned close to Leni; his shoulder brushed hers. "I say we make excuses and book it out of school today. I'll say I'm needed at home after lunch."

Leni felt a little thrill at the idea of skipping school. She'd never done it before. "I could say I have a headache. I'd just have to be back here at three for pick-up."

"Cool," Matthew said.

"Okay, okay," Ms. Rhodes said. "Enough of that. Leni, Axle, Matthew, turn to page one-seventeen in your Alaska state history book . . ."

For the rest of the morning, Leni and Matthew watched the clock nervously. Just before lunchtime, Leni pleaded a headache and said she needed to go home. "I can walk to the general store and call my parents on the ham radio."

"Sure," Ms. Rhodes said. The teacher didn't seem to question the lie, and Leni scooted out of the classroom and closed the door behind her. She walked down to the road and ducked into the trees, waiting.

A half hour later, Matthew strode out of the school, grinning widely.

"So what are we gonna do?" Leni asked. What choices were there? There was no TV, no movie theater, no paved roads for bike riding, no drive-ins for milkshakes, no roller rinks or playgrounds.

He took her by the hand and led her to a muddy all-terrain vehicle. "Climb on," Matthew said, swinging his leg over the ATV and settling on the black seat.

Leni did not think this was a good idea, but she didn't want him to think she was a scaredy-cat, so she climbed aboard. Awkwardly, she put her arms around his waist.

He twisted the throttle and they were off in a cloud of dust, the engine making a high-pitched whine, rocks flying out from beneath the wide rubber tires. Matthew drove through town, rumbled over the bridge, and onto the dirt road. Just past the airstrip, he veered into the trees, thumped over a ditch, and hurtled up a trail she didn't even see until they were on it.

They drove uphill, into thick trees, onto a plateau. From there, Leni saw a crook of blue, seawater carving into the land, waves crashing onto the shore. Matthew slowed the vehicle and expertly guided it over rough terrain, where there was no trail beneath their tires. Leni was thrown about; she had to hold tightly to him.

Finally he eased to a stop and clicked off the motor.

Silence enveloped them instantly, broken only by the waves crashing on the black rocks below. Matthew dug through the bag on his three-wheeler and pulled out a pair of binoculars. "Come on."

He walked ahead of her, his feet steady on the rough, rocky terrain. Twice Leni almost fell as rock gave way beneath her feet, but Matthew was like a mountain goat, perfectly at home.

He led her to a clearing perched like a scooped hand above the sea. There were two handmade wooden chairs positioned to face the trees. Matthew plopped down in one and indicated the other for her.

Leni dropped her backpack onto the grass and sat down, waiting as Matthew peered through the binoculars, and scanned the trees. "There they are." He handed her the binoculars, pointed to a stand of trees. "That's Lucy and Ricky. My mom named 'em."

Leni peered through the binoculars. At first all she saw was trees, trees, and more trees as she panned slowly from left to right, and then, a flash of white.

She eased back to the left a few degrees.

A pair of bald eagles perched on a bathtub-sized nest built high in the trees. One of the birds was feeding a trio of eaglets who jostled and lurched, beaks up, to get the regurgitated food. Leni could hear their squabbling, squawking cries over the crash of water below.

"Wow," Leni said. She would have pulled her Polaroid out of her backpack (she never went anywhere without it), but the eagles were too far away for the clunky camera to capture.

"They've been coming back here to lay eggs for as long as I can remember. Mom first brought me here when I was little. You should see them making the nest. It's amazing. And they mate for life. I wonder what Ricky would do if something happened to Lucy. My mom says that nest weighs almost a ton. I've watched eaglets leave that nest my whole life."

"Wow," Leni said again, smiling as one of the eaglets flapped its wings and tried to climb up over its siblings.

"We haven't come out here in a long time, though."

Leni heard something in Matthew's voice. She lowered the binoculars and looked at him. "You and your mom?"

He nodded. "Since she and Dad split up, it's been hard. Maybe it's 'cuz my sister, Alyeska, moved to Fairbanks to go to college. I miss her."

"You guys must be close."

"Yeah. She's cool. You'd like her. She thinks she wants to live in a city, but no way it will last. She'll be back. Dad says we both have to go to college so we know all our options. He's kind of pushy about it, actually. I don't need college to tell me what I want to be."

"You already know?"

"Sure. I want to be a pilot. Like my Uncle Went. I love being up in the sky. But my dad says it's not enough. I guess I need to know about physics and shit."

Leni understood. They were kids, she and Matthew; no one asked their opinion or told them anything. They just had to muddle along and live in the world presented to them, confused a lot of the time because nothing made sense, but certain of their subterranean place on the food chain.

She sat back in the splintery chair. He had told her something personal about himself, something that mattered. She needed to do the same thing. Wasn't that how true friendships worked? She swallowed hard, said quietly, "You're lucky your dad wants the best for you. My dad has been . . . weird since the war."

"Weird how?"

Leni shrugged. She didn't know exactly what to say, or how to say it without revealing too much. "He has—nightmares—and bad weather can set him off. Sometimes. But he hasn't had a nightmare since we moved here. So maybe he's better."

"I don't know. Winter is one big night up here. People go batshit in the dark, run screaming, open fire on their pets and friends."

Leni felt a tightening in her stomach. She had never really thought about the fact that in winter, it would be as dark as it was light now. She didn't want to think about that, *winter dark*. "What do you worry about?" she asked.

"I worry that my mom will leave us. I mean, I know she built a house and stayed on the homestead, and that my folks still love each other in some weird way, but it's not the same. She just came home one day and said she didn't love Dad anymore. She loves Cal the creep." He turned in his chair, looked at Leni. "It's scary that people can just stop loving you, you know?"

"Yeah."

"I wish school lasted longer," he said.

"I know. We have three more days before summer break. And then . . ."

Once school ended, Leni would be expected to work full-time at the homestead and so would Matthew at his place. They'd hardly see each other.

⊹⟨✿⟩⊹

ON THE LAST DAY OF SCHOOL, Leni and Matthew made all kinds of promises about how they would keep in touch until classes started again in September, but the truth shouldered in between them. They were kids and not in control of anything, their own schedules least of all. Leni felt lonely already as she walked away from Matthew on that last day and headed for the VW bus waiting on the side of the road.

"You look down in the dumps, baby girl," Mama said from her place in the driver's seat.

Leni climbed into the passenger seat. She didn't see the point in whining about something that couldn't be changed. It was three o'clock. There was an ocean of daylight left; that meant hours of chores to do.

As soon as they were home, Mama said, "I have an idea. Go get us that striped wool blanket and the chocolate bar in the cooler. I'll meet you down on the beach."

"What are we going to do?"

"Absolutely nothing."

"What? Dad will never agree to that."

"Well, he's not here." Mama smiled.

Leni didn't waste a second. She ran to the house (before Mama changed her mind). She grabbed the slim Hershey's chocolate bar from the cooler in the kitchen and the blanket from the back of the sofa. Wrapping it around her like a poncho, she headed for the rickety beach stairs, followed them down to the curl of water-stippled gray pebbles that was their own private beach. To the left were dark, enticing stone caves, carved by centuries of hurling water.

Mama stood in the tall grass up from the beach, a cigarette already lit. Leni was pretty sure that, to her, childhood would always smell like sea air and cigarette smoke and her mother's rose-scented perfume.

Leni spread out the blanket on the uneven ground and she and Mama sat down on it, their legs stretched out, their bodies angled into each other. In front of them, the blue sea rolled forward ceaselessly, washing over the stones, rustling them. Not far away an otter floated on its back, using its small black paws to crack open a clam.

"Where's Dad?"

"He went fishing with Mad Earl. I think Dad's hoping to ask the old man for a loan. Money is getting pretty tight. I've still got some of the money from my mom, but I've been using it for cigarettes and Polaroid film." She gave Leni a soft smile.

"I'm not sure Mad Earl is good for Dad," Leni said.

Mama's smile faded. "I know what you mean."

"He's happy here, though," Leni said. She tried not to think about the conversation she'd had with Matthew, about how winter was coming and winter was dark and cold and crazy-making.

"I wish you remembered your dad from before 'Nam."

"Yeah." Leni had heard dozens of stories of that time. Mama loved to talk about Before, about who they'd been in the beginning. The words were like a much-loved fairy tale.

Mama had been sixteen when she got pregnant.

Sixteen.

Leni would be fourteen in September. Amazingly, she'd never really thought about that before. She'd known her mama's age, of course, but she hadn't really put the facts together. *Sixteen.*

"You were only two years older than me when you got pregnant," Leni said.

Mama sighed. "I was a junior in high school. Christ. No wonder my parents threw a clot." She gave Leni a crooked, charming smile. "They were not the kind of people who could understand a girl like me. They hated my clothes and my music and I hated their rules. At sixteen, I thought I knew everything, and I told them so. They sent me away to a Catholic girls' school, where rebellion meant rolling up the waistband of your skirt to shorten the hem and show an inch of skin above your knees. We were taught to kneel and pray and marry well.

"Your dad came into my life like a rogue wave, knocking me over. Everything he said upended my conventional world and changed who I was. I stopped knowing how to breathe without him. He told me I didn't need school. I believed everything he said. Your dad and I were too in love to be careful, and I got pregnant. My dad exploded when I told him. He wanted to send me away to one of those houses for unwed mothers. I knew they'd take you away from me. I've never hated anyone more than I hated him in that moment."

Mama sighed. "So we ran away. I was sixteen—almost seventeen—and your dad was twenty-five. When you came along, we were flat broke and living in a trailer park, but none of that mattered. What was money or work or new clothes when you had the most perfect baby in the world?"

Mama leaned back. "He used to carry you all the time. At first in his arms and then on his shoulders. You adored him. We shut out the world and lived on love, but the world came roaring back."

"The war," Leni said.

Mama nodded. "I begged your dad not to go to Vietnam. We fought and fought about it. I didn't want to be a soldier's wife, but he wanted to go. So I packed my tears with his clothes and let him go. It was supposed to be for a year. I didn't know what to do, where to go, how to live without him. I ran out of money and moved back home with my parents, but I couldn't stand it there. All we did was fight. They kept telling me to divorce your father and think about you, and finally I left again. That's when I found the commune and people who didn't judge me for being a kid with a kid. Then your dad's helicopter got shot down and he was captured. I got one letter from him in six years."

Leni remembered the letter and how her mother had cried after reading it.

"When he came home, he looked like a dead man," Mama said. "But he loved us. Loved us like air. Said he couldn't sleep if I wasn't in his arms, although he didn't sleep much then, either."

As always, Mama's story came to a stumbling halt at this point, the fairy tale over. The witch's door slammed shut on the wandering kids. The man who'd come home from war was not the same man who'd boarded the plane for Vietnam. "He's better up here, though," Mama said. "Don't you think? He's almost himself again."

Leni stared down at the sea, rolling inexorably toward her. Nothing you did could hold back that rising tide. One mistake or miscalculation and you could be stranded or washed away. All you could do was protect yourself by reading the charts and being prepared and making smart choices. "You know it's dark up here for six months in the winter. And snowy and freezing cold and stormy."

"I know."

"You always said bad weather made him worse."

Leni felt her mother pull away from her. This was a fact she didn't want to confront. They both knew why. "It won't be like that here," Mama said, grinding out her cigarette in the rocks beside her. She said it again, just for good measure. "Not here. He's happier here. You'll see."

◈

As the long summer days passed, Leni's anxiety faded. Summer in Alaska was pure magic. The Land of the Midnight Sun. Rivers of light; eighteen-hour days with only a breath of dusk to separate one from the next.

Light, and work; that was summer in Alaska.

There was so much to get done. Everyone talked about it, all the time. In line at the diner, during checkout at the General Store, on the ferry to town. *How's the fishing going? Hunting good? How's the garden?* Every question was about stocking up on food, getting ready for winter.

Winter was a Big Deal. Leni had learned that. The coming cold was a constant subtext up here. Even if you were out fishing on a beautiful summer day, you were catching fish for winter. It might be fun, but it was serious business. Survival, it seemed, could hinge on the smallest thing.

She and her parents woke at five A.M. and mumbled through breakfast and then set out to do their chores. They rebuilt the goat pen, chopped wood, tended the garden, made soap, caught and smoked salmon, tanned hides, canned fish and vegetables, darned socks, duct-taped everything together. They moved, hauled, nailed, built, scraped. Large Marge sold them three goats and Leni learned how to care for them. She also learned to pick berries and make jam and shuck clams and cure salmon eggs into the best bait in the world. In the evenings, Mama made them new foods—salmon or halibut in almost everything, and vegetables from the garden. Dad cleaned his guns and fixed the metal traps Mad Earl had sold to him and read manuals on butchering animals. Barter and trade and helping out your neighbor was the way they all lived. You never knew when someone was going to drive up your driveway and offer extra meat or some mildewed planks of wood or a bucket of blueberries in exchange for something.

Parties sprouted like weeds in this wild place. People showed up with coolers full of salmon and a case of beer and a call was made on the ham radio. A boat full of fishermen pulled up to shore; a float plane landed in their cove. The next thing you knew, people were gathered around a fire on the beach somewhere, laughing and talking and drinking well past midnight.

Leni became an adult that summer; that was how it felt to her. In September, she turned fourteen, started her period, and finally needed a bra. Pimples popped out like tiny pink volcanoes on her cheeks, her nose, between her eyebrows. When it first happened, she worried about seeing Matthew, worried that he would change his opinion based on her awkward adolescence;

but he didn't seem to notice that her skin had become an enemy. Seeing him remained the highlight of her days up here. Whenever they got the chance to be together that summer, they ran off from the group and holed up and talked. He recited Robert Service poems to her and showed her special things like a nest full of blue duck eggs or a huge bear print in the sand. She took pictures of the things he showed her—and of him—in every light and tacked them into a giant collage on her loft bedroom wall.

Summer ended as quickly as it had begun. Autumn in Alaska was less a season and more an instant, a transition. Rain started to fall and didn't stop, turning the ground to mud, drowning the peninsula, falling in curtains of gray. Rivers rose to splash over their crumbling banks, tearing big chunks away, changing course.

All at once, it seemed, the leaves of cottonwood trees around the cabin turned golden and whispered to themselves, then curled into black flutes and floated to the ground in crispy, lacy heaps.

School started, and with it Leni felt her childhood return. She met Matthew in the classroom and took her seat beside him, scooting in close.

His smile reawakened her in a way, reminded her that there was more to life than work. He taught her something new about friendship: it picked right back up where you'd left off, as if you hadn't been apart at all.

⁕⤞❀⤝⁕

On a cold night in late September, after a long work day, Leni stood at the window, staring out at the dark yard. She and her mother were exhausted; they'd worked from sunup to sundown, canning the last of the season's salmon—preparing jars, scaling fish, slicing the plump pink and silver strips, and cutting off the slimy skin. They packed the strips in jars and put them into the pressure cooker. One by one, they carried the jars down to the root cellar and stacked them on newly built shelves.

"If there are ten smart guys in a room and one crackpot, you can bet who your dad will like best."

"Huh?" Leni asked.

"Never mind."

Mama moved in to stand by Leni. Outside, night had fallen. A full moon cast blue-white light on everything. Stars filled the sky with pinpricks and elliptical smears of light. Up here, at night, the sky was impossibly huge and never quite turned black, but stayed a deep velvet blue. The world beneath it dwindled down to nothing: a dollop of firelight, a squiggly white reflection of moonlight on the tarnished waves.

Dad was out there in the dark with Mad Earl. The two men stood beside each other at a fire burning in an oil drum, passing a jug back and forth. Black smoke billowed up from the garbage they were burning. Everyone else who had come by to help had gone home hours ago.

Mad Earl suddenly pulled out his pistol and shot at the trees.

Dad laughed uproariously at that.

"How long are they going to stay out there?" Leni asked. The last time she'd gone to the outhouse, she'd heard snippets of their conversation. *Ruining the country . . . keep ourselves safe . . . coming anarchy . . . nuclear.*

"Who knows?"

Mama sounded irritated. She'd fried the moose steaks Mad Earl had brought with him; then she'd made roasted potatoes and set the card table with their camping plates and utensils. One of Leni's paperback novels had been used to prop up the table's bad leg.

That had been hours ago. Now the meat was probably as dry as an old boot.

"Enough is enough," Mama finally said. She went outside. Leni sidled to the doorway, pushed the door open so she could hear. Goats bleated at the sound of footsteps.

"Hey, Cora," Mad Earl said, smiling sloppily. He stood unsteady on his feet, swayed to the right, stumbled.

"Would you like to stay for dinner, Earl?" Mama asked.

"Naw, but thanks," Mad Earl said, stumbling sideways. "My daughter will tan my hide if I don't make it home. She's making salmon chowder."

"Another time then," Mama said, turning back to the cabin. "Come on in, Ernt. Leni's starving."

Mad Earl staggered to his truck, climbed in, and drove away, stopping and starting, honking the horn.

Dad made his way across the yard in a mincing, overcautious way that meant he was drunk. Leni had seen it before. He slammed the door behind him and stumbled to the table, half falling into his chair.

Mama carried in a platter of meat and oven-browned potatoes and a warm loaf of sourdough bread, which Thelma had taught them how to make from the starter every homesteader kept on hand.

"Loo . . . s great," Dad said, shoveling a forkful of moose meat into his mouth, chewing noisily. He looked up, bleary-eyed. "You two have a lot of catching up to do. Earl and I were talking about it. When TSHTF, you two would be the first casualties."

"TSHTF? What in God's name are you talking about?" Mama said.

Leni shot her mother a warning look. Mama knew better than to say anything about anything when he was drunk.

"When the shit hits the fan. You know. Martial law. A nuclear bomb. Or a pandemic." He tore off a hunk of bread, dragged it in the meat juice.

Mama sat back. She lit up a cigarette, eyeing him.

Don't do it, Mama, Leni thought. *Don't say anything.*

"I don't like all of this end-of-the-world rhetoric, Ernt. And there's Leni to consider. She—"

Dad slammed his fist down on the table so hard everything rattled. "Damn it, Cora, can't you *ever* just support me?"

He got to his feet and went to the row of parkas hanging by the front door. He moved jerkily. She thought she heard him say, *G-damn stupid*, and mutter something else. He shook his head and flexed and unflexed his hands. Leni saw a wildness in him, barely contained emotion rising hard and fast.

Mama ran after him, reached out.

"Don't touch me," he snarled, shoving her away.

Dad grabbed a parka and stepped into his boots and went outside, slamming the door shut behind him.

Leni caught her mother's gaze, held it. In those wide blue eyes that held on to every nuance of expression, she saw her own anxiety reflected. "Does he believe all of that end-of-the-world stuff?"

"I think he does," Mama said. "Or maybe he just wants to. Who knows? It doesn't matter, though. It's all talk."

Leni knew what did matter.

The weather was getting worse.

And so was he.

✦✦⟨❀⟩✦✦

"WHAT'S IT REALLY LIKE?" Leni asked Matthew the next day at the end of school. All around them, kids were gathering up their supplies to go home.

"What?"

"Winter."

Matthew thought about it. "Terrible and beautiful. It's how you know if you're cut out to be an Alaskan. Most go running back to the Outside before it's over."

"The Great Alone," Leni said. That was what Robert Service called Alaska.

"You'll make it," Matthew said earnestly.

She nodded, wishing she could tell him that she'd begun to worry as much about the dangers inside of her home as outside of it.

She could tell Matthew a lot of things, but not that. She could say her father drank too much or that he yelled or lost his temper, but not that he sometimes scared her. The disloyalty of such a thing was impossible to contemplate.

They exited the schoolhouse together, walking shoulder to shoulder.

Outside, the VW bus waited for her. It looked bad these days, all dinged up and scraped. The bumper was duct-taped in place. The muffler had fallen off at a pothole, so now the poor old thing roared like a race car. Both of her parents were inside, waiting for her.

"'Bye," Leni said to Matthew, and headed to the vehicle. She tossed her backpack into the back of the bus and climbed in. "Hey, guys," Leni said.

Dad jammed the bus in reverse, backed up, and turned around.

"Mad Earl wants me to teach his family a few things," Dad said, turning onto the main road. "We talked about it the other night."

In no time, they were out of town and up the hill and pulling into the compound. Dad was the first one out of the bus. He grabbed his rifle from the back and slung it over his shoulder.

Mad Earl, seated on his porch, immediately rose and waved. He yelled something Leni couldn't hear and people stopped working. They put down their shovels and axes and chain saws and moved into the clearing in the center of the compound.

Mama opened the door and got out. Leni followed close behind, her waf-flestompers sinking into the wet, spongy ground.

A dented Ford truck pulled up beside the VW and parked. Axle and the two girls, Agnes and Marthe, got out of the truck and headed for the crowd gathering in front of Mad Earl's porch.

Mad Earl stood on the eroding, slanted porch, his bandy legs spaced a little farther apart than looked comfortable. His white hair hung limply around his loose-skinned face, greasy at the roots and frizzing at the ends. He wore dirty jeans tucked into brown rubber boots and a flannel work shirt that had seen better days. He made a sweeping motion with his hands. "Get closer, come on in. Ernt, Ernt, come up by me, son."

There was a murmur of sound through the crowd; heads turned.

Dad strode past Thelma and Ted, smiling at Clyde and thumping his back when he reached him. Dad stepped up onto the porch beside Mad Earl. He looked tall and rangy next to the diminutive old man. Super-handsome, with all that black hair and the bushy black mustache.

"We was talking last night, us boys, about the shit going on Outside," Mad Earl said. "Our president is a certified crook and a bomb blowed a TWA jet right outta the sky. Ain't nobody safe anymore."

Leni turned, looked up at Mama, who shrugged.

"My son, Bo, was the very best of us. He loved Alaska and he loved the good old US of A enough to volunteer to fight in that damn war. And we lost him. But even from that hellhole, he was thinking of us. His family. Our safety and security mattered to him. So he sent us his friend, Ernt Allbright, to be one of us." Mad Earl thumped Dad on the back, kind of pushed him forward. "I been watching Ernt all summer and now I know. He wants the best for us."

Dad pulled a folded newspaper from his back pocket, held it up. The headline read: *Bomb on TWA Flight 841 Kills 88.* "We might live in the bush, but we go to Homer and Sterling and Soldotna. We know what's going on in the Outside. Bombings by the IRA, the PLO, Weatherman. Folks killing each other, kidnappings. All those girls disappearing in Washington State; now someone is killing girls in Utah. The Symbionese Liberation Army. India testing nuclear bombs. It's only a matter of time before World War Three starts. It could be nuclear . . . or biological. And when that happens, the shit will really hit the fan."

Mad Earl nodded, murmured his agreement.

"Mama?" Leni whispered. "Is all that true?"

Mama lit up a cigarette. "A thing can be true and not the truth, now shush. We don't want to make him mad."

Dad was the center of attention, and he drank it up. "You all have done a great job of preparing for scarcity. You've excelled at homesteader self-reliance. You have a good water-collection system and good food stores. You've staked out freshwater sources and you're expert hunters. Your garden could be bigger, but it's well tended. You're ready to survive anything. Except the effects of martial law."

"Whaddaya mean?" Ted asked.

Dad looked . . . different somehow. Taller. His shoulders were higher and more square than she'd seen before. "Nuclear war. A pandemic. An electromagnetic pulse. Earthquake. Tidal wave. Tornado. Mount Redoubt blowing up, or Mount Rainer. In 1908 there was an explosion in Siberia that was a thousand times more powerful than the bomb dropped on Hiroshima. There are a million ways for this sick, corrupt world to end."

Thelma frowned. "Oh, come on, Ernt, there's no need to scare—"

"Shush, Thelma," Mad Earl snapped.

"Whatever comes, man-made tragedy or natural disaster, the first thing that happens is a breakdown of law and order," Dad said. "Think of it: No power. No communications. No grocery stores. No uncontaminated food. No water. No civilization. Martial law."

Dad paused, made eye contact with each person, one by one. "People like Tom Walker, with his big house and expensive boats and his excavator, will be caught off guard. What good will all that land and wealth do him when he runs out of food or medical supplies? None. And you know what will happen when people like Tom Walker realize they aren't prepared?"

"What?" Mad Earl stared up at Dad as if he'd just seen God.

"He'll come *here*, banging on our doors, begging for help from *us*, the people he thought he was better than." Dad paused. "We have to know how to protect ourselves and keep out the marauders who will want what we have. First off, we need to put together bug-out bags—packs that are already packed for survival. We need to be able to disappear at a moment's notice, with everything we need."

"Yeah!" someone yelled.

"But that's not enough. We have a good start here. But security is lax. I think Bo left me his land so I would find my way here, to you, and teach you that it's not enough to be prepared for survival. You have to fight for what's yours. Kill anyone who comes to take it from you. I know you all are hunters, but we'll need more than guns when TSHTF. Impact weapons break bones. Knives sever arteries. Arrows puncture. Before the first snowfall, I promise you, each one of us will be ready for the worst, every single one of you—from youngest to oldest—will be able to protect yourself and your family from the danger that's coming."

Mad Earl nodded.

"So. Everyone line up. I want to assess precisely how good each of you is with a gun. We'll start there."

EIGHT

B y the first of November, the days were shortening fast. Leni felt the loss of every moment of light. Dawn came reluctantly at nine A.M. and night reclaimed the world around five P.M. Barely eight hours of daylight now. Sixteen hours of darkness. Night swept in like nothing Leni had ever seen before, like the winged shadow of a creature too big and predatory to comprehend.

Weather had become impossible to predict. It had rained and snowed and rained again. Now the late-afternoon sky spit down at them, a freezing mixture of sleet and rain. Water pooled on the ground, turned to sheets of dirty, weed-studded ice. Leni had to do her chores in muck. After feeding the goats and chickens, she trudged into the woods behind the house, carrying two empty buckets. The cottonwoods were bare; autumn had turned them into skeletons. Everything with a heartbeat was hunkered down somewhere, trying to get out of the sleet and rain.

As she walked down toward the river, a cold wind pulled at her hair, whined across her jacket. She hunched her shoulders and kept her head down.

It took five trips to fill the steel water barrel they kept at the side of the house. Rain helped but couldn't be relied upon. Water, like firewood, could never be left to chance.

She was sweating hard, scooping a bucket of water from the creek, slopping it across her boots, when night fell. And she meant *fell*; it hit hard and fast, like a lid clanging down on its pot.

When Leni turned homeward, she saw an endless black expanse. Nothing distinguishable, no stars overhead, no moon to light a path.

She fumbled in her parka pocket for the headlamp her dad had given her. She adjusted the strap and put it on, snapping the light switch. She pulled a pistol out of its holster, stuck it in her waistband.

Her heart was hammering in her chest as she bent down and picked up the two buckets she'd filled with water. The metal handles bit into her gloved hands.

The icy rain turned to snow, stung her cheeks and forehead.

Winter.

The bears aren't in hibernation yet, are they? They are most dangerous now, feeding hungrily before going to sleep.

She saw a pair of yellow eyes staring at her from the darkness.

No. She was imagining it.

The ground beneath her changed, gave way. She stumbled. Water sloshed out of the buckets and onto her gloves. *Don'tpanicDon'tpanicDon'tpanic.*

Her headlight revealed a fallen log in front of her. Breathing hard, she stepped over it, heard the screech of bark against her jeans, and kept going; up a hill, down one, around a dense black thicket. Finally, up ahead, she saw a glimmer.

Light.

The cabin.

She wanted to run. She was *desperate* to get home, to feel her mother's arms around her, but she wasn't stupid. She had already made one mistake—she hadn't kept track of time.

As she neared the cabin, the night separated a little. She saw charcoal outlines against the black: the sheen of the metal stovepipe poking up through the roof, a side window full of light, the shadow of people inside. The air smelled of wood smoke and welcome.

Leni rushed around to the side of the cabin, lifted the barrel's makeshift lid, and poured what was left of her water into the barrel. The split second between her upending the bucket and the sound of the water splashing in told her the barrel was about three-quarters full.

Leni was shaking so hard it took two tries for her to unlatch the door.

"I'm back," she said, stepping into the cabin, her whole body shaking.

"Shut up, Leni," Dad snapped.

Mama stood in front of Dad. She was unsteady-looking, dressed in ragged sweats and a big sweater. "Hey, there, baby girl," she said. "Hang up your parka and take off your boots."

"I'm talking to you, Cora," Dad said.

Leni heard anger in his voice, saw her mother flinch.

"You have to take the rice back. Tell Large Marge we can't pay for it," he said. "And the pilot bread and powdered milk, too."

"But . . . you haven't gotten a moose yet," Mama said. "We need—"

"It's all my fault, is it?" Dad shouted.

"That's not what I meant, and you know it. But winter's bearing down on us. We need more food than we have, and our money—"

"You think I don't know we need money?" He swiped at the chair in front of him, sent it tumbling and cracking to the floor.

The sudden wildness in his eyes, the showing of the whites, scared Leni. She took a step backward.

Mama went to him, touched his face, tried to gentle him. "Ernt, baby, we'll figure it out."

He yanked back and headed for the door. Grabbing his parka from its place on the hook by the window, he pulled the door open, let in the sweeping cold, and slammed it shut behind him. A moment later, the VW bus engine roared to life; headlights stabbed through the window, turned Mama golden white.

"It's the weather," Mama said, lighting a cigarette, watching him drive away. Her beautiful skin looked sallow in the headlights' glow, almost waxen.

"It's going to get worse," Leni said. "Every day is darker and colder."

"Yeah," Mama said, looking as scared as Leni suddenly felt. "I know."

WINTER TIGHTENED ITS GRIP on Alaska. The vastness of the landscape dwindled down to the confines of their cabin. The sun rose at a quarter past ten in the morning and set only fifteen minutes after the end of the school day. Less than six hours of light a day. Snow fell endlessly, blanketed everything. It piled up in drifts and spun its lace across windowpanes, leaving them nothing to see except themselves. In the few daylight hours, the sky stretched gray overhead; some days there was merely the memory of light rather than any real glow. Wind scoured the landscape, cried out as if in pain. The fireweed froze, turned into intricate ice sculptures that stuck up from the snow. In the freezing cold, everything stuck—car doors froze, windows cracked, engines refused to start. The ham radio filled with warnings of bad weather and listed the deaths that were as common in Alaska in the winter as frozen eyelashes. People died for the smallest mistake—car keys dropped in a river, a gas tank gone dry, a snow machine breaking down, a turn taken too fast. Leni couldn't go anywhere or do anything without a warning. Already the winter seemed to have gone on forever. Shore ice seized the coastline, glazed the shells and stones until the beach looked like a silver-sequined collar. Wind roared across the homestead, as it had all winter, transforming the white landscape with every breath. Trees cowered in the face of it, animals built dens and burrowed holes and went into hiding. Not so different from the humans, who hunkered down in this cold, took special care.

Leni's life was the smallest it had ever been. On good days, when the bus would start and the weather was bearable, there was school. On bad days, there was only work, accomplished in this driving, demoralizing cold. Leni focused on what needed to be done—going to school, doing homework, feeding the animals, carrying water, cracking ice, darning socks, repairing clothes, cooking with Mama, cleaning the cabin, feeding the woodstove. Every day more and more wood had to be chopped and carried and stacked. There was no room in these shortened days to think about anything beyond the mechanics of survival. They were growing starter vegetables in Dixie cups on a table beneath the loft. Even the practice of survival skills at the Harlan compound on weekends had been suspended.

Worse than the weather was the confinement it caused.

As winter pared their life away, the Allbrights were left with only each other. Every evening was spent together, hours and hours of night, huddled around the woodstove.

They were all on edge. Arguments erupted between her parents over money, over chores, over the weather. Over nothing.

Leni knew how anxious Dad was about their inadequate supplies and their nonexistent money. She saw how it gnawed at him; she saw, too, how closely Mama watched him, how worried she was about his rising anxiety.

His struggle for calm was obvious in a dozen tics and in the way he seemed unwilling to look at them sometimes. He woke well before dawn and stayed outside working as long as he could, coming back in well after dark and covered in snow, his mustache and eyebrows frozen, the tip of his nose white.

The effort he made to keep his temper in check was apparent. As the days shortened and the nights lengthened, he began pacing after dinner, getting agitated and muttering to himself. On those bad nights, he took the traps Mad Earl had taught him to use and went trapping in the deep woods alone and came back exhausted, haggard-looking. Quiet. Himself. More often than not, he came home successful in the hunt, with fox or marten furs to sell in town. He made just enough money to keep them afloat; but even Leni could see the empty shelves in their root cellar. No meal was ever big enough to fill them up. The money Mama had borrowed from Grandma was long gone and there was none to take its place, so Leni had stopped taking pictures and Mama barely smoked. Large Marge sometimes gave them cigarettes and film for free—when Dad wasn't looking—but they didn't go into town often.

Dad's intentions were good, but even so, it was like living with a wild animal. Like those crazy hippies the Alaskans talked about who lived with wolves and bears and invariably ended up getting killed. The natural-born predator could seem domesticated, even friendly, could lick your throat affectionately or rub up against you to get a back scratch. But you knew, or should know, that it was a wild thing you lived with, that a collar and leash and a bowl of food might tame the actions of the beast, but couldn't change its essential nature. In a split second, less time than it took to exhale a breath, that wolf could claim its nature and turn, fangs bared.

It was exhausting to worry all the time, to study Dad's every movement and the tone of his voice.

It had obviously worn Mama down. Anxiety had pulled the light from her eyes and the glow from her skin. Or maybe the pallor came from living like mushrooms.

On an especially cold late November day, Leni woke to the sound of screaming. Something crashed to the floor.

She knew instantly what was happening. Her dad had had a nightmare. His third one this week.

She crawled out of her sleeping bag and went to the edge of the loft, peering down. Mama stood by the beaded door of their bedroom, holding a lantern high. In its glow, she looked scared, her hair a mess, wearing sweatpants and a sweatshirt. The woodstove was a dot of orange in the dark.

Dad was like an untamed animal, shoving, tearing, snarling, saying words she couldn't understand . . . then he was wrenching open boxes, looking for something. Mama approached him cautiously, laid a hand on his back. He shoved her aside so hard she cracked into the log wall, cried out.

Dad stopped, jerked upright. His nostrils flared. He was flexing and unflexing his right hand. When he saw Mama, everything changed. His shoulders rounded, his head hung in shame. "Jesus, Cora," he whispered brokenly. "I'm sorry. I . . . didn't know where I was."

"I know," she said, her eyes glistening with tears.

He went to her, enfolded her in his arms, held her. They sank to their knees together, foreheads touching. Leni could hear them talking but couldn't make out the words.

She returned to her sleeping bag and tried to go back to sleep.

✦✦〈✧〉✦✦

"LENI! GET UP. We're going hunting. I've got to get out of the g-damn house."

With a sigh, she dressed in the darkness. In the first months of this Alaskan winter, she had learned to live like one of those phosphorescent invertebrates that roamed the sea floor, their lives untouched by any light or color except that which they generated themselves.

In the living room, the woodstove offered light through a narrow window in the black metal door. She could make out the silhouettes of her parents standing beside it, could hear their breathing. Coffee gurgled in a metal pot on top of the stove, puffed its welcoming scent into the darkness.

Dad lit a lantern, held it up. In its orange glow, he looked haggard, tightly wound. A tic played at the corner of his right eye. "You guys ready?"

Mama looked exhausted. Dressed in a huge parka and insulated pants, she looked too fragile for the weather, and too tired to hike for much of a distance. In a week of rising nightmares and middle-of-the-night screaming, she wasn't sleeping well.

"Sure," Mama said. "I love to hunt at six A.M. on a Sunday morning."

Leni went to the hooks on the wall, grabbed the gray parka and insulated pants she'd found at the Salvation Army in Homer last month, and the secondhand bunny boots Matthew had given her. She pulled down-filled gloves out of her parka pockets.

"Good," Dad said. "Let's go."

This predawn world was hushed. There was no wind, no cracking branches, just the endless sifting downward of snow, the white accumulating everywhere. Leni trudged through the snow toward the animal pens. The goats stood huddled together, bleating at her arrival, bumping into each other. She tossed them a flake of hay and then fed the chickens and broke the ice on their water troughs.

When she got to the VW bus, Mama was already inside. Leni climbed into the backseat. In this cold, the bus took a long time to start and even longer for the windows to defrost. The vehicle was not good in this part of the world; they'd learned that the hard way. Dad put chains on the tires and tossed a gear bag in the well between the front seats. Leni sat in the back, her arms crossed, shivering, intermittently falling asleep and waking up.

On the main road, Dad turned right, toward town, but before the airstrip, he turned left onto the road that led to the abandoned chromium mine. They drove for miles on the hard-packed snow, the road a series of sharp switchbacks that seemed to be cut into the side of the mountain. Deep in the woods, high on the mountain, he parked suddenly, with a jarring stomp on the brakes, and handed them each a headlamp and a shotgun before hefting a pack and opening his door.

Wind and snow and cold swept into the bus. It couldn't be much above zero up here.

She fit the headlamp over her head, adjusted the strap, and turned on the light. It provided a bright thin beam of light directly ahead.

No stars, no starlight. Snow falling hard and fast. A deep, abiding black full of whispering trees and crouching, hidden predators.

Dad took off in front, trudging through the snow in his snowshoes, forging a path. Leni let Mama go next and then fell in step behind her.

They walked for so long that Leni's cheeks went from cold to hot to numb. Long enough that her eyelashes and nostril hairs froze, that she felt her own sweat accumulating under her long underwear, itching. At some point, she started to smell, and it made her wonder what else could smell her. It was easy to go from predator to prey out here.

Leni was so tired, just trudging forward, chin down, shoulders hunched, that it barely registered that at some point she began to see her own feet, her boots, her snowshoes. At first there was the gray, ambient glow, light that wasn't quite real, bleeding up from the snow, and then the dawn, pink as salmon meat, buttery.

Daylight.

Leni finally saw her surroundings. They were on a frozen river. It horrified her to realize she had followed Dad blindly onto its slick surface. What if the ice was too thin? One wrong step and someone could have plunged into the icy water and been swept away.

Beneath her, she heard a cracking sound.

Dad walked confidently forward, seemingly unconcerned about the ice beneath his feet. On the other shore, he cut a path through stubby, snow-coated brush, stared down, tilted his head as if he were listening. His face above the snowy beard was red with cold. She knew he was following sign—droppings, tracks. Snowshoe hares did most of their feeding and movement at dawn and dusk.

He stopped suddenly. "There's a hare over there," he said to Leni. "At the edge of the trees."

Leni looked in the direction he pointed. Everything was white, even the sky. Shapes were difficult to distinguish in this white-on-white world.

Then, movement: a plump white hare hopped forward.

"Yeah," she said. "I see it."

"Okay, Leni. This is your hunt. Breathe. Relax. Wait for the shot," Dad said.

She lifted her gun. She'd been target-shooting for months, so she knew what to do. She breathed in and out instead of holding her breath; she focused on the hare, aimed. She waited. The world fell away, became simple. There was just her and the hare, predator and prey, connected.

She squeezed the trigger.

It all seemed to happen simultaneously: the shot, the hit, the kill, the hare slumping sideways.

A good clean shot.

"Excellent," Dad said.

Leni slung her shotgun over her shoulder and the three of them set off single file for the tree line and Leni's kill.

When they reached the hare, Leni stared down at it, the soft white body sprayed with blood, lying in a pool of it.

She'd killed something. Fed her family for another night.

Killed something. Stopped a life.

She didn't know how to feel about it, or maybe she just felt two conflicting emotions at the same time—proud and sad. In truth, she almost wanted to cry. But she was Alaskan now, this was her life. Without hunting, there was no food on the table. And nothing would go to waste. The fur would be made into a hat; the bones would make a soup stock. Tonight Mama would fry the meat in home-churned butter made from goat's milk and season it with onions and garlic. They might even splurge and add a few potatoes.

Her dad knelt in the snow. She saw the shaking of his hands and could tell by the grim set to his mouth that he had a headache as he turned the dead hare onto its back.

He placed his blade at the tail and cut upward, through the skin and bone, in a single, sweeping cut. At the hare's breastbone, he slowed, positioned one bloody finger under the knife blade, and proceeded cautiously to avoid accidentally cutting any organs. He opened the animal, reached in and pulled out the entrails, which he left in a steaming red-pink pile on the snow.

He picked out the small, plump heart and held it up to Leni. Blood leaked between his fingers. "You're the hunter. Eat the heart."

"Ernt, please," Mama said, "we're not savages."

"That's exactly what we are," he said in a voice as cold as the wind at their back. "Eat it."

Leni's gaze cut to Mama, who looked as horrified as Leni felt.

"Are you going to make me ask again?" Dad said.

The quiet of his voice was worse than yelling. Leni felt a ridge of fear poke up, spread along her spine. She reached out, took the tiny blue-red organ in her hand. (Was it still beating or was she trembling?)

With her father's narrowed gaze steady on her, she put the heart in her mouth and forced her lips to close. Instantly, she wanted to gag. The heart was slippery and slimy; when she bit down it ruptured in her mouth, tasting metallic. She felt blood trickle out of the side of her mouth.

She swallowed, gagged, wiped the blood from her lips, felt its warmth smear across her cheek.

Her father looked up, just enough to make eye contact. He looked ruined, tired, but *present*; in his eyes, she saw more love and sadness than should be able to exist in one human being. Something was tearing him up inside, even now. It was the other man, the bad man, who lived inside of him and tried to break out in the darkness.

"I'm trying to make you self-sufficient."

It sounded like an apology, but for what? For being crazy sometimes or teaching her to hunt? Or for making her eat the hare's beating heart? Or for the nightmares that ruined all their sleep?

Or maybe he was apologizing for something he hadn't done yet but was afraid he would.

✦⟨✲⟩✦

DECEMBER.

Dad was edgy, tense; he drank too much and muttered under his breath. The nightmares became more frequent. Three a week, every week.

He was always moving, demanding, pushing. He ate, slept, breathed, and drank survival. He had become a soldier again, or that's what Mama said, and Leni found herself tongue-tied around him, afraid of saying or doing the wrong thing.

With as hard as she worked after school and on the weekends, Leni should have slept like the dead, but she didn't. Night after night she lay awake, worrying. Her fear and anxiety about the world had been sharpened to a knifepoint.

Tonight, as exhausted as she was, she lay awake, listening for his screams. When she did finally fall asleep, she landed in a dreamscape on fire, a place full of danger—a world at war, animals being slaughtered, girls being kidnapped, men screaming and pointing guns. She screamed for Matthew, but no one could hear one girl's voice in a falling-apart world. And besides, what good would he be? She couldn't tell Matthew this. Not this. Some fears you carried alone.

"Leni!"

She heard her name being called from far away. Where was she? It was the middle of the night. Was she still dreaming?

Someone grabbed her, yanked her out of bed. It was real this time. A hand clamped over her mouth.

She recognized his smell. "Dad?" she said through his hand.

"Come on," he said. "Now."

She stumbled over to the ladder, climbed down behind him in an utter darkness.

None of the lamps were lit downstairs, but she could hear her mother breathing heavily.

Dad led Leni to the newly fixed and steady card table; guided her to a seat.

"Ernt, really—" Mama said.

"Shut up, Cora," Dad said.

Something banged onto the table in front of Leni with a clatter and a clang. "What is it?" he said, standing right next to her.

She reached out, her fingers trailing across the rough surface of the card table.

A rifle. In pieces.

"You need better training, Leni. When TSHTF, we'll have to do things differently. What if it's winter? Everything might be dark. You'll be off guard, confused, sleepy. Excuses will get you killed. I want you to be able to do everything in the dark, when you're scared."

"Ernt," Mama said from the darkness, her voice uneven. "She's just a girl. Let her go back to bed."

"When men are starving and we have food, will they care that she's just a girl?"

Leni heard the click of a stopwatch. "Go, Leni. Clean your weapon, put it back together."

Leni reached out, felt for the cold pieces of the rifle, pulled them toward her. The darkness unnerved her, made her slow. She saw a match flare in the darkness, smelled a cigarette being lit.

"Stop," Dad said. A flashlight beam erupted, blared into being, focused on the rifle. "Unacceptable. You're dead. All of our food is gone. Maybe one of them is thinking of rape." He grabbed the rifle, disassembled it, and pushed the pieces to the center of the table. In the blast of light, Leni saw the rifle in parts, in addition to a cleaning rod, cloths, some Hoppes 9 solvent and rust protector, a few screwdrivers. She tried to memorize where everything was.

He was right. She needed to know how to do this or she could be killed. *Concentrate.*

The light clicked off. The stopwatch clicked on.

"Go."

Leni reached out, trying to remember what she'd seen. She pulled the rifle parts toward her, assembled it quickly, screwed the scope in place. She was reaching for the cleaning cloth when the stopwatch clicked off.

"Dead," Dad said in disgust. "Try again."

✦⟨❀⟩✦

YESTERDAY, on the second Saturday in December, they joined their neighbors for a tree-cutting party. They all hiked out into the wilderness and chose trees. Dad cut down an evergreen, dragged it onto their sled, and hauled it back to the cabin, where they placed it in the corner beneath the loft. They decorated it with family Polaroids and fishing lures. A few presents wrapped in yellowed pages from the *Anchorage Daily Times* were positioned beneath the fragrant green branches. Magic Marker lines pretended to be ribbon. The propane-fueled hanging lanterns created a warm interior, their light a sharp contrast to the still-dark morning. Wind clawed at the eaves; every now and then a tree branch smacked hard against the cabin.

Now, on Sunday afternoon, Mama was in the kitchen, making sourdough bread. The yeasty fragrance of baking bread filled the cabin. The bad weather kept them all inside. Dad was hunched over the ham radio, listening to scratchy voices, his fingers constantly working the knobs. Leni heard the staticky sound of Mad Earl's voice, his high-pitched cackle coming through loud and clear.

Leni sat huddled on the sofa, reading the ragged paperback copy of *Go Ask Alice* she'd found at the dump. The world felt impossibly small here; the drapes were drawn tightly for warmth and the door was locked shut against cold and predators.

"What was that, say again, over?" Dad said. He was hunched over the ham radio, listening. "Marge, is that you?"

Leni heard Large Marge's voice come through the radio, broken up, spangled with static. "Emergency. Lost . . . Search party . . . past Walker cabin . . . Meet on Mine Road. Out."

Leni put down her book, sat up. "Who is lost? In this weather?"

"Large Marge," Dad said. "Come in. Who is it? Who is lost? Earl, you there?"

Static.

Dad turned. "Get dressed. Someone needs help."

Mama took the half-baked bread out of the oven and set it on the counter, covering it with a dishcloth. Leni dressed in the warmest clothes she had: Carhartt insulated pants, rolled up at the hem, parka, bunny boots. Within five minutes of the call from Large Marge, Leni was in the back of the bus, waiting for the engine to start.

It would be a while.

Finally, Dad got the windshield scraped enough to see through. Then he checked the chains and climbed into the driver's seat. "It's a bad day for someone to get lost."

Dad slowly maneuvered around in the axle-deep snow, turned toward their driveway, which was a thick, unbroken layer of white without tire tracks, bracketed by snow-covered trees. Leni could see her breath; that was how cold it was inside the bus. Snow built up and disappeared on the windshield in between each swipe of the wiper blades.

As they neared town, vehicles appeared out of the curtain of falling snow in front of them, headlights glowing through the gloom. Up ahead, Leni saw amber and red lights flashing. That would be Natalie and her snowplow, leading the way onto a barely-there road that led toward the old mine.

Dad eased up on the gas. They slowed, pulled into line behind a big pickup truck that belonged to Clyde Harlan, and drove up the mountain.

When they reached a clearing, Leni saw a bunch of snow machines (Leni still thought of them as snowmobiles but no one called them that up here) parked in an uneven line. They belonged to the residents who lived in the bush, without roads to their homesteads. All of them had their lights on and their engines running. Falling snow braided through the light beams and gave it all an eerie, otherworldly look.

Dad parked alongside a snow machine. Leni followed her parents out into the falling snow and howling wind, into the kind of cold that burrowed deep. They saw Mad Earl and Thelma and made their way over to their friends.

"What's up?" Dad shouted to be heard above the wind.

Before Mad Earl or Thelma could answer, Leni heard the high-pitched wail of a whistle being blown.

A man in a heavy blue insulated parka and pants stepped forward. A wide-brimmed hat identified him as a policeman. "I'm Curt Ward. Thanks for coming. Geneva and Matthew Walker are missing. They were supposed to arrive at their hunting cabin an hour ago. This is their usual route. If they're lost or hurt, we should find them between here and the cabin."

Leni didn't realize she'd cried out until she felt her mother's reassuring touch.

Matthew.

She looked up at her mother. "He'll freeze out here," she said. "It will be night soon."

Before Mama could answer, Officer Ward said, "Space yourselves about twenty feet apart."

He began handing out flashlights.

Leni turned her flashlight on, stared out at the lane of snow-covered ground in front of her. The whole world spiraled down to a single strip of land. She saw it in layers—bumpy white snow-covered ground, snow-filled air, white trees pointing up to a gray sky.

Where are you, Matthew?

She moved slowly, doggedly forward, distantly aware of other searchers, other lights. She heard dogs barking and voices raised; searchlights crisscrossed each other. Time passed in a weird, surreal way—in light diminishing and breaths exhaled.

Leni saw animal tracks, a pile of bones mixed with fresh blood, fallen spruce needles. Wind had sculpted the snow into peaks and swirls with glazed and hardened icy tips. Tree wells were black with debris, made by animals into makeshift dens that gave them a place to sleep out of the wind.

The trees around her thickened. The temperature dropped suddenly; she felt a rush of cold as day gave way to night. It stopped snowing. Wind pushed the clouds away and left in their stead a navy-blue sky awash in swirls of starlight. A gibbous moon shone down, its light bright on the snow. Ambient silver light set the world aglow.

She saw something. Arms. Reaching up from the snow, thin fingers splayed out, frozen. She lunged forward through the deep snow, said, "I'm coming, Matthew," through wheezing, painful breaths, her light bobbing up and down in front of her.

Antlers. A full set, shed by a bull moose. Or maybe beneath this snow lay the bones left by a poacher. Like so many sins, the snow covered it all. The truth wouldn't be revealed until spring. If ever.

The wind picked up, banged through the trees, sent branches flying.

She trudged forward, one light amid dozens spread out through the glowing blue-white-black forest, pinpricks of yellow searching, searching . . . she heard Mr. Walker's voice call out, yelling Matthew's name so often he started to sound hoarse.

"There! Up ahead!" someone yelled.

And Mr. Walker yelled back, "I see him."

Leni plunged forward, trying to run through the deep snow.

Up ahead, she saw a shadowy lump . . . a person . . . kneeling by the side of a frozen river in the moonlight, head bowed forward.

Leni shoved through the crowd, elbowed her way to the front just as Mr. Walker squatted beside his son. "Mattie?" he shouted to be heard, laid a gloved hand on his son's back. "I'm here. I'm here. Where's your mom?"

Matthew's head slowly turned. His face was starkly white, his lips were chapped. His green eyes seemed to have lost their hue, taken color from the ice around him. The ice beneath him glowed with moonlight. He was shaking uncontrollably. "She's gone," he croaked, his voice raw. "Fell."

Mr. Walker hauled his son to his feet. Twice Matthew almost collapsed, but his dad held him upright.

Leni heard people talking in snippets.

". . . fell through the ice . . ."

". . . should know better . . ."

". . . Jesus . . ."

"Come on," Officer Ward said. "Let 'em through. We need to get this kid warmed up."

NINE

Winter had claimed one of them; one who had been born here, who knew how to survive.

Leni couldn't stop thinking about that, worrying about it. If Geneva Walker—*Gen, Genny, the Generator, I answer to anything*—could be lost so easily, no one was safe.

"My God," Thelma said as they walked solemnly back to their vehicles. "Genny didn't make mistakes on the ice."

"Everyone makes mistakes," Large Marge said, her dark face crumpled with grief.

Natalie Watkins nodded solemnly. "I've crossed that river a dozen times this month. Jesus. How could she fall through this time of year?"

Leni was listening and not listening. All she could think about was Matthew and what he must be going through now. He'd seen his mother fall through the ice and die.

How could you get over a thing like that? Every time Matthew closed his eyes, wouldn't he see it again? Wouldn't he wake screaming from nightmares for the rest of his life? How could she help him?

Back at home, shivering with cold and a new fear (you could lose your

parents or your life on a normal Sunday, just out walking in the snow . . .
gone), she wrote him a series of letters, each one of which she tore up because
it wasn't right.

She was still trying to compose the perfect letter two days later, when the
town came together for Geneva's funeral.

On this freezing cold afternoon, dozens of vehicles were in town, parked
wherever they could, on roadsides, in vacant lots. One was practically in the
middle of the street. Leni had never seen so many trucks and snow machines in town at one time. All of the businesses were closed, even the Kicking Moose Saloon. Kaneq was hunkered down for winter, glazed in snow
and ice, illuminated by the ambient glow of daylight.

The world could tumble, change radically in two days, with just one less
person living in it.

They parked on Alpine Street and got out of the bus. She heard the
whining drone of a generator's motor, grumbling loudly, powering the lights
in the church on the hill.

Single file, they trudged up the hill. Light filled the dusty windows of
the old church; smoke puffed up from the chimney.

At the closed door, Leni paused just long enough to peel the fur-trimmed
hood back from her face. She'd seen this church on every trip to town, but
she'd never been inside.

The interior was smaller than it looked from the outside, with chipped
white plank walls and a pine floor. There were no pews; people filled the
space from side to side. A man dressed in camouflage snow pants and a fur
coat stood up front, his face practically hidden by a mustache, beard, and
muttonchops.

Everyone Leni had ever met in Kaneq was here. She saw Large Marge,
standing between Mr. Rhodes and Natalie; the whole Harlan family was
here, squished in close to one another. Even Crazy Pete was here, with his
goose settled on his hip.

But it was the front row that held her attention. Mr. Walker stood beside
a beautiful blond girl who must be Alyeska, home from college, and alongside Walker relatives Leni hadn't met. Off to their right, standing together

with them and yet somehow alone, was Matthew. Calhoun Malvey, Geneva's boyfriend, kept shifting his weight, moving from foot to foot, as if he didn't know what to do. His eyes were red-rimmed.

Leni tried to get Matthew's attention, but even the opening and closing of the church's double doors and the subsequent sweep of cold and snow didn't faze him. He stood there, shoulders slumped, chin dropped, his profile veiled by hair that looked like it hadn't been washed in a week.

Leni followed her parents to an empty space behind Mad Earl's family and stood there. Mad Earl immediately handed Dad a flask.

Leni stared at Matthew, willing him to look at her. She didn't know what she'd say when they finally got to talk, maybe she wouldn't say anything, would just take his hand.

The priest—or was he a reverend, a minister, a father, what? Leni had no idea about things like this—started to talk. "We here all knew Geneva Walker. She wasn't a member of this church, but she was one of us, from the moment Tom brought her here from Fairbanks. She was game for anything and never gave up. Remember when Aly talked her into singing the national anthem at Salmon Days and she was so bad that the dogs started howling and even Matilda waddled away? And after it was all over, Gen said, 'Well, I can't sing a lick but who cares? It's what my Aly wanted.' Or when Genny hooked Tom in the cheek at the fishing derby and tried to claim the prize for biggest catch? She had a heart as big as Alaska." He paused, sighed. "Our Gen. She was a woman who knew how to love. We don't quite know whose wife she was at the end, but that doesn't matter. We all loved her."

Laughter, quiet and sad.

Leni lost track of the words. She wasn't even sure how much time had passed. It made her think of her own mother, and how it would feel to lose her. Then she heard people start to turn for the door, boots stomping, floorboards creaking.

It was over.

Leni tried to make her way to Matthew, but it was impossible; everyone was pushing toward the door.

As far as Leni could tell, no one had said anything about going down to the Kicking Moose Saloon afterward, but they all ended up there just the same. Maybe it was adult instinctive behavior.

She followed her parents down the hill and across the street and into the charred, tumbledown interior. The minute she crossed the threshold, she smelled the acrid, sooty smell of burnt wood. Apparently that smell never went away. The interior was cavelike, with propane-fueled lanterns swinging creakily from the rafters, throwing light like streams of water on the patrons below, set in motion by the tap of the wind every time the door opened.

Old Jim was behind the bar, serving drinks as fast as he could. A wet gray bar rag hung over one shoulder, dripped dark splotches down the front of his flannel shirt. Leni had heard someone say that he'd bartended here for decades. He'd started back when the few men who lived in this wilderness were either hiding out from or coming home from World War II. Dad ordered four drinks at once, downed them in rapid succession.

The sawdust floor gave off a dusty, barnlike scent and muffled the footsteps of so many people.

They were talking all at once, in the low voices of grief. Leni heard snippets, adjectives.

". . . beautiful . . . give you the shirt off her back . . . best damn nettle bread . . . tragedy . . ."

She saw how death impacted people, saw the glazed look in their eyes, the way they shook their heads, the way their sentences broke in half as if they couldn't decide if silence or words would release them from sorrow.

Leni had never known anyone who had died before. She had seen death on television and read about it in her beloved books (Johnny's death in *The Outsiders* had turned her inside out), but now she saw the truth of it. In literature, death was many things—a message, catharsis, retribution. There were deaths that came from a beating heart that stopped and deaths of another kind, a choice made, like Frodo going to the Grey Havens. Death made you cry, filled you with sadness, but in the best of her books, there was peace, too, satisfaction, a sense of the story ending as it should.

In real life, she saw, it wasn't like that. It was sadness opening up inside of you, changing how you saw the world.

It made her think about God and what He offered at times like this. She wondered for the first time what her parents believed in, what she believed in, and she saw how the idea of Heaven could be comforting.

She could hardly imagine a thing as terrible as losing your mother. The very thought of it made Leni sick to her stomach. A girl was like a kite; without her mother's strong, steady hold on the string, she might just float away, be lost somewhere among the clouds.

Leni didn't want to think about a loss like that, the bone-breaking magnitude of it, but at a time like this there was no looking away, and when she did look it in the face, without blinking or turning away, she knew this: if she were Matthew, she would need a friend right now. Who knew how the friend could help, whether offering silent companionship or a clatter of words was better? That, the how, she would have to figure out on her own. But the what—friendship—that she knew for sure.

She knew when the Walkers entered the tavern by the silence that fell. People turned to face the door.

Mr. Walker entered first; he was so tall and broad-shouldered, he had to duck to pass through the low door. Long blond hair fell across his face; he shoved it back. Looking up, he saw everyone staring at him, and he stopped, straightened. His gaze moved slowly around the room, from face to face; his smile faded. Grief aged him. The beautiful blond girl came up behind him, her face wet with tears. She had her arm around Matthew, was holding him like a Secret Service agent moving an unpopular Nixon through an angry mob. Matthew's shoulders were rounded, his body hunched forward, his face downcast. Cal hovered behind them, his eyes glassy.

Mr. Walker saw Mama, moved toward her first.

"I'm so sorry, Tom," Mama said, her face tilted up to him. Crying.

Mr. Walker looked down at her. "I should have been with them."

"Oh, Tom . . ." She touched his arm.

"Thanks," he said in a hoarse, lowered voice. He swallowed hard, seemed to stop himself from saying more. He looked at the friends gathered close.

"I know church funerals aren't our favorite, but it's so damn cold out, and Geneva did love the idea of church."

There was a murmur of agreement, a sense of restless motion contained, of relief mingled with grief.

"To Gen," Large Marge said, lifting her shot glass.

"To Gen!"

As the adults clinked their glasses and downed their drinks and turned their attention to the bar for another round, Leni watched the Walker family move through the crowd, stopping to talk to everyone.

"Pretty high-falutin' funeral," Mad Earl said loudly. Drunkenly.

Leni glanced sideways to see if Tom Walker had heard, but Mr. Walker was talking to Large Marge and Natalie.

"What do you expect?" Dad said, downing another whiskey. His eyes had the glazed look of drunkenness. "I'm surprised the governor didn't fly down to tell us how to feel. I hear he and Tom are fishing buddies. He loves to remind us peons of that."

Mama moved closer. "Ernt. It's the day of his wife's funeral. Can't we—"

"Don't you say a word," Dad hissed. "I saw the way you were hanging all over him—"

Thelma pushed in closer. "Oh, for God's sake, Ernt. This is a sad day. Stow the jealousy for ten minutes."

"You think I'm jealous of Tom?" Dad said. He glanced at Mama. "Should I be?"

Leni turned her back on them, watched Alyeska hustle Matthew through the mourners, over to a quiet corner in the back.

Leni followed, eased between people who stank of wood smoke and sweat and body odor. Bathing was a luxury in midwinter. No one did it often enough.

Matthew stood alone, staring blankly forward, with his back to the charred, black-peeling wall. Soot peppered his sleeves.

She was shocked by how changed he looked. He couldn't have lost that much weight in such a short time, but his cheekbones were like ridges above his hollow cheeks. His lips were chapped and bloodied. A patch of skin was white at his temple, the color a sharp contrast to his windburned cheeks. His hair was dirty, and hung in limp, thin strands on either side of his face.

"Hey," she said.

"Hey," he answered dully.

Now what?

Don't say, I'm sorry. That's what grown-ups say and it's stupid. Of course you're sorry. How does that help?

But what?

She edged forward cautiously, careful not to touch him, and sidled up beside him, leaning back against the burnt wall. From here, she could see everything—the lanterns hanging from burnt rafters, walls covered with dusty antique snowshoes and fishnets and cross-country skis, ashtrays overflowing, smoke blurring everything—and everyone.

Her parents were huddled with Mad Earl and Clyde and Thelma and the rest of the Harlan family. Even through the cigarette smoke haze, Leni could see how red her dad's face was (a sign of too much whiskey), how his eyes were narrowed in anger as he talked. Mama looked defeated beside him, afraid to move, afraid to add to the conversation or to look at anything except her husband.

"He blames me."

Leni was so surprised to hear Matthew speak that it took her a moment to process what he'd said. Her gaze followed his to Mr. Walker.

"Your dad?" Leni turned to him. "He couldn't. It's not anyone's fault. She just . . . I mean, the ice . . ."

Matthew started to cry. Tears streamed down his face as he stood there, stock-still, so tense he seemed to be vibrating. In his eyes, she glimpsed a bigger world. Being lonely, being afraid, a volatile, angry dad; these were bad things that gave you nightmares.

But they were nothing compared to watching your mother die. How would that feel? How would you ever get over it?

And how was she, a fourteen-year-old girl with troubles of her own, supposed to help?

"They found her yesterday," he said. "Did you hear? One of her legs was missing, and her face—"

She touched him. "Don't think—"

At her touch, he let out a howl of pain that drew everyone's attention. He roared with it again, shuddered. Leni froze, unsure of what to do—should she pull away or push forward? She reacted instinctively, took him in her arms. He melted into her, held her so tightly she couldn't breathe. She felt his tears on her neck, warm and wet. "It's my fault. I keep having these nightmares . . . and I wake up so pissed off I can't stand it."

Before Leni could say anything, the pretty blond girl moved in beside Matthew, put an arm around him, pulled him away from Leni. Matthew stumbled into his sister, moving unsteadily, as if even walking felt unfamiliar.

"You must be Leni," Alyeska said.

Leni nodded.

"I'm Aly. Mattie's big sister. He told me about you." She was trying hard to smile; that was obvious. "Said you were best friends."

Leni wanted to cry. "We are."

"That's lucky. I didn't have anyone my age in school when I lived here," Aly said, tucking her hair behind one ear. "I guess it's why Fairbanks seemed like a good idea. I mean . . . Kaneq and the homestead can feel as small as a speck sometimes. But I should have been here . . ."

"Don't," Matthew said to his sister. "Please."

Aly's smile wavered. Leni didn't know this girl at all, but her struggle for composure and her love for her brother were obvious. It made Leni feel strangely connected to her, as if they had this one important thing in common.

"I'm glad he has you. He's . . . struggling now, aren't you, Mattie?" Aly's voice broke. "But he'll be fine. I hope."

Leni saw suddenly how hope could break you, how it was a shiny lure for the unwary. What happened to you if you hoped too hard for the best and got the worst? Was it better not to hope at all, to prepare? Wasn't that what her father's lesson always was? Prepare for the worst.

"Of course he will," Leni said, but she didn't believe it. She knew what nightmares could do to a person and how bad memories could change who you were.

❖❖❖

ON THE DRIVE HOME, no one spoke. Leni felt the loss of every second of light as night fell, felt it as sharply as a mallet striking bone. She imagined her father could hear them, the lost seconds, like stones clattering down a rock wall, plunking somewhere into black, murky water.

Mama huddled in her seat, hunched over. She kept glancing at Dad.

He was drunk and angry. He bounced in his seat, thumped his hand on the steering wheel.

Mama reached out, touched his arm.

He yanked away from her, said, "You're good at that, aren't you? Touching men. You think I didn't see. You think I'm stupid."

Mama looked at him wide-eyed, fear etched onto her delicate features. "I don't think that."

"I saw how you looked at him. I saw it." He muttered something and pulled away from her. Leni thought he said, *Breathe,* under his breath, but she couldn't be sure. All she knew was that they were in trouble. "I saw you touch his hand."

This was bad.

He'd always been jealous of Tom Walker's money . . . this was something else.

All the way home, as he muttered under his breath, *whore, bitch, lied,* his fingers played piano keys on the steering wheel. At the homestead, he stumbled out of the bus and stood there swaying, looking at the cabin. Mama went up to him. They stared at each other, both breathing unsteadily.

"Make a fool of me again . . . will you?"

Mama touched his arm. "You don't really think I want Tom—"

He grabbed Mama by the arm and dragged her into the cabin. She tried to pull free, stumbled forward, put her hand over his in a feeble attempt to make him ease his grip. "Ernt, please."

Leni ran after them, followed them into the cabin, saying, "Dad, please, let her go."

"Leni, go—" Mama started to say.

Dad hit Mama so hard she flew sideways, cracked her head into the log wall, and crumpled to the floor.

Leni screamed. "Mama!"

Mama crawled to her knees, got unsteadily to her feet. Her lip was ripped, bleeding.

Dad hit her again, harder. When she hit the wall, he looked down, saw the blood on his knuckles, and stared at it.

A high, keening howl of pain burst out of him, ringing off the log walls. He stumbled back, putting distance between them. He gave Mama a long, desperate look of sorrow and hatred, then ran out of the cabin, slamming the door behind him.

⁘

LENI WAS SO SCARED and surprised and horrified by what she'd just seen, she did nothing.

Nothing.

She should have thrown herself at Dad, gotten between them, even gone for her gun.

She heard the door slam and it knocked her out of her paralysis.

Mama was sitting on the floor in front of the woodstove, her hands in her lap and her head forward, her face hidden by her hair.

"Mama?"

Mama slowly looked up, tucked the hair behind her ear. A red splotch marred her temple. Her lower lip was split open, dripping blood onto her pants.

Do something.

Leni ran into the kitchen, soaked a washcloth with water from the bucket, and went to Mama, kneeling beside her. With a tired smile, Mama took the rag, pressed it to her bleeding lip.

"Sorry, baby girl," she said through the cloth.

"He hit you," Leni said, stunned.

This was an ugliness she'd never imagined. A lost temper, yes. A fist? Blood? No . . .

You were supposed to be safe in your own home, with your parents. They were supposed to protect you from the dangers outside.

"He was agitated all day. I shouldn't have talked to Tom." Mama sighed. "And now I suppose he's gone to the compound to drink whiskey and eat hate with Mad Earl."

Leni looked at her mother's beaten, bruised face, the rag turning red with her blood. "You're saying it's your fault?"

"You're too young to understand. He didn't mean to do that. He just . . . loves me too much sometimes."

Was that true? Was that what love was when you grew up?

"He meant to," Leni said quietly, feeling a cold wave of understanding wash through her. Memories clicked into place like pieces of a puzzle, fitting together. Mama's bruises, her always saying, *I'm clumsy*. She had hidden this ugly truth from Leni for years. Her parents had been able to hide it from her with walls and lies, but here in this one-room cabin there was no hiding anymore. "He has hit you before."

"No," Mama said. "Hardly ever."

Leni tried to put it all together in her head, make it make sense, but she couldn't. How could this be love? How could it be Mama's fault?

"We have to understand and forgive," Mama said. "That's how you love someone who's sick. Someone who is struggling. It's like he has cancer. That's how you have to think of it. He'll get better. He will. He loves us so much."

Leni heard her mother start to cry, and somehow that made it worse, as if her tears watered this ugliness, made it grow. Leni pulled Mama into her arms, held her tightly, stroked her back, just like Mama had done so many times for Leni.

Leni didn't know how long she sat there, holding her mother, replaying the horrible scene over and over.

Then she heard her father's return.

She heard his uneven footsteps on the deck, his fumbling with the door latch. Mama must have heard it, too, because she was crawling unsteadily to her feet, pushing Leni aside, saying, "Go upstairs."

Leni watched her mama rise; she dropped the wet, bloody rag. It fell with a splat to the floor.

The door opened. Cold rushed in.

"You came back," Mama whispered.

Dad stood in the doorway, his face lined in agony, his eyes full of tears. "Cora, my God," he said, his voice scratchy and thick. "Of course I came back."

They moved toward one another.

Dad collapsed to his knees in front of Mama, his knees cracking on the wood so loudly Leni knew there would be bruises tomorrow.

Mama moved closer, put her hands in his hair. He buried his face in her stomach, started to shake and cry. "I'm so sorry. I just love you so much . . . it makes me crazy. Crazier." He looked up, crying harder now. "I didn't mean it."

"I know, baby." Mama knelt down, took him in her arms, rocked him back and forth.

Leni felt the sudden fragility of her world, of the world itself. She barely remembered Before. Maybe she didn't remember it at all, in fact. Maybe the images she did have—Dad lifting her onto his shoulders, pulling petals from a daisy, holding a buttercup to her chin, reading her a bedtime story— maybe these were all images she'd taken from pictures and imbued with an imagined life.

She didn't know. How could she? Mama wanted Leni to look away as easily as Mama did. To forgive even when the apology tendered was as thin as fishing line and as breakable as a promise to do better.

For years, for her whole life, Leni had done just that. She loved her parents, both of them. She had known, without being told, that the darkness in her dad was bad and the things he did were wrong, but she believed her mama's explanations, too: that Dad was sick and sorry, that if they loved him enough, he would get better and it would be like Before.

Only Leni didn't believe that anymore.

The truth was this: Winter had only just begun. The cold and darkness would go on for a long, long time and they were alone up here, trapped in this cabin with Dad.

With no local police and no one to call for help. All this time, Dad had taught Leni how dangerous the outside world was. The truth was that the biggest danger of all was in her own home.

TEN

—————=∞▷▷▷◎◇◎◁◁◁∞=—————

C ome on, sleepyhead!" Mama called up bright and early the next morn-
     ing. "Time for school."

It sounded so ordinary, something every mother said to every fourteen-
year-old, but Leni heard the words behind the words, the *please let's pretend*
that formed a dangerous pact.

Mama wanted to induct Leni into some terrible, silent club to which Leni
didn't want to belong. She didn't want to pretend what had happened was
normal, but what was she—a kid—supposed to do about it?

Leni dressed for school and climbed cautiously down the loft ladder,
afraid to see her father.

Mama stood beside the card table, holding a plate of pancakes bracketed by strips of crispy bacon. Her face was swollen on the right side,
purple seeping along the temple. Her right eye was black and puffy, barely
open.

Leni felt a rise of anger; it unsettled and confused her.

Fear and shame she understood. Fear made you run and hide and shame
made you stay quiet, but this anger wanted something else. Release.

"Don't," Mama said. "Please."

"Don't what?" Leni said.

"You're judging me."

It was true, Leni realized with surprise. She *was* judging her mother, and it felt disloyal. Cruel, even. She knew that Dad was sick. Leni bent down to replace the paperback book under the table's rickety leg.

"It's more complicated than you think. He doesn't mean to do it. Honestly. And sometimes I provoke him. I don't mean to. I know better."

Leni sighed at that, hung her head. Slowly, she got back to her feet and turned to face her mother. "But we're in Alaska now, Mama. It's not like we can get help if we need it. Maybe we should leave." She hadn't known it was even in her head until she heard herself say the terrible words. "There's a lot more winter to come."

"I love him. You love him."

It was true, but was it the right answer?

"Besides, we don't have anywhere to go and no money to go with. Even if I wanted to run home with my tail between my legs, how would I do it? We'd have to leave everything we own here and hike to town and get a ride to Homer and then have my parents wire us enough money for a plane ticket."

"Would they help us?"

"Maybe. But at what price? And . . ." Mama paused, drew in a breath. "He would never take me back. Not if I did that. It would break his heart. And no one will ever love me like he does. He's trying so hard. You saw how sorry he was."

There it was: the sad truth. Mama loved him too much to leave him. Still, even now, with her face bruised and swollen. Maybe what she'd always said was true, maybe she couldn't breathe without him, maybe she'd wilt like a flower without the sunshine of his adoration.

Before Leni could say, *Is that what love is?* the cabin door opened, bringing a rush of icy air with it, a swirl of snow.

Dad entered the cabin and shut the door behind him. Removing his gloves, blowing into the chapel of his bare hands, he stomped the snow from his mukluks. It gathered at his feet, white for a heartbeat before it melted into puddles. His woolen tuque was white with snow, as were his bushy mustache and beard. He looked like a mountain man. His jeans appeared almost frozen. "There's my little librarian," he said, giving her a sad, almost desperate smile. "I did your chores this morning, fed the chickens and goats. Mom said you needed your sleep."

Leni *saw* his love for her, shining through his regret. It eroded her anger, made her question everything again. He didn't want to hurt Mama, didn't mean to. He was sick . . .

"You're going to be late for school," Mama said quietly. "Here, take your breakfast with you."

Leni gathered up her books and her Winnie the Pooh lunch box and layered up in outerwear—boots, *qiviut* yarn tuque, Cowichan sweater, gloves. She ate a rolled-up jam-smeared pancake as she headed for the door and walked out into a white world.

Her breath clouded in front of her; she saw nothing but falling snow and the man breathing beside her. The VW bus slowly sketched itself into existence, already running.

She reached out with her gloved hand and opened the passenger door. It took a couple of tries in the cold, but the old metal door finally creaked open and Leni tossed her backpack and lunch box on the floor and climbed up onto the torn vinyl seat.

Dad climbed into the driver's seat and started the wipers. The radio came on, blastingly loud. It was the *Peninsula Pipeline* morning broadcast. Messages for people living in the bush without telephones or mail service. ". . . and to Maurice Lavoux in McCarthy, your mom says to call your brother, he's feeling poorly . . ."

All the way to school, Dad said nothing. Leni was so deep in her own thoughts, she was surprised when he said, "We're here."

She looked up, saw the school in front of her. The wipers made the building appear in a foggy fan and then disappear.

"Lenora?"

She didn't want to look at him. She wanted to be Alaska-pioneer-woman-survivor-of-Armageddon strong, to let him know that she was angry, let it be a sword she could wield, but then he said her name again, steeped in contrition.

She turned her head.

He was twisted around so that his back was pressed to the door. With the snow and fog outside, he looked vibrant, his black hair, his dark eyes, his thick black mustache and beard. "I'm sick, Red. You know that. The shrinks call it gross stress reaction. That's just a bunch of bullshit words, but the flashbacks and nightmares are real. I can't get some really bad shit out of my head and it makes me crazy. Especially now, with money so tight."

"Drinking doesn't help," Leni said, crossing her arms.

"No, it doesn't. Neither does this weather. And I'm sorry. I'm so damn sorry. I'll stop drinking. It will never happen again. I swear it by how much I love you both."

"Really?"

"I'll try harder, Red. I promise. I love your mom like . . ." His voice dropped to a whisper. "She's my heroin. You know that."

Leni knew it wasn't a good thing, not a *normal* mom-and-dad thing, to compare your love to a drug that could hollow your body and fry your brain and leave you for dead. But they said it to each other all the time. They said it the way Ali McGraw in *Love Story* said love means never having to say you're sorry, as if it were gospel true.

She wanted his regret, his shame and sadness to be enough for her. She wanted to follow her mother's lead as she always had. She wanted to believe that last night had been some terrible anomaly and that it wouldn't happen again.

He reached out, touched her cold cheek. "You know how much I love you."

"Yeah," she said.

"It won't happen again."

She had to believe him, to believe in him. What would her world be without that? She nodded and got out of the bus. She trudged through the snow and climbed the steps and entered the warm school.

Silence greeted her.

No one was talking.

Students were in their seats and Ms. Rhodes was at the chalkboard, writing, *WWII. Alaska was the only state invaded by Japanese.* The *skritch-skritch-skritch* of her chalk was the only sound in the room. None of the kids was talking or giggling or shoving each other.

Matthew sat at his desk.

Leni hung her Cowichan sweater on a hook alongside someone's parka, and stomped the snow from her bunny boots. No one turned to look at her.

She put away her lunch box and headed to her desk, taking her seat next to Matthew. "Hey," she said.

He gave her a barely-there smile and didn't make eye contact. "Hey."

Ms. Rhodes turned to face the students. Her gaze landed on Matthew, softened. She cleared her throat. "Okay. For Axle, Matthew, and Leni, turn to page 172 of your state history books. On the morning of June sixth, 1942, five hundred Japanese soldiers invaded Kiska Island, in the Aleutian chain. It is the only battle of that war fought on American soil. Many people have forgotten it, but . . ."

Leni wanted to reach under the table and hold Matthew's hand, to feel the comfort of a friend's touch, but what if he pulled away? What would she say then?

She couldn't complain that her family had turned out to be fragile and that she no longer felt safe in her home, not after what he'd been through.

She could have said it before—maybe—when life had felt different for both of them, but not now, when he was so broken he couldn't even sit up straight.

She almost said, *It will get better*, to him, but then she saw the tears in his eyes and she closed her mouth. Neither one of them needed platitudes right now.

What they needed was help.

⊹⟨❀⟩⊹

In January, the weather got worse. Cold and darkness isolated the Allbright family even more. Feeding the woodstove became priority number one, a constant round-the-clock chore. They had to chop and carry and stack a huge amount of wood each day, just to survive. And as if all of that weren't stressful enough, on bad nights—nightmare nights—Dad woke them in the middle of the night to pack and repack their bug-out bags, to test their preparedness, to take their weapons apart and put them back together.

Each day, the sun set before five P.M. and didn't rise until ten A.M., giving them a grand total of six hours of daylight—and sixteen hours of darkness—a day. Inside the cabin, the Dixie cups showed no new green starts. Dad spent hours hunched over his ham radio, talking to Mad Earl and Clyde, but more and more of the world was cut away. Nothing came easily—not getting water or cutting wood or feeding the animals or going to school.

But worst of all was the rapidly emptying root cellar. They had no vegetables anymore, no potatoes or onions or carrots. They were almost to the end of their fish stores, and a single caribou haunch hung in the cache. Since they ate almost nothing but protein, they knew the meat wouldn't last long.

Her parents fought constantly about the lack of money and supplies. Dad's anger—kept barely in check since the funeral—was slowly escalating again. Leni could feel it uncoiling, taking up space. She and Mama moved cautiously, tried never to aggravate him.

Today, Leni woke in the dark, ate breakfast and dressed for school in the dark, and arrived at her classroom in the dark. The bleary-eyed sun didn't appear until past ten o'clock, but when it did show up, sending streamers of brittle yellow light into the shadowy lantern- and woodstove-lit classroom, everyone perked up.

"It's a sunny day! The weatherman was right!" Ms. Rhodes said from her place at the front of the classroom. Leni had been in Alaska long enough to know that a sunny, blue-skied January day was noteworthy. "I think we need to get out of this classroom, get a little air in our lungs and some sunshine on our faces. Blow out the winter cobwebs. I've planned a field trip!"

Axle groaned. He hated anything and everything that had to do with school. He peered through the rat's-nest fringe of black hair he never washed. "Aw, come on . . . can't we just go home early? I could go ice fishing."

Ms. Rhodes ignored the scruffy-haired teenager. "The older of you—

Matthew, Axle, and Leni—help the littles put on their coats and get their backpacks."

"I'm not helping," Axle said flatly. "Let the lovebirds do everything."

Leni's face flamed at the comment. She didn't look at Matthew.

"Fine. Whatever," Ms. Rhodes said. "You can go home."

Axle didn't need more encouragement. He grabbed his parka and left the school in a rush.

Leni got up from her seat and went to help Marthe and Agnes with their parkas. No one else had shown up for school today; the trip from Bear Cove must have proven too harsh.

She turned back, saw Matthew standing by his desk, shoulders slumped, dirty hair fallen across his eyes. She went to him, reached out, touched his flannel sleeve. "You want me to get you your coat?"

He tried to smile. "Yeah. Thanks."

She got Matthew's camo parka and handed it to him.

"Okay, everyone, let's go," Ms. Rhodes said. She led the students out of the classroom and into the bright, sunlit day. They marched through town and down to the harbor, where a Beaver float plane was docked.

The plane was dented up and in need of paint. It rolled and creaked and pulled at its lines with every slap of the incoming tide. At their approach, the plane's door opened and a wiry man with a bushy white beard jumped down onto the dock. He wore a battered trucker's cap and mismatched boots. The smile he gave them was so big it bunched up his cheeks and turned his eyes into slits.

"Kids, this is Dieter Manse, from Homer. He used to be a Pan Am pilot. Climb aboard," Ms. Rhodes said. To Dieter, she said, "Thanks, man. I appreciate this." She glanced worriedly back at Matthew. "We needed to clear our heads a bit."

The old man nodded. "My pleasure, Tica."

In her previous life, Leni wouldn't have believed this man had been a captain at Pan Am. But up here, lots of people had been one thing on the Outside and became another in Alaska. Large Marge used to be a big-city prosecutor and now took showers at the Laundromat and sold gum, and Natalie had gone from teaching economics at a university to captaining her own fishing boat. Alaska was full of unexpected people—like the woman who lived in a broken-down school bus at Anchor Point and read palms. Rumor had it that she used to be a cop in New York City. Now she walked around with a parrot on her shoulder. Everyone up here had two stories: the life before and the life now. If you wanted to pray to a weirdo god or live in a school bus or marry a goose, no one in Alaska was going to say crap to you. No one cared if you had an old car on your deck, let alone a rusted fridge. Any life that could be imagined could be lived up here.

Leni stepped up into the plane, ducking her head, bending in half. Once inside, she took a seat in the middle row and snapped her seat belt in place. Ms. Rhodes sat down beside her. Matthew lumbered past them, head down, not making eye contact.

"Tom says he's not talking much," Ms. Rhodes said to Leni, leaning close.

"I don't know what he needs," Leni said, turning back, watching Matthew take a seat and strap his seat belt tight.

"A friend," Ms. Rhodes said, but it was a stupid answer. The kind of thing adults said. Obvious. But what was that friend supposed to *say*?

The pilot climbed aboard and strapped himself in and put on a headset, then started the engine. Leni heard Marthe and Agnes giggling in their seats behind her.

The float plane engine hummed, the metal all around her rattled. Waves slapped the floats.

The pilot was saying something about seat cushions and what to do in case of an unscheduled water landing.

"Wait. That means a crash. He's talking about what to do if we crash," she said, feeling the start of panic.

"We'll be fine," Ms. Rhodes said. "You can't be Alaskan and be afraid of small planes. This is how we get around."

Leni knew it was true. With so little of the state accessible by roads, boats and planes were important up here. In the winter, the vastness of Alaska was connected by frozen rivers and lakes. In the summer all of that fast-moving water separated and isolated them. Bush planes helped them get around.

Still, she hadn't been in an airplane before and it felt remarkably unsteady and unreliable. She clutched the armrests and held on. She tried to sweep fear out of her mind as the plane rambled past the breakwater, clattered hard, and began lifting into the sky. The plane swayed sickeningly, leveled out. Leni didn't open her eyes. If she did, she knew she'd see things that scared her: bolts that could pop out, windows that could crack, mountains they could crash into. She thought about that plane that had crashed in the Andes a few years ago. The survivors had become *cannibals*.

Her fingers ached. That was how tightly she was holding on.

"Open your eyes," Ms. Rhodes said. "Trust me."

She opened her eyes, pushed the vibrating curls out of her face.

Through a circle of Plexiglas, the world was something she'd never seen before. Blue, black, white, purple. From this vantage point, the geographical history of Alaska came alive for her; she saw the violence of its birth—volcanoes like Mounts Redoubt and Augustine erupting; mountain peaks thrust up from the sea and then worn down by rocky blue glaciers; fjords sculpted by rivers of moving ice. She saw Homer, huddled on a strip of land between high sandstone bluffs, fields covered in snow, and the Spit pointing out into the bay. Glaciers had formed all of this landscape, cut through and crunched forward, hollowing out deep bays, leaving mountains on either side.

The colors were spectacular, saturating. Across the blue bay, the Kenai Mountains rose like something out of a fairy tale, white sawlike blades that pushed high, high into the blue sky. In places, the glaciers on their steep sides were the pale blue of robins' eggs.

The mountains expanded, swallowed the horizon. Jagged, white peaks striated by black crevasses and turquoise glaciers. "Wow," she said, pressing closer to the window. They flew close to mountain peaks.

And then they were descending, gliding low over an inlet. Snow blanketed everything, lay in glittering patches on the beach, turned to ice and slush by the water. The float plane swerved and banked, lifted up again, and flew over a thicket of white trees. She saw a huge bull moose walking toward the bay.

They were over an inlet and descending fast.

She clutched the armrests again, closed her eyes, prepared.

They landed with a hard thump, and waves pounded the pontoons. The pilot killed the engine, jumped out of the plane, splashing into the ice-cold water, dragging the float plane higher onto the shore, tying it to a fallen log. Slush floated around his ankles.

Leni got out of the plane carefully (nothing was more dangerous up here than getting wet in the winter), walked along the float, and jumped out onto the slushy beach. Matthew was right behind her.

Ms. Rhodes gathered the few students together on the icy shore. "Okay, kids. The littles and I are going to hike over to the ridge. Matthew, you and Leni just go exploring. Have some fun."

Leni looked around. The beauty of this place, the majesty of it, was overwhelming. A deep and abiding peace existed here; there were no human voices, no thumping footsteps, no laughter or engines running. The natural world spoke loudest here, the breathing of the tide across the rocks, the slap of water on the float plane's pontoons, the distant barking of sea lions lumped together on a rock, being circled by chattering gulls.

The water beyond the shore ice was a stunning aqua, the color Leni imagined the Caribbean Sea to be, with a snowy shoreline decorated with huge white-covered black rocks. Snowcapped peaks muscled in close. Up high, Leni saw ivory-colored dots scattered on the impossibly steep sides— mountain goats. She reached into her pocket for her last, precious roll of film.

She couldn't wait to take some pictures, but she had to be judicious with the film.

Where would she start? The ice-glazed beach rocks that looked like seed pearls? The frozen fern fronds growing up from a snow-rounded black log? The turquoise water? She turned toward Matthew, started to say something, but he was gone.

She turned, felt icy water shushing over her boots, and saw Matthew standing far down the beach, alone, his arms crossed. He had dropped his parka; it lay inches away from the incoming waves. His hair whipped across his face.

She splashed through the water toward him, reached out. "Matthew, you need to put your coat on. It's cold—"

He yanked away from her touch, stumbled away. "Get away from me," he said harshly. "I don't want you to see . . ."

"Matthew?" She grabbed his arm, forced him to look at her. His eyes were red-rimmed from crying.

He shoved her away. She stumbled back, tripped over a piece of driftwood, and fell hard.

It happened fast enough to take her breath away. She lay there, sprawled on the frozen rocks, the cold water washing toward her, and stared up at him, her elbow stinging with pain.

"Oh, my God," he said. "Are you okay? I didn't mean to do that."

Leni got to her feet, stared at him. *I didn't mean to do that.* The same words she'd heard spoken by her dad.

"There's something wrong with me," Matthew said in a shaky voice. "My dad blames me and I can't sleep for shit, and without my mom, the house is so quiet that I want to scream."

Leni didn't know how to respond.

"I have nightmares . . . about Mom. I see her face, under the ice . . . screaming . . . I don't know what to do. I didn't want you to know."

"Why?"

"I want you to like me. Sometimes you're the only thing . . . Oh, shit . . . forget it." He shook his head, started crying again. "I'm a loser."

"No. You just need some help," she said. "Who wouldn't? After what you've been through."

"My aunt in Fairbanks wants me to come live with her. She thinks I should play hockey and learn to fly and see a shrink. I'd get to be with Aly. Unless . . ." He looked at Leni.

"So you'll go to Fairbanks," she said quietly.

He sighed heavily. She thought maybe it had already been decided and he'd been waiting to tell her all along. "I'll miss you."

He was going. Leaving.

At that, she felt an aching sense of sorrow expand in her chest. She would miss him so much, but he needed help. Because of her father, she knew what nightmares and sadness and a lack of sleep could do to a person, what a toxic combination that could be. What kind of friend would she be if she cared more about herself than him?

I'll miss you, she wanted to say back to him, but what was the point? Words didn't help.

⊰❖⊱

AFTER MATTHEW LEFT, January got darker. Colder.

"Leni, would you set the table for dinner?" Mama asked on a particularly cold and stormy night, with wind clawing to get in, snow swirling. She was frying up some Spam in a cast-iron skillet, pressing down on it with her spatula. Two slices of Spam for three people was all they had.

Leni put down her social studies book and headed for the kitchen, keeping her eye on Dad. He paced along the back wall, his hands flexing and fisting, flexing and fisting, shoulders hunched, muttering to himself. His arms were stringy and thin, his stomach concave beneath his stained thermal underwear top.

He hit his forehead hard with the heel of his palm, muttering something unintelligible.

Leni sidled around the table and turned into the small kitchen.

She gave Mama a worried look.

"What did you say?" Dad said, materializing behind Leni, looming.

Mama pressed the spatula down on a slice of Spam. A blob of grease popped up, landed on the back of her wrist. "Ouch! Damn it!"

"Are you two talking about me?" Dad demanded.

Leni gently took her father by the arm, led him to the table.

"Your mother was talking about me, wasn't she? What did she say? Did she mention Tom?"

Leni pulled out a chair, eased him into it. "She was talking about dinner, Dad. That's all." She started to leave. He grabbed her hand, pulled so hard she stumbled into him. "*You* love me, right?"

Leni didn't like the emphasis. "Mama and I both love you."

Mama showed up as if on cue, put the small plate of Spam alongside an enamel bowl of Thelma's brown-sugar baked beans.

Mama leaned down, kissed Dad's cheek, pressed her palm to his face.

It calmed him, that touch. He sighed, tried to smile. "Smells good."

Leni took her seat and began serving. She poured herself a glass of watery, powdered milk.

Mama sat across from Leni, picked at her beans, pushed them around on her plate, watching Dad. He muttered something under his breath. "You need to eat something, Ernt."

"I can't eat this shit." He swept his plate sideways, sending it crashing to the floor.

He shot up, strode away from the table, moving fast, grabbed his parka off of the wall hook, and wrenched the door open. "No g-damn *peace*," he said, leaving the cabin, slamming the door behind him. Moments later, they heard the bus start up, spin out, drive away.

Leni looked across the table.

"Eat," Mama said, and bent down for the fallen plate and glass.

After dinner, they stood side by side, washing and drying the dishes, putting them away on the shelves above the counter.

"You want to play Yahtzee?" Leni finally asked. Her question held as much enthusiasm as her mother's sad nod.

They sat at the card table, playing the game for as long as either could stand the pretense.

Leni knew they were both waiting to hear the VW rumble back into the yard. Worrying. Wondering which was worse: him being here or him being gone.

"Where is he, you think?" Leni asked after what seemed like hours.

"Mad Earl's, if he could get up there. Or the Kicking Moose, if the roads were too bad."

"Drinking," Leni said.

"Drinking."

"Maybe we should—"

"Don't," Mama said. "Just go to bed, okay?" She sat back, lit up one of her precious last cigarettes.

Leni gathered up the dice and scorecards and the little brown and yellow fake-leather shaker, and fit them all back into the red box.

She climbed up the loft ladder and crawled into her sleeping bag without even bothering to brush her teeth. Downstairs, she heard her mother pacing.

Leni rolled over for her paper and a pen. Since Matthew had been gone, she'd written him several letters, which Large Marge mailed for her. Matthew wrote back religiously, short notes about his new hockey team and how it felt to be in a school that actually had sports teams. His handwriting was so bad she could barely decipher it. She waited impatiently for each letter and ripped them open immediately. She read each one over and over, like a detective, looking for clues and hints of emotion. Neither she nor Matthew knew quite what to say, how to use something as impersonal as words to create a bridge between their disparate lives, but they kept writing. She didn't yet know how he felt about himself or the move or the loss of his mother, but she knew that he was thinking about her. That was more than enough to begin with.

Dear Matthew,

    Today we learned more about the Klondike Gold Rush in school.
Ms. Rhodes actually mentioned your grandma as an example
of the kind of woman who set out North with nothing and found—

She heard a scream.

Leni scrambled out of her sleeping bag and half slid down the ladder.

"There's something out there," Mama said, coming out of her bedroom, holding up a lantern. In its glow, she looked wild, pale.

A wolf howled. The wail undulated through the darkness.

Close.

Another wolf answered.

The goats screamed in response, a terrible keening cry that sounded human.

Leni grabbed the rifle from the rack and went to open the door.

"No!" Mama yelled, yanking her back. "We can't go out there. They could attack us."

They shoved the curtains aside and opened the window. Cold blasted them.

A sliver of moonlight shone down on the yard, weak and insubstantial but enough to show them glimmers of movement. Light on silver fur, yellow eyes, fangs. Wolves moving in a pack toward the goat pen.

"Get out of here!" Leni yelled. She pointed her rifle and aimed at something, movement, and fired.

The gunshot was a crack of sound. A wolf yelped, whined.

She shot again and again, heard the bullets thwack into trees, ping on metal.

The screaming and bleating of the goats went on and on.

✦⟨✾⟩✦

QUIET.

Leni opened her eyes and found that she was sprawled on the sofa, with Mama beside her.

The fire had gone out.

Shivering, Leni pushed back the pile of woolen and fur blankets and restarted the fire.

"Mama, wake up," Leni said. They were both wearing layers of clothing, but when they'd finally fallen asleep, they'd been so exhausted they'd forgotten the fire. "We have to check outside."

Mama sat up. "We'll go out when there's light."

Leni looked at the clock. Six A.M.

Hours later, when dawn finally shed its slow, tentative light across the land, Leni stepped into her white bunny boots and pulled the rifle down from the gun rack by the door, loading it. The closing of the chamber was a loud crack of sound.

"I don't want to go out there," Mama said. "And no. You're not going alone, Annie Oakley." With a wan smile, she pulled on her boots and put on her parka, flipping the fur-lined hood up. She loaded up a second rifle and stood beside Leni.

Leni opened the door, stepped out onto the snow-covered deck, holding the rifle in front of her.

The world was white on white. Snow falling. Muffled. No sounds.

They moved across the deck, down the steps.

Leni smelled death before she saw it.

Blood streaked the snow by the ruined goat pen. Stanchions and gates had been torn apart, lay broken. There were feces everywhere, in dark piles, mingled with blood and gore and entrails. Trails of gore led into the woods.

Wrecked. All of it. The pens, the chicken yard, the coop. Every animal gone, not even pieces left.

They stared at the destruction until Mama said, "We can't stay out here. The scent of blood will draw predators."

ELEVEN

O ut on the road with her mother, walking, the two of them holding hands, Leni felt like an astronaut moving through an inhospitable white landscape. Her breathing and their footsteps were all she heard. She tried to convince Mama to stop at either the Walker place or Large Marge's, but Mama wouldn't listen. She didn't want to admit what had happened.

In town, everything was hunkered down. The boardwalk was a strip of snow-covered ice. Icicles hung from the eaves of the buildings and snow coated every surface. The harbor was full of whitecaps that tossed the fishing boats from side to side, yanked at their lines.

The Kicking Moose was already—or still—open. Light bled through the amber windows. A few vehicles were parked out front—trucks, snow machines—but not many.

Leni elbowed Mama, cocked her head at the VW bus parked near the saloon.

Neither of them moved. "He won't be glad to see us," Mama said.

An understatement, Leni thought.

"Maybe we should go home," Mama said, shivering.

Across the street, the door to the General Store opened, and Leni heard the faraway tinkling of the bell.

Tom Walker stepped out of the store, carrying a big box of supplies. He saw them and stopped.

Leni was acutely aware of how she and Mama looked, standing knee-deep in snow, faces pink with cold, tuques white and frozen. No one went walking in weather like this. Mr. Walker put his box of supplies in the back of his truck, shoved it up against the cab. Large Marge came out of the store behind him. Leni saw the two of them look at each other, frown, and then head toward Leni and her mom.

"Hey, Cora," Mr. Walker said. "You guys are out on a bad day."

A shudder of cold made Mama shake; her teeth chattered. "Wolves were at our place last night. I d-don't know how many. They k-killed all the goats and chickens and ruined the pens and c-coop."

"Did Ernt kill any of them? Do you need help skinning? The pelts are worth—"

"N-no," Mama said. "It was dark. I'm just here . . . to put in an order for more chicks." She glanced at Large Marge. "Next time you go to Homer, Marge. And for more rice and beans, but . . . we're out of money. Maybe I can do laundry. Or darning. I'm good with a needle and thread."

Leni saw the way Large Marge's face tightened, heard the curse she muttered beneath her breath. "He left you alone, and wolves attacked your place. You could have been killed."

"We were fine. We didn't go out," Mama said.

"Where is he?" Mr. Walker asked quietly.

"W-we don't know," Mama lied.

"At the Kicking Moose," Large Marge said. "There's the VW."

"Tom, don't," Mom said, but it was too late. Mr. Walker was walking away from them, striding down the quiet street, his footsteps spraying up snow.

The women—and Leni—rushed along behind him, slipping and sliding in their haste.

"Don't, Tom, really," Mama said.

He wrenched open the saloon's door. Leni instantly smelled damp wool and unwashed bodies and wet dog and burnt wood.

There were at least five men in here, not counting the hunched, toothless bartender. It was noisy: hands thumping on whiskey-barrel tables, a battery-operated radio blaring out "Bad, Bad Leroy Brown," men talking all at once.

"Yeah, yeah, yeah," Mad Earl was saying, his eyes glazed. "The first thing they'll do is take over the banks."

"And seize our land," Clyde said, the words slurred.

"They won't take my g-damn land." This from her dad. He stood beneath one of the hanging lanterns, swaying unsteadily, his eyes bloodshot. "No one takes what's mine."

"Ernt Allbright, you piece of shit," Mr. Walker hissed.

Dad staggered, turned. His gaze went from Mr. Walker to Mama. "What the hell?"

Mr. Walker stormed forward, knocking chairs aside. Mad Earl scrambled to get out of his way. "A pack of wolves attacked your place last night, Allbright. Wolves," he said again.

Dad's gaze went to Mama. "Wolves?"

"You are going to get your family killed," Mr. Walker said.

"Look here—"

"No. *You* look," Mr. Walker said. "You aren't the first cheechako to come up here with no goddamn idea what to do. You aren't even the stupidest, not by a long shot. But a man who doesn't take care of his wife . . ."

"You got no right to say anything about keeping a woman safe, do you, Tom?" Dad said.

Mr. Walker grabbed Dad by the ear and yanked so hard he yelped like a girl. He dragged Dad out of the smelly bar and into the street. "I should kick your ass around the block," Mr. Walker said in a harsh voice.

"Tom," Mama pleaded. "*Please.* Don't make it worse."

Mr. Walker stopped. Turned. He saw Mama standing there terrified, nearly in tears, and Leni saw him pull himself from the brink of rage. She'd never seen a man do it before.

He stilled, frowned, then muttered something under his breath and yanked Dad to the bus. Opening the door, he lifted Dad as easily as if he were a kid and shoved him into the passenger seat. "You're a disgrace."

He slammed the door shut and then went to Mama.

"Will you be okay?" Leni heard him ask.

Mama whispered an answer Leni couldn't hear, but she thought she heard Mr. Walker whisper, *Kill him*, and saw Mama shake her head.

Mr. Walker touched her arm, barely, just for a second, but Leni saw.

Mama gave him an unsteady smile and said, "Leni, get in the bus," without looking away from him.

Leni did as she was told.

Mama climbed into the driver's seat and started the bus.

All the way home, Leni could see rage building in her father, see it in the way his nostrils flared every now and then, in the way his hands flexed and unflexed, hear it in the words he didn't say.

He was a man who talked, especially lately, especially in the winter, he always had something to say. Now his lips were pressed tightly together.

It made Leni feel as if she were a coil of rope drawn around a cleat with the wind pulling at it, tugging, the rope creaking in resistance, slipping. If the line wasn't perfectly tied down, it would all come undone, be torn away, maybe the wind would pull the cleat from its home in fury.

There was still a bright pink mark on his ear, like a burn, where Mr. Walker had taken hold and hauled Dad outside and humiliated him.

Leni had never seen anyone treat her father that way and she knew there would be hell to pay for it.

The bus jerked to a stop in front of the cabin, skidded sideways slightly in the snow.

Mama turned off the ignition, and the silence expanded, grew heavier without the rattle and rumble of the engine to hide even a layer of its depth.

Leni and Mama got out of the bus fast, left Dad sitting there, alone.

As they neared the cabin, they saw again the destruction the wolves had caused. Snow lay over it all, in heaping handfuls on posts and planks. Chicken wire stuck up in tangled heaps. A door lay half exposed. Here and there, in tree wells mostly, but on wood pieces, too, there was blood turned to pink ice and frozen clumps of gore. A few colorful feathers could be seen.

Mama took Leni by the hand and led her across the yard and into the cabin. She shut the door hard behind them.

"He's going to hurt you," Leni said.

"Your dad is a proud man. To be humiliated in that way . . ."

Seconds later, the door banged open. Dad stood there, his eyes bright with alcohol and rage.

He was across the room in less time than it took Leni to draw a breath. He grabbed Mama by the hair and punched her in the jaw so hard she slammed into the wall and collapsed to the floor.

Leni screamed and flew at him, her hands curling into claws.

"No, Leni!" Mama cried.

Dad grabbed Leni by the shoulders, shook her hard. Grabbing a handful of her hair, he yanked her across the floor, her feet tripping up on the rug, and shoved her outside into the cold.

He slammed the door shut.

Leni threw herself at the door, battering it with her body until there was no strength left in her. She slumped to her knees beneath the small overhang of the roof.

Inside, she heard a crash, something breaking, and a scream. She wanted to run away, get help, but that would only make everything worse. There was no help for them.

Leni closed her eyes and prayed to the God she had never been taught about.

She heard the door unlock. How long had it been?

Leni didn't know.

Leni stumbled to her feet, frozen, and went into the cabin.

It looked like a war zone. A broken chair, shattered glass across the floor, blood splattered on the sofa.

Mama looked even worse.

For the first time, Leni thought: *He could kill her.*

Kill her.

They had to get away. Now.

Leni approached her mother cautiously, afraid Mama was on the verge of collapse. "Where's Dad?"

"Passed out. In bed. He wanted . . . to punish me . . ." She turned away, ashamed. "You should go to bed."

Leni went to the hooks by the door, got Mama's parka and boots. "Here, dress warmly."

"Why?"

"Just do it." Leni moved quietly across the cabin, eased through the beaded curtain. Her heartbeat was a hammer hitting her rib cage as she looked around, saw what she'd come for.

Keys. Mama's purse. Not that there was any money in it.

She grabbed it all and started to leave and then stopped, turned back.

She looked at her dad, sprawled facedown on the bed, naked, his butt covered by a blanket. Burn scars puckered and twisted his shoulders and arms, the skin looked lavender-blue in the shadows. Blood smeared the pillow.

She left him there and went back to the living room, where Mama stood alone, smoking a cigarette, looking like she'd been beaten with a club.

"Come on," Leni said, taking her hand, giving a gentle, insistent tug.

Mama said, "Where are we going?"

Leni opened the door, gave Mama a little shove, then she reached down for one of the bug-out bags that were always by the door, a silent ode to the worst that could happen, a reminder that smart people were prepared.

Hefting it onto her shoulder, Leni leaned into the wind and snow and followed her mother out to the bus. "Get in," she said gently.

Mama climbed into the driver's seat and fit the key into the ignition, giving it a turn. As the VW warmed, she said dully, "Where are we going?"

Leni tossed the big pack into the back of the bus. "We're leaving, Mama."

"What?"

Leni climbed into the passenger seat. "We're leaving him before he kills you."

"Oh. That. No." Mama shook her head. "He would never do that. He loves me."

"I think your nose is broken."

Mama sat there a minute longer, her face downcast. Then, slowly, she put the old VW in gear, and turned toward the driveway. Headlights pointed to the way out.

Mama started to cry in that quiet way of hers, as if she thought Leni couldn't tell. As they drove into the trees, she kept glancing in the rearview mirror, wiping her tears away. When they reached the main road, a feral wind clawed at the bus. Mama worked the gas carefully, trying to keep the bus steady on the snow-packed ground.

They passed the Walker gate and kept going.

At the next bend in the road, a gust of wind punched the bus hard enough that they skidded sideways. A broken branch cracked into the windshield, got caught for a second in the wiper, was slammed up and down before it blew away, and revealed a giant bull moose in front of them, crossing the road on a turn.

Leni screamed a warning, but she knew it was too late. They had to either hit the moose or swerve too hard, and hitting an animal of that size would destroy the bus.

Mama turned the steering wheel, eased her foot off the accelerator.

The bus, never good in the snow, began a long, slow pirouette.

Leni saw the moose as they glided past him—his huge head inches from her window, his nostrils flaring.

"Hang on," Mama screamed.

They hit a berm of snow and flipped over; the bus cartwheeled and plummeted off the road, landing in a screech of metal.

Leni saw it in pieces—trees upside down, a snowy hillside, broken branches.

She cracked her head into the window.

When she regained consciousness, the first thing she noticed was quiet. Then the pain in her head and the taste of blood in her mouth. Her mother was slumped beside her; both of them were in the passenger seat.

"Leni? Are you okay?"

"I . . . think so."

She heard a hiss of sound—something gone wrong with the engine—and the whining creak of settling metal.

Mama said, "The bus is lying on its side. I think we're on solid ground, but there could be farther to fall."

Another way to die in Alaska. "Will someone find us?"

"No one is going to be out in weather like this."

"Even if they were, they wouldn't see us."

Moving cautiously, Leni felt around for the heavy, clanking backpack, found it, and burrowed through it for a headlamp. Fitting it onto her head, she flicked the switch. The glow was too yellow, otherworldly. Mama looked freakish, her bruised face waxlike and melting.

That was when Leni saw the blood in Mama's lap and her broken arm. A bone stuck out from a tear in her sleeve.

"Mama! Your arm. Your arm! Oh, my God—"

"Take a breath. Look at it, look good. It's a broken bone. And not my first."

Leni tried to settle her panic. She took a deep breath, submerged it. "What do we do?"

Mama unzipped the backpack, began pulling out gloves and neoprene face masks with her good hand.

Leni couldn't look away from the splintered bone, from the blood soaking her mother's sleeve.

"Okay. First I need you to bind up my arm to stop the bleeding. You've learned how to do this. Remember? Rip off the bottom of your shirt."

"I can't."

"Lenora," Mama said sharply. "Rip your shirt."

Leni's hands were shaking as she removed the knife from her belt and used it to start a rip in the fabric. When she had a long ribbon of flannel, she carefully scooted sideways.

"Above the break. Tie it as tightly as you can."

Leni fit the fabric around Mama's bicep, heard the groan of pain her mama made when Leni tightened it.

"Are you okay?"

"Tighter."

Leni yanked it as tightly as she could, tied it in a knot.

Mama let out a shaky sigh and climbed back into the driver's seat. "Here's what we have to do. I am going to break my window. You are going to climb over me and climb out."

"B-but—"

"No buts, Leni. I need you to be strong now, okay? *You* need it. I can't get out and if we both stay here, we'll freeze to death. You need to go for help. I can't climb out of the bus with this broken arm."

"I can't do it."

"You can do this, Leni." Mama clamped a bloody hand over the make-shift bandage on her arm. "I need you to do it."

"You'll freeze while I'm gone," she said.

"I'm tougher than I look, remember? Thanks to your dad's Armageddon phobia, we've got a bug-out bag. A survival blanket, and food and water." She gave a wan smile. "I will be fine. You go for help. Okay?"

"Okay." She tried not to be scared, but her whole body was shaking. She put on her gloves and her neoprene face mask and zipped up her parka.

Mama pulled a life hammer out from under her seat. "The Walker place is closest. It's probably less than a quarter of a mile from here. Go there. Can you make it?"

"Yeah."

The bus made a dull, creaking sound, settled a little, moved.

"I love you, baby girl."

Leni tried not to cry.

"Hold your breath. Go *up*."

Mama cracked the hammer against the window, hard, fast.

The glass crackled into a webbed pattern, sagged. For a second it held together, and then with a *snap!* it broke. Snow dumped into the bus, covering them.

The cold was shocking.

Leni lurched forward, climbing over her mother, trying not to hit her arm, hearing her moan in pain, feeling her mother's good hand come up through the snow to push her.

Leni shimmied through the window.

A branch smacked her in the face. She kept going, crawling on the side of the bus until she reached the hillside, which had been scraped and scarred by the plunging vehicle; black dirt and broken branches and exposed roots.

She launched herself forward, flailed for a higher foothold, climbed up the hillside.

It seemed to take forever. Clawing, clinging, hauling herself upward, breathing hard, sucking in snow. But finally she made it. She threw herself over the edge and landed facedown in the snow, on the road. Gasping, she climbed onto all fours and got to her feet.

Whiteout. Her headlamp threw out a razor-thin glow. Wind tried to shove her off the road as she started her trek. Trees shuddered all around her, bent and cracked. Branches flew past her, scraping the torn ground. One hit her hard in the side, almost knocked her over.

The light was her lifeline out here. Her chest began to ache from the frigid air she was breathing in, a stitch formed in her side. Sweat slid down her back and turned her hands clammy inside her gloves.

She had no idea how long she'd been trudging forward, trying not to stop or cry or scream, when she saw the silver gate up ahead, and the cow skull on it, wearing a bowler of snow.

Leni dragged the gate open, over the bumpy ground, bulldozing snow aside.

She wanted to run forward, scream *Help!* but she knew better. Running could be mistake number two. Instead, she trudged through the knee-high snow. The forest on her right blocked some of the wind.

It took at least fifteen minutes to get to the Walker house. As she neared it, saw light in the windows, she felt the sting of tears—tears that froze in the corners of her eyes, hurting, blurring her vision.

All at once the wind died; the world drew in a quiet breath, leaving a near-perfect silence, broken only by her ragged breathing and the distant purr of the waves on a frozen shore.

She stumbled past the snow-covered heaps of junk and old cars and past the beehives. At her approach, cows began lowing, stomping their hooves as they herded together in case she was a predator. Goats bleated.

Leni went up the ice-slick steps and pounded on the front door.

Mr. Walker answered quickly, opened the door. When he saw Leni, his face changed. "Jesus." He pulled her into the house, through the arctic entry lined with coats and hats and boots, and to the woodstove.

Her teeth were chattering so hard she was afraid she'd bite off her tongue if she tried to talk, but she had to.

"W-w-we cr-crashed th-the b-b-bus. M-Mama's stuck."

"Where?"

She couldn't stop her tears now, or her shaking. "By the b-bend in the road before Large Marge's p-place."

Mr. Walker nodded. "Okay." He left her standing there, shaking and shivering just long enough for him to return in snow gear, carrying a big mesh bag slung over one shoulder.

He went to the ham radio and found an open frequency. Staticky sound crackled through, then a high-pitched squeal. "Large Marge," he said into a handheld mouthpiece. "Tom Walker here. Car crash near my place on the main road. Need help. On my way. Over." He lifted his thumb from the button. Static again. Then he repeated the message and hung up the mouthpiece. "Let's go."

Could Dad hear that? Was he listening or still passed out?

Leni glanced worriedly outside, half expecting him to materialize.

Mr. Walker grabbed a striped red and yellow and white wool blanket from the back of the sofa and wrapped it around Leni.

"Her arm is broken. She's bleeding."

Mr. Walker nodded. Taking Leni's gloved hand in his own, he pulled her out of the warm house and back out into the frigid cold.

In the garage, his big truck started right up. The heat came on, blanketing the cab, making Leni shiver harder. She couldn't stop shaking as they drove down the driveway and turned out onto the main road, where wind beat at the windshield and whistled through every crevice in the metal frame.

Tom eased up on the gas; the truck slowed, grumbled, and whined.

"There!" she said, pointing to where they'd gone off the road. As Mr. Walker pulled over to the side, headlights appeared in front of them.

Leni recognized Large Marge's truck.

"You stay in the truck," Mr. Walker said.

"No!"

"*Stay* here." He grabbed his mesh bag and left the truck, slamming the door behind him.

In the glow of headlights, Leni saw Mr. Walker meet Large Marge in the middle of the road. He dropped his bag, took out some coiled-up rope.

Leni pressed herself to the window, her breath clouding the view. Impatiently she wiped it away.

Mr. Walker tied one end of the rope around a tree and the other end around his own waist in an old-school belay.

With a wave to Large Marge, he lowered himself over the embankment and disappeared.

Leni wrenched the door open and fought the wind, blinded by snow, to cross the road.

Large Marge stood at the edge of the embankment.

Leni peered over the edge, saw broken trees and the bus's shadowy bulk. She shined her flashlight down but it wasn't enough light. She heard metal creaking, a thump, and a woman's scream.

And then . . . Mr. Walker reappeared in the feeble beam of light, with Mama bound to his side, tied to him.

Large Marge grabbed the rope in her gloved hands, pulled them up, hand over hand, until Mr. Walker stumbled back up onto the road, Mama slumped at his side, unconscious, held up by Mr. Walker's grip. "She's in bad shape," Mr. Walker yelled into the wind. "I'll take her by boat to the hospital in Homer."

"What about me?" Leni screamed. They seemed to have forgotten she was there.

Mr. Walker gave Leni one of those *you-poor-kid* looks Leni knew so well. "You come with me."

⊹⟨❀⟩⊹

THE SMALL HOSPITAL waiting room was quiet.

Tom Walker sat beside Leni, his parka puffed up in his lap. First they had driven to Walker Cove, where Mr. Walker had carried Mama down to the dock and placed her gently on the bench seat in his aluminum boat. They had sped around the craggy shoreline to Homer.

At the hospital, Mr. Walker carried Mama up to the front desk. Leni ran along beside, touching Mama's ankle, her wrist, whatever she could reach.

A Native woman with two long braids sat at the desk, clacking away on a typewriter.

Within moments, a pair of nurses came to take Mama away.

"Now what?" Leni asked.

"Now we wait."

They sat there, not talking; each breath Leni took felt difficult, as if her lungs had a mind of their own and might stop working. There was so much to be afraid of: Mama's injury, losing Mama, Dad coming in (*Don't think about that, how mad he will be . . . what he'll do when he realizes they were leaving*), and the future. How would they leave now?

"Can I get you something to drink?"

Leni was so deep in the pit of her fear that it took her a second to realize Mr. Walker was talking to her.

She looked up, bleary-eyed. "Will it help?"

"Nope." He reached over for her hand, held it. She was surprised enough by the unexpected contact that she almost pulled away, but it felt nice, too, so she held his hand in return. She couldn't help wondering how different life would be with Tom Walker as her dad.

"How's Matthew?" she asked.

"He's getting better, Leni. Genny's brother is going to teach him to fly. Matthew is seeing a therapist. He loves your letters. Thanks for keeping in touch with him."

She loved his letters, too. Sometimes it felt like hearing from Matthew was the best part of her life. "I miss him."

"Yeah. Me, too."

"Will he come back?"

"I don't know. There's so much up there. Kids his age, movie theaters, sports teams. And I know Mattie, once he takes control of an airplane for the first time, he will fall in love. He's a kid who loves adventure."

"He told me he wanted to be a pilot."

"Yeah. I wish I'd listened to him a little better," Mr. Walker said with a sigh. "I just want him to be happy."

A doctor walked into the waiting room, approached them. He was a heavyset man with a barrel chest that strained to be freed from the confines of his blue scrubs. He had the rugged, hard-drinking look of a lot of the men who lived in the bush, but his hair was closely cropped and, except for a bushy gray mustache, he was clean-shaven. "I'm Dr. Irving. You must be Leni," he said, pulling off his surgical cap.

Leni nodded, got to her feet. "How is she?"

"She's going to be fine. Her arm is set in a cast now, so she'll need to slow down for six weeks or so, but there should be no lasting damage." He looked at Leni. "You saved her, young lady. She wanted to make sure I told you that."

"Can we see her?" Leni asked.

"Of course. Follow me."

Leni and Mr. Walker followed Dr. Irving down the white hallway and into a room with a sign that read RECOVERY on the door. He pushed open the door.

Mama was in a fabric-curtained cubicle. She was sitting upright in a narrow bed, wearing a hospital gown; a warming blanket lay across her lap. Her left arm was bent at a ninety-degree angle and was encased in a cast of white plaster. Something wasn't quite right with her nose and both eyes showed signs of bruising.

"Leni," she said, her head lolling a little to the right on the stack of pillows behind her. She had the lazy, unfocused look of someone who'd been drugged. "I told you I was tough," she said. Her voice was a little misshapen. "Ah, baby girl, don't cry."

Leni couldn't help herself. Seeing her mother like this, living through the crash, all she could think about was how fragile Mama was and how easily she could be lost. It made her think sharply, keenly, of Matthew and how quickly and unexpectedly death could sweep in.

She heard the doctor say goodbye and leave the room.

Mr. Walker went to Mama's bedside. "You were leaving him, weren't you? What other reason would there be to be out in this weather?"

"No." Mama shook her head.

"I could help you," he said. "We could help you. All of us. Large Marge used to be a prosecutor. I could call the police, tell them he hurt you. He does, doesn't he? You didn't break your nose in the accident, did you?"

"The police can't help," Mama said. "I know the system. My dad's a lawyer."

"They'd put him in jail."

"For what? A day? Two? He'd come back for me. Or you. Or Leni. Do you think I could live with putting other people at risk? And . . . well . . ."

Leni heard Mama's unspoken words: *I love him.*

Mr. Walker stared down at Mama, who was so bruised and bandaged she barely looked like herself. "All you have to do is ask for help," he said quietly. "I want to help you, Cora. Surely you know I—"

"You don't know me, Tom. If you did . . ."

Leni saw tears gather in her mother's eyes. "There's something wrong with me," she said slowly. "Sometimes it feels like a strength and sometimes like a weakness, but I don't know how to stop loving him."

"Cora!" Leni heard her father's voice and saw how Mama shrank into the pillows behind her.

Mr. Walker lurched away from her bedside.

Dad ignored Mr. Walker completely, shoved past him. "Oh, my God, Cora? Are you okay?"

Mama seemed to melt in front of him. "We crashed the bus."

"What were you doing out in that weather?" he said, but he knew. Leni saw it in his eyes. There was a deep scratch on his cheek.

Mr. Walker backed toward the door, a big man trying to disappear. He gave Leni a sad, knowing look and left the room, closing the door quietly behind him.

"We needed food," Mama said. "I wanted to make you a special d-dinner."

Dad laid his work-callused hand against her bruised, swollen cheek, as if his touch could heal her. "Forgive me, baby. I'll kill myself if you don't."

"Don't say that," Mama said. "Don't ever say that. You know I love you. Only you."

"Forgive me," he said. He turned. "And you, too, Red. Forgive a stupid man who can't get his shit together sometimes, but who loves you. And who will do better."

"I love you," Mama said, and she was crying now, too, and suddenly Leni understood the reality of her world, the truth that Alaska, in all its beautiful harshness, had revealed. They were trapped, by environment and finances, but mostly by the sick, twisted love that bound her parents together.

Mama would never leave Dad. It didn't matter that she'd gone so far as to take a backpack and run to the bus and drive away. She would come back, always, because she loved him. Or she needed him. Or she was afraid of him. Who knew, really?

Leni couldn't begin to understand the hows and whys of her parents' love. She was old enough to see the turbulent surface, but too young to know what lay beneath.

Mama could never leave Dad, and Leni would never leave Mama. And Dad could never let them go. In this toxic knot that was their family, there was no escape for any of them.

✦⤙❀⤚✦

THAT NIGHT, they took Mama home from the hospital.

Dad held Mama as if she were made of glass. So careful, so concerned for her well-being. It filled Leni with an impotent rage.

And then she'd get a glimpse of him with tears in his eyes and the rage would turn soft and slide into something like forgiveness. She didn't know how to corral or change either of these emotions; her love for him was all tangled up in hate. Right now she felt both emotions crowding in on her, each jostling for the lead.

He got Mama settled in bed and immediately went out to chop wood. There was never enough on the pile and Leni knew that physical exertion helped him somehow. Leni sat by her mother's bedside for as long as she could, holding her mother's cold hand. She had so many questions she wanted to ask, but she knew the ugly words would only make her mother cry, so Leni said nothing.

The next morning, Leni was climbing down the ladder when she heard Mama crying.

Leni went into Mama's bedroom and found her sitting up in bed (just a mattress on the floor), leaning back against the skinned log wall, her face swollen, both eyes black and blue, her nose just slightly to the left of where it belonged.

"Don't cry," Leni said.

"You must think the worst of me," Mama said, gingerly touching the split in her lip. "I baited him, didn't I? Said the wrong thing. I must have?"

Leni didn't know what to say to that. Did Mama mean that it was her fault, that if Mama was quieter or more supportive or more agreeable, Dad wouldn't explode? It didn't seem true to Leni, not at all. Sometimes he snapped and sometimes he didn't, that was all there was. Mama taking the blame seemed wrong. Dangerous, even.

"I love him," Mama said, staring down at her cast-encased arm. "I don't know how to stop. But I have you to think about, too. Oh, my God . . . I don't know why I'm like this. Why I let him treat me this way. I just can't forget who he was before the war. I keep thinking he'll come back, the man I married."

"You won't ever leave him," Leni said quietly. She tried not to make it sound like an indictment.

"Would you really want that? I thought you loved Alaska," Mama said.

"I love you more. And . . . I'm afraid," Leni said.

"This time was bad, I'll admit, but it scared him. Really. It won't happen again. He's promised me."

Leni sighed. How was Mama's unshakable belief in Dad any different than his fear of Armageddon? Did adults just look at the world and see what they wanted to see, think what they wanted to think? Did evidence and experience mean nothing?

Mama managed a smile. "You want to play crazy eights?"

So that was how they would do it, merge back into the driving lane after a blown tire. They would say ordinary things and pretend none of it had happened. Until the next time.

Leni nodded. She retrieved the cards from the rosewood box that held her mother's favorite things and sat down on the floor beside the mattress.

"I'm so lucky to have you, Leni," Mama said, trying to organize her cards with one hand.

"We're a team," Leni said.

"Peas in a pod."

"Two of a kind."

Words they said all the time to each other; words that felt a little hollow now. Maybe even sad.

They were halfway through the first game when Leni heard a vehicle drive up. She tossed the cards on the bed and ran to the window. "It's Large Marge," she yelled back to Mama. "And Mr. Walker."

"Shit," Mama said. "Help me get dressed."

Leni ran back to Mama's bedroom and helped her take off her flannel pajamas and get into a pair of faded jeans and an oversized hooded sweatshirt with sleeves big enough to accommodate the cast. Leni brushed Mama's hair and then helped her out to the living room, got her situated on the ragged sofa.

The cabin door opened. Snow fluttered inside on a wave of icy air, brushed across the plywood floor.

Large Marge looked like a grizzly in her huge fur parka and mukluks, with a wolverine hat that looked to have been handmade. Earrings made of antler bone hung from her sagging earlobes. She stomped the snow from her boots and started to say something. Then she saw Mama's bruised face and muttered, "Son of a freaking bitch. I should kick his beef-jerky ass."

Mr. Walker came in to stand behind her.

"Hey," Mama said, not quite making eye contact with him. She didn't stand; maybe she wasn't strong enough. "Would you like some—"

Dad pushed his way in, slammed the door shut behind him. "I'll get 'em coffee, Cora. You stay put."

The tension between the adults was unbearable. What was happening here? Something, that was for sure.

Large Marge took Mr. Walker by the arm—a firm, fish-landing grip—and led him to a chair by the woodstove. "Sit down," she said, shoving him into the chair when he didn't move fast enough.

Leni grabbed a stool from beside the card table and dragged it into the living room for Large Marge.

"That itty-bitty thing?" Large Marge asked. "My ass is going to look like a mushroom on a toothpick." Still, she sat down. Planting her fleshy hands on her hips, she looked at Mama.

"It's worse than it looks," Mama said in an uneven voice. "We had a car crash, you know."

"Yeah. I know," Large Marge said.

Dad came into the living room, carrying two blue-speckled cups full of coffee. Steam rose up from them, scented the air. He handed Tom and Large Marge each a cup.

"So," he said uneasily. "We haven't had winter guests in a while."

"Sit down, Ernt," Large Marge said.

"I don't—"

"Sit down or I'll knock you down," Large Marge said.

Mama gasped.

Dad sat down on the sofa beside Mama. "That's not really the way to talk to a man in his own home."

"You don't want to get me started on what a real man is, Ernt Allbright. I'm holding on to my temper, but it could run away with me. And you do not want to see a big woman come at you. Trust me. So shut your trap and listen." She glanced at Mama. "Both of you."

Leni felt the air leave the room. A chilling, weighted silence came in, pressed down on them.

Large Marge looked at Mama. "I know you know I'm from D.C. and that I used to be a lawyer. Big-city prosecutor. Wore designer suits and high heels. The whole shebang. I loved it. And I loved my sister, who married the man of her dreams. Only he turned out to have a few problems. A few quirks. Turned out he drank too much and liked to use my baby sis as a punching bag. I tried everything to get her to leave him, but she refused. Maybe she was scared, maybe she loved him, maybe she was as sick and broken as he was. I don't know. I know that when I called the police it was worse for her and she begged me not to do it again. I backed off. Biggest mistake of my life. He went after her with a hammer." Large Marge flinched. "We had to have a closed-casket funeral. That was what he'd done to her. He claimed he'd taken the hammer from her and protected himself. The law isn't kind to battered women. He's still out there. Free. I came up here to get away from all that." She looked at Ernt. "And here you are."

Dad started to rise.

"I'd sit, if I were you," Mr. Walker said.

Dad slowly sat back down. Anxiety shone in his eyes, showed in the hands he flexed and unflexed. His booted foot tapped nervously on the floor. They had no idea what this little meeting would cost Mama. As soon as they left, he'd explode.

"You probably mean well," Leni said. "But—"

"No," Mr. Walker said in a kind voice. "This isn't for you to solve, Leni. You're a kid. Just listen."

"Tommy and I have talked about this," Large Marge said. "Your situation here. We have a couple of solutions, but really, Ernt, our favorite one is we take you out and kill you."

Dad laughed once, then went silent. His eyes widened when he realized they weren't joking.

"That's my choice, actually," Mr. Walker said. "Large Marge has a different plan."

"Ernt, you're going to pack your shit up and go to the slope," Large Marge said. "The pipeline is hiring men like you—it's a Sodom and Gomorrah up there—and they need mechanics. You'll make a pile of money, which you need, and you'll be gone until spring."

"I can't leave my family alone until spring," Dad said.

"How thoughtful you are," Mr. Walker muttered.

"You think I'll just leave her to you?" Dad said.

"Enough, boys," Large Marge said. "You can clank antlers later. For now, Ernt is leaving and I'm moving in. I'll stay with your girls for the winter, Ernt. I'll keep them safe from everything and everyone. You can come back in the spring. By then, maybe you'll know what you've got and treat your wife as she deserves."

"You can't make me go," Dad said.

"That's not the A answer," Large Marge said. "Look, Ernt. Alaska brings out the best and the worst in a man. Maybe if you'd stayed Outside you never would have become who you are now. I know about 'Nam, and it breaks my heart what you boys went through. But you can't handle the dark, can you? It's nothing to be ashamed of. Most folks can't. Accept it and do what's best for your family. You love Cora and Leni, don't you?"

Dad's expression changed as he looked at Mama. Everything about him softened; for an instant, Leni saw her dad, the real him, the man he would have been if the war hadn't ruined him. The man from Before. "I do," he said.

"Perfect. You love them enough to leave and provide for them," she said. "Go pack your shit and hit the road. We'll see you again at breakup."

1978

TWELVE

Seventeen-year-old Leni drove the snow machine with confidence in the falling snow. She was all alone in the vastness of winter. Following the glow of her headlights in the predawn dark, she turned onto the old mine road. Within a mile or so the road became a trail that twisted and turned and rose and fell. The plastic sled behind her thumped on the snow, empty now, but she hoped that soon it would hold her latest kill. If there was one thing her dad had been right about, it was this: Leni had learned to hunt.

She hurtled over embankments and around trees and across frozen rivers, airborne on the snow machine sometimes, skidding out of control, sometimes shrieking in joy or fear or a combination of the two. She was completely in her element out here.

As the elevation increased, the trees became sparser, scrawnier. She began to see cliffs and snow-covered rock outcroppings.

She kept going: up, down, around, bursting through banks of snow, careening around fallen logs. It took so much concentration, she couldn't think or feel anything else.

On a hill, the snow machine slid left, lost traction. She eased back on the gas, slowed. Stopped.

Breathing hard through the slits in her neoprene face mask, Leni looked around. Sharp white mountain peaks, blue-white glaciers, black shadows.

She dismounted, shivering. Bracing against the wind, she untied her pack and put on snowshoes, then pushed the snow machine into the limited protection afforded by a large tree and tarped it. This was as far as the vehicle could take her.

The sky overhead was lightening by degrees. Daylight expanded with each breath.

The trail turned upward, narrowed. She saw her first clot of frozen sheep scat within half a mile and followed the hoofprints higher uphill.

She brought out her binoculars and scanned the white landscape around her.

There. A cream-colored Dall sheep with huge curving horns, walking along a high ledge, its hooves dainty on the rough, snowy terrain.

She moved carefully, made her way along the narrow ridge, and hiked up into the trees. There, she found tracks again and followed them to a frozen river.

Fresh scat.

The sheep had crossed the river here, crashing through the ice, splashing through the river. Big chunks of ice poked up, bobbed, held in place by the solid ice around them.

An old tree lay across the ice, its frozen limbs splayed out, water stirring in patches alongside.

Snow swirled across the ice, collecting on one side of the log, fanning away in tiny whirlwinds on the other side. Here and there, the wind had brushed all of the snow away, leaving glistening, cracked patches of silver-blue ice. She knew it was unsafe to cross here, but anywhere else could cost her hours. And who knew if there would even be a good crossing point? She hadn't come all this way to quit.

Leni tightened her pack and tied down her hunting rifle, took off her snowshoes and tied them to her pack, too.

Staring down at the log, which was about two feet in diameter, its bark peeling away, frozen, covered with snow and ice, she took a deep breath and climbed onto it on all fours.

The world became as narrow as the log, as wide as the river. Rough icy bark bit into her knees. The cracking of the ice was like gunfire exploding around her.

She stared down the barrel of the log.

There. The other shore. That was all she would think about. Not the creaking ice or the frigid water running beneath. Certainly not the idea of falling through.

She crawled forward inch by inch, wind whipping across her, snow peppering her.

The ice cracked. Hard. Loud. The log crashed downward, breaking through the ice in front of her. Water splashed up, pooled on the ice, caught what little light there was.

The log made a deep snapping sound and thunked down deeper, hit something.

Leni lurched to her feet, found her balance, held her arms out. The log seemed to be breathing beneath her.

The ice cracked again. A roar of sound this time.

There were maybe seven feet between her and the shore. She thought of Matthew's mother, whose body had been found miles from where she had gone through the ice, and ravaged by animals. You didn't want to fall through the ice. There was no telling where your body would be found; water ran everywhere in Alaska, revealed things that should stay hidden.

She inched forward. When she neared the opposite shore, she launched herself upward, arms and legs flailing as if she could will herself to take flight, and crashed into the snow-covered rocks on the other side.

Blood.

She tasted it, warm and metallic in her mouth, felt it sliding down one ice-cold cheek.

Suddenly she was shivering, aware of the dampness of her clothes, whether from sweat or water droplets on her wrists or in her boots, she didn't know. Her gloves were wet, as were her boots, but both were water-proof.

She crawled to her feet and assessed the damage. She had a superficial forehead laceration and she'd bitten her tongue. The cuffs of her parka sleeves were wet and she thought some water had splashed down her neck. Nothing bad.

Resettling her pack and repositioning her rifle, she went off again, began hiking away from the river, while keeping it in view. She followed the tracks and scat, up and up, across jutting shelves of rock. This high up, the world was dead quiet. Everything was blurred by the falling snow and her breath.

Then: a sound. The crack of a branch, a snap of hooves sliding on rock. She smelled the musky scent of her prey. She eased between two trees, lifted her weapon.

She peered through the sight, found the male sheep, took aim.

She breathed evenly.

Waited.

Then pulled the trigger.

The sheep didn't make a sound. *A perfect shot, right on target.* No suffering. The sheep crashed to its knees, crumpled, slid down the rock face, and came to a stop at a snowy ledge.

She trudged through the snow toward her kill. She wanted to field-dress the animal and get the meat in her pack as quickly as possible. This was technically an illegal kill—the hunting season for sheep was in the fall—but an empty freezer was an empty freezer. She guessed that the animal would dress out at about one hundred pounds. It would be a long trek back to the snow machine, carrying all that weight.

⊹⊱❈⊰⊹

LENI MANEUVERED THE SNOW MACHINE down the long white driveway toward the cabin. She kept a light hand on the throttle, moved slowly, aware of every dip and turn.

In the past four years, she had grown like everything grew in Alaska: wild. Her hair hung almost to her waist (she never saw any reason to cut it) and had turned a deep mahogany red. Her pudgy, little-girl face had thinned, her freckles had faded away, left her with a milky complexion that accentuated the aqua of her eyes.

Next month, her father would return to the cabin. For the past few years, Dad had followed the rules laid down by Tom Walker and Large Marge. Grudgingly, and with a bad attitude, he'd done as they "recommended." After Thanksgiving every year (usually just as his nightmares were starting to increase and when he started muttering to himself and picking fights), he left for the North Slope to work on the pipeline. He made good money, which he sent home every week. Money they'd used to better their life up here. They now had goats and chickens, and an aluminum skiff for fishing, and a garden that thrived inside a domed greenhouse. The VW had been traded in for a reasonably good truck. An old hermit lived in the bus now, up in the woods around McCarthy.

Dad was still a hard man to live with, volatile and moody. He hated Mr. Walker with a dangerous intensity, and the smallest disappointment (or whiskey and Mad Earl) could still set him off, but he wasn't stupid. He knew Tom Walker and Large Marge were watching him closely.

Mama still said, *He's better, don't you think?* and Leni sometimes believed it. Or maybe they'd adapted to their environment, like the ptarmigans who turned white in the winter.

In the darkening month before he left for the pipeline, and on the winter weekends when he came home to visit, they studied Dad's moods like scientists, noting the tiniest twitch of an eye that meant his anxiety was rising. Leni learned how to defuse her father's temper when she could and get out of the way when she couldn't. Her interference—she had learned the hard way—only made things worse for Mama.

Leni pulled into the white yard, noticed Tom Walker's big truck parked alongside Large Marge's International Harvester.

Parking between the chicken coop and the cabin, Leni stepped off the snow machine, her booted foot sinking into the crusty, dirty snow. Down here, the weather was changing fast: warming. It was late March. Soon the icicles would start to drip water from the eaves in a constant patter, and snow-melt in the higher elevations would run downhill and turn their yard to mud.

She untied the field-dressed carcass from the red plastic sled that the snow machine towed. Hefting the bloody, white-bagged meat over her shoulder, she trudged past the animals—clucking, bleating at her arrival—and went up the now-solid stairs and into the cabin.

Warmth and light immediately enfolded her. Her breath, which she'd seen only seconds before, disappeared. She heard the hum of the generator, which powered the lights. The little black woodstove—the one that had always been here—pumped out heat.

Music blared from a big portable radio on the new dining room table. Some disco song by the Bee Gees was cranked up. The cabin smelled of baking bread and roasting meat.

You could always tell when Dad was gone. Everything was easier and more relaxed in his absence.

Large Marge and Mr. Walker sat at the big rectangular dining table Dad had made last summer, playing cards.

"Hey, Leni. Make sure they're not cheating," Mama yelled from the kitchen alcove, which had been redesigned piecemeal over the years—a propane oven had been hauled in, as well as a refrigerator. Mr. Walker had tiled the counter and put in a better dry sink. There was still no running water and no bathroom in the cabin. Large Marge had built a rack for the dishes they bought when they went to the Salvation Army in Homer.

"Oh, they're cheating," Leni said, smiling.

"Not me," Large Marge said, popping a chunk of reindeer sausage in her mouth. "I don't need to cheat to beat these two. Come on over, Leni. Give me a run for my money."

Chuckling, Mr. Walker got up, his chair screeching across the plank floor. "Looks like someone bagged a sheep." He pulled a big white plastic sheet out from underneath the sink and spread it out on the floor.

Leni thumped her load down onto the plastic and knelt beside it. "I did," she said. "Up by Porter Ridge." She opened the bag and pulled out the field-dressed carcass.

Mr. Walker sharpened an *ulu*, handed it to her.

Leni set about her task of cutting the haunch into steaks and roasts and tearing away the silvery skeins from the meat. Once it had seemed weird to butcher meat in the house, on a sheet of plastic. No more. This was life in the winter months.

Mama came out of the kitchen, smiling. In the winter, it seemed, she was always smiling. She had bloomed here in Alaska, just as Leni had. Ironically, they both felt safest in the winters, when the world was at its smallest and most dangerous. With Dad gone, they could breathe easily. They were the same height now, she and Leni. Their protein-heavy diet had made them both as lean and lithe as ballerinas.

Mama took her place at the table and said, "I'm shooting the moon this time. Just letting you get your strategy set."

"All the way?" Mr. Walker said. "Or just most of the way, like usual?"

Mama laughed. "You'll eat those words, Tom." She started dealing.

Leni did some pretending in the winter, just as she did in the summer. Like now, she pretended not to notice how Mama and Mr. Walker looked at each other, how careful they were never to actually touch each other. How Mama sometimes sighed when she mentioned his name.

Some things were dangerous; they all knew that.

Leni bent to her task. She was concentrating so keenly on making her cuts that it was a moment before she noticed the sound of an engine. Then she saw a flash of headlights come through the window, illuminating the cabin in a staccato burst.

Moments later, the cabin door opened.

Dad walked in. He wore a faded, frayed trucker's hat, pulled low on his brow, his long beard and mustache untended. After months on the pipeline, he had the sinewy, hard look of a man who drank too much and ate too little. The harsh Alaska weather had given his skin a lined, leathery look.

Mama shot to her feet, looking instantly anxious. "Ernt! You're home early! You should have told me you were coming."

"Yeah," he said, looking at Mr. Walker. "I can see why you'd want to know."

"It's just a hand of cards with neighbors," Mr. Walker said, pushing to his feet. "But we'll leave you to your reunion." He walked past Dad (who didn't take a step backward, forced Mr. Walker to change course), took his parka from the hook by the door, and put it on. "Thanks, gals."

When he was gone, Mama stared at Dad, her face pale, her mouth parted slightly. She had a breathless, worried look about her.

Large Marge stood up. "I can't get my stuff together quick enough, so I'll just stay tonight, if you don't mind. I'm sure you don't."

Dad didn't spare Large Marge a glance. He had eyes only for Mama. "Far be it for me to tell a fat woman what to do."

Large Marge laughed and walked away from the dining table. She plopped onto the sofa Dad had bought from a hotel going out of business in Anchorage, put her slippered feet up on the new coffee table.

Mama went to Dad, put her arms around him, pulled him close. "Hey, you," she whispered, kissing his throat. "I missed you."

"They fired me. Sons of bitches."

"Oh, no," Mama said. "What happened? Why?"

"A lying son of a bitch said I was drinking on the job. And my boss is a prick. It wasn't my fault."

"Poor Ernt," Mama said. "You never get a break."

He touched Mama's face, tilted her chin up, kissed her hard. "God, I missed you," he said against her lips. She moaned at his touch, molded her body to his.

They drifted toward the bedroom, pushed through the clacking beads, apparently unaware that anyone else was in the cabin. Leni heard them fall on the bed with a thump, heard their breathing accelerate.

Leni sat back on her heels. Good God. She would never understand her parents' relationship. It shamed Leni; that unshakable love both she and Mama had for Dad gave her a bad, heartsick feeling. There was something wrong with them; she knew it. Saw it in the way Large Marge sometimes looked at Mama.

"It ain't normal, kid," Large Marge said.

"What is?"

"Who the hell knows? Crazy Pete is the happiest married person I know."

"Well, Matilda's no ordinary goose. You hungry?"

Large Marge patted her big belly. "You bet. Your mama's stew is my favorite."

"I'll get us some. God knows they won't be out of the bedroom for a while." Leni wrapped up the meat she'd butchered, then washed her hands with water from the bucket by the sink. In the kitchen, she cranked up the radio as loud as it would go, but it wasn't enough to drown out the reunion in the bedroom.

BREAKUP IN ALASKA. The season of melting, movement, noise, when the sunlight tenatively came back, shone down on dirty, patchy snow. The world shifted, shrugging off the cold, making sounds like great gears turning. Blocks of ice as big as houses broke free, floated downstream, hitting anything in their way. Trees groaned and fell over as the wet, unstable ground moved beneath them. Snow turned to slush and then to water that collected in every hollow and indentation in the land.

Things lost in the snow were found again: a hat taken by the wind, a coil of rope; beer cans that had been tossed into snowbanks floated to the muddy surface of the road. Black spruce needles lay in murky puddles, branches broken by storms floated in the water that ran downhill from every corner of their land. The goats stood knee-deep in a sucking muck. No amount of hay could soak it up.

Water filled tree wells and ran along roadsides and pooled everywhere, reminding everyone that this part of Alaska was technically a rain forest. You could stand anywhere and hear ice cracking up and water sluicing from tree limbs and eaves, along the sides of the road, running in rivulets along every indentation in the oversaturated ground.

The animals came out of hiding. Moose ambled through town. No one ever took a turn too quickly. Sea ducks returned in squawking flocks and settled on waves in the bay. Bears came out of their dens and lumbered down hillsides looking for food. Nature was spring-cleaning, scrubbing away the ice and cold and frost, clearing the windows to let in the light.

On this beautiful blue evening, beneath a cerulean sky, Leni stepped into her rubber Xtratuf boots and went outside to feed the animals. They had seven goats now and thirteen chickens and four ducks. Slogging through ankle-deep mud, along watery tire grooves, she heard voices. She turned toward the sound, toward the cove that was their family's link to the outside world. Although they had spent years here, the property remained stubbornly wild. Even in her own backyard Leni had to be careful, but on days like this, when the tide was in and water lapped up on the shell-strewn shore, it still took her breath away.

Now she saw canoes down on the water, a flotilla of brightly colored boats gliding past.

Tourists. Probably unaware of how fast things could change in Alaska. The water beneath them was calm, but the small bay filled and emptied twice a day in fast, rushing tides that could strand or drown the unwary before they recognized the danger.

Mama came up beside Leni. She smelled the familiar combination of cigarette smoke, rose-hip soap, and lavender hand cream that would always remind her of her mother. Mama looped one arm over Leni's shoulder, gave her a playful hip bump.

They watched the tourists glide into the cove, heard their laughter echo across the water. Leni wondered what their lives were like, those Outside kids, who came up here for a vacation and backpacked up mountainsides and dreamed of living "off the land," and then went back to their suburban homes and their changing lives.

Behind them, the red truck rumbled to life. "It's time to go, girls," Dad yelled.

Mama took Leni's hand. They began walking toward Dad.

"We shouldn't go to the meeting," Leni said when they reached him.

Dad looked at her. In their years in Alaska, he had aged, turned thin and wiry. Fine lines bracketed his eyes, creased his sunken cheeks. "Why?"

"It will upset you."

"You think I'd run from a Walker? You think I'm a coward?"

"Dad—"

"This is our community, too. No one loves Kaneq more than I do. If Walker wants to act like a big shot and call a meeting, we're going. Get in the truck."

They crammed into the old truck.

Kaneq was a different town than it had been when they moved here, and her father hated each and every change. He hated that there was now a foot ferry that brought tourists from Homer. He hated that you had to slow down for them because they walked in the middle of the road and wandered around googly-eyed, pointing to every eagle and hawk and seal. He hated that the new fishing-charter business in town was thriving and sometimes there wasn't an empty seat at the diner. He hated people who came to visit—lookie-loos, he called them—but even more, he hated the outsiders who'd moved in, building houses near town, taming their lots with fences and building garages.

On this warm evening, a few hardy tourists moved down Main Street, taking pictures and talking loudly enough to startle the dogs tied up along the roadside. They gathered outside the brand-new Snackle Shop (where you could buy snacks and fishing tackle).

A sign on the Kicking Moose Saloon read TOWN MEETING SUNDAY NIGHT. 7 P.M.

"What are we? Seattle?" Dad muttered.

"Our last meeting was two years ago," Mama said. "When Tom Walker donated the lumber to repair the transient dock."

"You think I don't know that?" he said, pulling into a parking space. "You think I need you telling me that? I can hardly forget Tom Walker acting like a big shot, shoving his money in our noses." He parked in front of the burnt-out Kicking Moose Saloon. The bar's door was flung wide open in welcome.

Leni followed her parents into the saloon.

For all the changes that had taken place in town, this was the one place that had remained the same. No one in Kaneq cared about the blackened walls or the smell of char, as long as the booze flowed.

The place was already packed. Men and women (mostly men) in flannel shirts were bellied up to the bar. A few scrawny dogs lay curled beneath the barstools and out of the way. Everyone was talking at once and music played in the background. A dog whined along to the sound, howled once before a boot shut him up.

Mad Earl saw them and waved.

Dad nodded and headed to the bar.

Old Jim was bartending, as he had for decades. With no teeth and rheumy eyes and a beard as sparse as his vocabulary, he was slow behind the bar but congenial. Everyone knew Old Jim would give them a drink on credit or take some moose meat in trade. Rumor was, it had been that way at the Moose since Tom Walker's dad built the saloon in 1942.

"Whiskey, double," Dad yelled out to Jim. "And a Rainier beer for the missus." He slapped a handful of wadded-up pipeline bills on the table.

Taking his drink and Mama's beer, he headed to the corner, where Mad Earl and Thelma and Ted and Clyde and the rest of the Harlan clan had staked out a collection of chairs clustered around an overturned barrel.

Thelma smiled up at Mama, pulled a white chair in beside her. Mama sat down and the two women immediately bent their heads together and started talking. In the past few years, they had become good friends. Thelma, Leni had learned over the years, was like most of the Alaskan women who dared to live in the bush—tough and steady and honest to a fault. But you didn't want to mess with her.

"Hey, Leni," Moppet said, smiling up with her mouthful of which-a-ways teeth. Her sweatshirt was too big and her pants were too short, exposing at least three inches of pipe-cleaner-thin shins above her slumped woolen socks and ankle boots.

Leni smiled down at the eight-year-old. "Hey, Mop."

"Axle was home yesterday. I almost shot him with my arrow," she said with a grin. "Boy, was he piss-a-rood."

Leni bit back a smile.

"You got new pictures to show me?"

"Sure. I'll bring 'em next time we come up." Leni leaned back against the burnt log wall. Moppet tucked in close beside her.

At the front of the bar, a bell clanged.

The conversations around the bar quieted but didn't silence. Town meetings might be an accepted custom off the grid, but you could never really shut up a room full of Alaskans.

Tom Walker moved into place behind the bar, smiled. "Hey, neighbors. Thank you for coming. I see a lot of old friends in this room and plenty of new faces. To our new neighbors, hello and welcome. For those of you who don't know me, I'm Tom Walker. My father, Eckhart Walker, came to Alaska before most of you were born. He panned for gold but found his real wealth in land, here in Kaneq. He and my mom homesteaded one hundred and sixty acres and staked their claim."

"Here we go," Dad said sourly, downing his drink. "Now we're gonna hear all about his buddy the governor, and how they went crab fishing when they were kids. Good God . . ."

"Three generations of my family have lived on the same land. This place is not just where we live, it's who we are. But times are changing. You know what I'm talking about. New faces attest to the changes. Alaska is the last frontier. People are hungry to see our state before it changes even more."

"So what?" someone yelled.

"Tourists are flooding the banks of the Kenai River during king season, they're navigating our waters, they're packing the marine ferry system and coming to our dock in droves. Cruise ships are going to start bringing thousands of people up here, not just hundreds. I know Ted's charter business has doubled in the last two years and you can't get a seat at the diner in the summer. Word is that the foot ferry between us and Seldovia and Homer could be filled every day."

"We came up here to get away from all that," Dad shouted.

"Why are you telling us all this, Tommy?" Large Marge called out from the corner.

"Glad you asked, Marge," Mr. Walker said. "I've finally decided to spend some money on the Moose, fix the old girl up. It's about time we had a bar that didn't blacken our palms and the seat of our pants."

Someone whooped out in agreement.

Dad got to his feet. "You think we need a citified bar, that we need to *welcome* the idiots who come up here in sandals, with cameras hanging around their necks?"

People turned to look at Dad.

"I don't think a little paint and some ice behind the bar will hurt us," Mr. Walker said evenly.

The crowd laughed.

"We came here to get away from the Outside and that screwed-up world. I say we say no to Mr. Big Shot *improving* this saloon. Let cheechakos go to the Salty Dawg to drink."

"I'm not building a bridge to the mainland, for God's sake," Mr. Walker said. "My dad built this town, don't forget. I was working at the saloon when you were trying out for Little League in the Outside. It's all mine." He paused. "All of it. Did you forget that? And now that I think of it, I better fix up the old boardinghouse, too. People need somewhere to sleep. Hell, I'll call it the Geneva. She'd like that."

He was needling Dad; Leni saw it in Mr. Walker's eyes. The animosity between the two men was ever-present. Oh, they tried to walk a wide berth around each other, but it was always there. Only now Mr. Walker wasn't moving aside.

"Do you frigging believe this?" Dad turned to Mad Earl. "What's next? A casino? A Ferris wheel?"

Mad Earl frowned, got to his feet. "Hold on a sec, here, Tom—"

"It's just ten rooms, Earl," Mr. Walker said. "It welcomed guests a hundred years ago when Russian fur traders and missionaries walked these streets. My mother made the stained-glass windows in the lobby. The inn is a part of our history and now she's all boarded up like a widow in black. I'll make her shine again." He paused, looked right at Dad. "No one can stop me from improving this town."

"Just 'cause you're rich, you don't get to shove us all around," Dad yelled.

"Ernt," Thelma said. "I think you're making too much of this."

Ernt shot Thelma a sharp look. "We don't want a bunch of tourists climbing up our asses. We say no to this. No, g-damn it—"

Mr. Walker reached up to the bell above the bar, clanged it. "Drinks are on the house," he said with a smile.

There was an immediate uproar: people clapping and whooping and bellying up to the bar.

"Don't let him buy you with a few free drinks," Dad shouted. "This idea of his is bad. If we wanted to live in a city, we'd be somewhere else, damn it. And what if he doesn't stop there?"

No one was listening. Even Mad Earl was moving toward the bar for his free drink.

"You never did know when to shut up, Ernt," Large Marge said, sidling up to him. She was wearing a knee-length, hand-beaded suede coat over flannel pajama pants tucked into mukluks. "Does anyone make you get a business license to fix boat engines down at the dock? No. We don't. If Tom wants to turn this place into Barbie's Dream House, none of us will tell him otherwise. *That's* why we're here. To do whatever we want. Not to do what you want us to."

"I've taken shit from men like him all of my life."

"Yeah. Well. Maybe that's more about you than him," Large Marge said.

"Shut your fat mouth," Dad snapped. "Come on, Leni." He grabbed Mama by the bicep and pulled her through the crowd.

"Allbright!"

Leni heard Mr. Walker's big voice behind them.

Almost to the door, Dad stopped, turned. He yanked Mama close in beside him. She stumbled, almost fell.

Mr. Walker moved toward Dad, and people came with him, stood close, drinks in hand. Mr. Walker looked casual until you saw his eyes and the way his mouth tightened when he looked at Mama. He was pissed.

"Come on, Allbright. Don't run off. Be neighborly," Mr. Walker said. "There's money to be made, man, and change is natural. Unavoidable."

"I won't let you change our town," Dad said. "I don't care how much money you have."

"Yes, you will," Mr. Walker said. "You have no choice. So let it go and lose gracefully. Have a drink."

Gracefully?

Didn't Mr. Walker know by now?

Dad wasn't one to let things go.

THIRTEEN

All the next day, Dad paced and fumed and railed about dangerous changes and the future. At noon, he got on the ham radio and called for a meeting at the Harlan family compound.

For the entirety of the day, Leni had a bad feeling, a hollowness in the pit of her stomach. The hours passed slowly, but still they passed. After dinner, they drove up to the compound.

Now they were all waiting impatiently for the meeting to start. Chairs had been dragged out of cabins and unstacked from sheds and set up in a haphazard fashion on the muddy ground facing Mad Earl's porch.

Thelma sat in an aluminum chair, with Moppet sprawled uncomfortably across her, the girl too big for her mother's lap. Ted stood behind his wife, smoking a cigarette. Mama sat beside Thelma in an Adirondack chair with only one arm, and Leni was beside her, sitting in a metal fold-out chair that had sunk into the muck. Clyde and Donna stood like sentinels on either side of Marthe and Agnes, both of whom were carving sticks of wood into spikes.

All eyes were on Dad, who stood on the porch, alongside Mad Earl.

There was no sign of whiskey between them, but Leni could tell they had been drinking.

A dreary rain fell. Everything was gray—gray skies, gray rain, gray trees lost in a gray haze. Dogs barked and snapped at the ends of rusty chains. Several stood atop small doghouses and watched the proceedings in the center of the compound.

Dad looked out over the crowd gathered in front of him, which was the smallest it had ever been. In the last few years, the young adults had ventured off their grandfather's land in search of their own lives. Some fished in the Bering Sea, others rangered up in the national park. Last year Axle had impregnated a Native girl and was now living in a Yupik settlement somewhere.

"We all know why we're here," Dad said. His long hair was a dirty mess and his beard was thick and untrimmed. His skin was winter pale. A red bandanna covered most of his head, kept his hair out of his face. He patted Mad Earl's scrawny shoulder. "This man saw the future long before any of the rest of us. He knew somehow that our government would fail us, that greed and crime would destroy everything we love about America. He came up here—brought you all here—to live a better, simpler life, one that went back to the land. He wanted to hunt his food and protect his family and be away from the bullshit that goes on in cities." Dad paused, looked out at the people gathered in front of him. "It's all worked. Until now."

"Tell 'em, Ernt," Mad Earl said, leaning forward, reaching down for a jug hidden beneath his chair, uncorking it with a *thunk*.

"Tom Walker is a rich, arrogant prick," Dad said. "We've all known men like him. He didn't go to 'Nam. Guys like him had a million ways to dodge the draft. Unlike me and Bo and our friends, who stood up for our country. But, hey, I can get over that, too. I can get over his holier-than-thou attitude and his rubbing his money in my face. I can get over him leering at my wife." He stepped down the rickety porch steps, splashed into the murky water that pooled along the bottom step. "But I will *not* let him destroy Kaneq and our way of life. This is our *home*. We want it to stay wild and free."

"He's fixing up the tavern, Ernt, not building a convention center," Thelma said. At her raised voice, Moppet got up and walked away, went over to play with Marthe and Agnes.

"And a hotel," Mad Earl said. "Don't forget that, missy."

Thelma looked at her father. "Come on, Dad. You guys are making a mountain out of a molehill. There are no roads over here, no services, no electricity. All this complaining is counterproductive. Just let it go."

"I don't want to complain," Dad said. "I want to *do* something, and by Christ, I will. Who's with me?"

"Damn right," Mad Earl said, his voice a little slurred.

"He'll raise the price of drinks," Clyde complained. "You watch."

"I didn't move out into the bush so I could have a *hotel* nearby," Dad said.

Mad Earl grumbled something, took a long drink.

Leni watched the men come together, each one clapping Dad on the back as if he had said the perfect thing.

Within moments the women were left sitting alone in the muddy center of the compound.

"Ernt is pretty worked up over a little fixing-up of the saloon," Thelma said, watching the men. You could see them ingesting righteous anger, puffing up with it, passing the jug from one to the other. "I thought he'd let it go."

Mama lit a cigarette. "He never lets anything go."

"I know you two don't have much influence with him," Thelma said, looking from Mama to Leni. "But he could start a shitstorm up here. Tom Walker may have a new truck and own the best land on the peninsula, but he'll give you the shirt off his back. Last year when Mop was so sick, Tom heard about it from Large Marge and showed up here on his own and flew her to Kenai."

"I know," Mama said quietly.

"Your husband's going to rip this town apart if we aren't careful."

Mama gave a tired laugh. Leni understood. You could be as careful as a chemist with nitroglycerin around Dad. It wouldn't change a thing. Sooner or later, he was going to blow.

ONCE AGAIN, Leni's parents got so drunk she had to drive them home. Back at the cabin, she parked the truck and helped Mama into her room, where she collapsed into bed, laughing as she reached for Dad.

Leni climbed up to her own bed, to the mattress they'd salvaged from the dump and cleaned with bleach, and lay beneath her army surplus blankets and tried to fall asleep.

But the incident at the saloon and the meeting with the Harlans stayed with her. Something about it was deeply unsettling, although she couldn't quite put her finger on any one moment and say, *There, that's what bothered me.* Maybe just a sense of imbalance in her dad that was, if not new, a magnification.

Change. Slight, but apparent.

Her dad was angry. Maybe furious. But why?

Because he'd been fired from the pipeline? Because he'd seen Mama and Tom Walker together in March, seen Mr. Walker sitting at their table?

It had to be something more than what it seemed. How could a few businesses in town upset him so much? God knew he liked to drink whiskey at the Kicking Moose more than most men.

She rolled over for the box by her bed, the one that held Matthew's letters from the last few years. Not a month had gone by without word from him. She had each letter memorized and could pull them up at will. Some sentences never left her. *I'm getting better . . . I thought of you last night when I was out to dinner, this kid had a huge Polaroid camera . . . I scored my first goal yesterday, I wish you'd been there . . .* and her favorites, when he said things like, *I miss you, Leni.* Or, *I know it sounds lame, but I dreamed of you. Do you ever dream of me?*

Tonight, though, she didn't want to think about him and how far away he was or how lonely she felt without him and his friendship. In the years he'd been gone, no new kids had moved in to Kaneq. She had learned to love Alaska, but she was lonely a lot, too. On bad days—like today—she didn't want to read his letters and wonder if he would ever come back, and she worried that if she wrote to him, she would accidentally say what was really on her mind. *I'm afraid,* she might say, *I'm lonely.*

Instead, she opened her latest book—*The Thorn Birds*—and lost herself in the story of a forbidden love in a harsh and inhospitable land.

She was still reading well past midnight, when she heard the rustling of beads. She expected to hear the clank of the woodstove door opening and closing, but all she heard were footsteps moving across the wooden floor. She eased out of bed and crawled to the edge of the loft and peered down.

In the dark, with only the woodstove's glow for light, it took her eyes a moment to adjust.

Dad was dressed all in black, with an Alaska Aces baseball cap pulled low on his forehead. He was carrying a big gear bag that clanked as he walked.

He opened the front door and stepped out into the night.

Leni climbed down the loft stairs and went quietly to the window and peeked out. A full moon shone down on the muddy yard; here and there, stubborn patches of crusty brown snow caught the light. There were piles of junk all around: boxes of fishing tackle and camping supplies, rusting metal crates and contraptions, a broken gate, another bicycle Dad had never gotten around to fixing, a stack of blown-out tires.

Dad tossed the gear bag into the bed of the truck, then slogged over to the plywood shed where they kept their tools.

A moment later he came out carrying an ax over one shoulder.

He climbed into the truck and drove away.

✦⟨✻⟩✦

THE NEXT MORNING, Dad was in a good mood. His shaggy black hair was drawn into a weirdo Jesus-samurai topknot that had fallen to one side and looked like a puppy's ear. His thick black beard was full of wood shavings, and so was his mustache. "There's our sleepyhead. Did you stay up reading last night?"

"Yeah," Leni said, eyeing him uneasily.

He pulled her into his arms, danced with her until she couldn't help smiling.

The worry she'd had since last night slowly released.

What a relief. And on the first Saturday in April; one of her favorite days of the year.

Salmon Days. Today the town would come together to celebrate the upcoming salmon season. The festivities had begun under another name, started by the Native tribe that had once lived here; they had come together to ask for a good fishing season. Now, though, it was just a town party. On today of all days, the unpleasantness of last night would be forgotten.

A little after two o'clock, after all their chores were done, Leni loaded her arms with containers of food and followed her parents out of the cabin. Blue sky stretched as far as the eye could see; the pebbled beach looked iridescent in the sunlight, with its broken clamshells scattered like pieces of wedding lace.

They loaded food and blankets and a bag full of rain gear and extra coats (the weather wasn't reliable this time of year) into the back of the truck. Then they squished into the cab's bench seat and Dad drove off.

In town, they parked by the bridge and walked toward the General Store.

"What in the world?" Mama said when they rounded the corner.

Main Street was crowded, but not in the way it should be. There should have been men gathered around barbecues, grilling moose burgers and reindeer sausage and fresh clams, swapping fish tales, drinking beers. The women should have been by the diner, fussing over long tables set up with food—halibut sandwiches, platters of Dungeness crab, buckets of steamed clams, vats of baked beans.

Instead, half the townspeople stood on the boardwalk on the water side of town and the other half stood in front of the saloon. It was like some weird O.K. Corral showdown.

Then Leni saw the saloon.

Every window was broken, the door had been hacked to bits, left as sharp shards of wood hanging from brass hinges, and white spray-painted graffiti covered the burnt walls. THIS IS A WARNING. STAY AWAY. ARROGANT PRICK. NO PROGRESS.

Tom Walker stood in front of the ruined saloon, with Large Marge and Natalie standing to his left and Ms. Rhodes and her husband on his right. Leni recognized the rest of the people standing with him: most of the town's merchants and fishermen and outfitters. These were the people who'd come to Alaska *for* something.

Across the street, on the boardwalk, stood the off-the-gridders; the outcasts, the loners. Folks who lived in the bush, with no access to their property except by sea or air and who had come here to get away from something—creditors, the government, the law, child support, modern life. Like her dad, they wanted Alaska to remain wild to her fingertips forever. If they had their way, there would never be electricity or tourists or telephones or paved roads or flush toilets.

Dad walked confidently forward. Leni and Mama rushed to keep up with him.

Tom Walker strode out to meet Dad in the middle of the street. He threw a can of spray paint onto the ground at Dad's feet. It clanged in the dirt, rolled sideways. "You think I don't know it was you? You think everyone doesn't know it was you, you crazy asshole?"

Dad smiled. "Something happen last night, Tom? Vandalism? What a shame."

Leni noticed how powerful Mr. Walker looked beside her father, how steady. Leni couldn't imagine Tom Walker ever stumbling around drunk or talking to himself or waking up screaming and crying. "You're worse than a coward, Allbright. You're stupid. Sneaking around in the dark to break windows and spray-paint words on wood I'm going to tear down anyway."

"He wouldn't do that, Tom," Mama said, taking care to keep her gaze downcast. She knew better than to look at Tom directly, especially not at a time like this. "He was home last night."

Mr. Walker took a step forward. "Listen closely, Ernt. I'm going to let this go as a mistake. But progress is coming to Kaneq. You do anything—

anything—to hurt my business from here on out, and I'm not going to call a town meeting. I'm not going to call the cops. I'm coming for *you*."

"You don't scare me, rich boy."

This time Mr. Walker smiled. "Like I said. Stupid."

Mr. Walker turned back to the crowd, many of whom had drawn in close to hear the argument. "We're all friends here. Neighbors. A few words painted on wood don't mean anything. Let's get this party started."

People reacted immediately, rearranged themselves. Women drifted over to the food tables while men fired up the barbecues. Down at the end of the street, the band started up.

Lay down, Sally, and rest you in my arms . . .

Dad took Mama by the hand and led her down the street, bobbing his head in time to the beat.

Leni was left standing alone, a girl caught between two factions.

She felt the schism in town, the disagreement that could easily become a fight for the soul of what Kaneq should be.

This could get ugly.

Leni knew what her father had done and the vandalism revealed a new side to his rage. It terrified her that he had done such a public thing. Ever since Mr. Walker and Large Marge had first sent Dad to the pipeline for the winter, Dad had been on his guard. He never hit Mama in the face, or anywhere that a bruise could be seen. He worked hard—beyond hard—at controlling his temper. He walked a wide, respectful berth around Mr. Walker.

No more, it seemed.

Leni didn't realize that Tom Walker had come up beside her until he spoke.

"You look scared," Mr. Walker said.

"This thing between you and my dad could tear Kaneq apart," she said. "You know that, right?"

"Trust me, Leni. There's nothing for you to worry about."

Leni looked up at Mr. Walker. "You're wrong," she said.

⊷⟨※⟩⊶

"YOU WORRY TOO MUCH," Large Marge said to Leni the next day, when Leni showed up to work. For the past year, Leni had worked part-time at the General Store, stocking shelves, dusting supplies, ringing up sales on the antique cash register. She made enough money to keep herself well stocked with film and books. Dad had been against it, of course, but this one time, Mama had stood up to him, told him a seventeen-year-old girl needed an after-school job.

"That vandalism is a bad thing," Leni said, staring through the window, down the street toward the ruined saloon.

"Aw. Men are stupid. You might as well learn that now. Look at bull moose. They ram into each other at full speed. Same with Dall sheep. This will be a lot of sound and fury, signifying nothing."

Leni didn't agree. She saw what her father's vandalism had done, the effects of it on the people around her. A few painted words had become bullets hurtled into the heart of a town. Although the party last night on Main Street had raged as it always did, clattering on until daylight began at last to dim, she had seen how the townspeople divided themselves into teams, one that believed in change and growth and another that didn't. When the party had finally ended, everyone had gone their separate ways.

Separate. In a town that used to be about being together.

⊷⟨※⟩⊶

ON SUNDAY NIGHT, Leni and her parents went to the Harlan compound for a barbecue dinner. Afterward, as usual, they built a big bonfire in the mud and stood around it, talking and drinking as evening fell around them, turning the people into violet silhouettes.

From her place on Thelma's porch, rereading Matthew's latest letter by lantern light, Leni could see the adults gathered near the flames. A jug that looked from here like a black wasp moved from hand to hand. She heard the men's voices above the snapping, hissing flames, a din of rising anger.

". . . take over our town . . ."

". . . arrogant prick, think he owns us . . ."

". . . next he'll want to bring in electricity and television . . . turn us into Las Vegas."

Headlights speared through the darkness. Dogs went crazy in the yard, barked and howled as a big white truck rumbled through the mud, parked with a splash.

Mr. Walker got out of his expensive new truck, strode confidently toward the bonfire, calm as you please, as if he belonged here.

Uh-oh.

Leni folded up her letter, jammed it in her pocket, and stepped down into the mud.

Dad's face was orange in the firelight. His topknot had fallen, now lay in a lump of hair behind his left ear. "Looks like someone is lost," he said, his voice pulled out of shape by booze. "You don't belong here, Walker."

"Says the cheechako," Mr. Walker said. His broad smile took some of the sting out of the insult. Or maybe it added to it; Leni wasn't sure.

"I've been here four years," Dad said, his mouth flattening until his lips almost disappeared.

"That long, huh?" Mr. Walker said, crossing his big arms across his chest. "I got boots that have covered more ground in Alaska than you have."

"Now, look—"

"Down, boy," Mr. Walker said, grinning, although the smile didn't reach his eyes. "I'm not here to talk to you. I'm here to talk to them." He lifted his chin to indicate Clyde and Donna and Thelma and Ted. "I've known them all of my life. Hell, I taught Clyde how to hunt duck, remember, Clyde? And Thelma smacked me a good one for getting fresh when we were kids. I came to talk to my friends."

Dad looked uncomfortable. Irritated.

Mr. Walker smiled at Thelma, who smiled back. "We drank our first beers together, remember? The Moose is *our* place. Ours. Hell, Donna, you guys got married there."

Donna glanced at her husband, smiled uncertainly.

"Here's the thing. It's time we fixed the old girl up. We deserve a place where we can gather and talk and have fun without smelling like burnt wood and having soot all down ourselves when we leave. It will take a lot of work, though." Mr. Walker paused, his gaze moving from face to face. "And a lot of workers. I can hire people from Homer, pay them the four bucks an hour to rebuild the place, but I'd rather keep my money here, in town, with my friends and neighbors. We all know how nice it is to have some change in our jeans come winter."

"Four bucks an hour? That's high," Ted said, shooting Thelma a look.

"I want to be more than fair," Mr. Walker said.

"Ha!" Dad said. "He's trying to manipulate you. Buy you. Don't listen to him. We know what's good for our town. And it isn't his money."

Thelma shot Dad an irritated look. "How long will the job last, Tom?"

He shrugged. "Gotta be done before the weather turns, Thelma."

"And how many workers do you need?"

"As many as I can get."

Thelma stepped back, turned to Ted, whispered something to him.

"Earl?" Dad said. "You're not going to let him do this?"

Mad Earl's pale, wrinkled face squelched up, looked like one of those dried-apple carvings. "Jobs is scarce up here, Ernt."

Leni saw the effect those few words had on her father.

"I'll take a job," Clyde said.

Mr. Walker smiled triumphantly. Leni saw his gaze cut to Dad, stay there. "Great. Anyone else?"

When Clyde had come forward, Dad made a sound like a tire blowing and grabbed Mama by the arm and pulled her across the compound. Leni had to run through the mud to keep up. They all climbed into the truck.

Dad hit the gas too hard and the tires spun through the mud before finding traction. He shoved the pickup into reverse, lurched back, spun around, and hurtled through the open gates.

Mama reached over and held Leni's hand. They both knew better than to say anything as he started muttering to himself, thumping his palm hard on the steering wheel to punctuate his thoughts.

Damn idiots . . . letting him win . . . g-damn rich men think they own the world.

At the cabin, he skidded to a stop and rammed the gearshift in park.

Leni and Mama sat there, afraid to breathe too loudly.

He didn't move, just stared through the dirty, mosquito-splattered windshield at the shadowy smokehouse and the stand of black trees beyond. The sky was a deep purple-brown, strewn with pinprick stars.

"Go," he said, his teeth gritted. "I need to think."

Leni opened the door and she and Mama practically tumbled out of the pickup in their haste to disappear. Hand in hand, they slogged through the mud and climbed the steps and opened the door, slamming it shut behind them, wishing they could lock it, but they knew better. In one of his rages, he might burn the place down to get to Mama.

Leni went to the window, peeled the curtain aside, looked out.

The truck was there, puffing into the night, its headlights two bright beams.

She could see him in silhouette, talking to himself.

"He did it," Leni said, standing close. "Vandalized the tavern."

"No. He was home. In bed with me. And it's not the kind of thing he would do."

A part of Leni wanted to keep this from her mother, to spare her pain, but the truth was burning a hole in Leni's soul. Sharing it was the only way to put out the flames. They were a team, she and Mama. Together. They didn't keep secrets from each other. "After you fell asleep, he took the truck to town. I saw him leave, with an ax."

Mama lit a cigarette. Exhaled heavily. "I thought for once . . ."

Leni got it. Hope. A shiny thing, a lure for the unwary. She knew how seductive it could be, and how dangerous. "What do we do?"

"Do? He was already pissed about losing his pipeline job, and now this thing with the saloon—with Tom—could push him over the edge."

Leni felt her mother's fear, and the shame that was its silent twin. "We are going to have to be very careful. This thing could blow up."

FOURTEEN

——— ∞∘≫≫◈⊙◈≪≪∘∞ ———

April in Fairbanks was an unreliable month. This year, an unseason-
able cold gripped the town, snow fell, the birds stayed away, the rivers
stayed frozen. Even the old-timers began to complain, and they had spent
decades in this town that was called the coldest in America.

Matthew walked away from the ice rink after practice, his hockey stick
slung over his shoulders. He knew he looked like an ordinary seventeen-
year-old in a sweat-dampened hockey uniform and boots but looks could be
deceiving. He knew it, and they knew it, the kids he'd gone to school with
for the past few years. Oh, they were friendly enough (no one judged anyone this far from civilization; you could be whoever you wanted to be), but
they gave him a wide berth. Rumors of his "breakdown" had spread faster
than a wildfire on the Kenai. Before he took his seat in his first class in ninth
grade, he'd already had a reputation. High school kids, even in the wilds of
Alaska, were still herd animals. They sensed when there was a weak member in their midst.

Ice fog, a gray heavy haze peppered with tiny particles of frozen pollut-
ants, turned Fairbanks into a fun-house version of itself where nothing was

quite solid, no line distinct. The place smelled of trapped exhaust, like a race-track.

The squat, two-story buildings across the street appeared to be holding each other up, forlorn in the fog. Like many of the buildings in town, they looked temporary, hastily built.

Through the gloom, people were charcoal drawings, lines and slashes, the homeless who huddled in doorways, the drunks who sometimes stumbled out of taverns late at night and froze to death. Not all of those Matthew saw now would survive the day or the week, let alone this unexpected cold in a town where winter lasted from September through April, and night lay across the land for eighteen hours. There were casualties every day. People went missing all the time.

As he walked to the pickup truck, night fell. Just like that, in a blink. Streetlamps created the only light there was—dots here and there—aside from the occasional snake of headlights in the glow. He wore a parka; beneath that, his hockey sweater, long underwear, and his hockey pants, and mukluks. It wasn't that cold, not by Fairbanks standards. Barely below freezing. He didn't bother with gloves.

It didn't take long for the truck to start, not this time of year; not like in the deep midwinter, when you left your truck running while you were at the store or running errands, when the thermostat often dropped to twenty-five below.

He climbed into his uncle's big extended-cab pickup and drove through town slowly, alert, always looking for animals or sliding cars or kids playing where they shouldn't be playing.

A banged-up Dodge pulled out in front of him. It had a sign in the back window that read WARNING. IN CASE OF RAPTURE, THIS CAR WILL BE UNMANNED.

There were a lot of bumper stickers like that out here, deep in Alaska's wild interior, far from the tourist destinations of the coast or the majestic beauty of Denali. Alaska was full of fringe-ists. People who believed in weirdo things and prayed to exclusionary Gods and filled their basements with equal measures of guns and Bibles. If you wanted to live in a place where no one told you what to do and didn't care if you parked a trailer in your yard or had a fridge on your porch, Alaska was the state for you. His aunt said it was the romance of adventure that attracted so many individualists. Matthew didn't know if he agreed (actually, he didn't expend much energy thinking about stuff like that), but he did know that the farther away you got from civilization, the stranger things got. Most people spent one dark, bleak, eight-month winter in Fairbanks and left the state screaming. The few who stayed—misfits, adventurers, romantics, loners—rarely left again.

It took him almost fifteen minutes to reach the homestead road, and five more minutes to get to the house he'd called home for the last few years. Two decades ago, when his mother's family had homesteaded out here, the land had been remote; over the years, town had crept closer, spread out. Fairbanks might be in the middle of nowhere, fewer than 120 miles from the Arctic Circle, but it was the second largest city in the state and growing fast because of the pipeline.

He drove up the long, winding, tree-shrouded driveway and parked in the huge, plank-sided garage/workshop between Uncle Went's ATV and his snow machine.

Inside the house, the walls were roughly hewn planks that looked messy in the combination of light and shadow. His aunt and uncle had always intended to drywall them but never had. The kitchen was delineated by L-shaped polished wood counters set atop green cabinets that had come from an abandoned house in Anchorage, one of those "dream" homes built by lowlanders who couldn't last through their first winter. A bar with three barstools separated it from the dining area. Beyond that was the living room; a big plaid sectional (complete with movable footrests) and two well-worn La-Z-Boy chairs faced a window that overlooked the river. There were bookcases everywhere, overflowing with books; lanterns and flashlights decorated almost every surface for when the power went out, and it went out often, with so many big trees and bad weather. The house had electricity and running water and even a television, but no flush toilets. Truthfully, no

Walker ever cared. They'd all been raised with outhouses and were happy to live that way. People down south had no idea how clean an outhouse could be if you took care of it.

"Hey, you," Aly said, looking up from the sofa. She was doing homework, by the looks of it.

Matthew dropped his gear bag by the door and propped his hockey stick in the arctic entry—a corridor full of coats and boots that separated the outside from the inside. He hung up his coat on a hook and kicked off his boots. He was so tall now—six-foot-two—that he had to duck to enter the house.

"Hey." He plopped down beside her.

"You smell like a goat," she said, closing her textbook.

"A goat who scored two goals." He leaned back, laid his head on the sofa back, stared up at the big wood crossbeams that traversed the ceiling. He didn't know why, but he felt nervous, a little raw. He tapped his foot, played an arpeggio on the worn armrest with his fingers.

Aly stared at him. As usual, she had applied her makeup sporadically, as if she'd lost interest halfway through the process. Her blond hair was drawn back into a messy ponytail that hung a little to the left. He had no idea if that was intentional. She was beautiful in the natural, rough-hewn way of Alaskan girls, who were more likely to hunt on the weekends than go to a shopping mall or movie theater.

"You're doing it again," he said.

"What?"

"Watching me. Like you think I'm going to explode or something."

"No," she said, trying to smile. "It's just . . . you know. Are you having a bad day?"

Matthew closed his eyes, sighed. His older sister had been his salvation; there was no doubt about that. Back when he'd first moved here, when he'd been unable to deal with his grief and been beset by terrible nightmares, Aly had been his steadying hand, the voice that could get through to him. Although it had taken time. For the first three months, he pretty much hadn't talked at all. The therapist they sent him to was no help. He'd known from the first session that it wouldn't be a stranger's hand he'd reach out to, especially not one who talked to him as if he were a kid.

It was Aly who had saved him. She never gave up, never stopped asking how he felt. When he finally found the words to express himself, his grief had shown itself to be bottomless, terrifying.

He still cringed at the way he'd cried.

His sister had held him when he cried, rocked him as their mother would have done. Over the years, the two of them had fashioned a vocabulary for grief, learned how to talk about their loss. He and Aly had talked about their pain until there were no words left to say. They'd also spent hours in silence, standing side by side on the river, fly-fishing, and hiking rough trails in the Alaska Range. In time, his grief had turned to anger and then drifted toward sorrow, and now, finally, it had settled into a lingering sadness that was a part of him, not the whole. Lately, they'd begun to talk about the future instead of the past.

It was big, that change, and they knew it. Aly had been hiding out in school, using the classroom as a shield against the hard realities of life as a motherless girl, and she'd stayed here, in Fairbanks, to be at Matthew's side. Before Mom's death, Aly had dreamed big, of moving to New York or Chicago, someplace that had bus service and live theater and opera halls. But, as with Matthew, loss had rearranged her from the inside out. Now she knew how much family mattered and how important it was to hang on to the people you loved. Lately she'd begun to talk about moving back onto the homestead with Dad, and maybe working with him. Matthew knew that his presence here was holding his sister back. It could go on this way forever if he let it, and a part of him wanted to do just that. But he was almost eighteen years old. If he didn't push his way out of the nest, she'd stay next to him forever.

"I want to finish the school year in Kaneq," he said into the silence. He heard the question she didn't ask and answered it. "I can't hide out forever," he said.

Aly looked frightened. She'd seen him through the worst of times, and he knew that she was terrified of him sliding back into depression. "But you love hockey and you're good at it."

"The season ends in two weeks. And I start college in September. "

"Leni."

Matthew wasn't surprised that she understood. He and Aly had talked about everything, including Leni and how much her letters meant to Matthew. "What if she goes off to college somewhere? I want to see her. I might not get another chance."

"Are you sure you're ready? Everywhere you look, you'll see Mom."

And there it was. The big question. The truth was, he didn't know if he could handle any of it—going back to Kaneq, seeing the river that swallowed his mother, seeing his father's grief in Technicolor, up close—but he knew one thing. Leni's letters had mattered to him. Maybe they'd saved him as much as Aly had. For all their separate miles, and their different lives, Leni's letters and the photographs she sent reminded him of who he'd been.

"I see her everywhere *here*. Don't you?"

Aly nodded slowly. "I swear I see her out of the corner of my eye all of the time. I talk to her at night."

He nodded. Sometimes in the morning when he woke up, he had a split second where he thought the world was upright, that he was an ordinary kid in an ordinary house and that his mom would soon be calling him down for breakfast. The silence on mornings like that was awful.

"You want me to come with you?"

He did. He wanted her beside him, holding his hand, keeping him steady. "No. You don't get out of school until June," he said, hearing the unsteadiness in his voice, knowing she heard it, too. "Besides, I think I have to do this by myself."

"You know Dad loves you. He'll be thrilled to have you back."

He did know that. He also knew that love could freeze over, become a kind of thin ice all its own. He and Dad had had a tough time talking in the past few years. Grief and guilt had bent them out of shape.

Aly reached out for him, took his hand in hers.

He waited for her to speak, but she didn't say anything. They both knew why: there was nothing to say. Sometimes you had to go backward in order to go forward. This truth they knew, even as young as they were. But there was another truth, one they shied away from, one they tried to protect each other from. Sometimes it was painful to go back.

Maybe grief had been waiting for Matthew to return all this time, waiting, in the dark, in the cold. Maybe in Kaneq he'd undo all this progress and break down again.

"You're stronger now," Aly said.

"I guess we'll find out."

❖❖⟨✿⟩❖❖

TWO WEEKS LATER, Matthew flew his uncle's float plane over Otter Point and banked right, lowered, touched down on the flat blue water below. He killed the engine and floated toward the big silvered-wood arch that read WALKER COVE.

His father stood at the end of the dock, his arms at his sides.

Matthew jumped off the pontoon and onto the dock and tied the float plane down. He remained that way, bent over, his back to his father, for a moment longer than necessary, gathering the strength he needed to really be here.

At last he straightened, turned.

His father was close now; he pulled Matthew into a bone-jarring hug that went on so long Matthew had to gasp for breath. Dad drew back finally, looked at him, and love took shape in the air around them, a regret- and memory-filled version, maybe, sad around the edges, but love.

It had been only a few months since they'd seen each other. (Dad made it a point to come to several of Matthew's hockey games and visit in Fairbanks as often as the harsh weather and homesteading chores allowed, but they had never really talked about anything that mattered.)

Dad seemed older, his skin more lined and creased. He smiled in that way of his, the way he did everything in life, full tilt, no explanations, no regrets, no safety nets. You knew Tom Walker in a glance, because he let you in. You knew instantly that this was a man who always told the truth as he saw it, whether it was popular or not, who had a set of rules to guide his life and no other rules mattered. He laughed harder than any man Matthew had ever met, and Matthew had only seen him cry once. On that day out on the ice.

"You're even taller than the last time I saw you."

"I'm like the Hulk. I keep tearing through my clothes."

Dad grabbed Matthew's suitcase and led him up the dock, past the fishing boat straining at its lines; seabirds cawed overhead, waves slapped the pilings. The smell of kelp baking in the sun and eelgrass beaten down by waves greeted him.

At the top of the stairs, Matthew got his first glimpse of the big log home with the soaring bowed front and wraparound deck. A welcoming light illuminated the pots hanging from the eaves, still full of last year's dead geraniums.

Mom's pots.

He paused, caught his breath.

He hadn't realized how time could unspool the years of your life until for a second you were fourteen again, crying from a place so deep it seemed to predate you, desperate to be whole again.

Dad went on ahead.

Matthew forced himself to move. He passed by the weather-grayed picnic table and climbed the wooden steps to the purple-painted front door. Beside it hung a metal cutout of an orca that read WHALECOME! (That had been a gift from Matthew; it always cracked his mother up.)

It brought tears to his eyes. He wiped them away, embarrassed by the display in front of his stoic father, and went inside.

The house looked the same as it always had. A cluster of reclaimed and antique furniture in the living room, an old picnic table draped in bright yellow fabric with a vase of blue flowers placed in its center. A collection of candles stood like a medieval village around the flowers. His mother's touch was everywhere. He could almost hear her.

The interior of the house, bark-darkened log walls, windows large enough to capture the view, a pair of brown leather couches, a piano Grandma had

had shipped in from the Outside. He walked over to the window, stared out, saw the cove and the dock through a watery image of his own face.

He felt his father come up behind him. "Welcome home."

Home. The word had layers of meaning. A place. An emotion. Memories. "She was out ahead of me," he said, hearing the unsteadiness of his voice.

He heard the way his father drew in a sharp breath. Would he stop Matthew, abort this conversation they'd never dared to have?

There was a moment, a pause that lasted less time than an indrawn breath; then Dad laid a heavy hand on Matthew's shoulder. "No one could contain your mother," he said quietly. "It wasn't your fault."

Matthew didn't know how to respond. There was so much to say, but they'd never talked about any of it. How could you even start a conversation like that?

Dad pulled Matthew into a fierce embrace. "I'm glad as hell you're back."

"Yeah," Matthew said hoarsely. "Me, too."

⊹⊰⟨❀⟩⊱⊹

MID-APRIL. Dawn washed across the land well before seven A.M. When Leni first opened her eyes, even though it was to darkness, she felt the buoyancy that came with the changing of the seasons. As an Alaskan, she could feel the nascent light, see it in the lessening of the inky black to a charcoal hue. It carried with it a sense of hope, of daylight coming, of everything would be better now. Of *he* would be better.

But none of that was true this spring. Even as sunlight was returning, her dad was getting worse. Angry and intense. More jealous of Tom Walker.

Leni had a terrible, building feeling that something bad was going to happen.

All day at school she battled a headache. On her bike ride home, she started getting a stomachache. She tried to tell herself it was her period, but she knew better. It was stress. Worry. She and Mama had gone into alert mode again. They made eye contact constantly, walked carefully, tried to be invisible.

She rode expertly over the bumpy driveway, taking care to stay on the high ground between the two muddy tire ruts.

In her yard—a morass of mud and running water—she saw that the red truck was gone, which meant that Dad was either hunting or had gone to see the Harlans.

She slanted her bike against the cabin and did her chores, feeding the animals, checking their water, bringing in the dry sheets from the line, dropping them into a willow basket. Holding the laundry basket on her hip, she heard the high, rubber-band sound of a boat engine, and stared out at the water, tenting a hand across her eyes. High tide.

An aluminum skiff turned into their cove. The *put-put-put* of the engine was the only sound for miles. Leni tossed the laundry basket onto the porch and headed for the beach stairs, which they'd strengthened over the years. Almost all of the boards were new; only here and there could you see the tarnished gray of the original stairs. She descended the zigzag steps in her muddy boots.

The boat puttered forward, its sharp prow angled up proudly on the waves. A man stood at the console, guided the boat forward, beached it.

Matthew.

He killed the engine and stepped out into the ankle-deep water, held on to the boat's ragged white line.

She touched her hair in embarrassment. She hadn't bothered to braid it or brush it this morning. And she was wearing the exact same outfit she'd worn to school today and the day before. Her flannel shirt probably smelled like wood smoke.

Oh, God.

He pulled the boat up onto the beach, dropped the rope, and walked toward her. For years she'd imagined this moment; in her musings, she always knew exactly what to say. In the privacy of her imagination, they just started talking, picked up the thread of their friendship as if he'd never been gone.

But in her mind, he was Matthew, the fourteen-year-old kid who'd showed her frogs' eggs and baby eagles, the boy who'd written her every week. *Dear Leni, it's hard at this school. I don't think anyone likes me . . .* And to whom she'd written back. *I know a lot about being the new kid in school. It blows. Let me give you a few tips . . .*

This . . . man was someone else, someone she didn't know. Tall, long blond hair, incredibly good-looking. What could she say to this Matthew?

He reached into his backpack, pulled out the worn, banged-up, yellowed version of *The Lord of the Rings* that Leni had sent him for his fifteenth birthday. She remembered the inscription she'd written in it. *Friends forever, like Sam and Frodo.*

A different girl had written that. One who hadn't known the ugly truth about her toxic family.

"Like Sam and Frodo," he said.

"Sam and Frodo," Leni repeated after him.

Leni knew it was crazy, but it seemed to her as if they were having a conversation without saying anything, talking about books and durable friendships and overcoming insurmountable odds. Maybe they weren't talking about Sam and Frodo at all, maybe they were talking about themselves and how they had somehow grown up and stayed kids at the same time.

He pulled a small, wrapped box out of his backpack and handed it to her. "This is for you."

"A present? It's not my birthday."

Leni noticed that her hands were shaking as she tore open the paper. Inside, she found a heavy black Canon Canonet camera in a leather case. She looked up at him in surprise.

"I missed you," he said.

"I missed you, too," she said quietly, knowing even as she said it that things had changed. They weren't fourteen anymore. More important, her father had changed. Being friends with Tom Walker's son would cause trouble.

It worried her that she didn't care.

⊰⊹✦⊹⊱

AT SCHOOL THE NEXT DAY, Leni could hardly concentrate. She kept glancing sideways at Matthew, as if to assure herself that he was really there. Ms. Rhodes had had to yell at Leni several times to get her attention.

At the end of class, they walked out of the schoolhouse together, emerged side-by-side into the sunshine, and walked down the wooden steps and into the muddy ground.

"I'll come back for my ATV," he said when she pulled her bike away from its place along the chain-link fence that had been built two years ago after a sow and her cubs walked right up to the school door, looking for food. "I'll walk you home. If that's okay."

Leni nodded. Her voice seemed inaccessible. She hadn't said two words to him all day; she was afraid of embarrassing herself. They weren't children anymore and she had no idea how to talk to a boy her own age, especially one whose opinion of her mattered so much.

She had a solid hold on her plastic handlebar grips, with her dump-recycled bicycle clanging along the gravel road beside her. She said something about her job at the General Store, just to break the quiet.

She was aware of him physically in a way she'd never experienced before. His height, the breadth of his shoulders, the sure, easy way he walked. She smelled spearmint gum on his breath and the complex scents of store-bought shampoo and soap on his hair and skin. She was attuned to him, connected in that weird way of predator and prey, a sudden, dangerous circle-of-life type of connection that made no sense to her.

They turned off Alpine Street and walked into town.

"Town sure has changed," Matthew said.

At the saloon, he stopped, tented his hand over his eyes, read the grafitti spray-painted across the charred wooden front. "Some people don't want change, I guess."

"Guess not."

He looked down at her. "My dad said your dad vandalized the saloon."

Leni stared up at him, felt shame twist her gut. She wanted to lie to him, but she couldn't. Neither could she say the disloyal words out loud. People assumed her dad had vandalized the saloon; only she and her mother knew it for sure.

Matthew started walking again. Relieved to be past the evidence of her father's anger, she fell into step beside him. When they passed the General Store, Large Marge emerged with a bellow, her big arms outflung. She gave Matthew a hug, then thumped him on the back. When she stepped back, she gazed at the two of them.

"Be careful, you two. Things aren't good between your dads."

Leni started off. Matthew followed her.

She wanted to smile, but the vandalized tavern and Large Marge's warning had taken the shine off the day. Large Marge was right. Leni was playing with fire right now. Her dad could drive up this road at any minute. It would not be good for him to see her walking home with Matthew Walker.

"Leni?"

She realized Matthew had run to catch up with her. "Sorry."

"Sorry for what?"

Leni didn't know how to answer; she was sorry for things he knew nothing about, for a future she was probably dragging him into that would surely sour. Instead, she said some lame thing about the latest book she'd read; for the remainder of the way home they talked about superficial things—the weather, the movies he'd seen in Fairbanks, the latest lures for king salmon.

It seemed that no time had passed, even though they had walked together for almost an hour, when Leni saw the metal gate with the cow skull on it up ahead. Mr. Walker was standing beside a big yellow excavator that was parked beside the gate that marked the entrance to his land.

Leni came to a stop. "What's your dad doing?"

"He's clearing some acreage to build cabins. And he's putting up an arch over the driveway so guests will know how to find us. He's calling it the Walker Cove Adventure Lodge. Or something like that."

"A lodge for tourists? Right here?"

Leni felt Matthew's gaze on her face, as strongly as any touch. "You bet. There's money to be made."

Mr. Walker walked toward them, pulling the trucker's cap off his head, revealing a white strip of skin along his forehead, scratching his damp hair.

"My dad won't like that arch," Leni said as he approached.

"Your dad doesn't like much," Mr. Walker said with a smile, mopping the sweat from his brow with a bunched-up bandanna. "And you being friends with my Mattie is going to be at the top of his hate list. You know that, right?"

"Yeah," Leni said.

"Come on, Leni," Matthew said. He took her by the elbow and led her away from his father, with the bicycle clattering alongside. When they came to Leni's driveway, she stopped, stared down the tree-shaded road.

"You should leave now," she said, pulling away.

"I want to walk you home."

"No," she said.

"Your dad?"

She wished the world would just open up and swallow her. She nodded. "He would not want me to be friends with you."

"Screw him," Matthew said. "He can't tell us we can't be friends. No one can. Dad told me about the stupid feud going on. Who cares? What's it to us?"

"But—"

"Do you like me, Leni? Do you want to be friends?"

She nodded. The moment felt solemn. Serious. A pact being made.

"And I like you. So there. It's done. We're friends. There's nothing anyone can do about it."

Leni knew how naïve he was, how wrong. Matthew knew nothing about angry, irrational parents, about punches that broke noses and the kind of rage that began with vandalism and might go places he couldn't imagine.

"My dad is unpredictable," Leni said. It was the only equivocal word she could come up with.

"What does that mean?"

"He might hurt you if he found out we liked each other."

"I could take on your dad."

Leni felt a little burst of hysterical laughter rise up. The idea of Matthew "taking on" Dad was too terrible to contemplate.

She should walk away right now, tell Matthew they couldn't be friends.

"Leni?"

The look in his eyes was her undoing. Had anyone *ever* looked at her like that? She felt a shiver of something, longing maybe, or relief, or even desire. She didn't know. She just knew she couldn't turn away from it, not after so many lonely years, even though she felt danger slip silently into the water and swim toward her. "We can't let my dad know we're friends. Not at all. Not ever."

"Sure," Matthew said, but she could see that he didn't understand. Maybe he knew about pain and loss and suffering; that knowledge of darkness was in his eyes. But he didn't know about fear. He thought her warnings were melodramatic.

"I mean it, Matthew. He can never know."

FIFTEEN

Leni dreamed it was raining. She stood on a riverbank, getting drenched. Rain slicked her hair, blurred her vision.

The river rose, made a great, cracking thunderous sound, and suddenly it was breakup. House-sized chunks of ice broke free of the land, careening downstream, taking everything in their path—trees, boats, houses.

You need to cross.

Leni didn't know if she heard the words or if she'd said them. All she knew was that she needed to cross this river before the ice swept her away and the water rushed into her lungs.

But there was nowhere to cross.

Ice-cold waves arched up into walls, ground fell away and trees crashed. Someone screamed.

It was her. The river hit her like a shovel to the head, knocked her sideways.

She flailed, screamed, felt herself falling, falling.

Over here, a voice yelled.

Matthew.

He could save her. She gasped, tried to claw her way to the surface, but something had a hold of her feet, dragged her down, down until she couldn't breathe. Everything went dark.

Leni woke with a gasp and saw that she was safe in her room, with her stacks of books and the notebooks full of her pictures along the wall, and the box full of Matthew's letters beside her.

Bad dream.

Already fading from memory. Something about a river, she thought. Spring breakup. Another way to die in Alaska.

She dressed for school in denim overalls and a plaid flannel shirt. She pulled the hair back from her face and wove it into a loose French braid. Without any mirrors in the house (Dad had broken them all over the years), she couldn't assess how she looked. Leni had gotten used to seeing herself in shards of glass. Herself in pieces. She hadn't cared at all until Matthew's return.

Downstairs, she dropped the stack of her schoolbooks on the kitchen table and took a seat. Mama set a plate of reindeer sausage, biscuits, and gravy in front of her, alongside a bowl full of blueberries they'd picked from the sandy bluffs above Kachemak Bay last fall.

While Leni ate her breakfast, Mama stood nearby watching her.

"You carted water for an hour last night so you could take a bath. And you've braided your hair. It looks beautiful, by the way."

"It's called ordinary hygiene, Mama."

"I heard Matthew Walker is back in town."

Leni should have known Mama would put two and two together. Sometimes, because of Dad and all, Leni forgot how smart Mama was. How perceptive.

Leni kept eating, careful not to make eye contact. She knew what Mama would say about this, so Leni wasn't going to tell her. Alaska was a big place; there were plenty of places to hide something as small as a friendship.

"Too bad your dad hates his dad so much. And too bad your dad has a temper problem."

"Is that what we're calling it?"

Leni felt Mama eyeing her, like an eagle watching waves for a splash of silver. It was the first time Leni had hidden something from her mother and it felt uncomfortable. "You're almost eighteen. A young woman. And you and Matthew must have written each other a hundred letters over the years."

"What does that have to do with anything?"

"Hormones are like afterburners. The right touch and you're in outer space."

"Huh?"

"I'm talking about love, Lenora. Passion."

"Love? Jeez Louise. I don't know why you'd bring that up. There's nothing to worry about, Mama."

"Good. You stay smart, baby girl. Don't make the same mistake I did."

Leni finally looked up. "What mistake? Dad? Or me? Are you—"

The door opened and in walked her father, who had washed his hair this morning and put on relatively clean brown canvas pants and a T-shirt. He kicked the door shut behind him, said, "Something smells good, Cora. Morning, Red. Did you sleep well?"

"Sure, Dad," she said.

He kissed the top of her head. "You ready for school? I'll drive you."

"I can ride my bike."

"Can't I take my second-best girl out on a sunny day?"

"Sure," she said. She picked up her books and lunch box (still the Winnie the Pooh; she loved it now) and got to her feet.

"You be careful at school," Mama said.

Leni didn't glance back. She followed Dad out to the truck and climbed in.

He popped an eight-track tape into the stereo and cranked up the sound. "Lyin' Eyes" blared through the speakers.

Dad started singing along, going strong, saying, "Sing with me," as he turned out onto the main road and rumbled toward town.

Suddenly he slammed on the brakes. "Son of a *bitch*."

Leni was thrown forward.

"Son of a *bitch*," Dad said again.

Mr. Walker stood beneath the rough-timbered arch he'd erected over his driveway. Hand-carved into the top beam were the words WALKER COVE AD-VENTURE LODGE.

Dad jammed the truck in park and got out, striding across the bumpy road, not even trying to avoid the muddy potholes.

Mr. Walker saw him coming and stopped work, shoved his hammer through his belt, so that it hung from the leather like a weapon.

Leni leaned forward, peered intently through the dirt-and-squished-mosquito-filled windshield.

Dad was screaming at Mr. Walker, who smiled and crossed his arms.

Leni was put in mind of a Jack Russell terrier straining aggressively at the end of his leash, yapping at a Rottweiler.

Dad was still yelling when Mr. Walker turned his back and walked to the arch and returned to his work.

Dad stood there a minute. Finally he stalked back to the truck, climbed in, slammed the door shut. He rammed the truck into gear and hit the gas. "Someone needs to knock that son of a bitch down a peg. I knew guys like him in 'Nam. Shitty, cowardly officers who got better men killed and got medals for it."

Leni knew better than to say anything. All the way to school, he muttered under his breath. *Son of a bitch, arrogant prick, thinks he's better* . . . Leni knew he would head straight to the compound from here, to find people to join in his bitching. Or maybe, talk wouldn't be enough anymore.

He stopped at the school. "I'm taking the ferry into Homer today. I'll pick you up from work at five."

"Okay."

Leni gathered her books and lunch box and climbed out of the truck. On her way to the schoolhouse she didn't look back, and Dad didn't honk in goodbye. He drove away so fast gravel sputtered out from his tires.

She came into the classroom, saw everyone was already seated. Ms. Rhodes was at the blackboard writing, *iambic pentameter in Shakespeare.*

Matthew turned in his chair to face her. His smile was like the gravitational pull from one of her science fiction novels; she moved toward him, sat down.

He stared at her. Was it the way Dad stared at Mama? She thought so. Sometimes. It made her feel unsettled, kind of anxious.

He ripped off a piece of notebook paper and scrawled a note, which he passed to her. It read: *Want to skip work after school? We could do something.*

Say no, she thought. What she said was, "My dad is picking me up at five."

"So that's yes?"

She couldn't help smiling. "Yeah."

"Cool."

For the rest of the day, Leni felt both nervous and energized. She could hardly sit still, found it difficult to answer questions about *Hamlet*. Still, she read her passages aloud and made notes and tried not to reveal to Matthew or anyone else how weird she felt.

When school ended, she was the first one out of her chair. She bolted out of the school and ran for the General Store, pushed through the narrow door, and yelled, "Large Marge!"

Large Marge was unpacking a case of toilet paper. Like all of her supplies, she purchased it in Soldotna, marked it up, and shelved it for sale. "What's up, kiddo?"

"I can't work today."

"Oh. Okay."

"Don't you want to know why?"

Large Marge smiled, straightened, placed a hand at the small of her back, as if it hurt her to bend over. "Nope."

The bell clanged again. Matthew walked into the store.

"Like I said," Large Marge said. "I don't want to know." She turned her back on Leni and Matthew and walked down the crowded aisle, disappearing behind a stack of crab pots.

"Let's go," Matthew said. "Follow me."

They slipped out of the store and hurried past the workers at the Kicking Moose Saloon and up the hill by the Russian Orthodox church. There they were hidden from view.

They hiked out to the point and found a clearing, where the blue waters of Kachemak Bay spread out in front of them. At least a dozen small boats were out on the water.

Matthew took the big serrated knife from the sheath at his belt and hacked down a bunch of evergreen branches. He laid them on the ground, creating a bower of fragrant green. "Here. Sit."

Leni sat down; the greenery was buoyant beneath her, springy.

He sat down beside Leni, wishboned his arms to cradle his head in his hands, and lay back. "Look up."

She looked up.

"No. Lie down."

Leni followed his lead. Above them, white clouds drifted across a pale blue sky.

"You see the poodle?"

Leni saw the sculpted cloud shape that looked like a groomed poodle. "That one looks like a pirate ship."

She watched clouds move slowly across the sky, change shapes, become something new before her eyes. She wished change were so easy for people. "How was Fairbanks?"

"Crowded. For me, anyway. I guess I like the empty and the quiet. And it was rough. Full of pipeline workers who drank a lot and started fights. But my aunt and uncle were great, and it was cool to be with Aly. She worried about me a lot."

"So did I."

"Yeah. I know. And. I wanted to say I'm sorry," he said.

"What for?"

"That day on the field trip when I shoved you. I thought I was holding it together—I mean, I wasn't, but I thought I was."

"I understood," she said.

"How could you?"

"My dad has nightmares from the war. It makes him crazy sometimes."

"I saw her. My mom. Under the ice, floating beneath my feet. Her hair was all splayed out. She was clawing for a way out. Then she was gone." He let out a ragged breath. She felt him leave her behind, journey into the landscape of dark, thorny memories. Then she felt him come back. "I don't know if I would have made it without my sister and . . . your letters. I know that sounds weird, but it's true."

At his words, Leni felt as if the ground beneath her had fallen away (just like in her dream). She knew things now she hadn't known at fourteen—about ice and loss and even fear. She couldn't imagine losing her mother in *any* way, but that, watching her under the ice, unable to save her . . .

She turned her head, stared at his profile, the sharp line of his nose, the shadow of a shaven blond beard, the ridge of his lips. She saw the tiny scar that bisected his eyebrow, and the brown mole that peeked out from his hairline. "You are lucky to have a sister like Alyeska."

"Yeah. She used to want to work for *Vogue* or something. Now she wants to come back to the homestead and work with Dad. They're going to build an adventure lodge on the property. So another generation of Walkers can live in the same place." He laughed at the idea.

"You don't like that?"

"I do," he said quietly. "I want to teach my kids the things my dad taught me."

Leni drew away from him at that. That was the last thing in the world she wanted. She turned her attention to the sky again. At the poodle that had become a spaceship.

"I read this cool book, *Childhood's End*, about the last man alive on earth. I wonder how that would feel. Or to be clairvoyant . . ."

When he reached for her hand, she didn't draw away. Holding his hand—touching him—seemed like the most natural thing in the world.

⚬⟨❀⟩⚬

IT DIDN'T TAKE LENI LONG to know that she was in trouble. She thought about Matthew constantly. At school she began to study his every move; she watched him as she would a prey animal, trying to glean intent from action. His hand sometimes brushed hers beneath the desk, or he touched her shoulder as he passed by her in the classroom. She didn't know if those brief contacts were intentional or meaningful, but her body responded instinctively to each fleeting touch. Once she'd even risen from her chair, pushed her shoulder into his palm like a cat seeking attention. It wasn't a thought, that lifting up, that unknown need; it just happened. And sometimes, when he talked to her, she thought he stared at her lips the way she stared at his. She found herself secretly mapping his face, memorizing every ridge and hollow and valley, as if she were an explorer and he her discovery.

She couldn't stop thinking about him, not at school while she was supposed to be reading or at home when she was supposed to be working. She'd lost track of the amount of times Mama had had to raise her voice to get Leni's attention.

She might have talked to Mama, asked her about this edgy restlessness she felt, the dreams of touching and kissing that left her feeling unsettled when she woke, needful of something she couldn't name, but Dad was obviously getting worse, and the cabin felt charged with bad energy. Mama didn't need more to worry about, so Leni kept her weird, inexplicable longings to herself and tried to make sense of them alone.

Now Leni and her mother and Thelma were out at the stainless steel table at the Harlan compound, gutting fish, slicing the meat into strips. They would soak the strips in marinade, then smoke them in the smokehouse for at least thirty-six hours.

Ted was repairing one of the doghouses, while Clyde worked a cowhide, preparing to make it into ropes of rawhide. Off to the left, thirteen-year-old Agnes was practicing throwing sharp silver stars into trees. *Thunk-thunk-thunk.* Marthe was whittling wood to make a slingshot. Donna was over at the clothesline, pinning up sheets. Dad and Mad Earl had gone into Homer.

Thelma threw a bucket of sudsy water over the table, sent the fish innards sliding to the muddy ground, where the dogs fought over them.

Seated in a chair, with Moppet on the ground beside her, chattering away about some bird's nest she'd found, Leni worked at repairing a crab pot.

There was an uneasiness in camp now. Ever since Mr. Walker had shown up at the compound and reminded the Harlans that his place in their lives had been secured long ago—and offered well-paying jobs—Leni had seen the way the adults looked at one another. Or, to be more precise, didn't look at one another.

A schism had opened. Not only in town, but also here, at the Harlan compound. Leni wasn't always sure who was on what side, but the adults knew. She was pretty sure Dad hadn't spoken to Thelma or Ted since that night.

A horn honked loudly enough to startle Leni. She dropped the crab pot, which landed hard on her ankle. She yelped and kicked it aside.

Dad's truck rolled in and parked by the toolshed.

Both doors opened at once; Dad and Mad Earl exited the pickup.

Dad reached into the back, grabbed a big cardboard box, hefted it into his arms. The box rattled and clanged as Dad carried it into the compound. He went to the high ground by the beehives and looked out at the people. Mad Earl stepped up and stood beside him. The old man looked tired, or more tired than usual. He'd lost most of his hair in the past year and the lines in his forehead looked like they'd been etched in place. White hair sprouted from his jaw, his cheeks, his nose, his ears.

"Gather 'round," Mad Earl said, gesturing.

Thelma wiped her hands on her dirty pant leg and joined her husband.

Leni sidled up to Mama. "They look drunk," she said.

Mama nodded, lit a cigarette. They walked forward, stood beside Thelma.

Standing on the ridge above them like some high priest, Dad smiled down at the people gathered before him.

Leni recognized his Big Idea smile. She'd seen it lots of times. A beginning; he loved them.

Dad placed a hand on Earl's shoulder, gave a meaningful squeeze. "Earl here has welcomed me and my family into this safe, wonderful place you've created. We almost feel like Harlans. That's how warm you've all been. I know how much Thelma's friendship means to Cora. Honestly, we have never felt that we belonged anywhere until now." He put the box down with a rattling clank, pushed it aside with the blunt toe of his rubber boot. "Bo wanted me to have his cabin. Why? So I could bring what I know to this family. He wanted someone here he could trust to protect his family. As you all know, I have taken that responsibility seriously. Each of you is a crack shot. You are also adept with a bow and arrow. Your bug-out bags are packed and ready to go at a moment's notice. We are ready for martial law or nuclear war or a pandemic. Or so I thought."

Leni saw Thelma frown.

"What do you mean?" Clyde asked, uncrossing his beefy arms.

"Last week, an enemy walked onto this land as easy as you please. No one stopped him. Nothing stopped him. He came in here and used words—and bribes—to put a wedge between us. You know it's true. You feel the dissension. It's all because of Tom Walker."

Thelma muttered, "Here we go."

"Ernt," Ted said. "It's just a job. We need the money."

Dad raised his hands, smiling.

(Leni knew that smile: it was not a sign of happiness.)

"I am not blaming anyone. I understand. I'm just pointing out a danger you've missed. When TSHTF, our neighbors will all have sob stories to tell. They'll want what we have and you'll want to give it to them. You've known them a long time. I get it. So I'm here to protect you from yourselves, too."

"Bo woulda wanted that," Mad Earl said. He rolled a cigarette and lit it up, taking a drag so deep Leni thought he might die on the spot. "Tell 'em," Mad Earl said, finally exhaling.

Dad squatted down, opened the cardboard flaps of the box, and reached in. He then got back to his feet, holding a plank of wood that had been studded with hundreds of nails, hammered in close to each other to make what looked like a weapon. In his other hand, he held a hand grenade. "No one is ever going to just walk into this place again. First, we're going to build a wall and put razor wire on top. Then we'll dig a ditch around the perimeter, in the places where attackers will come in. We'll fill it with these nail beds, broken glass, spikes. Anything we can think of."

Thelma laughed.

"This ain't no joke, missy," Mad Earl said.

"You put the grenade in a mason jar," Dad said, beaming at his cleverness. "We remove the pin, put the grenade in the jar, and compress the safety lever. Then we bury it. When someone steps on it, the jar breaks, and kablooey."

No one spoke. They just stood there, dogs barking in the background.

Mad Earl clapped Dad on the back. "Hell of an idea, Ernt. Hell of an idea."

"No," Thelma said. And then: "No. *No.*"

With Mad Earl's cackle going full volume, it took a moment for Thelma's quieter voice to be heard. She pushed her way to the front, then took another step, until she was standing alone, the point of the arrow. "No," she said again.

"No?" her father said, his mouth squelching up.

"He's off his rocker, Dad," Thelma said. "We have children here. And, let's face it, more than a few drinkers. We can't booby-trap the perimeter of our *home* with buried explosives. We'll kill one of us, most likely."

"Your job isn't security, Thelma," Dad said. "It's mine."

"No, Ernt. My job is keeping my family safe. I'll go along with stockpiling food and creating water filtration. I'll teach my daughter useful skills, like shooting and hunting and trapping. I'll even let you and my dad yammer on about nuclear war and pandemics, but I am not going to worry every day of my life that we could accidentally kill someone for no reason."

"'Yammer on'?" Dad said, his voice going low.

Everyone started talking at once, arguing. Leni felt the schism between them rip free, crack wide open; they separated into two groups. Those who wanted to be a family (most of them) versus those who wanted to be able to kill anyone who came close (Dad and Mad Earl and Clyde).

"We've got kids here," Thelma said. "You have to remember that. We can't have bombs or booby traps."

"But they could just walk in here with machine guns," Dad said, looking for support. "Kill us and take what we have."

Leni heard Moppet say, "Could they, Mom? Could they?"

The argument re-erupted. The adults clotted together, went toe-to-toe, voices raised, faces red.

"Enough!" Mad Earl finally said, raising his skeletal hands in the air. "I can't have this happening to my family. And we do got little ones." He turned to Dad. "Sorry, Ernt. I gotta side with Thelma."

Dad took a step back, put distance between him and the old man. "Sure, Earl," he said tightly, "whatever you say, man."

Just like that, the argument ended for the Harlans. Leni saw the way they came together as a family, forgave each other, began talking about other things. Leni wondered if any of them even noticed how her father hung back, how he watched them, the way his mouth flattened into an angry line.

SIXTEEN

In May, the sandpipers returned by the thousands, flying overhead in a swarm of wings, touching down briefly in the bay before continuing their journey north. So many birds returned to Alaska in this month that the sky was constantly busy and the air was loud with birdsong and squawking and cawing.

Usually, this time of year, Leni would lie in bed listening to the noises, identifying each bird by its song, noting the season's passing by their arrivals and departures, looking forward to summer.

This year was different.

There were only two weeks of school left.

"You're awfully quiet," Dad said as he turned the truck into the school parking lot. He parked next to Matthew's pickup.

"I'm fine," she said, reaching for the door handle.

"It's the security, isn't it?"

Leni turned to look at him. "What?"

"You and your mom have been sorta mopey and glum since our last time at the Harlans' place. I know you're scared."

Leni just stared at him, unsure of what the right answer was. He had been extra edgy since the fallout at the Harlan place.

"Thelma's an optimist. One of those head-in-the-sanders. Of course she doesn't want to face the truth head-on. 'Cuz it's ugly. But looking away is no answer. We need to prepare for the worst. I would die before I'd let anything happen to you or your mom. You know that, right? You know how much I love you both." He tousled her hair. "Don't worry, Red. I'll keep you safe."

She got out of the truck and slammed the door shut behind her, then hauled her bicycle out from the truck bed. Settling her backpack strap over one shoulder, she leaned her bike against the fence and headed toward the school.

Dad honked the horn and drove away.

"Pssssst! Leni!"

She glanced sideways.

Matthew stood hidden in the trees across from the school. He waved her over.

Leni waited for her dad's truck to disappear around the corner and then hurried over to Matthew. "What's up?"

"Let's skip school today and take the *Tusty* into Homer."

"Skip school? Homer?"

"Come on! It'll be fun."

Leni knew all the reasons to say no. She also knew that today was a minus tide and her dad was going to be clamming all morning.

"We won't get caught, and even if we do, big whoop. We're seniors. It's May. Don't seniors in the Outside skip all the time?"

Leni didn't think it was a good idea, thought it might even be dangerous, but she couldn't say no to Matthew.

She heard the low, elegiac honking of the ferry's horn as it neared the dock.

Matthew reached out for Leni's hand, and the next thing she knew they were running out of the school's parking lot and up the hill, past the old church, and out onto the waiting ferry.

Leni stood on the deck, holding on to the railing as the boat eased away from land.

All summer, the trusty *Tustamena* hauled Alaskans around—fishermen, adventurers, laborers, tourists, even high school sports teams. The hull was full of cars and supplies: construction equipment, tractors, backhoes, steel beams. To the few hardy tourists who used the boat as a blue-collar cruise to remote destinations, the ferry crossing was a pretty way to spend the day. To locals, this was simply the way to town.

Leni had ridden this ferry hundreds of times in her life, but never had she felt the sense of freedom on it that she felt now. Or possibility. As if maybe this old ship could sail her right into a brand-new future.

Wind ruffled her hair. Gulls and shorebirds squawked overhead, wheeling and diving, floating on tufts of wind. The seawater was flat and green, only a few motor ripples on the surface.

Matthew moved in behind her, put his arms around her, held on to the railing. She couldn't help leaning back into him, letting his body warm her. "I can't believe we're doing this," she said. For once, she felt like an ordinary teenager. This was as close as she and Matthew could get to that, to being the kind of kids who went to the movies on a Saturday night and went for milkshakes at the A&W afterward.

"I got into the university in Anchorage," Matthew said. "I'll be playing hockey for their team."

Leni turned. With him still holding on to the railing, it meant she was in his arms. Her hair whipped across her face.

"Come with me," he said.

It was like a beautiful flower, that idea; it bloomed and then died in her hand. Life was different for Matthew. He was talented and wealthy. Mr. Walker wanted his son to go to college. "We can't afford it. And they need me to work the homestead, anyway."

"There are scholarships."

"I can't leave," she said quietly.

"I know your dad is weird, but why can't you leave?"

"It's not him I can't leave," Leni said. "It's my mama. She needs me."

"She's a grown-up."

Leni couldn't say the words that would explain it.

He would never understand why Leni sometimes believed she was the only thing keeping her mother alive.

Matthew pulled her into his arms, held her. She wondered if he could feel the way she was trembling. "Jeez, Len," he whispered into her hair.

Had he meant that, to shorten her name, to claim it somehow as something new in his hands?

"I would if I could," she said. After that, they fell silent. She thought about how different their worlds were, and it showed her how big the world was Outside; they were just two kids among millions.

When the boat docked in Homer, they disembarked with a throng of people. Holding hands, they lost themselves among the crowd of bright-eyed tourists and drably dressed locals. They ate halibut and chips on the restaurant's deck at the tip of the Spit, tossing salty, greasy fries to the birds waiting nearby. Matthew bought Leni a photo album at a souvenir shop that sold Alaska-themed Christmas ornaments and T-shirts that said things like DON'T MOOSE WITH ME and GOT CRABS?

They talked about nothing and everything. Inconsequential things. The beauty of Alaska, the craziness of the tide, the clog of cars and people on the Spit.

Leni took a picture of Matthew in front of the Salty Dawg Saloon. One hundred years ago, it had been the post office and grocery store for this out-of-the-way spot that even Alaskans called Land's End. Now the old girl was a dark, twisty tavern where locals rubbed elbows with tourists and the walls were decorated in memorabilia. Matthew wrote LENI AND MATTHEW on a dollar bill and pinned it to the wall where it was immediately lost among the thousands of bills and scraps of paper around it.

It was the single best day of Leni's life. So much so that when it ended, and they were on a water taxi, seated on a bench in the aft, heading for Kaneq, she had to battle a wave of sadness. On the *Tusty* and in town, they'd been two kids in a crowd. Now, it was just them and the water-taxi captain and a lot of water around them.

"I wish we didn't have to go back," she said.

He put an arm around her, pulled her close. The boat rose and fell with the waves, unsteadying them. "Let's run away," he said.

She laughed.

"No, really. I can see us traveling the world, backpacking through Central America, climbing up to Machu Picchu. We'll settle down when we've seen it all. I'll be an airline pilot or a paramedic. You'll be a photographer. We'll come back here to where we belong and get married and have kids who won't listen to us."

Leni knew he was just playing around, daydreaming, but his words sparked a deep yearning in her; one she'd never known existed. She had to force herself to smile, to play along as if this hadn't struck her in the heart. "I'm a photographer, huh? I like the idea of that. I think I'll wear makeup and high heels to pick up my Pulitzer. Maybe I'll order a martini. But I don't know about kids."

"Kids. Definitely. I want a daughter with red hair. I'll teach her to skip rocks and hook a king salmon."

Leni didn't answer. It was such a silly conversation, how could it break her heart? He should know better than to dream so big and to give voice to those dreams. He had lost his mother and she had a dangerous father. Families and the future were fragile.

The water taxi slowed, drifted sideways into the dock. Matthew jumped off and looped a line around a metal cleat. Leni stepped out onto the dock as Matthew tossed the line back on board.

"We're home," he said.

Leni stared up at the buildings perched on barnacled, muddy stilts above the water.

Home.

Back to real life.

✦⟨❀⟩✦

AT WORK THE NEXT AFTERNOON, Leni made one mistake after another. She mismarked the boxes of three-penny nails and put them in the wrong place and then stood there staring at her mistake, thinking, *Could I go to college?* Was it possible?

"Go home," Large Marge said, coming up behind her. "Your mind is somewhere else today."

"I'm fine," Leni said.

"No. You're not." She gave Leni a knowing look. "I saw you and Matthew walking through town yesterday. You're playing with fire, kid."

"W-what do you mean?"

"You know what I mean. Do you want to talk about it?"

"There's nothing to talk about."

"You must think I was born yesterday. Be careful, that's all I'll say."

Leni didn't even respond. Words were beyond her, as was logical thought. She left the store and retrieved her bicycle and rode home. Once there, she fed the animals, carted water from the spring they'd dug a few years ago, and opened the cabin door. Her mind was so overrun by thoughts and emotions that honestly the next thing she knew she was in the kitchen with her mama, but she had no memory of getting there.

Mama was kneading bread dough. She looked up as the door banged shut, her floury hands lifting from the mound of dough. "What's wrong?"

"Why do you say that?" Leni asked, but she knew. She was close to tears—although *why*, she wasn't sure. All she knew was that Matthew had pulled her world out of shape. He had altered her view of things, opened her up. Suddenly all she could think about was the end of school and him going away to college without her.

"Leni?" Mama wiped her floury hands on a washrag and tossed it aside. "You look brokenhearted."

Before Leni could answer, she heard a vehicle drive up. She saw a shiny white pickup truck pull into the yard.

The Walker truck.

"Oh, no." Leni ran for the cabin door, flung it open.

Matthew stepped out of the truck, into their yard.

Leni crossed the deck, rushed down the steps. "You shouldn't have come here."

"You were so quiet at school today and then you ran off to work. I thought . . . did I do something wrong?"

Leni was happy to see him and scared that he was here. It felt to her like all she did was say no and goodbye to him, and she wanted so, *so* much to say yes.

Dad came around from the side of the cabin, holding an ax. He was flushed with exertion, damp with sweat. He saw Matthew and came to a sudden stop. "You aren't welcome on this land, Matthew Walker. If you and your dad want to pollute your own place, apparently I can't stop you, but you stay off my land and you stay away from my daughter. You understand? You Walkers are a blight on our landscape, with your saloon upgrades and your hotel and your damn adventure lodge plans. You'll ruin Kaneq. Turn it into g-damn Disneyland."

Matthew frowned. "Did you say Disneyland?"

"Get the hell out of here before I decide you're trespassing and shoot you."

"I'm going." Matthew didn't sound scared at all, but that was impossible. He was a kid, being threatened by a man holding an ax.

Watching him go hurt more than Leni would have thought possible. She turned away from her father and went into the house and just stood there, staring at nothing, missing Matthew in a way that pushed everything else away.

Mama came in a moment later. She crossed the room, opened her arms, saying, "Oh, baby girl."

Leni burst into tears. Mama tightened her hold, stroked Leni's hair, then led her to the sofa, where they sat down.

"You're attracted to him. How could you not be? He's gorgeous. And you alone and lonely all these years."

Leave it to Mama to say the words out loud.

Leni *had* felt alone for a long time.

"I understand," Mama said.

It helped, those few words, reminded Leni that in the vast landscape of Alaska, this cabin was a world of its own. And her mama understood.

"It's dangerous, though. You see that, right?"

"Yeah," Leni said. "I see it."

❖❖❖

For the first time, Leni understood all the books she'd read about broken hearts and unrequited love. It was physical, this pain of hers. The way she missed Matthew was like a sickness.

When she woke the next morning, after a restless night, her eyes felt gritty. Light blared down through the skylight, bright enough to force her to shield her eyes from it. She dressed in yesterday's clothes and climbed down from the loft. Without bothering to eat breakfast, she went outside and fed the animals and jumped onto her bike and rode away. In town, she waved to Large Marge, who was outside the General Store washing windows, and pedaled past Crazy Pete and turned into the school parking lot. Leaving her bicycle in the tall grass by the chain-link fence, she clamped her backpack to her chest and went into the classroom.

Matthew's desk was empty.

"Makes sense," she muttered. "He's probably halfway to Fairbanks after seeing how crazy my dad is."

"Hey, Leni," Ms. Rhodes said brightly. "Can you handle teaching today? An injured eagle needs help at the center in Homer. I thought I'd go."

"Sure. Why not?"

"I knew you'd be my ace in the hole. Moppet is doing some long division and Agnes and Marthe are working on their history papers; you and Matthew are supposed to read T. S. Eliot today."

Leni forced a smile as Ms. Rhodes left the classroom. She glanced at the clock, thought, *Maybe he's late,* and then set about helping the girls with their assignments.

The day crawled forward, with Leni constantly looking at the clock until it finally struck three o'clock.

"That's it, kiddos. School's done."

When the kids were gone and the classroom fell silent, Leni packed up her stuff and was the last person to leave the school.

Outside, she retrieved her bicycle and pedaled idly down the center of Main Street, in no hurry to get home. Overhead, a bush plane puttered in a lazy arc, giving its passengers a good view of the small town perched on a boardwalk along the water's edge. The marshes behind town were in full bloom, clumps of grass fluttering in the breeze. The air smelled of dust and new grass and murky water. In the distance, a red boat moved among the thick growth on its way out to the sea. She heard hammering at the saloon, but there were no workers to be seen outside.

She came to the bridge. Normally, on a day this bright at the start of the season, it would be crammed with men and women and children standing shoulder to shoulder, lines in the water, the kids on tiptoes, peering over the edge into the crystal-clear river below.

Now there was only one person standing here.

Matthew.

She coasted to a stop, stepped down on one foot, rested the other on the pedal. "What are you doing?"

"Waiting."

"For what?"

"You."

Leni dismounted the bike and fell into step beside him as he led her back toward town. The bicycle clanged and thumped over the bumpy gravel of Main Street. Every now and then the bell made a shivering little ringing sound.

Leni glanced nervously at the saloon as they passed it, but didn't see Clyde or Ted working. She didn't want anyone to tell her dad they'd seen her with Matthew.

They hiked up the hill past the church and ducked into the Sitka spruce trees. Leni set her bike down and followed Matthew to the point that jutted out over a black rock cliff.

"I didn't sleep last night," Matthew said at last.

"Me, either."

"I was thinking about you."

She could have said the same thing but didn't dare.

He took her by the hand, led her to the bower he'd made before. They sat down, leaned back against a crumbling, moss-draped nurse log. Leni heard the waves on the rocks below. The ground smelled fecund and sweet. Shade fell in star-shaped patches between the strands of sunlight. "I talked to my dad last night about us. I even went to the diner to call my sister."

Us.

"Uh-huh?"

"Dad said I was playing with fire wanting you."

Wanting you.

"Aly asked if I'd kissed you yet. When I said no, she said, 'What the hell, baby brother, get going.' She knows how much I like you. So. Can I kiss you?"

She barely nodded, but it was enough. His lips brushed tentatively against hers. It was like every love story she'd ever read; this first kiss changed her, opened her up to a world she'd never imagined, a big, bright, shining universe full of unexpected possibilities.

When he drew back, Leni stared at him. "Us. This. It's dangerous."

"Yeah, I guess. But it doesn't matter, does it?"

"No," Leni said quietly. She knew that she was making a decision she might regret, but it felt inevitable. "Nothing matters except us."

⁙

COME AWAY TO COLLEGE WITH ME, Len. Please . . .

U of A is beautiful . . . you could still get in for fall. We could go together.

Together . . .

At home, she put her bicycle away and fed the animals, but she was so distracted she dropped an entire bucket of grain. Then she hauled water from the spring at the top of the hill. An hour later, when she'd finished her chores, she saw her parents go down to the beach and stand by the boat. They were going fishing.

They'd be gone for hours.

She could ride her bike to Matthew's house, let him kiss her again. Her parents wouldn't even know she'd been gone.

Stupid plan. She would see Matthew tomorrow.

Tomorrow felt like a lifetime away.

She yanked up her bicycle and jumped aboard and pedaled away, past the canoe Dad had dragged home from the dump last week and the rotting husk of a dirt bike he'd been unable to get running again. The shadows of the driveway plunged down around her, chilled her.

She pedaled out onto the main road, back into the sunshine, and rode the quarter mile to the gated driveway. Wheeling around the open gate, she passed beneath the painted arch, with its tanned silver salmon carved into the wood, and kept going.

This is dangerous, she thought, but she couldn't make herself care. All she could think about now was Matthew, and how it had felt when he kissed her, and how much she wanted to kiss him again.

Here, the road was not so muddy. Someone had obviously taken the time to regrade the earth and put down gravel. It was the kind of thing her father would never do: smooth out a road to make life easier.

She came to a bumpy, breathless stop in front of the Walker house.

Matthew was carrying a huge bale of hay over to the cattle pen. He saw her and dropped the bale and came toward her. He wore an oversized hockey sweater and shorts and rubber boots. "Len?" She loved how he had renamed her, made her into someone else, someone only he knew. "Are you okay?"

"I missed you," she said. *Stupid.* They had barely been apart. "I wish . . . we need *time* together."

"I'll come over to see you tomorrow night," he said, taking her in his arms. It was where she wanted to be.

"Wh-what do you mean?"

"I'll sneak over to see you." He said it with such conviction that she didn't know what to say. "Tomorrow night."

"You can't."

"At midnight. Sneak out to meet me."

"It's too dangerous."

"You guys have an outhouse, right? So it's no big deal to go out. And do they ever look up in the loft for you in the middle of the night?"

She could dress warmly and go out and just not come back for a while. They could steal an hour together, maybe more. Alone.

If she said no right now, it would prove that Leni could live a sensible life, with the kind of love that no one would ever compare to heroin and she would never cry herself to sleep.

"Please? I need to see you."

"Leni!"

She heard her father's voice yelling at her. She pushed Matthew away, but too late. Her father had seen them together and now he was striding toward them, while Mama ran along behind him.

"What the *hell* are you doing over here?" Dad said.

"I—I—" She couldn't answer. *Stupidstupidstupid*. She shouldn't have come here.

"I thought I told you to stay away from my Lenora," Dad said. He grabbed Leni by the bicep, yanked her to his side.

Leni bit down hard, so she wouldn't make a sound. She didn't want Matthew to know her dad had hurt her.

"Leni," Matthew said, frowning.

"Stay back," she said. "Please."

"Come on, Leni," Dad said, pulling her away.

Leni stumbled along beside her father, crashing into him and pulling away on the uneven ground. If she got too far, he wrenched her back to his side. Mama hurried along beside, walking with Leni's bicycle.

Back in their yard, Leni yanked free and almost fell, scrambled across the muddy grass, faced him. "I didn't do anything wrong," she cried.

"Ernt," Mama said, trying to sound reasonable. "They're just friends—"

Dad turned to Mama. "So you knew about them?"

"You're overreacting," Mama said evenly. "He's in Leni's class. That's all."

"You knew," Dad said to her again.

"No," Leni said, suddenly afraid.

"I saw her leave," Dad said. "But you saw her go, too, didn't you, Cora? And you knew where she was going."

Mama shook her head. "N-no. I thought she was going to work, maybe. Or to pick some balm-of-Gilead."

"You're lying to me," he said.

"Dad, please, it's my fault," Leni said.

He wasn't listening. His eyes had that wild, desperate look. "You know better than to hide things from me." He grabbed Mama and dragged her toward the cabin.

Leni followed them, tried to pull Mama away.

Dad shoved Mama inside and Leni out of the way.

The door slammed shut. The bolt came down hard, with a clank, and locked them inside.

Then, from behind the door, a loud crash, a bitten-off scream.

Leni hurled herself at the door, banged on it, screaming to be let in.

SEVENTEEN

The next morning, the left side of Mama's face was swollen and purple; one eye was blackening. She sat alone at the table, a cup of coffee in front of her. "What were you thinking? He saw you leave and followed your tire tracks in the mud."

Leni sat down at the table, ashamed of herself. "I wasn't thinking."

"Hormones. I told you they were wicked dangerous." Mama leaned forward. "Here's the thing, baby girl. You are on thin ice. You know it. I know it. You need to stay away from this boy or something bad is going to happen."

"He kissed me." *He wants me to sneak out to meet him tonight.*

Mama sat there a long time. Quiet. "Well. One kiss can change a girl's world. Don't I know that? But you're not an ordinary girl in the suburbs with a Mr. Cleaver dad. Choices have consequences, Leni. Not just for you, either. For your boy. For me." She touched her bruised cheekbone, wincing. "You need to stay away from him."

MEET ME. Midnight.

All day, Leni thought about it. At school, every time she looked at Matthew, she knew what he was thinking.

"Please" was the last thing he said to her.

She'd said no and meant it, but when she got home and started on her long list of chores, she found herself waiting impatiently for the sun to set.

Time was not something she usually paid much attention to. On the homestead, the bigger picture mattered—the darkening of the sky, the ebbing of the tide, the snow hares changing color, the birds returning or flying south. That was how they marked the passage of time, in growing seasons and salmon runs, and the first snowfall. On school days, she took notice of the clock, but in a lackadaisical way. No one much cared if you got to school on time, not in the winter when some days it was so cold the trucks wouldn't start, and not in the spring and fall when there were so many chores to do.

But now time commanded her attention. Down in the living room, Mama and Dad were cuddled together on the couch, talking quietly. Dad kept touching Mama's bruised face and murmuring apologies, telling her how much he loved her.

At just past ten P.M., she heard Dad say, "Well, Cora, I am about to drop," and Mama answered, "Me, too."

Her parents turned off the generator and fed the fire one last time. Then Leni heard the rattle of the beaded curtain being pushed aside as they went into their room.

Then, quiet.

She lay there, counting whatever she could: her breaths, her heartbeats. She willed time to pass even as its passage frightened her.

She imagined different scenarios—going to meet Matthew, staying in bed, not getting caught, getting caught.

She told herself repeatedly that she was *not* waiting for midnight, that she wasn't stupid and reckless enough to sneak out.

Midnight came. She heard the last little click of the hand on her clock.

She heard a birdcall through her window, a little trill of sound that wasn't quite real.

Matthew.

She climbed out of bed and dressed warmly.

Every creak of the ladder terrified her, made her freeze in place. Every footstep on the floor did the same thing, so that it took her forever to reach the door. She stepped into her rubber boots and slipped into a down vest.

Holding her breath, she unclicked the lock, slid the bar latch, and opened the door.

Night air rushed in to greet her.

She could see Matthew standing on the crest of the hill above the beach, his outline against a pink and amethyst sky.

Leni closed the door and ran to him. He took her hand and together they ran through the grassy, wet yard, slipped over the rise, and down the stairs to the beach, where Matthew had laid out a blanket and set big rocks on each of the four corners.

She lay down. He did the same. Leni felt the warmth of his body along hers and it made her feel safe even with all the risk they were taking. Normal kids would probably be talking nonstop, or laughing. Something. Maybe drinking beer or smoking pot or making out, but Leni and Matthew both knew they weren't ordinary kids for whom sneaking out was expected. The crazy wildness of her father's anger hung in the air between them.

She could hear the sea washing toward them and the spruce trees creaking in the murmur of a spring breeze. A pale ambient light shone on everything, illuminated the lavender night sky. Matthew pointed out constellations, told her their stories.

The world around them felt different, magical, a place of infinite possibility instead of hidden dangers.

He turned onto his side. They were nose to nose now; she could feel his breathing on her face, feel a strand of his hair across her cheek.

"I talked to Ms. Rhodes," he said. "She said you could still get into U of A. Think of it, Len. We could be together, away from all of this."

"It's expensive."

"They have scholarships and low-interest loans. We could do it. Totally."

Leni dared—just for a second—to imagine it. A life. *Her* life. "I could apply," she said, but even as she heard her dream given voice, she thought of the price. Mama would be the one to pay it. How could Leni live with that?

But was she supposed to be trapped forever by her mother's choice and her father's rage?

He slipped a necklace around her throat, fumbled to clasp it in the dark. "I carved it," he said.

She felt it, a heart made of bone, hanging on a metal chain as thin as cobweb.

"Come to college with me, Len," he said.

She touched his face, felt how different his skin was from hers, rougher, whiskery here and there.

He pressed his body to hers, hip to hip. They kissed; she felt his breathing turn ragged.

She hadn't known until now how love could erupt into existence like the big bang theory and change everything in you and everything in the world. She believed in Matthew suddenly, in the possibility of him, of them. The way she believed in gravity or that the earth was round. It was crazy. *Crazy.* When he kissed her, she glimpsed a whole new world, a new Leni.

She drew back. The depth of this new feeling was terrifying. Real love grew slowly, didn't it? It couldn't be this fast, like a crashing together of planets.

Yearning. She knew what it felt like now. *Yearning.* An old word, from Jane Eyre's world, and as new to Leni as this second.

"Leni! Leni!"

Her father's voice. Yelling.

Leni jackknifed up. *Oh, God.* "Stay here." She scrambled up and ran for the weathered steps. She rushed up their zigzagged path, her down vest flapping open, her boots clomping on the chicken-wire-covered steps. "Here I am, Dad," she yelled, out of breath, waving her arms.

"Thank *God*," he said. "I got up to take a leak and saw that your boots were gone."

Boots. That was her mistake. Such a small thing.

She pointed skyward. Did he notice how hard she was breathing? Could he hear the thud of her heart? "Look at the sky. It's so beautiful."

"Ah."

She stood beside him, trying to calm down. He put an arm around her shoulders. She felt claimed by the hold. "Summer is magical, isn't it?"

The grassy hillside hid the beach from view, thank God. Leni couldn't see the curl of pebbled stone and crushed shells, or the blanket Matthew had carried over. Nor could she see Matthew. He was well below the crest of the hill between the cabin and the beach.

She clasped the bone heart around her neck, felt its sharp point burrow into her palm.

"Don't do that again, Red. You know better. The bears are dangerous this time of year. I almost grabbed my gun and came looking for you."

PERSONAL STATEMENT
by Lenora Allbright

"It's a dangerous business, Frodo, going out your door. You step onto the road and if you don't keep your feet, there's no knowing where you might be swept off to."

If you knew me, you wouldn't be surprised at all that I start my college essay off with a quote from Tolkien. Books are the mile markers of my life. Some people have family photos or home movies to record their past. I've got books. Characters. For as long as I can remember, books have been my safe place. I read about places I can barely imagine and lose myself in journeys to foreign lands to save girls who didn't know they were really princesses.

Only recently have I learned why I needed those faraway worlds.

I was taught by my father to be afraid of the world, and some of the lessons stuck. I read about Patty Hearst and the Zodiac Killer and the massacre at the Munich Olympics and Charles Manson, and I knew the world was a terrifying place. He said it all of the time, reminded me that mountains could blow up and kill people in their sleep. Governments were corrupt. A flu could come out of nowhere and kill millions. A nuclear bomb could fall at any second, obliterating everything.

I learned to shoot the head off of a paper target while on the run. I have a bug-out bag full of survival supplies by my front door. I can start a fire with flint and put a gun together blindfolded. I know how to adjust a gas mask for the perfect fit. I have grown up preparing for a war or anarchy or worldwide tragedy.

But none of it is true. Or it's true but not the truth, which is the kind of distinction adults make.

My parents left Washington State when I was thirteen. We came to Alaska and forged a subsistence life in the bush. I love it. I do. I love the harsh, uncompromising beauty of Alaska. I love the women most of all, women like my neighbor, Large Marge, who used to be a lawyer and now runs a grocery store. I love how tough she is and how compassionate. I love how my mom, who is as fragile as a fern frond, has still managed to survive out here in a climate designed to destroy her.

I love all of it, and I love this state that has given me a place to belong, a home, but it's time for me to leave the homestead and make my own way, to learn about the real world.

That's why I want to go to college.

⊹⟨◉⟩⊹

IN THE DAYS AFTER that night on the beach, Leni became a thief, invisible when she wanted to be. It was an illusion she'd practiced all of her life, and now, as she became a stealer of time, it served her well.

She also became a liar. Straight-faced, even smiling, she lied to her father to steal the time she needed. There was a test to be taken early—at least an hour—a field trip that would keep her at school late. A research project that required her to take the skiff to the library in Seldovia. She met Matthew in the woods, in the shadowy stacks at Large Marge's store, or in the abandoned cannery. In class, they were always touching under the desk. They celebrated his birthday together after school, sitting on the dock behind an aging metal boat.

It was wonderful, exhilarating. She learned things no book had ever taught her—how falling in love felt like an adventure, how her body seemed to change at his touch, the way her armpits ached after an hour of holding him tightly, how her lips puffed and chapped from his kisses, and how his rough beard-growth could burn her skin.

Stolen time became the engine that powered her world; on weekends, when hours without Matthew stretched out before her, she felt an almost unbearable need to leave the homestead, run to him, find a way to steal just ten more minutes.

The specter of school's end cast a long shadow. Today, when Leni slid into her desk at school, she looked at Matthew and almost started to cry.

He reached across the desk, took her hand in his. "Are you okay?"

Leni couldn't help thinking how small they were in this big dangerous world, just kids who wanted to be in love.

Ms. Rhodes clapped her hands at the front of the room, demanded attention. "There's only a week of school left, and I thought it would be a good day for a boat ride and a hike. So, everyone, grab your coats and let's go."

Ms. Rhodes herded her chattering charges out of the classroom and through town and down to the docks. Everyone boarded Ms. Rhodes's aluminum fishing boat.

They motored out into the bay and sped up, bumping across the waves, water splashing at their sides. The teacher guided the boat up the waters of the fjord, mountains all around them, down one stretch of water and up another, until they stopped seeing any cabins or boats at all. Here the water was aquamarine. Leni could see a sow and two black cubs walking along an isolated shore.

Ms. Rhodes pulled up to a dock in a narrow cove. Matthew jumped onto the weathered dock and tied the boat down.

"Matthew's grandparents homesteaded this land in '32," Ms. Rhodes said. "It was their first family homestead. Who wants to see a pirate cave?"

Pandemonium.

Ms. Rhodes led the younger kids up the beach, marching through the heavy sand, stepping over huge pieces of driftwood.

When they rounded the corner of the bay and disappeared, Matthew took Leni by the hand. "Come on," he said at last. "I'll show you something cool."

He led her upland, into knee-deep grass that ended at a sparse forest of stunted trees.

"Shhh," he said, pressing a finger to his lips.

After that Leni noticed every twig that broke beneath her and every whisper of the wind. Occasionally a bush plane puttered overhead. At a wall of greenery, bushes grown to Alaskan size from all the water that ran down from the mountains, he showed her a path she wouldn't have seen on her own. They ducked into it, walked hunched over in the cool shadows.

A small seam of light drew them forward. Leni's eyes adjusted slowly.

A vista opened up in the break between the bushes: marshland, as far as the eye could see. Tall, waving green grass through which meandered a lazy, motionless river. Mountains were tucked in close, arms drawn protectively around the marshes.

Leni counted fifteen huge brown bears in the marshes, munching on the grass, pawing for fish in the stagnant water. They were great, shaggy creatures—called grizzly bears by most of the world—with giant heads. They moved in a shambling way, as if their bones were held together with rubber bands. Mama bears kept their cubs close and away from the males.

Leni watched the majestic animals move through the tall grass. "Wow."

A bush plane banked overhead, began its descent.

"My grandpa took me here when I was just a kid," Matthew whispered. "I remember telling him he was crazy to homestead land so close to the bears, and he said, *It's Alaska*, as if that were the only answer that mattered. My grandparents relied on their dogs to run off the bears if they came too close. The government created a national refuge around us."

"Only here," Leni said with a laugh.

She leaned against Matthew. *Only here.*

God, she loved this place; she loved Alaska's wild ferocity, its majestic beauty. Even more than the land, she loved the people to whom it spoke. She hadn't realized until just this moment how deep her love for Alaska ran.

"Matthew! Leni!"

They heard Ms. Rhodes yelling for them.

They ducked back through the scrub brush and came out on the beach. Ms. Rhodes was there, with the younger girls gathered around her. Off to her left, a float plane was pulled up onto the beach. "Hurry!" Ms. Rhodes said, waving her hand. "Marthe, Agnes, get in the plane. We have to get back to Kaneq. Mad Earl has had a heart attack."

⊷⊰⊱⊱⊷

MAD EARL DIED.

Leni couldn't quite wrap her mind around it. Yesterday, the old man had been alive, vibrant, drinking moonshine, telling stories. The compound had been a busy place, a hive of activity: chain saws whirring, steel being fired into blades over open flames, axes chopping wood, dogs barking. Without him, it fell into quiet.

Leni didn't cry for Mad Earl. She wasn't that much of a hypocrite, but she wanted to weep for the loss she saw in the faces around her. For Thelma and Ted and Moppet and Clyde and the rest of the people who lived at the compound; the blank space left by Mad Earl would hurt for a long time.

Now they were all out in the bay, near the boat launch below the Russian church.

Leni sat in the dented aluminum canoe that her father had salvaged, with Mama in front of her. Dad was behind Leni, keeping them steady in the water.

There were boats all around them, floating in the calm of this bright day. They had gathered for their version of a funeral. It was almost summer; you could feel it in the sun's heat. Hundreds of snow geese had returned to the head of the bay. The craggy shoreline, empty and slicked with ice all winter, now bore all manner of life. On a rock in the middle of the water, a green and black tower of stone that rose up from the deep, sea lions crowded over one another. Seagulls flew above them in lazy white arcs, yapping like terriers. She saw nesting gulls and diving cormorants. Seals, with black or silver cocker spaniel faces, poked their noses up from the water alongside otters who lay lazily on their backs, cracking clams in quick-moving paws.

Not far away, Matthew sat in a shiny aluminum skiff with his father. Every time Matthew looked at Leni, she looked away, afraid to reveal her feelings for him in such a public place.

"My daddy loved this place," Thelma was saying, her words swaying in time to the music made by her oar in the water. "He will be missed."

Leni watched Thelma pour a stream of ashes from a cardboard box. They floated for a moment, fanned out, creating a murky stain, then slowly sank.

Silence fell.

Most of Kaneq was out here, or so it seemed. The Harlans, Tom and Matthew Walker; Large Marge; Natalie; Calhoun Malvey and his new wife; Tica Rhodes and her husband; and all the merchants. There was even a bunch of old-timers, men who lived so far off the grid and so deep in the bush they were hardly ever seen. They had few teeth and lots of stringy hair and hollowed-out cheeks. Several had dogs in their boats. Crazy Pete and Matilda stood on the shore, side by side.

One by one the boats floated back to shore, were beached. Mr. Walker carried Thelma's canoe up the beach and tossed it into the back of a rusted pickup.

People instinctively looked to Mr. Walker to say something more, to bring them all together. They gathered close to him.

"I'll tell you what, Thelma," Mr. Walker said. "Why don't you all come over to my place? I'll throw some salmon on the fire and get out a case of cold beer. We can give Earl a send-off he'd love."

"The big man, offering to host the wake for a man he looked down on," Dad said. "We don't need your charity, Tom. We will say goodbye in our own way."

Leni wasn't the only one who flinched at the stridency of her father's voice. She saw shock on the faces around her.

"Ernt," Mama said. "Not now."

"Now is the perfect time. We are saying goodbye to a man who came up here because he wanted a simpler way of life. The last thing he'd want us to do is celebrate by drinking with the man who wants to turn Kaneq into Los Angeles."

Dad seemed to grow while he stood there, fueled by rage and animosity. He moved forward, went to Thelma, who looked as broken as a used Popsicle stick, her hair dirty, her shoulders slumped, her eyes watery.

Dad squeezed Thelma's shoulder. She flinched, looked frightened. "I'll take Earl's place. You don't have to worry. I'll make sure we stay ready for anything. I'll teach Moppet—"

"You'll teach my daughter what?" Thelma asked in an unsteady voice. "The way you teach your wife? You think we haven't seen the way you treat her?"

Mama froze, a flush colored her cheeks.

"We're done with you," Thelma said, her voice strengthening. "You scare the kids, especially when you're drinking. My dad put up with you because of what you did for my brother, and I'm grateful for that, too, but there's something wrong with you. I don't want to rig the outside of our land with explosives, for God's sake, and no eight-year-old needs to put on a gas mask at two A.M. and get to the gate with her bug-out bag. My dad did things one way. I'm doing them another." She drew in a deep breath. Her eyes glittered with tears, but Leni saw relief, too. How long had Thelma wanted to say all this? "And now I am taking my dad's old friends to Tom's place to celebrate his life. We've known the Walkers forever. We were all friends, a *community*, before you showed up. If you can come and be civil, come. If you just want to tear this town apart, stay home."

Leni saw the way people backed away from Dad. Even the bushy-bearded off-the-gridders took a step back.

Thelma looked at Mama. "Come with us, Cora."

"What? But—" Mama shook her head.

"My wife stays with me," Dad said.

There was a long moment. No one moved or spoke. Then, slowly, the Harlans began to walk away.

Dad looked around, saw how easily they'd culled him from the herd.

Leni watched their friends and neighbors get into their vehicles and drive away, boats thumping along behind them on trailers or in pickup beds. Matthew gave Leni a long, sad look and finally turned away.

When they were alone, just the three of them, Leni glanced at Mama, who looked as worried and scared as Leni felt. Neither had any doubt: this would push him over the edge.

Dad stood still, eyes blazing with hatred, staring down the empty road.

"Ernt," Mama said.

"Shut up," he hissed. "I'm thinking."

After that and all the way home, he said nothing, which should have been better than yelling, but it wasn't. Yelling was like a bomb in the corner: you saw it, watched the fuse burn, and you knew when it would explode and you needed to run for cover. Not speaking was a killer somewhere in your house with a gun when you were sleeping.

Inside the cabin, he paced and paced. He muttered to himself, shook his head as if he were hearing something he didn't like.

Leni and Mama stayed out of his way.

At suppertime, Mama put some leftover moose stew on the stove to heat up, but the rich aroma did nothing to ease the tension.

When Mama put dinner on the table, Dad stopped suddenly, looked up; the light in his eyes was scary. Muttering something about ingratitude and bitches with bad attitudes and pricks who thought they owned the world, he stormed out of the house.

"We should lock him out," Leni said.

"And let him break a window or tear a wall away to get in?"

Outside, they heard a chain saw whir to life.

"We could run away," Leni said.

Mama gave her a wan smile. "Sure. Yeah. He won't come after us."

They knew, both of them, that Leni might (might) be able to get away and have a life. Not Mama. He would track her down wherever she went.

They ate dinner in silence, each watching the door carefully, listening for an early warning sign of trouble.

Then the door cracked open against the wall. Dad stood there, crazy-eyed, hair covered in sawdust, holding a hatchet.

Mama lurched to her feet, backed away. He swept in, muttering, yanked Mama into him, drew her outside, and dragged her down the driveway. Leni ran behind them. She heard Mama talking to him in that soothing voice of hers.

He pulled Mama toward a pair of skinned logs that created a giant barricade at the end of their driveway.

"I can build a wall. Put spikes on the top, maybe razor wire. Keep us safe inside. We don't need the g-damn compound. Screw the Harlans."

"B-but Ernt . . . we can't live—"

"Think of it," he said, pulling her close, a hatchet hanging from one hand. "Nothing to fear from the outside world anymore. We will be safe inside. Just us. That son of a bitch can turn Kaneq into Detroit and we won't care. I'll protect you, Cora. From all of them. That's how much I love you."

Leni stared in horror at the logs, imagining it: this thumbprint piece of land walled off at the joint, cut off from the bit of civilization that would now be Out There.

There was no one who would stop her dad from building a wall or shutting them away, no police who would protect them or come in an emergency.

And once he finished it, bolted the gate shut, would Leni—or Mama—ever get out?

Leni glanced at her parents: two thin figures, angled together, touching with lips and fingers, murmuring about love, Mama trying to keep him calm, Dad trying to keep her close. They would always be the way they'd been, nothing would ever change.

In the naïveté of youth, her parents had seemed like towering presences, omnipotent and all-knowing. But they weren't that; they were just two broken people.

She could leave them. She could break free and go her own way. It would be frightening, but it couldn't be worse than staying, watching this toxic dance of theirs, letting their world become her world until there was nothing left of her at all, until she was as small as a comma.

EIGHTEEN

At ten P.M., the night of Mad Earl's funeral, the sky above Walker Cove was a layer of deep blue, fading to lavender at the edges. The evening's bonfire had burned down; logs turned to ash and crumbled into one another.

An extreme low tide had pulled back the sea, revealing a wide swath of mud, a mirror of slick gray that reflected the color of the sky and the snow-covered mountains that rose up on the opposite shore. Clumps of shiny black mussels clung to exposed pilings; the aluminum drift boat lay angled in the mud, its line tied to the buoy.

For hours there had been talk. Stories about Mad Earl, told in halting voices. Some had made them laugh. Most had made them all fall silent and remember. Mad Earl hadn't always been the crotchety, angry man he'd become in old age. Grief over the loss of his son had twisted him. Once, he'd been Grandad Eckhart's best friend. Alaska was tough on people, especially once they got old.

Now, quiet. There was only the occasional popping of the fire, the thunk of a falling bit of burnt wood, the lapping of the outgoing tide.

Matthew sat in one of their old beach chairs, his legs stretched out, crossed at the ankles, watching a young eagle picking at a salmon carcass on the beach. A pair of seagulls flew close, waiting for scraps.

There were only three of them left now. Dad and Large Marge and Matthew.

"Are we going to talk about it, Tom?" Large Marge said after so long a silence that Matthew was sure they'd kicked out the fire and climbed the beach stairs. "Thelma pretty much as banished Ernt from their place."

"Yeah," Dad said.

Matthew didn't like the way his father looked at Large Marge. The worry in his eyes.

"What are you two talking about?" Matthew asked.

Dad said, "Ernt Allbright is an angry man. We all know he vandalized the saloon. Thelma said tonight that he's been trying to get the Harlans to plant trip wires and explosives to 'protect' them in case of war."

"Yeah. He's crazy like Mad Earl, but—"

"Mad Earl was harmless," Large Marge said. "Ernt will not take this banishment well. It will piss him off. When he gets mad he gets mean, and when he gets mean, he hurts people."

"People?" Matthew said, feeling a chill go through him. "You mean Leni? He'll hurt Leni?"

Matthew didn't wait for them to answer. He ran up the stairs to the yard, where he snagged his bicycle and climbed aboard. Pedaling hard on the wet, spongy ground, he reached the main road in less than ten minutes.

At the Allbright driveway, he skidded to a stop so fast his bike almost slipped out from underneath him. Two skinned logs barricaded the scrawny necklike entrance to the land. They were the color of salmon meat, freshly cut, a fleshy pink, studded here and there with bits of bark.

What the hell?

Matthew looked around, saw no movement, heard nothing. He pedaled around the logs and kept going, more slowly now, his heart thumping in his chest, worry expanding.

At the end of the driveway, he dismounted, laid his bike on its side. A cautious examination of the Allbright land showed no sign of trouble. Ernt's truck was parked in front of the cabin.

Matthew crept forward slowly, wincing every time a twig snapped beneath his foot or he stepped on something—a beer can, a comb someone had dropped—he couldn't see in the shadows. The goats bleated. Chickens squawked in alarm.

He was about to take a step when he heard a sound.

The cabin door opening.

He threw himself into the tall grass, lay still.

Footsteps on the deck. Creaking.

Scared to move and more scared not to, he lifted his head, looked out above the grass.

Leni stood at the edge of the porch, with a wool blanket wrapped around her in a cape of red and white and yellow stripes. She was holding a roll of toilet paper; moonlight set it aglow.

"Leni," he said.

She looked over, saw him. Worriedly, she glanced back at the cabin, then ran for him.

He stood, pulled her into his arms, held her tightly. "Are you okay?"

"He's building a wall," Leni said, glancing back.

"That's what those logs are for out at the road?"

Leni nodded. "I'm scared, Matthew."

Matthew started to say, *It will be all right*, but he heard the cabin lock hitch.

"*Go*," Leni whispered, shoving him away.

Matthew threw himself into the cover of trees just as the door opened. He saw Ernt Allbright step out onto the porch, dressed in a ragged T-shirt and baggy boxer shorts. "Leni?" he called out.

Leni waved. "I'm here, Dad. Just dropped the TP." She cast a desperate glance back at Matthew. He hid behind a tree.

Leni walked over to the outhouse, disappeared inside of it. Ernt waited for her on the porch, herded her back inside as soon as she was done. The door lock latched with a click behind them.

Matthew retrieved his bicycle and rode home as fast as he could. He found Large Marge and his dad standing together in the yard, beside Marge's truck.

"H-he's building a wall," Matthew said, his breath coming in gasps. He jumped off his bike and dropped it in the grass by the smokehouse.

"What do you mean?" Dad said.

"Ernt. You know how their land is a bottleneck and then flares out over the water? He's skinned two logs and laid them across the driveway. Leni says he's building a wall."

"Jesus," Dad said. "He'll cut them off from the world."

✦❖✦

Leni woke to the high-pitched whirring of the chain saw and the occasional *whack* of a hatchet splitting wood. Dad had been up for hours, all weekend, building his wall.

The only bright spot was that she had survived the weekend and now it was Monday again, a school day.

Matthew.

Joy pushed aside the cramped, hopeless feeling of loss this weekend had birthed. She dressed for school and climbed down the ladder.

The cabin was quiet.

Mama came out of her bedroom dressed in a turtleneck and baggy jeans. "Morning."

Leni went to her mother. "We have to do something before the wall is finished."

"He won't really do it. He was just crazed. He'll see reason."

"That's what you're going to rely on?"

Leni saw for the first time how old her mother looked, how drawn and defeated. There was no light in her eyes anymore, no ready smile.

"I'll get you coffee."

Before Leni made it to the kitchen, a knock rattled the cabin door. Almost simultaneously the door swung open. "Hullo, the house!"

Large Marge strode forward. A dozen bracelets clattered on her fleshy wrists, earrings bobbed up and down like fishing lures, catching the light. Her hair was growing out again. She'd parted it down the middle and tied it into two pom-pom balls that flopped as she moved.

Dad pushed in behind the black woman, put his hands on his bony hips. "I said you couldn't go in, g-damn it."

Large Marge grinned and handed Mama a bottle of lotion. She pressed it into her hands, closed her big hands over Mama's small ones. "Thelma made this from the lavender growing in her backyard. She thought you'd love it."

Leni could see what this small kindness meant to her mother.

"We don't want your charity," Dad said. "She smells just fine without putting on that shit."

"Girlfriends give each other gifts, Ernt. And Cora and I are friends. That's why I'm here, in fact. I thought I'd have coffee with my neighbors."

"Would you get Marge some coffee, Leni?" Mama said. "And maybe a piece of cranberry bread."

Dad crossed his arms, standing with his back to the door.

Large Marge led Mama to the sofa, helped her to sit, then sat beside her. The cushion popped beneath the woman's weight. "Really, I wanted to talk to you about my diarrhea."

"Good Christ," Dad said.

"It's been explosive. I wondered if you'd come across any home remedies. Good Lord, the cramping has been awful."

Dad muttered an expletive and left the cabin, slamming the door shut behind him.

Large Marge smiled. "Men are so easy to outthink. So, now it's just us."

Leni handed out coffees and then sat down in the old Naugahyde recliner they'd bought at a junk store in Soldotna last year.

Large Marge's gaze moved from Cora, to Leni, and back to Cora. Leni was sure that it missed nothing. "I don't imagine Ernt was pleased about Thelma's decision at Earl's funeral."

"Oh. That," Mama said.

"I see the posts he's dug out on the main road. Looks like he's building a wall around this place."

Mama shook her head. "He won't."

"You know what walls do?" Large Marge said. "They hide what happens behind them. They trap people inside." She put her cup down on the coffee table, leaned toward Mama. "He could put a lock on that gate and keep the key and how would you escape?"

"H-he wouldn't do that," Mama said.

"Oh, really?" Large Marge said. "That's what my sister said the last time I talked to her. I would do anything to go back in time and change what happened. She'd finally left him, but it was too late."

"She left him," Mama said quietly. For once, she didn't look away. "That's what got her killed. Men like that . . . they don't stop looking for you until they find you."

"We can protect you," Large Marge said.

" 'We'?"

"Tom Walker and me. The Harlans. Tica. Everyone in Kaneq. You're one of us, Cora, you and Leni. He's the outsider. Trust us. Let us help."

Leni thought about it for real, seriously; they could leave him.

It would mean leaving Kaneq and probably Alaska.

Leaving Matthew.

And, what? Would they have to be on the run forever, hiding out, changing their names? How did that work? Mama had no money, no credit card. She didn't even have a valid driver's license. Neither of them did. On paper, did she and Mama even exist?

And what if he found them anyway?

"I can't," Mama finally said, and Leni thought they were the saddest, most pathetic words she'd ever heard.

Large Marge stared at Mama a long time, disappointment etched in the lines of her face. "Well. These things take time. Just know that we are here. We'll help you. All you have to do is ask. I don't care if it's the middle of the night in January. You come to me, okay? I don't care what you've done or what he's done. You come to me and I'll help."

Leni couldn't help herself. She launched herself around the coffee table and into Large Marge's arms. The woman's comforting bulk enfolded her, made her feel safe. "Come on," Large Marge said. "Let's get you to school. There aren't many days left before you graduate."

Leni grabbed her backpack and slung it over her shoulder. After a fierce hug for her mother, a whispered, *We need to talk about this,* Leni followed Large Marge outside. They were halfway to the truck when Dad appeared, holding a five-gallon jug of gasoline.

"Leaving so soon?" he said.

"Just a cup of coffee, Ernt. I'll drive Leni to school. I'm heading to the store."

He dropped the plastic jug. It sloshed beside him. "No."

Large Marge frowned. "No, what?"

"No one leaves this place without me anymore. There's nothing out there for us."

"She's five days away from graduating. Of course she's going to finish."

"Fat chance, fat lady," Dad said. "I need her at the homestead. Five days is nothing. They'll give her the damned piece of paper."

"You want to fight this battle?" Large Marge advanced, bracelets clattering. "If this young woman misses a single day of school, I will call the state and turn you in, Ernt Allbright. Don't think for one second I won't. You can be as batshit crazy and mean as you want, but you are not going to stop this beautiful girl from finishing high school. You got it?"

"The state won't care."

"Oh. They will. Trust me. You want me talking to the authorities about what goes on here, Ernt?"

"You don't know shit."

"Yeah, but I'm a big woman with a big mouth. You want to push me?"

"Go ahead. Take her to school, if it means so damned much to you." He looked at Leni. "I'll pick you up at three. Don't keep me waiting."

Leni nodded and climbed into the old International Harvester, with its ragtag cloth-covered seats. They drove down the bumpy driveway, past the newly skinned log poles. Out on the main road, rambling through a cloud of dust, Leni realized she was crying.

It felt overwhelming suddenly. The stakes were too high. What if Mama ran and Dad really did find her and kill her?

Large Marge pulled up in front of the school and parked. "It's not fair that you have to deal with this. But life ain't fair, kid. You know that, I guess. You could call the police."

"And if I get her killed? How's my life after that?"

Large Marge nodded. "You come to me if you need help. Okay? Promise?"

"Sure," Leni said dully.

Large Marge leaned toward Leni, popped open the creaky glove box, took out a thick envelope. "I have something for you."

Leni was used to Large Marge's gifts. A candy bar, a paperback novel, a shiny barrette. Large Marge often had something to press in Leni's palm at the end of the workday at the store.

Leni looked down at the envelope. It was from the University of Alaska. It had been mailed to Lenora Allbright, in care of Marge Birdsall at the Kaneq General Store.

Her hands were shaking as she tore it open and read the first line. *We are pleased to offer you . . .*

Leni looked at Large Marge. "I got in."

"Congratulations, Leni."

Leni felt numb. She'd been *accepted*.

To college.

"Now what?" Leni said.

"You go," Large Marge said. "I've talked to Tom. He's going to pay for it. Tica and I are buying your books and Thelma is giving you spending money. You're one of us and we have your back. No excuses, kid. You leave this place the second you can. Run like hell, kid, and don't look back. But Leni—"

"Yeah?"

"You be careful as hell until the day you leave."

❖❖❦〈❀〉❦❖❖

ON THE LAST DAY OF SCHOOL, Leni thought her heart might explode. Maybe she would pitch face-first into the ground and be another Alaskan statistic. The girl who died for love.

The idea of summer, all those long hot days spent working from sunup to sundown, made her insane to contemplate. How could she last until September without seeing Matthew?

"We will hardly see each other," she said, feeling sick. "We'll both be working constantly. You know how summer is." From now on, life would be chores.

Summer. The season of salmon runs and gardens that needed constant tending, of berries ripening on hillsides, of canning fruits and vegetables and fish, of salmon that needed to be cut into strips, marinated, and smoked, of repairs that needed to be made while the sun shone.

"We'll sneak out," he said.

Leni couldn't imagine taking that risk now. The banishment from the Harlans had broken the last thread of her father's control. He cut trees and skinned logs daily and woke in the middle of the night to pace. He muttered under his breath constantly and hammered, hammered, hammered on his wall.

"We're going to college together in September," Matthew said (because he knew how to dream and to believe).

"Yeah," she said, wanting it more than she had ever wanted anything. "We'll be normal kids in Anchorage." It was what they said to each other all the time.

Leni walked beside him to the door, mumbled goodbye to Ms. Rhodes, who gave her a fierce hug and said, "Don't forget the graduation party at the saloon tonight. You and Mattie are the guests of honor."

"Thanks, Ms. Rhodes."

Outside, Leni's parents were waiting for her, holding a sign that read HAPPY GRAD DAY! She stumbled to a stop.

Leni felt Matthew's hand at the small of her back. She was pretty sure he gave her a push. She moved forward, forcing a smile.

"Hey, guys," she said as her parents rushed at her. "You didn't have to do this."

Mama beamed at her. "Are you kidding? You graduated at the top of your class."

"A class of two," she pointed out.

Dad put an arm around her, drew her close. "I've never been number one at anything, Red. I'm proud of you. And now you can leave that pissant school behind. Sayonara, bullshit."

They packed into the truck and headed out. Overhead, a plane flew low, making a dull *putt-putt-putt* sound.

"Tourists." Dad said the word as if it were a curse, loud enough that people heard. Then he smiled. "Mom made your favorite cake and strawberry *akutaq*."

Leni nodded, too depressed to force a fake smile.

Down the street, a banner hung across the half-finished saloon. CONGRATULATIONS LENI AND MATTHEW!!! GRAD PARTY FRIDAY NIGHT! 9 P.M. FIRST DRINK FREE!

"Leni, baby girl? You look sad as a lost dollar."

"I want to go to the graduation party at the saloon," Leni said.

Mama leaned forward to look at Dad. "Ernt?"

"You want me to walk into Tom Walker's damn saloon and see all the people who are ruining this town?" Dad said.

"For Leni," Mama said.

"No way, José."

Leni tried to see past his anger to the man Mama claimed he used to be, before Vietnam had changed him and Alaska's winters had revealed his own darkness. She tried to remember being Red, his girl, the one who'd ridden his shoulders on The Strand in Hermosa Beach. "Please, Dad. *Please.* I want to celebrate graduating from high school in my town. The town you brought me to."

When Dad looked at her, Leni saw what she saw so rarely in his eyes: love. Tattered, tired, shaved small by bad choices, but love just the same. And regret.

"Sorry, Red. I can't do it. Not even for you."

NINETEEN

———————⇒⟫⟩⊕⟨⟪⟸———————

E vening.

The sound of a chain saw whirring, sputtering, going silent.

Leni stood at the window staring out at the yard. It was seven o'clock: the dinner hour, a break in this season's long workday. Any minute now, Dad would come back into the cabin, bringing tension in with him. The remnants of Leni's three-person graduation party—carrot cake and strawberry *akutaq*, a kind of ice cream made from snow and Crisco and fruit— lay on the table.

"I'm sorry," Mama said, coming up to stand beside her. "I know how badly you wanted to go to the party. I'm sure you considered sneaking out. I would have at your age."

Leni scooped out a spoonful of *akutaq*. Usually, she loved it. Not tonight. "I planned a dozen ways to do it."

"And?"

"They all end the same way: with you alone in a room full of his fists."

Mama lit a cigarette, exhaled smoke. "This . . . wall of his. He's not giving up on it. We're going to have to be more careful."

"More careful?" Leni turned to her. "We think about every single thing we say. We disappear in an instant. We pretend we don't need anything or anyone except him and this place. And none of it is enough, Mama. We can't be good enough to keep him from losing it."

Leni saw how difficult this conversation was for her mother; she wished she could do what she'd always done. Pretend it would get better, that he'd get better, pretend it hadn't been on purpose or it wouldn't happen again. Pretend.

But things were different now.

"I got into the University of Alaska at Anchorage, Mama."

"Oh, my *God*, that's great!" Mama said. A smile lit up her face and then faded. "But we can't afford—"

"Tom Walker and Large Marge and Thelma and Ms. Rhodes are paying for it."

"Money isn't the only issue."

"No," Leni said, not looking away. "It's not."

"We will have to plan this carefully," Mama said. "Your dad can never know Tom is paying. Never."

"It doesn't matter. Dad won't let me go. You know he won't."

"Yes, he will," Mama said in a firmer voice than Leni had heard from her in years. "I'll make him."

Leni cast out the dream, let the hook of it sail over blue, blue water and splash down. College. Matthew. A new life.

Yeah. Right. "You'll make him," she said dully.

"I can see why you have no faith in me."

Leni's hold on resentment lessened. "That's not it, Mama. How can I leave you here alone with him?"

Mama gave her a sad, tired smile. "There will be no talk of that. None. You're the chick. I'm the mama bird. Either you take flight on your own or I shove you out of the nest. It's your choice. Either way, you're going off to college with your boy."

"You think it's possible?" Leni let the amorphous dream turn solid enough that she could hold it in her hands, look at it from different angles.

"When do classes start?"

"Right after Labor Day."

Mama nodded. "Okay. You're going to have to be careful. Smart. Don't risk everything for a kiss. That's the kind of thing I would have done. Here's what we'll do: You stay away from Matthew and the Walkers until September. I will squirrel away enough money to buy you a bus ticket to Anchorage. We'll fill your bug-out bag with what you need. Then, one day, I'll arrange for a trip to Homer for all of us. You'll say you have to use the bathroom and slip away. Later, when Dad calms down, I'll find a note you left, saying that you've gone to college—without saying where—and you'll promise to be back on the homestead for summer. It will work. You'll see. If we're careful, it will work."

Don't see Matthew until September.

Yes. That was what she would need to do.

But could she do it, really? Her love for Matthew was elemental, as powerful as the tide. No one could hold back the tide.

It reminded her of that movie she'd watched with Mama a lifetime ago. *Splendor in the Grass.* In it, Natalie Wood had loved Warren Beatty in that overwhelming way, but she lost him and ended up in a loony bin. When she got out, he was married, with a kid, but you knew neither one of them would love anyone else in that way again.

Mama had cried and cried.

Leni hadn't understood then. Now she did. She saw how love could be dangerous and beyond control. Ravenous. Leni had it in her to love the way her mother did. She knew that now.

"Seriously, Leni," Mama said, looking worried. "You will need to be smart."

⊹⟨❀⟩⊹

In June, Dad worked on his wall every day. By the end of the month, the skinned log stanchions were all in place; they stuck up from the ground every ten feet along the property line, an elliptical boundary between their land and the main road.

Leni tried to submerge her longing for Matthew, but it was buoyant, prone to bobbing up. Sometimes, when she was supposed to be working, she stopped and pulled the secret necklace out of her hip pocket and held it so tightly the sharp point drew blood. She made lists in her head of things she wanted to say to him, had whole conversations by herself, over and over. At night she read paperback novels that she'd found in the FREE box at the General Store. One after another. *Devil's Desire*, *The Flame and the Flower*, *Moonstruck Madness*: historical romances about women who had to fight for love and ultimately were saved by it.

She knew the difference between fact and fiction, but she couldn't abandon her love stories. They made her feel as if women could be in control of their destinies. Even in a cruel, dark world that tested women to the very limits of their endurance, the heroines of these novels could prevail and find true love. They gave Leni hope and a way to fill the lonely hours of the night.

During the endless daylight hours, she worked: she tended to the garden, carried trash to the oil drum and burned it to ash, which she used to fertilize the garden and make soap and block pests from the vegetable beds. She hauled water and repaired crab pots and untangled skeins of fishing nets. She fed the animals and gathered eggs and fixed fencing and smoked the fish they caught.

All the while she thought: *Matthew*. His name became a mantra.

Over and over, she thought: *September isn't that far away.*

But as June passed into July, with Leni and Mama trapped on the homestead behind the wall her father was building, Leni started to lose her grasp on common sense. On the Fourth of July, she knew the town was celebrating on Main Street and she longed to be there.

Night after night, week after week, she lay in her bed, missing Matthew. Her love for him—a warrior, hiking mountains, crossing streams—strode into the wild borderlands of obsession.

Near the end of July, she began to have negative fantasies—him finding someone else, falling in love, deciding Leni was too much trouble. She ached for his touch, dreamed of his kiss, talked to herself in his voice. She began to get a vague, discomforting feeling that her endless yearning had combined with fear to taint her, that her breath had killed the tomatoes that never turned red, that tiny beads of her sweat had soured the blueberry jam, and next winter, when they ate all this food she had touched, her parents would wonder what had gone so wrong.

By August, she was a wreck. The wall was almost finished. The entire property line along the main road, from cliff to cliff, was a wall of freshly cut planks. Only a ten-foot-wide opening across the driveway allowed them to go in or out.

But the wall hardly concerned Leni. She had lost five pounds and was barely sleeping. Every night she woke at three or four and went out to stand on the deck, thinking, *He's there . . .*

Twice, she'd put on her boots; once she'd made it as far as the end of their driveway before turning back.

She had Mama's safety to consider, and Matthew's.

Labor Day was less than a month away.

She should just wait to see Matthew in Anchorage, when time would be on their side.

That was the smart move. But she wasn't smart in love.

She had to see him again, make sure he still loved her.

When did it become more than a longing? When did it solidify into a plan?

I need to see him.

Be with him.

Don't do it, the old Leni said, the girl shaped by Dad's violence and her mother's fear.

Just once, came the answer from the Leni reformed by passion.

Just once.

But how?

✦⟨✲⟩✦

In early August, during the eighteen-hour days, stocking up on food for the winter was paramount. They harvested the garden and canned vegetables; picked berries and made jam; fished in the ocean and the rivers and the bay. They smoked salmon and trout and halibut.

Today they'd woken early and spent all day on the river catching salmon. Fishing was serious business and no one bothered to talk much. Afterward, they hauled their catch home and got started on preserving the meat. Another in a string of long, exhausting days.

They finally took a break for dinner and went into the cabin. At the table, Mama set down a dinner of salmon pot pie and green beans cooked in bacon fat. She smiled at Leni, trying to pretend everything was okay. "Leni, I bet you're excited for moose season to start."

"Yeah," she said. Her voice was shaky. All she could think about anymore was Matthew. Missing him made her physically ill.

Dad poked his fork through the flaky crust, looking for fish. "Cora, we're going to Sterling on Saturday. There's a snow machine for sale, and ours is going to shit. And I need some hinges for the gate. Leni, you'll need to stay here and take care of the critters."

Leni almost dropped her fork. Did he mean it?

Sterling was at least an hour and a half away by road, and if Dad wanted to bring home a snow machine, he'd need to drive his truck, which meant the ferry, which was a half an hour ride each way. From here to Sterling and back would take all day.

Dad went back to picking through his pot pie. When his fish was all gone, he went through looking for potatoes, then carrots, and finally peas.

Mama looked at Leni. "I don't think it's a good idea, Ernt. Let's all go. I don't like the idea of Leni home alone."

Leni felt suspended on the silence while Dad dragged a piece of bread across his plate. "It's uncomfortable for all three of us to be crammed into the truck for so long. She's fine."

❄

SATURDAY FINALLY ARRIVED.

"Okay, Leni," Dad said in his sternest voice. "It's summer. You know what that means. Black bears. The guns are loaded. Keep the door locked if you're inside. When you go for water, make lots of noise, take your bear whistle. We should be home by five, but if we're late, I want you in the cabin with the door locked by eight. I don't care how light it is outside. No fishing from the shore. Okay?"

"Dad, I'm almost eighteen. I know all that."

"Yeah. Yeah. Eighteen only sounds old to you. Humor me."

"I won't leave the property and I'll lock the door," Leni promised.

"Good girl." Dad grabbed a box full of pelts that he would sell to the furrier in Sterling and headed for the door.

When he was gone, Mama said, "Please, Leni. Don't screw up. You're so close to leaving for college. Just a few weeks." She sighed. "You are not listening."

"I am listening. I won't do anything stupid," Leni lied.

Outside, the truck horn honked.

Leni hugged her mother and literally shoved her toward the door.

Leni watched them drive away.

Then she waited, counted down the minutes until the ferry's departure time.

Precisely forty-seven minutes after they left, she jumped onto her bicycle and pedaled down the bumpy driveway, through the opening in the plank wall and onto the main road. She turned onto the Walker's road. She came to a thumping stop in front of the two-story log house and stepped off her bike, glancing around. No one would be inside on a day like this, not with so many chores to do. She saw Mr. Walker off to the left, near the trees, driving a bulldozer, moving piles of dirt around.

Leni dropped her bike in the grass and walked over the grassy berm and stared down the wide, weathered gray steps that led to the pebbled beach. Broken mussel shells lay scattered across the kelp and mud and rocks.

Matthew stood in the shallow water at a sloping metal table, filleting big silver and red salmon, pulling sacs of bright orange eggs out, carefully laying them out to dry. Seagulls cawed overhead, swooping and flapping, waiting for scraps. Guts floated in the water, brushed up against his boots.

"Matthew!" she yelled down at him.

He looked up.

"My parents are on the ferry. Going to Sterling. Can you come over? We have all day together."

He put down his *ulu*. "Holy shit! I'll be there in thirty minutes."

Leni went back to her bike and jumped on.

At the homestead, she fed and watered the animals and then ran around like a madwoman, trying to get ready for her first real date. She packed a picnic basket full of food and brushed her teeth—*again*—and shaved her legs and dressed in a pretty, off-white Gunne Sax dress Mama had given her for her seventeenth birthday. She twined her waist-length hair into a single wrist-thick braid and tied the end with a piece of grosgrain ribbon. Her stretched-out gray wool socks and wafflestompers kind of ruined the romantic effect, but it was the best she could do.

Then she waited. Holding her picnic basket and blanket, she stood on the deck, tapping her foot. Off to her right, the goats and chickens seemed agitated. They were probably sensing her nervousness. Overhead, a sky that should have been cornflower blue darkened. Clouds rolled in, stretched out, dimmed the sun.

They were on the ferry now, pulling into Homer; they had to be. *Please don't let them come back for something.*

While she was staring down the shadowy driveway, she heard a distant motor whirring. Fishing boat. The sound was as common here in the summer as the drone of mosquitoes.

She ran to the edge of the property just as an aluminum fishing boat puttered into their cove. Nearing the beach, the motor clicked off and the boat glided soundlessly forward, beaching itself on the pebbled shore. Matthew stood at the console, waving.

She hurried down the stairs to the beach.

Matthew jumped down into the shallow water and came toward Leni, dragging the boat higher on the beach behind him, mesmerizing her with his smile, his confidence, the love in his eyes.

In an instant, a glance, the tension that had held her in its maw for months released. She felt giddy, young. In love.

"We have until five," she said.

He swept her off her feet and kissed her.

Laughing at the sheer *joy* she felt, Leni took him by the hand and led him past the caves on the beach to an inland trail that led to a stub of forested land that overlooked the other side of the bay. Cliffs jutted out beneath them, defiant slabs of stone. Here, the ocean crashed against the rocky shore, sprayed up and landed like wet kisses on their skin.

She laid out the blanket she'd brought and set down the picnic basket.

"What did you bring?" Matthew asked, sitting down.

Leni knelt on the blanket. "Easy stuff. Halibut sandwiches, crab salad, some fresh beans, sugar cookies." She looked up, smiling. "This is my first date."

"Mine, too."

"We've lived weird lives," she said.

"Maybe everyone does," he said, sitting down beside her, and then lying down, pulling her into his arms. For the first time in months, she could breathe.

They kissed so long she lost track of time, of fear, of everything except the softness of his tongue against hers and the taste of him.

He loosened one pearl button on her dress, just enough to slip his hand inside. She felt his rough, work-callused fingers glide across her skin; goose bumps changed the feel of her flesh. She felt him touch her breasts, slip beneath the worn cotton of her bra to touch her nipple.

A crack of thunder.

For a second she was so sluggish with desire, she thought she'd imagined it.

Then the rain hit. Hard, fast, pelting.

They scrambled to their feet, laughing. Leni grabbed the picnic basket and together they ran along the winding beach trail, and emerged on the bluff by the outhouse.

They didn't stop until they were in the cabin, standing face-to-face, staring at each other. Leni felt raindrops sliding down her cheeks, dripping from her hair.

"Alaska in the summer," Matthew said.

Leni stared at him, realizing *now*, all at once in a sweep of goose bumps, *how* she loved him.

Not in the toxic, needy, desperate way her mother loved her father.

She needed Matthew, but not to save her or complete her or reinvent her.

Her love for him was the clearest, cleanest, strongest emotion she'd ever felt. It was like opening your eyes or growing up, realizing that you had it in you to love like this. Forever. For all time. Or for all the time you had.

She started to unbutton her wet dress. The lacy collar fell down her shoulder, exposed her bra strap.

"Leni, are you sure—"

She silenced him with a kiss. She had never been more sure of anything. She finished unbuttoning her dress, which fell down her body, landed like a parachute of lace at her booted feet. She stepped out of it, kicked it aside.

She unlaced her boots, pulled them off, threw them aside. One hit the cabin wall with a thunk. Down to her bra and cotton panties, she said, "Come on," and led him up the loft ladder to her bedroom, where Matthew hurriedly undressed and pulled her down onto the fur-covered mattress.

He undressed her slowly. His hands and mouth explored her body until every nerve in her tightened. When he touched her: music.

She lost herself in him. Her body was autonomous, moving in some instinctive, primal rhythm it must have known all along, edging into a pleasure so intense it was almost pain.

She was a star, burning so brightly it broke apart, pieces flying, light spraying. Afterward, she fell back to earth a different girl, or a different version of herself. It scared her even as it exhilarated her. Would anything else in her life ever change her so profoundly? And now that she had had this, had him, how was she supposed to leave him? Ever?

"I love you," he said quietly.

"I love you, too."

The word felt too small, too ordinary to contain all of this emotion.

She lay against him staring up at the skylight, watching rain boil across the glass. She knew she would remember this day all of her life.

"What do you think college will be like?" she asked.

"Like you and me. Like this all the time. Are you ready to go?"

Truthfully, she was afraid that when it was time to actually go, she wouldn't be able to leave her mother. But if Leni stayed, if she gave up this dream, she would never recover. She couldn't look that harsh future in the eyes.

Here, in his arms, with the magical possibility of *time* between them, she didn't want to say anything at all. She didn't want words to turn into walls that separated them.

"Do you want to talk about your dad?" he asked.

Leni instinctively wanted to say no, to do what she'd always done: keep the secret. But what kind of love was that? "The war screwed him up, I guess."

"And now he hits you?"

"Not me. My mom."

"You and your mom need to get out of here, Len. I've heard my dad and Large Marge talking about it. They want to help you guys but your mom won't let them."

"It's not as easy as people think," Leni said.

"If he loved you guys, he wouldn't hurt you."

He made it sound so simple, as if it were a mathematical equation. But the connection between pain and love wasn't linear. It was a web. "What's it like?" she asked. "To feel safe?"

He touched her hair. "Do you feel it now?"

She did. Maybe for the first time, but that was crazy. The last place Leni was safe was here, in the arms of a boy her dad hated. "He hates you, Matthew, and he doesn't even know you."

"I won't let him hurt you."

"Let's talk about something else."

"Like . . . how I think about you all of the time? It makes me feel crazy, how much I think about you." He pulled her in for a kiss. They made out forever, time slowing down just for them; tasting each other, taking each other in. Sometimes they talked, whispered secrets or made jokes, or stopped talking altogether and just kissed. Leni learned the magic of knowing someone else through touch.

Her body wakened again in his arms, but lovemaking was different the second time. Words had changed it somehow, real life had pushed its way in.

She was scared that this was all they would ever have. Just this day. Scared that she'd never get to go to college or that Dad would kill Mama in her absence. Scared even that this love she felt for Matthew wasn't real, or that it was real and flawed, that maybe she'd been so damaged by her parents that she couldn't know what love really was.

"No," she said to herself, to him, to the universe. "I love you, Matthew."

It was the only thing she knew for sure.

TWENTY

A hand clamped over Leni's mouth; a voice whispered harshly, "Len, wake up."

She opened her eyes.

"We fell asleep. Someone's here."

Leni gasped into Matthew's palm.

It had stopped raining. Sunlight poured through the skylight.

Outside, she heard a truck engine, heard the rattle of the metal bed on the axle as the truck rolled over the ground.

"Oh, my God," Leni said. She scrambled over Matthew, snatched up some clothes and dressed quickly. She was almost to the railing when she heard the door open.

Dad walked in, stopped, looked down.

He was standing on the wet heap of her dress.

Shit.

She launched herself over the side of the railing and half climbed, half slid down the loft ladder.

Dad bent down for her soggy dress, lifted it up. Water dripped from the eyelet hem.

"I—I got caught in that squall," Leni said. Her heartbeat was so hard, she was breathless. Dizzy. She glanced around for anything that might give them away and saw Matthew's boots.

She let out a little cry.

The rack to Dad's left was full of guns, the shelf beneath them layered with boxes of ammunition. He barely had to turn, reach out, and he'd be armed.

Leni rushed over and grabbed her soaking-wet dress.

Mama frowned. Her gaze followed Leni's, landed on the boots. Her eyes widened. She looked at Leni and then at the loft. Her face went pale.

"Why did you wear your good dress?" Dad asked.

"G-girls are funny that way, Ernt," Mama said, sidling sideways, blocking Dad's view of the boots.

Dad looked around; his nostrils flared. Leni was reminded of a predator on the scent. "Something smells different in here."

Leni hung her dress up on a hook by the door. "It's the picnic I packed for us," Leni said. "I—I wanted to surprise you."

Dad walked over to the table, flipped open the picnic basket, looked inside. "There are only two plates."

"I got hungry and ate mine. That's for you guys. I—I thought you'd enjoy it after the haul to Sterling."

A creak from upstairs.

Dad frowned, stared up at the loft, headed toward the ladder.

Sit still, Matthew.

Dad touched the loft ladder, looked up. Frowned. Leni saw him lift a foot, place it on the bottom rung.

Mama bent down, picked up Matthew's boots, and dropped them in the big cardboard boot box by the door. She did it in a gliding, single motion, and then slipped in beside Dad. She said, "Let's show Leni the snow machine," loud enough for Matthew to hear. "It's parked out over by the goat pen."

Dad let go of the loft ladder and turned to them. There was a strange look in his eyes. Did he suspect? "Sure. Come on."

Leni followed her dad to the door. When he opened it, she glanced back, looked up at the loft.

Go, Matthew, she thought. *Run.*

Mama held Leni's hand tightly as they walked across the deck and down into the grass, as if she feared Leni might turn and run.

In the cove, Matthew's aluminum boat captured the sunlight, glittered silver against the shore. The sudden squall had scrubbed the landscape, left everything shiny. Light glinted off a million drops of water, on blades of grass and wildflowers.

Leni said something quickly—she didn't even know what, just something to make her dad turn to her and away from the beach.

"There she is," he said when they came to the rusted trailer hitched to the truck. A dented snow machine sat there, its seat a torn-up mess, missing its headlight. "Duct tape will fix that seat so it's practically new."

Leni thought she heard the cabin door click open and the creak of a footfall on the deck.

"It's *great*!" she yelled. "We can use it for ice fishing and caribou hunting. It'll come in handy to have two snow machines."

She heard the distinct whine of an outboard motor starting up and the *scree* of it winding up for speed.

Dad pushed Leni aside. "Is that a boat in our cove?"

Below, the aluminum skiff was planed high, pointed bow lifted proudly out of the water, speeding for the point.

Leni held her breath. There was no doubt it was Matthew, his blond hair, his brand-new boat. Would Dad recognize him?

"Damn tourists," Dad said at last, turning away. "Those rich college kids think they own this state in the summer. I'm putting up NO TRESPASSING signs."

They'd done it. Gotten away with it. *We did it, Matthew.*

"Leni."

Her mama's voice. Sharp. She sounded angry, or maybe scared.

Mama and Dad were both staring at her.

"What?" Leni said.

"Your dad was talking to you," Mama said.

Leni smiled easily. "Oops. Sorry."

Dad said, "I guess you were woolgathering, as my old man used to say."

Leni shrugged. "Just thinking."

"About what?"

Leni heard the tone change in his voice, and it concerned her. She saw now how intently he was staring at her. Maybe they hadn't gotten away with it after all. Maybe he knew . . . maybe he was toying with her.

"Oh, you know teenagers," Mama said, her voice fluttery.

"I am asking Leni, not you, Cora."

"I was thinking it would be fun to go out, spend the day together. Maybe try our luck at Pedersen's Resort on the Kenai. We've always had good luck there."

"Good thought." Dad stepped back from the new snow machine, glanced down the driveway. "Well. It's summer. I have work to do."

He left them standing there alone, went to the toolshed, and retrieved his chain saw. Hefting it over his shoulder, he headed toward the driveway and disappeared into the trees.

Mama and Leni stood there, barely breathing, until they heard the chain saw whir to life.

Mama turned to Leni, whispered harshly, "Stupid, stupid, stupid. You could have gotten caught."

"We fell asleep."

"Fatal mistakes often look ordinary. Come," Mama said, leading her into the cabin. "Sit by the fire. I'll comb your hair. It's a mess. You're lucky he's not one to notice a thing like that."

Leni grabbed a three-legged stool and dragged it over to the woodstove. She sat down on it, hooking her bare feet on the bottom rung, unbraiding her hair as she waited.

Mama pulled a wide-toothed comb from the blue coffee can on her makeshift vanity and slowly began combing the tangles out of Leni's waist-length hair. Then she massaged Leni's scalp with oil and smoothed some of the fragrant balm-of-Gilead rub they made from the buds onto Leni's rough hands. "You think you got away with it this time and so you want to see Matthew again. That's what you were really thinking, right?"

Of course Mama knew.

"I'll be smarter next time," Leni said.

"There won't be a next time, Leni." Mama took Leni by the shoulders, turned her around on the stool. "You will wait until college, like we talked about. We will do as we planned. In September, you'll see Matthew in Anchorage and start your life."

"I'll die if I don't see him."

"No. You won't. Please, Leni, think about me instead of yourself."

Leni was ashamed of herself, embarrassed by her selfishness. "I'm sorry, Mama. You're right. I don't know what came over me."

"Sex changes everything," Mama said quietly.

◆―〈※〉―◆

A WEEK LATER, while Mama and Leni were eating oatmeal for breakfast, the cabin door opened. Dad strode inside, his dark hair and flannel shirt dusted with wood chips. "Come with me. Both of you. Hurry!"

Leni followed her parents out of the cabin and toward the driveway. Dad was walking fast, really covering ground. Mama stumbled along beside him, struggling to keep up on the spongy ground.

Leni heard her mother say, "Oh, my God," in a whisper, and Leni looked up.

The wall her dad had been building all summer was in front of them. Finished. Plank after plank of newly milled wood ran in a straight line, topped in coiled razor wire. It looked like something out of the Gulag.

But that wasn't the worst of it. Now there was a gate across the driveway; a length of heavy metal chain kept the gate closed. A metal lock hung from loops in the chain. Leni saw the key hanging from a chain around her father's throat.

Dad pulled Mama in close. He was smiling now. He leaned in, whispered something in Mama's ear, and kissed the small purple bruise at the base of her throat.

"Now it's just us, in here, cut off from the whole damn backstabbing world," he said. "We'll be safe now."

⊷⟨❀⟩⊶

FEAR, LENI LEARNED, was not the small, dark closet she'd always imagined: walls pressed in close, a ceiling you bumped your head on, a floor cold to the touch.

No.

Fear was a mansion, one room after another, connected by endless hall-ways.

In the days following the closing of the gate, with its rattling chain, Leni learned the feel of those rooms. At night, in her bed, she lay in the loft and tried not to sleep, because sleep brought on nightmares. The fear she battled during daylight besieged her at night. She dreamed of her death in a hun-dred ways—drowning, falling through ice, plummeting down a mountain-side, being shot in the head.

Metaphors, all of them. The death of every dream she'd ever had and those she'd yet to dream.

Dad hovered beside them all the time, talking as if nothing were wrong, in a good humor for the first time since his banishment from the Harlan place. He teased, he laughed, he worked alongside them. At night Leni lay listening to the sound of her parents' voices, of their lovemaking. Mama was good at pretending everything was normal. Leni had lost that childhood ability.

What she thought, over and over and over again, was: *We need to run.*

⊷⟨❀⟩⊶

"WE HAVE TO LEAVE HIM," Leni said on Saturday morning, a week to the day since he'd locked the gate shut. It was the first time Dad had left them alone together.

Mama paused, her hands softening on the pile of dough she was knead-ing. "He'll kill me," she whispered.

"Don't you get it, Mama? He's going to kill you in here. Sooner or later. Think about winter coming. The dark. The cold. And us in here, locked behind that wall. He's not going to work the pipeline this winter. It'll be just him and us in the dark. Who will stop him or help us?"

Mama glanced nervously at the door. "Where would we go?"

"Large Marge offered to help. So did the Walkers."

"Not Tom. That would make it worse."

"College starts in three and a half weeks, Mama. I have to leave as soon as I can. Will you go with me?"

"Maybe you should go without me."

Leni had known this was coming. She had wrestled with it and finally come to an answer. "I have to go, Mama. I can't live this way, but I need you. I'm afraid . . . I won't be able to leave you."

"Peas in a pod," Mama said, sounding sad. But she understood. They had always been together. "You need to go. I want you to go. I couldn't forgive myself if you didn't, so what's your plan?"

"The first chance we get, we run. Maybe he goes hunting and we take the boat. Whatever the opportunity is, we take it. If we're still here when the first leaf falls, it's all over."

"So we just run. With nothing."

"We run with our lives."

Mama glanced away. It was a long, long time before she nodded and said, "I'll try."

It was not the answer Leni wanted, but it was the best she was going to get. She only prayed that when the opportunity for escape arose, Mama would go with her.

◆⟨❁⟩◆

THE WEATHER BEGAN to change. Here and there, bright green leaves turned golden, tangerine, scarlet. Birch trees that had been invisible all year, lost amid the other trees, appeared boldly in the forefront, their bark white as the wings of a dove, their leaves like a million candle flames.

With every leaf that changed color, Leni's tension increased. It was nearing the end of August now—early for autumn to arrive, but Alaska was capricious that way.

Although she and Mama had never spoken of their escape plan again, it lived in the air between sentences. Every time Dad left the cabin they looked at each other, and in that look, a question. *Is this the time?*

Today Leni and her mother were making blueberry syrup when Dad came in from outside. He was dirty and sweaty, with a fine layer of black dust on his damp face. For the first time, Leni noticed gray strands in his beard. He wore his hair in a low, haphazard ponytail and had tied a bicentennial bandanna across his forehead. He came forward, his rubber boots clomping on the plywood floor. He went into the kitchen, saw what Mama was making for dinner. "Again?" he said, peering down at the salmon croquettes. "No vegetables?"

"I'm conserving. We're out of flour and low on rice. I've told you that," Mama said wearily. "If you'd let me go to town . . ."

"You should go to Homer, Dad. Stock up for winter," Leni said, hoping she sounded casual.

"I don't think it's safe to leave you two here alone."

"The wall keeps us safe," Leni said.

"Not completely. At high tide someone could come in by boat," Dad said. "Who knows what could happen when I'm gone? Maybe we all should go. Get what we need from that bitch in town."

Mama looked at Leni.

This is it, Leni's gaze said.

Mama shook her head. Her eyes widened. Leni understood her mother's fear; they had talked about the both of them sneaking away while he was gone, not running away while he was with them. But the weather was changing; the nights were growing cold, which meant that winter was approaching. Classes at U of A started in less than a week. This was their chance to run. If they planned it right—

"Let's go," Dad said. "Right now." He clapped his hands. At the sharp sound, Mama flinched.

Leni glanced longingly at her bug-out bag, full—always—of everything she needed to survive in the wild. She couldn't bring it without arousing suspicion.

They would have to make their escape with nothing except the clothes they were wearing.

Dad grabbed a shotgun from the rack by the door and held it over his shoulder.

Was it a warning?

"Let's go."

Leni went to her mother, placed a hand on her thin wrist, felt how she was trembling. "Come on, Mama," Leni said evenly.

They walked to the cabin door. Leni couldn't help stopping, turning back just for a second to stare at the cabin's warm, cozy interior. For all the pain and heartache and fear, this was the only real home she'd ever known.

She hoped she would never see it again. How sad that her hope felt like loss.

In the truck, seated between her parents on the ragged bench seat, Leni could sense her mother's fear; it gave off a sour smell. Leni wanted to reassure her, say it would be okay, that they'd escape and move to Anchorage and everything would be fine, but she just sat there, breathing shallowly, holding on, hoping that when the time came to run they would make their feet move.

Dad started up the truck and drove out to the gate.

There he stopped, got out, left his door open, and went to the gate, grabbing the lock. He removed the key from around his neck and fit it into the lock, giving it a hard turn.

"This is it," Leni said to her mother. "In town, we are going to run. The ferry docks in forty minutes. We'll find a way to be on it."

"It won't work. He'll catch us."

"Then we'll go to Large Marge. She'll help us."

"You'd risk her life, too?"

The huge metal lock clanked open. Dad pushed the gate open, over the bumpy muskeg, until the main road was visible again.

"We might only get one chance," Mama said, chewing worriedly on her lower lip. "It better be the right one or we wait."

Leni knew it was good advice, but she didn't know if she could wait anymore. Now that she'd allowed herself to actually *think* about freedom, the idea of returning to captivity seemed impossible. "We can't wait, Mama. The leaves are falling. Winter could come early this year."

Dad climbed into the cab and shut the door. They drove forward. When they'd passed through the gate, Leni twisted around in her seat, stared through the guns in the gun rack. Words in black had been spray-painted across the newly cut wood.

STAY OUT. NO TRESPASSING. VIOLATERS WILL BE SHOT.

She made a mental note of the fact that he hadn't closed the gate behind them. They turned onto the main road and rumbled past the arch at the entrance to Walker land, past Marge Birdsall's driveway.

Just past the airstrip, new gravel had been laid down, crunching beneath their tires. Up ahead was the newly painted wooden bridge, where a few people dressed in colorful rain jackets stood at the rail, staring down at the river, pointing at the bright red salmon swimming through the clear water, on their way to spawn and die.

Dad rolled down his window, yelled, "Go back to California," as they rumbled past, spitting black smoke at them.

In town, a barricade ran down the middle of Main Street—a collection of sawhorses and white buckets and orange cones kept tourists away from the backhoe that was digging a trench in front of the diner. Behind it, running the length of the street, was a yawning scar of cut-up earth, with dirt piled alongside.

Dad stomped on the brake so hard the old truck came to a skidding stop in the tall grass on the side of the road. From here, they could see the backhoe operator: Tom Walker.

Dad wrenched the truck into park and shut off the engine. Slamming his body into the reluctant door, he jumped out of the truck and slammed the door shut behind him. Just as Leni said, "Stay with me, Mama, hold my hand," Dad appeared at the passenger door, opened it, and grabbed Mama's wrist and pulled her out of the truck.

Mama looked back, wild-eyed, *Go*, she mouthed. Dad yanked on Mama's wrist, made her stumble forward to keep up with him.

"Shit," Leni said.

She saw her parents making their way through the few tourists that were here on this bright late August day, her dad elbowing his way harder than he needed to, pushing people aside.

Leni couldn't help herself; she sidled out of the truck and followed them. Maybe there was still a way to get Mama away from him. They didn't need long, just enough time to disappear. Hell, they'd steal a boat if they had to. Maybe this was the distraction they needed.

"Walker!" Dad shouted.

Mr. Walker shut the backhoe down and pushed the trucker's cap back from his sweaty forehead. "Ernt Allbright," he said. "What a pleasant surprise."

"What in the *hell* are you doing?"

"Digging a trench."

"Why?"

"Electricity for town. I'm putting in a generator."

"What?"

Mr. Walker said it again, pronouncing *e-lec-tri-city* with care, as if speaking to someone who barely understood English.

"What if we don't *want* electricity in Kaneq?"

"I bought easements from every business in town, Ernt. Paid cash money," Mr. Walker said. "From people who want lights and refrigerators and heat in the winter. Oh, and streetlamps. Won't that be great?"

"I won't let you."

"What are you going to do? Spray-paint again? I wouldn't recommend it. I won't be so forgiving a second time."

Leni came up behind Mama, grabbed her sleeve, tried to pull her away while Dad was fixated on something else.

"Leni!"

Matthew's voice rang out. He was standing in front of the saloon, holding a big cardboard box.

"Help us," she screamed.

Dad grabbed Leni by the bicep and pulled her against him. "You think you need help? What for?"

She shook her head, croaked, "Nothing. I didn't mean it." She glanced at Matthew, who had put down the box and was coming toward them, stepping down from the boardwalk.

"You'd better tell that boy to stop walking, or so help me God . . ." Dad put a hand on the knife at his waist.

"I'm fine," she yelled to Matthew, but she could see that he didn't believe her. He saw that she was crying. "S-stay there. Tell your dad we're okay."

Matthew said her name. She saw it form on his lips, but couldn't hear it.

Dad tightened his grip on Leni's upper arm until it felt like pliers clamping down. He guided Leni and Mama back to the truck, shoved them inside, slammed the door shut behind them.

It took less than two minutes: all of it. The arrival in town, the scene, the shouted plea to *help us*, and the return to the truck.

All the way home, Dad muttered under his breath. The only words she got were *liar* and *Walker*.

Mama held Leni's hand as they bounced over the rutted road and turned onto their land. Leni tried to think of a way to calm her dad down. What had made her cry out like that? She knew better than to ask for help.

Love and fear.

The most destructive forces on earth. Fear had turned her inside out, love had made her stupid.

Dad drove through the open gate, still muttering to himself. Leni thought: *When he gets out to close the gate, I'll grab the wheel and put the truck in reverse and stomp on the gas*, but he left the gate open behind him.

Open. They could run in the middle of the night . . .

In the clearing, he threw the gearshift into park and killed the engine, then grabbed Leni and pulled her across the grass and up the steps and across the deck. He shoved her into the cabin so hard she stumbled and fell.

Mama came up behind him, moving cautiously, her face studiously calm. How she could pull that off, Leni didn't know. "Ernt, you're overreacting. Please. Let's talk about this." She laid a hand on his shoulder.

"Do you think you need help, Cora?" he said in a strangely taut voice.

"She's young. She didn't mean anything by it."

Leni saw the violence of his breathing, the way his fingers spasmed. He was on the balls of his feet, energy pouring out of him, anger transforming him. "You're lying to me," he said.

Mama shook her head. "No. I'm not. I don't even know what you mean."

"It's always the Walkers," he muttered.

"Ernt, this is crazy—"

He hit her so hard she slammed into the wall. Before Mama could get to her feet, he was on her again, yanking her hair back, exposing the pale skin of her throat. Wrapping his hand in her hair, he smashed his fist down, cracked the side of her head on the floor.

Leni hurled herself at her father, landed on his back. She clawed at him, pulled his hair, screamed, "Let her go!"

He wrenched free, cracked Mama's forehead into the floor.

Leni heard the door open behind her; seconds later she was yanked off her dad. She got a glimpse of Matthew, saw him pull Dad off Mama, spin him around, and punch him in the jaw so hard Dad staggered sideways and crumpled to his knees.

Leni ran to her mother, helped her to her feet. "We need to go. Now."

"You go," Mama said, looking nervously toward Dad, who moaned in pain. "Go." Her face was bloodied, her lip torn.

"I'm not leaving you," Leni said.

Tears filled Mama's eyes and fell, mixing with the blood. "He'll never let me go. You go. *Go.*"

"No," Leni said. "I'm not leaving you."

"She's right, Mrs. Allbright," Matthew said. "You can't stay here."

Mama sighed. "Fine. I'll go to Large Marge's. She'll protect me, but Leni, I don't want you anywhere near me. You understand? If he comes after me, I don't want you there." She looked to Matthew. "I want her *gone* for at least twenty-four hours. Hidden someplace he can't find her. I'll go to the police this time. Press charges."

Matthew nodded solemnly. "I won't let anything happen to her, Mrs. Allbright. I promise."

Dad made a groaning sound, cursed, tried to get up.

Mama hefted up Leni's bug-out bag and handed her the pack. "*Now,* Leni. We need to run."

They ran out of the cabin and into the bright sunlit yard toward Matthew's truck. "Get in," he yelled, then raced over to Dad's truck. He opened the hood, did something to the engine.

Behind them, the cabin door cracked open. Dad staggered out.

Leni heard the cracking sound of a gun being cocked. "Cora, damn it." Dad was on the deck, bleeding profusely from his forehead, blinded by blood, holding a shotgun. "Where are you?"

"Get in!" Matthew yelled, throwing something into the trees. He jumped into the driver's seat and started his truck.

In a spray of shotgun pellets pinging loudly, Leni leaped onto the seat and Mama crammed in beside her. Matthew jammed the gearshift into drive and stomped on the gas. The truck fishtailed in the deep grass before the wheels grabbed hold. He sped down the driveway and through the open gate and turned onto the main road.

They turned again at Large Marge's driveway and drove to the end of it, honking the horn. "You keep her safe and away from me," Mama said to Matthew, who nodded.

Leni stared at her mother. The whole of their lives—and all of their love—was in that look. "You won't go back to him," Leni said. "You'll call the police. Press charges. We'll meet up in twenty-four hours. Then we'll run away. You promise?"

Mama nodded, hugged her fiercely, kissed her tears away. "Go," she said in a sharp voice.

After Mama got out of the truck, and they drove away, Leni sat there, replaying it all in her mind, crying quietly. Every breath hurt and she had to fight the urge to go back, to be with her mother. Had she done the wrong thing by leaving her?

Matthew turned at the Walker gate, rumbled beneath the welcoming arch.

"We can't go here! He'll look for us here!" Leni said. "Mama said we needed to disappear for a day."

He parked, got out. "I know. But it's low tide. We can't use the boats or the float plane. I only know one place to disappear. Stay here."

Five minutes later, Matthew was back with a backpack, which he tossed into the bed of the truck.

Leni kept looking behind them, down the Walker driveway.

"Don't worry. He won't find the distributor cap for a while," Matthew said.

And they were off again, turning onto the main road, then left, toward the mountain.

Turns. Switchbacks. River crossings. Up and up they went.

Finally, they pulled into a dirt parking lot and stopped abruptly. There were no other vehicles. A sign at the trailhead read:

BEAR CLAW WILDERNESS AREA
ALLOWABLE USES: Hiking, Camping, Rock Climbing.
DISTANCE: 2.8 miles one way.
DIFFICULTY: Challenging. Steep climbs.
ELEVATION GAIN: 2600 feet
CAMPING: Sawtooth Ridge, near marked Eagle Creek crossing.

Matthew helped Leni out of the truck. Kneeling, he checked her waffle-stompers, retied her laces. "You okay?"

"What if he—"

"She got away. Large Marge will protect her. And she wanted you safe."

"I know. Let's go," she said dully.

"We've got a long hike ahead of us. Can you make it?"

Leni nodded.

They headed for the trail, with Matthew leading and Leni following along behind him, struggling to keep up.

They climbed for hours, saw no one. The trail snaked along a sheer stone cliff. Below them was the sea, waves crashing into rocks. The ground trembled at each wave's impact, or maybe Leni just thought it did because life felt so unstable now. Even the ground felt unreliable.

Finally, Matthew came to what he'd been looking for: a huge, grassy field, thick with purple lupine. Snow whitened the peaks; below lay folds of rock, dotted here and there by the white dots that were Dall sheep.

He dropped his pack into the grass and turned to face Leni. He handed her a smoked salmon sandwich and a can of warm Coke, and while she ate he set up a pup tent deep in the grass.

Later, with a fire crackling in front of the tent and the orange flaps pinned open, Matthew sat on the grass beside her. He put an arm around her. She leaned into him.

"You don't have to be the only one protecting her, you know," he said. "We'll all take care of you. It's always been that way in Kaneq."

Leni wanted that to be true. She wanted to believe there was a safe place for her and Mama, a do-over of their lives, a beginning that didn't rise from the ashes of a violent, terrible ending. Mostly, she didn't want to feel solely responsible for her mama's safety anymore.

She turned to Matthew, loving him so much, so desperately, it felt like she was being held underwater and needed oxygen. "I love you."

"Me, too," he said.

Up here, in the vastness of Alaska, the words sounded infinitesimal and small. A fist shaken at the gods.

TWENTY-ONE

His job was to keep her safe.

Leni was his North Star. He knew it sounded stupid and girlie and romantic and that people would say he was too young to know these things, only he wasn't. When your mom died, you grew up.

He hadn't been able to protect his mom, to save her.

He was stronger now.

He held Leni in his arms all night last night, loved her, felt her twitch at bad dreams, listened to her sobs. He knew how that was, nightmares like that about your mom.

Finally, when the first glimmer of daylight pulsed through the pup tent's tangerine nylon sides, he eased away from her, smiling at the muffled sound of her snoring. He dressed in yesterday's clothes, put on his hiking boots, and stepped outside.

Gray clouds muscled across the sky, lowered over the trail. The breeze was more a sigh than anything else, but it was the end of August. The leaves were changing color at night. They both knew what that meant. Change came even faster up here.

Matthew busied himself building a fire on the black remnants of last night's blaze. Sitting on a rock, leaning forward, he stared into the wavering flames. The breeze kicked up, taunted the flames.

Now, sitting by the fire alone, he admitted to himself that he was afraid he'd done the wrong thing by bringing Leni here, afraid he'd done the wrong thing by leaving Cora in Kaneq. Afraid he'd turn around and see Ernt barreling up the trail with a rifle in one hand and a bottle of whiskey in the other.

Mostly he was afraid for Leni, because no matter how this all worked out, no matter if she did everything perfectly and got away and saved her mom, Leni's heart would always have a broken place. It didn't matter how you lost a parent or how great or shitty that parent was, a kid grieved forever. Matthew grieved for the mother he'd had. He figured Leni would grieve for the dad she wanted.

He settled a camp coffeepot in the fire, right in the flames.

Behind him, he heard rustling, the zipping sound of nylon being moved. Leni pushed back the flaps and stepped out into the morning. A raindrop splatted into her eye as she braided her hair.

"Hey," he said, offering her coffee. Another raindrop fell on the metal cup.

She took the cup in both hands, sat beside him, leaned against him. Another raindrop fell, pinged on the coffeepot, sizzled and turned to steam.

"Great timing," Leni said. "It's going to dump on us any second."

"There's a cave up at Glacier Ridge."

She looked up at him. "I can't stay away."

"But your mom said—"

"I'm scared," she said in a small voice.

He heard the spike of uncertainty in her voice, recognized that she was asking him something, not simply telling him that she was afraid.

He understood.

She didn't know what the right answer was and she was afraid to be wrong.

"You think I should go back for her?" she asked.

"I think you stand by the people you love."

He saw her relief. And her love.

"I might not be able to go to college. You know that, right? I mean, if we have to run, we'll have to go somewhere he won't look."

"I'll go with you," he said. "Wherever you go."

She drew in a breath, looked shaky enough that he thought she might collapse. "You know what I love most about you, Matthew?"

"What?"

She knelt in the wet grass in front of him, took his face in her cold hands, and kissed him. She tasted of coffee. "Everything."

After that, there didn't seem to be much to say. Matthew knew Leni was distracted, that she couldn't think about anything but her mom and that her eyes kept filling with tears as she brushed her teeth and rolled up her sleeping bag. He also knew how relieved she was to be going back.

He would save her.

He *would*. He'd find a way. He'd go to the police or the press or his dad. Hell, maybe he'd go to Ernt himself. Bullies were always cowards who could be made to back down.

It would work.

They'd separate Ernt from Leni and Cora and let them start a new life. Leni *could* go to college with Matthew. Maybe it wouldn't be in Anchorage. Maybe it wouldn't even be in Alaska, but who cared? All he wanted was to be with her.

Somewhere in the world they would find a fresh start.

They ate breakfast, packed up camp, and made it about fifty feet back down the trail before the storm hit for real. They were in a place so narrow they had to walk single file.

"Stay close," Matthew shouted above the driving rain and screeching wind. His jacket made a sound like cards being shuffled. Rain plastered his hair to his face, blinded him. He reached back, took Leni's hand. It slipped free.

Rain ran in rivulets over the trail, turned the rocks slippery. To their left, fireweed quivered and lay flattened, broken by wind and rain.

The trail darkened; mist rolled in, obscured everything. Matthew blinked, tried to see.

Rain hammered his nylon hood. His face was wet, rain running down his cheeks, burrowing beneath his collar, beading his eyelashes.

He heard something.

A scream.

He spun around. Leni wasn't behind him. He started back, shouting her name. A tree limb smacked him in the face. Hard. Then he saw her. She was about twenty feet away, off the trail, too far to the right. He saw her make a mistake. She slipped, started to fall.

She screamed, fought for balance, tried to right herself, reaching for something—anything.

There was nothing.

"Le—ni!" he yelled.

She fell.

⁕⊰⟨۞⟩⊱⁕

PAIN.

Leni woke in a stinking darkness, sprawled in the mud, unable to move without pain. She heard the *drip-drip-drip* of water. Rain falling on rock. The air smelled fetid, of dead things and decay.

Something in her chest was broken, a rib, maybe; she was pretty sure. And maybe her left arm. It was either broken or her shoulder was dislocated.

She was on her backpack, splayed above it. Maybe it had saved her life.

Ironic.

She peeled the bug-out bag's straps away from her shoulders, ignoring the seizing, scalding pain that came with the smallest movement. It took forever to free herself; when she did it, she lay there, arms and legs sprawled out, panting, sick to her stomach.

Move, Leni.

She gritted her teeth and rolled sideways, plopped into a deep and slimy mud.

Breathing hard, hurting, trying not to cry, she lifted her head, looked around.

Darkness.

It smelled bad down here, of rot and mold. The ground was deep mud and the walls were slick wet rock. How long had she been unconscious?

She crawled slowly forward, holding her broken arm close to her body. She made her slow, agonizing way to a slice of light that illuminated a slab of stone carved by time and water into a saucer shape.

It hurt so much she puked, but kept going.

She heard her name being yelled.

She crawled onto the concave stone slab, looked up. Rain blinded her.

Way up above her, she saw the blurry red of Matthew's jacket. "Le . . . nn . . . ii!"

"I'm here!" She tried to scream the words, but the pain in her chest made it impossible. She waved her good arm but knew he couldn't see her. The opening in the crevice above her head was slim, no wider than a bathtub. Through it, rain fell hard, its percussive sound a roar of noise in the dark cave. "Go for help," she yelled as best she could.

Matthew leaned over the sheer edge, trying to reach down for a tree that grew stubbornly from the rock.

He was going to come for her.

"*No!*" she shouted.

He eased one leg over the rock ledge, inched downward, looking for someplace to put his foot. He paused, maybe reassessing.

That's right. Stop. It's too dangerous. Leni wiped her eyes, trying to focus in the downpour.

He found a foothold and climbed over the ledge and hung there, suspended on the rock wall.

He stayed there a long time, a red and blue *X* on the gray stone wall. Finally he reached to his left for the tree, tugged on it, testing it. Holding it, he moved to another foothold a little lower.

Leni heard a clatter of stones and knew what was happening, saw it in a kind of stunned, horrified slow motion.

The tree pulled out of the rock side.

Matthew was still holding on to it when he fell.

Rock, shale, mud, rain, and Matthew crashed down, his scream lost in the avalanche of falling rock. He tumbled downward, his body cracking branches, thudding into stone, ricocheting.

She threw an arm across her face and turned her head as the debris landed on her, stones hit her; one cut her cheek. "Matthew. *Matthew!*"

She saw the final falling rock too late to duck.

⤛⟨❀⟩⤜

LENI IS OUT in Tutka Bay with Mama, in the canoe Dad salvaged. Mama is talking about her favorite movie, Splendor in the Grass. *The story of young love gone wrong. "Warren loves Natalie, you can tell, but it isn't enough."*

Leni is hardly listening. The words aren't what matter. It is the moment. She and Mama are playing hooky, living another life, ignoring the list of chores that awaits them at the cabin.

It is what Mama calls a bluebird day, except the bird Leni sees in the crystal-blue sky is a bald eagle with a six-foot wingspan gliding overhead. Not far away on a jagged outcropping of black rock, seals lie together, barking at the eagle. Shorebirds caw but keep away. A small pink dog collar glitters in the uppermost branches of a tree, near a huge eagle's nest.

A boat chugs past the canoe, upsetting the calm water.

Tourists wave, cameras raised.

"You'd think they'd never seen a canoe before," Mama says, then picks up her paddle. "Well, we'd best get home."

"I don't want this to end," Leni whines.

Mama's smile is unfamiliar. Something isn't quite right. "You need to help him, baby girl. Help yourself."

Suddenly the canoe tilts sideways so hard everything tumbles into the water—bottles, thermoses, a day pack.

Mama somersaults past Leni, screaming, and splashes into the water, disappears.

The canoe rights itself.

Leni scrambles to the side, peers over, yells, "Mama!"

A black fin, sharp as a knife blade, comes up from the water, rising, rising, until it is almost as tall as Leni. Killer whale.

The fin blots out the sun, darkens the sky all at once; everything goes black.

Leni hears the gliding of the orca, the splash as it emerges, the snort of air through its blowhole. She smells the decaying fish on its breath.

Leni opened her eyes, breathing hard. A headache pounded in her skull and the taste of blood filled her mouth.

The world *was* dark and fetid-smelling. Putrid.

She looked up. Matthew hung in the crevice above her, caught between the two rock walls, suspended, his feet hanging above her head, stuck in place by his backpack.

"Matthew? Matthew?"

He didn't answer.

(Maybe he couldn't. Maybe he was dead.)

Something dripped onto her face. She wiped it away, tasted blood.

She struggled to sit up. The pain was so violent, she vomited all over herself and passed out. When she came to, she almost puked again at the smell of her own vomit splattered across her chest.

Think. Help him. She was Alaskan. She could survive, damn it. It was the one thing she knew how to do. The one thing her father had taught her.

"It's a crevice, Matthew. Not a bear cave. So that's good." No brown bear would be ambling in, looking for a place to sleep. She moved inch by inch around the entire interior, her hands feeling the slick rock walls. No exit.

She crawled back onto the saucer rock and looked up at Matthew. "So. The only way out is up."

Blood dripped down his leg, plopped onto the rock beside her.

She stood up.

"You're blocking the only way out. So I need to get you unstuck. The pack is the problem." The added width had him pinned. "If I can get the pack off you, you'll fall."

Fall. That didn't sound like a great plan, but she couldn't think of anything better.

Okay.

How?

She moved gingerly, wedged her numb hand into the waistband of her pants. She slid/fell off the saucer-shaped rock, splashed into the squishy mud. A sharp pain jabbed her in the chest, made her gasp. She dug through her bug-out bag and found her knife. Biting down on it, she crawled to a place directly below Matthew's feet.

Now all she had to do was get to him and cut him free.

How? She couldn't reach his feet.

Climb. How? She had one good arm and the stone wall was slick and wet.

On rocks.

She found some large flat rocks and dragged them to the wall and stacked them as best she could. It took forever; she was pretty sure that twice she passed out and awoke and started again.

When she had built a stack that was about a foot and a half high, she took a deep breath and stepped on top of it.

At her weight, one of the rocks slid out from under her.

She fell hard, cracked her bad arm on something, and screamed.

She tried four more times, falling each time. It wasn't going to work. The rocks were too slippery and they were unstable when stacked.

"Okay." So she couldn't climb layered rocks. Maybe that should have been obvious.

She slogged to the wall, reached out to touch its cold, clammy surface. She used her good hand to trace the wet stone, feeling for every bump and ridge and indentation. A little light bled down on either side of Matthew. She burrowed through her pack, found a headlamp, put it on. With light, she saw differences in the slab—ledges, holes, footholds.

She felt upward, sideways, out, found a small lip of stone for her foot, and stepped up onto it. She steadied herself, then felt for another.

She fell hard, lay there stunned, breathing hard, staring up at him. "Okay. Try again."

With every attempt, she memorized a new bump in the wall of the crevice. On her sixth try, she made it all the way up, high enough to grab his backpack to steady herself. His left leg was terrible to look at—bone sticking out, torn flesh, his foot almost backward.

He hung limply, his head lolling to the side, blood smearing his face into something completely unrecognizable.

She couldn't tell if he was breathing.

"I'm here, Matthew, hang on," she said. "I'm going to cut you loose." She drew in a deep breath.

Using the pocketknife blade, she sawed through the pack's straps, shoulder and waist. It took forever to do with one hand, but finally she was done.

Nothing happened.

She cut all the straps and he didn't move. Nothing changed.

She yanked on his good leg as hard as she could.

Nothing.

She pulled again, lost her balance, and fell into the mud and rocks.

"What?" she screamed at the opening. "*What?*"

Metal snapped; something clanged against the rock.

Matthew plummeted, banged into the wall, thudded hard into the mud beside Leni. The pack landed beside her, splashing mud.

Leni scrambled over to him, pulled his head onto her lap, wiped his bloody face with her muddy hand. "Matthew? Matthew?"

He wheezed, coughed. Leni almost burst into tears.

She dragged him through the mud to the saucer-shaped rock. There, she struggled and fought to get his body up onto the indented stone surface.

"I'm here," she said, climbing up beside him. She didn't even realize she was crying until she saw her tears splash on his muddy face. "I love you, Matthew," Leni said. "We're going to be okay. You and me. You'll see.

We'll . . ." She tried to keep talking, wanted to, *needed* to, but all she could think was that it was her fault he was here. Her fault. He'd fallen trying to save her.

❧❀❧

SHE SCREAMED UNTIL her throat hurt, but there was no one up there to hear. No help coming. No one even knew they were on the trail, let alone that they'd fallen into a crevice.

She'd fallen.

He'd tried to save her.

And here they were. Battered. Bleeding. Huddled together on this cold, flat rock.

Think.

Matthew lay beside her, his face bloodied and swollen and unrecognizable. A huge flap of skin had split away from his face and lay like a bloody dog's ear, exposing the white-red bone beneath.

It was raining again. Water sluiced down the rock walls, turned the mud into a viscous pool. There was water all around them, swirling in the indentation in the rock, splashing, dripping, pooling. In the wan daylight that drifted down with the rain, she saw that Matthew's blood had turned it pink.

Help him. Help us.

She crawled over him, slipped down off the rock, and dug through his pack for a tarp. It took a long time to tie it in place with only one good hand, but she finally did it, created a gulley to catch rainwater into two big thermoses. When one was full, she positioned the other thermos to collect water and then climbed back up onto the rock.

She tilted his chin, made him drink. He swallowed convulsively, gagged, coughed. Setting the thermos aside, she stared at his left leg. It looked like a pile of hamburger with a shard of bone sticking out.

She went to the packs, salvaged what she could. The first-aid kit was well stocked. She found Bactine, gauze, aspirin, and sanitary pads. She removed her belt. "This is not going to feel good. How about a poem? We used to love Robert Service, remember? When we were kids, we could recite the good ones by heart."

She put her belt around his thigh and yanked it so tight he screamed and thrashed. Crying, knowing how much it had to hurt, she tightened it again and he lost consciousness.

She packed his wound with gauze and sanitary pads and bound it all in place with duct tape.

Then she held him as best she could with her broken arm and cracked rib.

Please don't die.

Maybe he couldn't feel her. Maybe he was as cold as she was. They were both soaking wet.

She had to let him know she was there.

The poems. She leaned close, whispered in his ear with her hoarse, failing voice, over the sound of her chattering teeth. *"Were you ever out in the Great Alone when the moon was awful clear . . ."*

✦⟨❋⟩✦

HE HEARS SOMETHING. *Jumbled sounds that mean nothing, letters flung in a pool, floating apart.*

He tries to move. Can't.

Numb. Pins and needles in his skin.

Pain. Excruciating. Head exploding, leg on fire.

He tries again to move, groans. Can't think.

Where is this?

Pain is the biggest part of him. All there is. All that's left. Pain. Blind. Alone.

No.

Her.

What does that mean?

✦⟨❋⟩✦

"MATTHEWMATTHEWMATTHEW."

He hears that sound. It means something to him, but what?

Pain obliterates everything else. A headache so bad he can't think. The smell of vomit and mold and decay. His lungs and nostrils ache. He can't breathe without gasping.

He is beginning to study his pain, see nuances. His head is pressure building, pounding, squeezing; leg is sharp, stabbing, fire and ice.

"Matthew."

A voice. (Hers.) Like sunshine on his face.

"I'mhere. I'mhere."

Meaningless.

"Ssshitsokay. I'mhere. I'lltellyouanotherstory. MaybeSamMcGee."

A touch.

Agony. He thinks he screams.

But maybe it's all a lie . . .

❖⟨❀⟩❖

DYING. He can feel the life draining out of him. Even the pain is gone.

He is nothing, just a lump in the wet and cold, pissing himself, vomiting, screaming. Sometimes his breathing just stops and he coughs when it starts again.

The smell is terrible. Mold, muck, decay, piss, vomit. Bugs are crawling all over him, buzzing in his ears.

The only thing keeping him alive is Her.

She talks and talks. Familiar rhyming words that almost make sense. He can hear her breathing. He knows when she is awake and when she's asleep. She gives him water, makes him drink.

He is bleeding now, through his nose. He can taste it, feel its viscous slime.

She is blearying.

No. That's a wrong word.

Crying.

He tries to hold on to that, but it goes like everything else, at a blur, too fast to grasp. He is floating again.

Her.

IloveyouMatthewdon'tleaveme.

Consciousness pulls away from him. He fights for it, loses, and sinks back into the smelly darkness.

TWENTY-TWO

After two terrible, freezing nights, Matthew moved for the first time. He didn't wake up, didn't open his eyes, but he moaned and made this terrible clicking sound, like he was suffocating.

A trapezoid of blue sky hung above them. It had finally stopped raining. Leni saw the rock face clearly, all the ridges and indentations and footholds.

He was burning up with fever. Leni made him swallow more aspirin and poured the last of the Bactine on his wound and rewrapped it in new gauze and duct tape.

Still, she could feel the life ebbing out of him. There was no *him* in the broken body beside her. "Don't leave me, Matthew . . ."

A distant whirring sound reached down into the darkness, the *thwop-thwop-thwop* of a helicopter.

She unwound from Matthew and scrambled into the mud. "We're here!" she shouted, sloshing to the break in the rocks where the sky showed.

She flattened herself to the sheer rock wall, waved her good arm, screaming, "We're here! Down here!"

She heard dogs barking, the buzz of human voices.

A flashlight shone down on her.

"Lenora Allbright," yelled a man in a brown uniform. "Is that you?"

✦✧〈❀〉✧✦

"WE'RE TAKING YOU UP FIRST, Lenora," someone said. She couldn't see his face in the mix of sunlight and shadow.

"No! Matthew first. He's . . . worse."

The next thing she knew, she was being strapped into a cage and hauled up the sheer wall. The cage banged into rock, clanged. Pain ricocheted in her chest, down her arm.

The cage landed on solid ground with a clatter. Sunlight blinded her. There were men in uniforms all around, dogs barking wildly. Whistles being blown.

She closed her eyes again, felt herself being transported to the grassy patch up the trail, heard the *thwop-thwop-thwop* of a helicopter. "I want to wait for Matthew," she yelled.

"You'll be fine, miss," someone in a uniform said, his face too close, his nose spread like a mushroom in the middle of his face. "We're airlifting you to the hospital in Anchorage."

"Matthew," she said, clutching his collar with her one good hand, yanking him close.

She saw his face change. "The boy? He's behind you. We've got him."

He didn't say Matthew would be fine.

✦✧〈❀〉✧✦

LENI OPENED HER EYES SLOWLY, saw a strip of overhead lighting above her, a line of glowing white against an acoustical tile ceiling. The room smelled cloyingly sweet, full of flower arrangements and balloons. Her ribs were wrapped so tightly it hurt to breathe and her broken arm was in a cast. The window beside her revealed a pale purple sky.

"There's my baby girl," Mama said. The left side of her face was swollen and her forehead was black and blue. Wrinkled, dirty clothes told the tale of a mother's worry. She kissed Leni's forehead, pushed the hair gently away from her eyes.

"You're okay," Leni said, relieved.

"I'm okay, Leni. You're the one we've been worried about."

"How did they find us?"

"We looked everywhere. I was beside myself with worry. Everyone was. Tom finally remembered a place his wife had loved to camp. He went looking and found the truck. Search and Rescue saw some broken branches on Bear Claw Ridge where you fell. Thank God."

"Matthew tried to save me."

"I know. You told the paramedics about a dozen times."

"How is he?"

Mama touched Leni's bruised cheek. "He's in bad shape. They don't know if he'll make it through the night."

Leni struggled to sit up. Every breath and movement hurt. There was a needle stuck in the back of her hand, and around it a strip of flesh-colored tape over a purple bruise. She eased the needle out, threw it aside.

"What are you doing?" Mama asked. "You have two broken ribs."

"I need to see Matthew."

"It's the middle of the night."

"I don't care." She swung her bare, bruised, scratched legs over the side of the bed and stood. Mama moved in close, became a stanchion of support. Together, they shuffled away from the bed.

At the door, Mama lifted the curtain and looked through the window, then nodded. They slipped out; Mama closed the door quietly behind them. Leni inched painfully forward on stockinged feet, following her mother down one corridor to the next until they came to the brilliantly lit, coldly efficient-looking area called the intensive care unit.

"Wait here," Mama said. She went on ahead, checking rooms. At the last one on the right, she turned back, motioned for Leni to follow.

On the door behind her mother, Leni saw WALKER, MATTHEW written on a clipboard in a clear plastic sleeve.

"This may be hard," Mama said. "He looks bad."

Leni opened the door, went inside.

There were machines everywhere, thunking and humming and whirring, making a sound like human breathing.

The boy in the bed couldn't be Matthew.

His head was shaved and covered in bandages; gauze crisscrossed his face, the white fabric tinged pink by blood seepage. One eye was covered by a protective cup; the other was swollen shut. His leg was elevated, suspended about eighteen inches above the bed by a leather sling, and so swollen it looked more like a tree trunk than a boy's leg. All she could see of it were his big, purple toes peeking out from the bandages. A tube in his slack mouth connected him to a machine that lifted and fell in breaths, inflated and deflated his chest. Breathing for him.

Leni took hold of his hot, dry hand.

He was here, fighting for his life because of her, because he loved her.

She leaned down, whispered, "Don't leave me, Matthew. Please. I love you."

After that, she didn't know what to say.

She stood there as long as she could, hoping he could feel her touch, hear her breathing, understand her words. It felt like hours had passed when Mama finally pulled her away from the bed, said, "No arguments," firmly, and led her back to her own room and helped her back into bed.

"Where's Dad?" Leni said at last.

"He's in jail, thanks to Marge and Tom." She tried to smile.

"Good," Leni said, and saw her mother flinch.

✦✧⟨❀⟩✧✦

THE NEXT MORNING, Leni woke slowly. She had a split second of blessed amnesia, then the truth tackled her. She saw Mama slumped in a chair by the door.

"Is he alive?" Leni asked.

"He made it through the night."

Before Leni could process this, there was a knock at the door.

Mama turned as Mr. Walker entered. He looked exhausted, as haggard and unmoored as Leni felt.

"Hey, Leni." He pulled the trucker's cap off his head, crushed it nervously in his big hands. His gaze moved to Mama, barely landing before it returned to Leni. A wordless conversation took place between them, excluded Leni. "Large Marge and Thelma and Tica are here. Clyde is taking care of your animals."

"Thank you," Mama said.

"How is Matthew?" Leni asked, struggling to sit up, wheezing at the pain in her chest.

"He's in a medically induced coma. There's a problem with his brain, something called shearing, and he might be paralyzed. They are going to try to wake him. See if he can breathe on his own. They don't think he'll be able to."

"They think he'll die when they unplug him?"

Mr. Walker nodded. "He'd want you there, I think."

"Oh, Tom," Mama said. "I don't know. She's hurt, and it will be too much for her to see."

"No looking away, Mama," Leni said, and climbed out of bed.

Mr. Walker took her arm, steadied her.

Leni looked at him. "I'm the reason he's hurt. He tried to save me. It's my fault."

"He couldn't do anything else, Leni. Not after what happened to his mom. I know my son. Even if he'd known the price, he would have tried to rescue you."

Leni wished that made her feel better, but it didn't.

"He loves you, Leni. I'm glad he found that."

He was already talking as if Matthew were gone.

She let Mr. Walker lead her out of the room and down the hall. She felt her mother behind her; every now and then she would reach out, brush her fingertips against the small of Leni's back.

They entered Matthew's room. Alyeska was already there, with her back to the wall. "Hey, Len," Alyeska said.

Len.

Just like her brother.

Alyeska hugged Leni. They didn't know each other well, but tragedy created a kind of family relationship between them. "He would have tried to save you no matter what. It's who he is."

Leni couldn't answer.

The door opened and three people came into the room, dragging equipment with them. In the lead was a man in a white coat; behind him were two nurses in orange scrubs.

"You'll need to stand over there," the doctor said to Leni and Mama. "Except for you, Dad. You come stand by the bed."

Leni moved to the wall, stood with her back pressed to it. There was barely any distance between her and Alyeska, but it seemed like an ocean; on one shore, the sister who loved him, on the other, the girl who'd been the cause of his fall. Alyeska reached over and held Leni's hand.

The medical team moved efficiently around Matthew's bed, nodding and talking to one another, taking notes, checking machines, recording vital signs.

Then the doctor said, "Okay?"

Mr. Walker leaned down and whispered something to Matthew and kissed his bandaged forehead, murmured words Leni couldn't hear. When he drew back, he was crying. He turned to the doctor and nodded.

Slowly, the tube was pulled out of Matthew's mouth.

An alarm sounded.

Leni heard Alyeska say, "Come on, Mattie. You can do it." She pulled away from the wall, stepped forward, brought Leni with her.

And Mr. Walker: "You're a tough kid. *Fight.*"

An alarm sounded.

Beep. Beep. Beep.

The nurses exchanged a knowing look.

Leni knew she shouldn't speak, but there was no way to hold back. "Don't leave us, Matthew . . . please . . ."

Mr. Walker gave Leni a terrible, agonized look.

Matthew took a great, gulping, gasping breath.

The alarm silenced itself.

"He's breathing on his own," the doctor said.

He's back, Leni thought with a staggering relief. *He'll be fine.*

"Thank God," Mr. Walker said on a sigh.

"Don't get your hopes up," the doctor said, and the room went quiet. "Matthew may breathe on his own but never wake up. He may remain in a persistent vegetative state. If he does wake, he may have substantial cognitive impairment. Breathing is one thing. Life is another."

"Don't say that," Leni said too softly for anyone to hear. "He might hear you."

"He *will* be okay," Aly murmured. "He'll wake up and smile and say he's hungry. He's always hungry. He'll want one of his books."

"He's a fighter," Mr. Walker added.

Leni couldn't say anything. The high she'd felt when he took that first breath had gone. Like getting to the top of a roller coaster: there was a nanosecond of pure exhilaration before the headlong plunge into fear.

⁘⟨❀⟩⁘

"THEY'RE DISCHARGING YOU TODAY," Mama said while Leni stared up at the television suspended on the wall in her hospital room. Radar was babbling some story to Hawkeye on *M*A*S*H*. Leni hit the off button. She'd spent years wishing she could watch TV. Now she couldn't care less.

Really, she had trouble caring about anything except Matthew. Her emotions were impossible to access. "I don't want to go."

"I know," Mama said, stroking her hair. "But we have to leave."

"Where will we go?"

"Home. But don't worry. Your dad's in jail."

Home.

Four days ago, when she'd been in that crevice with Matthew, hoping against hope that they'd be rescued before he died in her arms, she'd told herself they'd be okay. Matthew would be fine, they'd go to college together, and Mama would come to Anchorage with them, get an apartment, maybe serve drinks at Chilkoot Charlie's and collect big tips. Two days ago, when she'd watched them pull the tube from Matthew's mouth and seen him breathe on his own, she'd had a split second of hope, and then it had crashed on the rocks of *may never wake up.*

Now she saw the truth.

There would be no college for her and Matthew, no do-over as a pair of ordinary kids in love.

There was no way to lie to herself anymore, to dream of happy endings. All she could do was be there for Matthew and keep on loving him.

I think you stand by the people you love. That was what he'd said, and it was what she would do.

"Can I see Matthew before I go?"

"No. He's got an infection in his leg. They won't even let Tom get near him. But we'll come back as soon as we can."

"Okay."

Leni felt nothing as she dressed to go home.

Nothing.

She shuffled through the hallway beside her mother, the casted arm held in close to her body, nodding at the nurses who told her goodbye.

Did she smile in acknowledgment? She didn't think so. Even that small a thing was beyond her. This grief was unlike any emotion she'd experienced before, suffocating, weighty. It pulled the color from everything.

They found Mr. Walker in the main waiting area, pacing, drinking black coffee from a Styrofoam cup. Alyeska was seated in a chair beside him, reading a magazine. At their entrance, both tried to smile.

"I'm sorry," Leni said to them.

Mr. Walker came closer. He touched her chin, forced her to look up. "No more of that," he said. "We Alaskans are tough, right? Our boy will pull through. He'll survive. You'll see."

But wasn't it Alaska that had nearly killed him? How could a place be as alive as Alaska, as beautiful and cruel?

No. It wasn't Alaska's fault. It was hers. Leni was Matthew's second mistake.

Alyeska moved in beside her father. "Don't you give up on him, Leni. He's a tough kid. He made it through Mom's death. He'll get through this, too."

"How will I know how he's doing?" Leni asked.

"I'll give updates on the radio. *Peninsula Pipeline.* Seven P.M. broadcast. Listen for them," Mr. Walker said. "We'll bring him home as soon as we can. He'll recover better around us."

Leni nodded numbly.

Mama led her out to the truck and they climbed in.

On the long drive home, Mama chatted nervously. She pointed out the extreme low tide in Turnagain Arm and the cars parked at the Bird House Tavern in the middle of the day and the crowd of people fishing at the Russian River (combat fishing, they called it, people stood so close together). Usually Leni loved this drive. She'd search the high ridges for specks of white that were Dall sheep and she'd scour the inlet for the sleek, eerie-looking white beluga whales that sometimes appeared.

Now she just sat silently, her one good hand lying in her lap.

In Kaneq, they drove off the ferry, rumbled over the textured metal ramp, and rolled past the old Russian church.

Leni took care not to look at the saloon as they drove past. Even so, she saw the CLOSED sign on its door and the flowers laid in front. Nothing else had changed. They drove to the end of the road and through the open gate onto their property. There, Mama parked in front of the cabin and got out. She came around to Leni's side, opened the door.

Leni slid sideways, grateful for her mother's firm grip as they walked through the tall grass. The goats bleated, packed in together, and stood in a clot at the chicken-wire gate.

Inside the cabin, buttery August sunlight streamed through the dirty windows, thickened by motes of dust.

The cabin was spotless. No broken glass, no lanterns fallen on the floor, no overturned chairs. No sign of what had happened here.

And it smelled good, of roasting meat. Almost exactly when Leni noticed the scent, Dad came out of the bedroom.

Mama gasped.

Leni felt nothing, certainly not surprise.

He stood there facing them, his long hair pulled back into a squiggly ponytail. His face was bruised, a little misshapen. One eye was black. He was wearing the same clothes Leni had last seen him in and there were dried flecks of blood on his neck.

"Y-you're out," Mama said.

"You didn't press charges," he answered.

Mama's face turned red. She didn't look at Leni.

He moved toward Mama. "Because you love me and you know I didn't mean any of it. You know how sorry I am. It won't happen again," he promised as he reached for her.

Leni didn't know if it was fear or love or habit or a poisonous combination of all three, but Mama reached out, too. Her pale fingers threaded through his dirty ones, curled in to take hold.

He pulled her into his arms, held on to her so tightly he must have thought they'd be swept away, one without the other. When they finally pulled apart, he turned to Leni. "I heard he's going to die. I'm sorry."

Sorry.

Leni felt something then, a seismic shift in her thinking; like spring breakup, a changing of the landscape, a breaking away that was violent, immediate. She wasn't afraid of this man anymore. Or if she was, the fear was submerged too deeply to register. All she felt was hatred.

"Leni?" he said, frowning. "I'm sorry. Say something."

She saw what her silence did to him, how it shredded his confidence, and she decided right then: she would never speak to her father again. Let Mama slink back, let her twine herself back into this toxic knot that was their family. Leni would stay only as long as she had to. As soon as Matthew was better she would leave. If this was the life Mama chose for herself, so be it. Leni was going to leave.

As soon as Matthew was better.

"Leni?" Mama said, her voice uncertain. She, too, was confused and frightened by this change in Leni. She sensed an upheaval in emotion that could move the continents of their past.

Leni walked past them both, climbed awkwardly up the loft ladder, and crawled into bed.

Dear Matthew,

I never really knew the weight of sorrow before, how it stretches you out like an old, wet sweater. Every minute that passes with no word from you, without hope of word from you, feels like a day, every day feels like a month. I want to believe that you will just sit up one day and say you're starving, that you'll swing your legs out of bed and get dressed and come for me, maybe carry me off to your family's hunting cabin, where we will burrow under the furs and love each other again. That's the big dream. Strangely, it doesn't hurt as much as the little dream, which is just that you open your eyes.

I know what happened to us was my fault. Meeting me ruined your life. No one can argue with that. Me, with my screwed-up family, with my dad, who wanted to kill you for loving me and who beat my mother for simply knowing about it.

My hatred of him is a poison burning me from the inside out. Every time I look at him something in me hardens. It scares me how much I hate him. I haven't spoken to him since I got back.

He doesn't like that, I can tell.

Honestly, I don't know what to do with all these emotions. I'm furious, I'm desperate, I'm sad in a way I never knew existed.

There's no outlet for my feelings, no valve to shut them down. I listen to the radio every night at seven P.M. Last night, your dad broadcast how you're doing. I know you're out of the coma and not paralyzed and I try to make that good enough, but it's not. I know you can't walk or talk and that your brain is probably irreparably damaged. That's what the nurses said.

None of it changes how I feel. I love you.

I'm here. Waiting. I want you to know that. I'll wait forever.

Leni

LENI SAT IN THE BOW of the fishing skiff, leaned over, fluttering bare fingers through cool water, watching it cascade and pool. The cast on her other arm looked starkly white against her dirty jeans. Her broken ribs made her conscious of every breath.

She could hear her parents talking softly together; her mama was closing the cooler, full now of silvery fish. Dad started up the engine.

The boat motor started; the bow planed up as they sped for home.

At their beach, the boat crunched up onto the pebbles and sand, made a sound like sausage sizzling in a cast-iron pan. Leni jumped into the ankle-deep water, grabbed the frayed line with her one good hand, and pulled the skiff aground. She tied it to a huge, limbless driftwood log that lay angled on the beach and went back for the dripping metal net.

"That was quite a silver Mom landed," Dad said to Leni. "I guess she's the day's big winner."

Leni ignored him. Slinging the gear bag over her shoulder, she headed up the steps, making her way slowly to dry land.

Once there, she put her gear away and headed to the animal pens to check that their water was okay. She fed the goats and the chickens, stayed to turn the compost in the bin, and then started hauling water from the river. It took longer with only one strong arm. She stayed outside as long as she could, but finally she had to go inside.

Mama was in the kitchen making dinner: pan-fried, fresh-caught salmon, drizzled with homemade herb butter; green beans fried in preserved moose fat; a salad of freshly picked lettuce and tomatoes.

Leni set the table, sat down.

Dad took a seat across from her. She didn't look up, but she heard the clatter of chair legs on the wood, the squeak of the seat as he sat down. She smelled the familiar combination of perspiration and fish and cigarette smoke. "I was thinking we would head over to Bear Cove tomorrow, pick blueberries. I know how much you love them."

Leni didn't look at him.

Mama came up beside Leni, holding a pewter tray of the crispy-skinned fish, with bright green beans tucked in alongside. She paused, then set it down in the middle of the table next to an old soup can full of flowers.

"Your favorite," she said to Leni.

"Uh-huh," Leni said.

"G-damn it, Leni," her father said. "I can't abide this moping. You ran off. The kid fell. What's done is done."

Leni ignored him.

"Say something."

"Leni," Mama said. "Please."

Dad shoved back from the table and stormed out of the cabin, slamming the door shut behind him.

Mama sank into her chair. Leni could see how tired her mother was, how her hands trembled. "You have to stop this, Leni. It's upsetting him."

"So?"

"Leni . . . you'll be gone soon. He'll let you go to college now. He feels terrible about what happened. We can get him to agree. You can leave. Just like you wanted. All you have to do is—"

"No," she said more forcefully than she meant to, and she saw the effect her shouting had on Mama, how she instinctively shrank back.

Leni wanted to care that she was frightening her mother, but she couldn't hold on to that caring. Mama had chosen to dig for treasure through the dirt of Dad's toxic, porous love, but not Leni. Not anymore.

She knew what her silence was doing to him, how it angered him. Each hour she didn't speak to him, he became more agitated and irritable. More dangerous. She didn't care.

"He loves you," Mama said.

"Ha."

"You're lighting a fuse, Leni. You know that."

Leni couldn't tell Mama how angry she was, the sharp, tiny teeth that gnawed at her all the time, shredding a little more of her away every time she looked at her father. She pushed back from the table and went to the loft to write to Matthew, trying not to think about her mother sitting down there all alone.

Dear Matthew,

I am trying not to lose hope, but you know how hard it has always been for me. Hope, I mean. It's been four days since I last saw you. It feels like forever.

It's funny, now that hope has become so slippery and unreliable, I realize that all those years, when I was a kid thinking I didn't believe in hope, I was actually living on it. Mama fed me a steady diet of he's trying *and I lapped it up like a terrier. Every day I believed her. When he smiled at me or gave me a sweater or asked me how my day was, I thought,* See? He cares. *Even after I saw him hit her for the first time, I still let her define the world for me.*

Now it is all gone.

Maybe he's sick. Maybe Vietnam broke him. And maybe those are all excuses set at the feet of a man who is just rotting from the inside.

I don't know anymore and as much as I try, I can't care.

I have no hope left for him. The only hope I can hold on to is for you. For us.

I'm still here.

TWENTY-THREE

Dear Admissions Director:
University of Alaska, Anchorage.

I am very sorry to say that I will not be able
to attend classes at the University this quarter.
   I am hopeful—although doubtful—that winter quarter
will see a change in my circumstances.
   I will be forever grateful for my acceptance and
hope that another lucky student can take my spot.
                              Sincerely,
                              Lenora Allbright

In September, cold winds roared across the peninsula. Darkness began its slow, relentless march across the land. By October, the moment that was autumn in Alaska had passed. Every night, at seven P.M., Leni sat close to the radio, the volume cranked high, static popping, listening for

Mr. Walker's voice, waiting for news on Matthew. But week after week, there was no improvement.

In November, the precipitation turned to snow, light at first, goose down fluttering from white skies. The muddy ground froze, turned hard as granite, slippery, but soon a layer of white lay over everything, a new beginning of sorts, a camouflage of beauty over whatever lay hidden beneath.

And still Matthew wasn't Matthew.

On an ice-cold evening that followed the first vicious storm of the season, Leni finished her chores in a sooty darkness and returned to the cabin. Once inside, she ignored her parents and stood in front of the woodstove, her hands outstretched to its warmth. Gingerly she flexed the fingers of her left hand. The arm still felt weak, foreign somehow, but it was a relief to have the cast off.

She turned, saw her own reflection in the window. Pale, thin face with a knifepoint chin. She'd lost weight since the accident, and rarely bothered to bathe. Grief had upset everything—her appetite, her stomach, her sleep. She looked bad. Drained and exhausted. Bags under her eyes.

She went to the radio at exactly 6:55 and turned it on.

Through the speaker, she heard Mr. Walker's voice, steady as a trawler in calm seas. "To Leni Allbright in Kaneq: We're moving Matthew to a long-term facility in Homer. You can visit on Tuesday afternoon. It's called Peninsula Rehabilitation Center."

"I'm going to see him," Leni said.

Dad was sharpening his *ulu*. He stopped. "The hell you are."

Leni didn't glance at him or flinch. "Mama. Tell him if he wants to stop me, he'll have to shoot me."

Leni heard her mother draw in a sharp breath.

Seconds passed. Leni felt her father's anger and his uncertainty. She could feel the war waging within him. He wanted to explode, to exert his will, to hit something, but she meant it and he knew it.

He hit the coffeepot, sent it flying, muttered something they couldn't quite hear. Then he cursed, threw up his hands, and backed away, all in a single jerking movement. "Go," Dad said. "Go see the boy, but get your chores done first. And you." He turned to Mama, pointed a finger at her, thumped it on her chest. "She goes *alone*. You hear me?"

"I hear you," Mama said.

⊶⊰✧⊱⊷

Tuesday finally came.

"Ernt," Mama said after lunch. "Leni needs a ride to town."

"Tell her to take the old snow machine, not the new one. And be back by dinner." He gave Leni a look. "I mean it. Don't make me come looking for you." Yanking his iron animal traps from their hooks on the wall, he went outside, banging the door behind him.

Mama moved forward, glancing uncertainly behind her. She pressed two folded-up pieces of paper in Leni's hand. "Letters. For Thelma and Marge."

Leni took the letters, nodded.

"Don't be stupid, Leni. Be back before dinner. That gate could close again anytime. They're only open because he feels bad for what he did and he's trying to be good."

"Like I care."

"*I* care. And you should care *for* me."

Leni felt the sting of her selfishness. "Yeah."

Outside, Leni angled into the wind and trudged through the snow.

When she finished feeding the animals, she pulled the starter on the snow machine and climbed aboard.

In town, she pulled up in front of the harbor dock entrance and parked. A water taxi was waiting for Leni. Mama had called for it on the ham radio. The sea was too rough to take the skiff out.

Leni slung her backpack over her shoulder and headed down the slick, icy dock ramp.

The water-taxi captain waved at her. Leni knew he wasn't going to charge her for the ride. He was in love with Mama's cranberry relish. Every year she made two dozen jars of it just for him. That was how the locals did it: trading.

Leni handed him a jar and climbed aboard. As she sat on the bench in the back, staring up at the town perched on stilts above the sea, she told herself not to have any hopes for today. She knew Matthew's condition, had heard the words so often they'd worn a groove in her consciousness. *Brain damage.*

Even so, at night, after writing her daily letter to Matthew, she often fell asleep dreaming it was a Sleeping Beauty kind of thing, a dark spell that the kiss of true love could undo. She could marry him and hope that her love would waken him.

Forty minutes later, after a bumpy, splashing crossing of Kachemak Bay, the water taxi pulled up to the dock and Leni jumped out.

On this ice-cold winter day, fog coiled along the waterline of the Spit. There were only a few locals out in this weather and no tourists. Most of the businesses were closed for the season.

She left the road and began the uphill climb into Homer proper. She'd been told that if she came to the house with the pink boat in the yard and Fourth of July decorations still up, she'd gone too far on Wardell.

The care facility sat at the edge of town, on a wildly overgrown lot with a gravel parking lot.

She stopped. A huge bald eagle perched on a telephone pole watching her, its golden eyes bright in the gloom.

Forcing herself to move, she went into the building, spoke to the receptionist, and followed her directions down to the room at the end of the hall.

There, at the closed door, she paused, took a steady breath, and opened the door.

Mr. Walker stood by the bed. At Leni's entrance, he turned. He didn't look like himself. The months had whittled him away; his sweater and jeans bagged. He had grown a beard that was half gray. "Hi, Leni."

"Hey," she said, her gaze cutting to the bed.

Matthew lay strapped down. There was a cagelike thing around his bald head. It was *bolted* in with screws; they'd drilled into his skull. He looked thin and scrawny and old, like a plucked bird. For the first time she saw his face, crisscrossed by red zipper scars. A pucker of folded skin pulled one corner of his eye downward. His nose was flattened.

He lay motionless, his eyes open, his mouth slack. A line of drool beaded down from his full lower lip.

Leni went to the bed, stood beside Mr. Walker.

"I thought he was better."

"He is better. Sometimes I swear he looks right at me."

Leni leaned down. "H-hey, Matthew."

Matthew moaned, bellowed. Words that weren't words, just apelike sounds and grunts. Leni drew back. He sounded angry.

Mr. Walker placed his hand on Matthew's. "It's Leni, Matthew. You know Leni."

Matthew screamed. It was a heartrending sound that reminded her of an animal caught in a trap. His right eye rolled around in the socket. "Waaaaath."

Leni gaped down at him. This wasn't *better*. This wasn't Matthew, not this screaming, moaning husk of a person.

"Blaaaa . . ." Matthew moaned, his body buckling. A terrible smell followed.

Mr. Walker took Leni by the arm, led her out of the room.

"Susannah," Tom said to the nurse. "He needs a diaper change."

Leni would have collapsed if not for Mr. Walker, who held her up. He led her over to a waiting area with vending machines and eased her into a chair.

He sat in the chair beside her. "Don't worry about the screaming. He does it all the time. The doctors say it's purely physical, but I think it's frustration. He's in there . . . somewhere. And he is in pain. It's killing me to see him like this and not to be able to help."

"I could marry him, take care of him," Leni said. In her dreams she'd imagined it, being married, her caring for him, her love bringing him back.

"That's a really nice thing, Leni, and it tells me Matthew loves the right girl, but he may never get out of that bed or be able to say 'I do.'"

"But people get married, people who are injured and can't talk and are dying. Don't they?"

"Not to eighteen-year-old girls with their whole lives in front of them. How's your mom? I hear she took your dad back."

"She always takes him back. They're like magnets."

"We're all worried about you two."

"Yeah." Leni sighed. What good had worry ever done? Only Mama could change their situation, and she refused to do it.

In the silence that followed that unanswerable comment, Mr. Walker reached into his pocket and pulled out a thin package wrapped in newsprint. Written across the top in red marker was: *HAPPY BIRTHDAY, LENI.* "Alyeska found this in Mattie's room. I guess he got it for you . . . before."

"Oh" was all she could say. Her birthday had been forgotten in all the drama this year. She took the gift, stared down at it.

The nurse exited Matthew's room. Through the open door, Leni heard Matthew screaming. "Waaaa . . . Na . . . sher . . ."

"The brain damage . . . it's bad, kiddo. I won't lie to you. I was sorry to hear you decided not to go to college."

She shoved the present in her parka pocket. "How could I? It was supposed to be both of us."

"He'd want you to go. You know he would."

"We don't know what he wants anymore, do we?"

She got up, went back into Matthew's room. He lay rigid, his fingers flexed. The bolts in his head and scars on his face gave him a Frankenstein appearance. His one good eye stared dully ahead, not at her.

She leaned over and picked up his hand. It was a deadweight. She kissed the back of it, saying, "I love you."

He didn't respond.

"I'm not going anywhere," she promised in a thick voice. "I'll always be here. This is me, Matthew, climbing down to save you. Like you did for me. You did it, you know? You saved me. I'm standing here, by the one I love. I hope you hear that."

She stayed by him for hours. Every now and then he screamed and struggled. Twice, he cried. Finally, they asked her to leave so they could bathe him.

It wasn't until later, after she'd flagged down the water taxi and climbed aboard, as she was listening to the boat hull thumping over the whitecaps, with water spraying her in the face, that she realized she hadn't said good-bye to Mr. Walker. She'd just walked through the care facility and gone outside, past a man standing in front of a shack held together with duct tape and plastic sheeting, past a group of kids playing four-square in the school playground, wearing arctic camo clothes, past an old Native woman walking two huskies and a duck—all on leashes.

She thought she had grieved for Matthew, cried all the tears she had, but now she saw the desert of grief that lay before her. It could go on and on. The human body was eighty percent water; that meant she was literally made of tears.

In Kaneq, as she walked off the water taxi, it started to snow. The town gave off a slight humming: the sound of the big generator that fueled the new lights. Snow fell like sifting flour in the glow of Mr. Walker's new streetlamps. She barely noticed the cold as she walked up to the General Store.

The bell rang at her entrance. It was four-thirty, technically still daytime, but night was coming in fast.

Large Marge was dressed in a thigh-length fringed suede jacket over insulated pants. Her hair looked like shavings from an Etch A Sketch that had been glued to her skull. In places she had no hair at all, patches where she'd cut too zealously down to her brown scalp, probably because she didn't own a mirror. "Leni! What a nice surprise," she said in a foghorn voice that would have sent birds into the air. "I miss my best-ever employee."

Leni saw compassion in the woman's dark eyes. She meant to say, *I saw Matthew*, but to her horror what she did was burst into tears.

Large Marge led Leni over to the cash register, eased her to a sitting position on the old-fashioned settee and handed her a Tab.

"I just saw Matthew," Leni said, slumping forward.

Large Marge sat down beside her. The settee creaked angrily. "Yeah. I was in Anchorage last week. It's hard to see. It's killing Tom and Aly, too. How much heartache can one family handle?"

"I thought a care facility meant he was better. I thought . . ." She sighed. "I don't know what I thought."

"He's as good as he's going to get, from what I hear. Poor kid."

"He was trying to save me."

Large Marge was quiet for a moment. In the silence, Leni wondered if one person could ever really save another, or if it was the kind of thing you had to do for yourself.

"How's your mom? I still can't believe she let Ernt come back."

"Yeah. The cops can't do anything if she won't." Leni didn't know what else to say. She knew it was impossible for someone like Large Marge to understand why a woman like Cora stayed with a man like Ernt. It should have been as easy as an elementary math equation: he hits you x broken bones = leave him.

"Tom and I begged your mama to press charges. I guess she's too afraid."

"It's about more than fear." Leni was about to say more when her stomach seized. She thought she might throw up. "Sorry," she said when the nausea passed. "I feel terrible lately. Worry is making me physically sick, I guess."

Large Marge sat there a long time, then pushed to her feet. "Wait here." She left Leni sitting on the settee, breathing carefully. She walked back toward the store's shelving, bumping into one of the steel animal traps hanging on the wall.

Leni kept reliving the scene with Matthew, hearing his screams, seeing his eye roll around in the socket. *He needs a diaper change.*

Her fault. All of it.

Large Marge returned, her rubber boots squeaking on the sawdust floor. "You might need this, I'm afraid. I always keep one in stock."

Leni looked down, saw the slim box in Large Marge's palm.

And just like that, Leni's life got even worse.

⊹⟨❁⟩⊹

IN THE DARK of an early-fallen night, Leni made her way from the outhouse to the cabin beneath a starlit velvet blue sky. It was one of those vibrant, clear-skied Alaskan nights that were otherworldly. Moonlight reflected on snow and set the world aglow.

Once inside the cabin, she latched the door behind her and stood by the row of parkas and Cowichan sweaters and rain jackets, the box of mittens and gloves and hats at her feet. Unable to move, to think, to feel.

Until now, this second, she would have said blue was her favorite color. (A stupid thought, but there it was.) Blue. The color of morning, of twilight, of glaciers and rivers, of Kachemak Bay, of her mother's eyes.

Now blue was the color of a ruined life.

She didn't know what to do. There was no good answer. She was smart enough to know that.

And dumb enough to be in this situation.

"Leni?"

She heard her mother's voice, recognized the concerned tone, but it didn't matter. Leni felt distance spreading between them. That was how change came, she supposed: in the quiet of things unspoken and truths unacknowledged.

"How was Matthew?" Mama asked. She walked over to Leni, peeled off her parka, hung it up, and led her to the sofa, but neither of them sat down.

"He's not even him," Leni said. "He can't think or talk or walk. He didn't look at me, just screamed."

"He's not paralyzed, though. That's good, right?"

That was what Leni had thought, too. Before. But what good was being able to move if you couldn't think or see or talk? It might have been better if he'd died down there. Kinder.

But the world was never kind, especially not to kids.

"I know you think it's the end of the world, but you're young. You'll fall in love again and . . . What's that in your hand?"

Leni held out her fist, uncurled her fingers to reveal the thin vial in her hand.

Mama took it, studied it. "What is this?"

"It's a pregnancy test," Leni said. "Blue means positive."

She thought about the chain of choices that had led her here. A ten-degree shift anywhere along the way and everything would be different. "It must have happened the night we ran away. Or before? How do you know a thing like that?"

"Oh, Leni," Mama said.

What Leni needed now was Matthew. She needed him to be *him,* whole. Then they would be in this together. If Matthew were Matthew, they'd get married and have a baby. It was 1978, for God's sake; maybe they didn't even have to get married. The point was, they could make it. They'd be too young and college would have to wait, but it wouldn't be the tragedy it was now.

How was she supposed to do this without him?

Mama said, "It's not like in my day when they sent you away in shame and nuns took your baby. You have choices now. It's legal to—"

"I'm having Matthew's baby," Leni said. She didn't even know until then that all of this had already gone through her brain and she'd decided.

"You can't raise a baby alone. Here."

"You mean with Dad," Leni said, and there it was: the thing that made this even worse. Leni was carrying a Walker baby. Her father would blow a gasket when he found out.

"I don't want him anywhere near this baby," Leni said.

Mama pulled Leni into her arms, held her tightly.

"We will figure this out," Mama said, stroking her hair. Leni could tell that her mother was crying, and that made her feel even worse.

"What's this?" Dad said, his voice booming loud.

Mama sprang back, looking guilty. Her cheeks shone with tears, her smile was unsteady. "Ernt!" Mama said. "You're back."

Leni shoved the vial into her pocket.

Dad stood by the door, unzipped his insulated coveralls. "How is the kid? Still a vegetable?"

Leni had never felt such hatred. She pushed Mama aside and went to him, saw his surprise as she neared him and said, "I'm pregnant."

She never saw the hit coming. One minute she was standing there, staring at her father, and the next minute his fist hit her chin so hard she tasted blood. Her head snapped back, she stumbled, lost her balance, crashed into an end table, and fell to the floor. As she landed, she thought, oddly, *He's so fast.*

"Ernt, no!" Mama screamed.

Dad unbuckled his belt, pulled it loose, came at Leni.

She tried to get up, but her head was ringing and she was dizzy. Her vision was off.

The first crack of his belt buckle hit her across the cheek, breaking the skin. Leni cried out, tried to scuttle away.

He hit her again.

Mama threw herself at Dad, clawing at his face. He shoved her away and went after Leni again.

He yanked her to her feet, backhanded her across the face. She heard the cartilage crack, pop. Blood gushed from her nose. She staggered back, instinctively protecting her stomach as she fell to her knees.

A gun fired.

Leni heard the loud *craaaack* and smelled the shot. Glass shattered.

Dad stood there, his legs braced wide, his right hand still curled into a fist. For a second nothing happened; no one moved. Then Dad stumbled forward, toward Leni. Blood pulsed from a wound in his chest, stained his shirt. He looked confused, surprised. "Cora?"

Mama stood behind him, the gun still pointed at him. "Not Leni," she said, her voice steady. "Not my Leni."

She shot him again.

TWENTY-FOUR

H e's dead," Leni said. Not that there was much doubt. The gun Mama had chosen could kill a bull moose.

Leni realized she was kneeling in a pool of gore. Bits of bone and cartilage looked like maggots in the blood. Ice-cold air swept into the room through the broken window.

Mama dropped the weapon. She moved toward Dad, her eyes wide, her mouth trembling. She scratched nervously at her throat, turned the pale skin red in streaks.

Leni climbed woodenly to her feet and walked into the kitchen. She ought to be thinking, *We're fine, he's gone*, but she felt nothing, not even relief.

Her face hurt so much it made her sick to her stomach. The taste of blood was making her gag, and with every breath her nose made a whistling sound. She got a rag wet and pressed it to her face, wiped blood away.

How had Mama endured this pain over and over?

She rinsed the rag, twisted out the pink water of her blood, and dampened it again, then returned to the living room, which smelled of gun smoke and gore and blood.

Mama knelt on the floor. She'd pulled Dad into her lap and was rocking him back and forth, crying. There was blood everywhere: on her hands, her knees. She'd smeared it across her eyes.

"Mama?" Leni leaned down, touched her mother's shoulder.

Her mother looked up, blinking groggily. "I didn't know how else to stop him."

"What do we do?" Leni said.

"Get on the ham radio. Call the police," Mama said in a lifeless voice.

The police. Finally. After all these years, they would get some help. "We will be okay, Mama. You'll see."

"No, we won't, Leni."

Leni wiped blood from her mother's face, just as she'd done so often before. Mama didn't even flinch. "What do you mean?"

"They'll call it murder."

"Murder? But he was beating us. You saved my life."

"I shot him in the back, Leni. Twice. Juries and defense attorneys don't like people shot in the back. It's fine. I don't care." She pushed the hair out of her face, left bloody streaks. "Go tell Large Marge. She's a lawyer, or was. She'll handle it." Mama sounded drugged; her speech was slow. "You'll have your fresh start. You'll raise your baby here in Alaska, among our friends. Tom will be like a father to you. I know it. And Large Marge adores you. Maybe college is still a possibility." She looked at Leni. "It was worth it. I want you to know that. I'd do it again for you."

"Wait. Are you talking about *leaving* me? About prison?"

"Just go get Large Marge."

"You are not going to prison for killing a man that everyone in town knew was abusive."

"I don't care. You're safe. That's all that matters."

"What if we get rid of him?"

Mama blinked. "Get rid of him?"

"We could make it so this never happened." Leni got to her feet. *Yes.* This was the answer. They would devise a way to erase what they'd done. Then they could stay here, she and Mama, and live among their friends, in this place they'd grown to love. The baby would be loved by all of them, and when Matthew finally got better, Leni would be waiting.

"That's not as easy as it sounds, Leni," Mama said.

"This is Alaska. Nothing is easy, but we're tough, and if you go to prison, I'll be alone. With a baby to raise. I can't do it without you. I *need* you, Mama."

It was a moment before Mama said, "We'd need to hide the body, make sure it never gets found. The ground is too frozen to bury him."

"Right."

"But Leni," she said evenly. "You're talking about another crime."

"Letting you be called a murderer? *That* would be a crime. You think I'm going to trust the law with your life? The *law*? You told me the law didn't protect abused women, and you were right. He got out of jail in a few days. When did the law ever protect you from him? No. *No.*"

"Are you sure, Leni? It means you'll have to live with it."

"I can live with it. I'm sure."

Mama took a while to consider, then extracted herself from Dad's limp, bloody body, and stood. She went into her bedroom and came out a few moments later dressed in insulated pants and a turtleneck. She dumped her bloody clothes in a heap by Dad's body. "I'll be back as soon as I can. Don't open the door to anyone except me."

"What do you mean?"

"Step one is to dispose of the body."

"And you think I'm going to sit here while you do it?"

"*I* killed him. I'll do this."

"And I'm helping you cover it up."

"We don't have time to argue."

"Exactly." Leni stripped out of her bloody clothes. Within moments she was in her insulated pants and parka and bunny boots, ready to go.

"Get his traps," Mama said, and left the cabin.

Leni gathered the heavy traps from their hooks on the cabin wall and carried them outside. Mama had already hooked the big red plastic sled to the snow machine. It was the one Dad had used for hauling wood. It could hold two large coolers, a lot of chopped wood, and a moose carcass.

"Lay the traps in the sled. Then go get the chain saw and the auger."

When Leni returned with the tools, Mama said, "You ready for the next part?"

Leni nodded.

"Let's go get him."

It took them thirty minutes to drag Dad's lifeless body from the cabin and across the snowy deck, and then another ten minutes to get him settled on the sled. A bloody trail in the snow revealed their path, but within the hour, with snow falling this heavily, it would be gone. Come spring, the rains would wash it away. Mama covered Dad with a tarp and lashed him and it down with bungee cords.

"Okay, then."

Leni and her mother exchanged a look. In it was the truth that this act, this decision, would change them forever. Without words, Mama gave Leni the chance to change her mind.

Leni stood firm. She was in this. They would dispose of the body, clean the cabin, and tell everyone he left them, say he must have fallen through the ice while hunting or lost his way in the snow. No one would question or care. Everyone knew there were a thousand ways to disappear up here.

Leni and her mama would finally—*finally*—be unafraid.

"Okay, then."

Mama pulled the cord to start the snow machine, then took her place on the two-person seat and grasped the throttle. She fitted a neoprene face mask over her bruised, swelling face, and gingerly pulled on her helmet. Leni did the same. "This is going to be cold as hell," Mama yelled over the roar of the engine. "We're going up the mountain."

Leni climbed aboard, put her arms around her mother's waist.

Mama revved the engine and they were off, driving through the virgin snow, through the open gate. They turned right on the main road and left onto the road that led up to the old chromium mine. By then it was deep night and blowing snow and cold. The thread of yellow from the snow machine's headlight led the way.

In weather like this, they didn't need to worry much about being seen. For more than two hours, Mama drove high up the mountain. Where the snow was deep, her touch on the throttle was light. They rode up hills, down valleys, across frozen rivers, and around cliffs of soaring rock. Mama kept the snow machine's speed so low it was barely faster than walking; speed wasn't their objective now. Invisibility was. And the sled needed to stay steady.

They came at last to a small lake high on the mountain, ringed by tall trees and cliffs. Sometime in the last hour the snow had stopped falling and the clouds had departed to reveal a velvety blue night sky awash in swirls of starlight. The moon came out, as if to watch two women in the midst of all this snow and ice or to mourn their choices. Full and bright, it shone down on them, its light reflected across the snow, seeming to lift skyward, a radiant glow illuminating the snowy landscape.

In the sudden clarity of the night, they were visible now, two women on a snow machine in a glowing, silver-white world with a dead body on a sled.

At the frozen lakeshore, Mama eased off of the gas, came to a trembling stop. The insect drone of the engine was the loudest noise out here. It drowned out the harsh sound of Leni's breathing through the neoprene face mask and helmet.

Was the lake fully frozen? There was no way to know for sure. It should be, at this high elevation, but it was early, too. Not midwinter. The snow radiated with moonlight across the flat, frozen lake.

Leni tightened her hold.

Mama barely turned the throttle, then inched forward. In this dark, they were like astronauts, moving through a strange, impossibly illuminated world, like deepest space, the sound of cracking ice all around them. In the center of the lake, Mama killed the engine. The snow machine slid to a stop. Mama dismounted. The cracking sound was loud, insistent, but not the kind of sound that mattered. It was just the ice breathing, stretching; not breaking.

Mama took off her helmet, hung it on the throttle, and removed her face mask. Her breath shot out in humid plumes. Leni set her helmet on the duct-taped vinyl seat.

In the silver-blue-white light of the moon, ice crystals sparkled across the surface of the snow, glittered like gemstones.

Quiet.

Only their breathing.

Together they pulled Dad's body off the sled. Leni used the emergency shovel to clear a divot in the snow. When she came to the glassy silver ice, she put her shovel away and retrieved the auger and the chain saw. Mama used the auger to drill an eight-inch hole in the ice. Slushy water seeped up, bounced the round disc of ice.

Leni pulled off her face mask and shoved it in her pocket, then started up the chain saw, the *wa-na-na-na* excruciatingly loud out here.

She pointed the blade downward, stuck it in the hole, and began the long, arduous process of turning the hole into a big square opening in the ice.

When Leni finished, she was sweating hard. Mama dropped the animal traps beside the hole. They landed with a clank.

Then Mama went back for Dad. Grabbing hold of his cold white hands, she dragged him over to the hole, tucked him up close to it.

Dad's body was stiff and still, his face as white and hard as a tusk carving.

For the first time, Leni really thought about what they were doing. The bad thing they'd done. From now on, they would have to live with the knowledge that they were capable of *this,* all of it. The shooting, the carrying of a dead man, the covering up of a crime. Although they'd had a lifetime of covering up for him, looking away, pretending, this was different. Now they were the criminals and the secret Leni had to protect was her own.

A good person would feel ashamed. Instead she was angry. Howlingly so.

If only they had walked away years ago, or called the police, asked for help. Any small course correction on Mama's part might have led to a future where there wasn't a dead man on the ice between them.

Mama dragged the traps apart, forced the black jaws open. She pushed Dad's forearm into the maw. The trap closed with a *snap* of breaking bone. Mama paled, looking sick. Traps broke both of Dad's legs—*sn-ap*—became weights.

The northern lights appeared overhead, cascading in swirls of yellow, green, red, and purple. Impossible, magical color; lights fell like silken scarves across the sky, skeins of yellow, neon-green, shocking pink. The electric-bright moon seemed to watch it all.

Leni stared down at her father. She saw the man who had used his fists when he was angry, saw the blood on his hands and the mean set to his jaw. But she saw the other man, too, the one she'd crafted from photographs and her own need, the one who'd loved them as much as he could, his capacity for love destroyed by war. Leni thought maybe that he would haunt her. Not just him, but the idea of him, the sad and scary truth that you could love and hate the same person at the same time, that you could feel a deep and abiding loss and shame for your own weakness and still be glad that this awful thing had been done.

Mama dropped to her knees beside him, bent close. "We loved you."

She looked up at Leni, wanting—maybe needing—Leni to say the same thing, to do what Leni had always done. Peas in a pod.

It was between them now, years of yelling and hitting, of being afraid . . . and smiles and laughter, Dad saying, *Heya, Red*, and begging for forgiveness.

" 'Bye, Dad" was all Leni could summon. Maybe, in time, this wouldn't be her last memory of him; maybe, in time, she would remember how it felt when he held her hand or put her on his shoulders as he walked along The Strand.

Mama pushed him across the ice, traps clanking, into the open hole. His body plunged down, snapping his head back.

His face peered up at them, a cameo in cold black water, skin white in the moonlight, beard and mustache frozen. Slowly, slowly he sank into the water and disappeared.

There would be no trace of him tomorrow. The ice would close up long before anyone else came out here. His body would be dragged by the heavy traps to the lake floor. In time, he would be worn down by the water and become only bones, and bones could wash ashore, but the predators would likely find them before the authorities would. By then no one would be looking, anyway. Five out of every thousand people went missing in Alaska every year, were lost. That was a known fact. They fell down crevasses, lost their way on trails, drowned in a rising tide.

Alaska. The Great Alone.

"You know what this makes us," Mama said.

Leni stood beside her, imagining the sight of her dad's pale, stiff body being dragged down into the dark. The thing he hated most. "Survivors," Leni said. The irony was not lost on her. It was what her dad had wanted them to be.

Survivors.

⊹•⟨❀⟩•⊹

LENI KEPT REPLAYING IT in her mind, seeing the last glimpse of her dad's face before the black water pulled him under. The image would haunt her for the rest of her life.

When they finally returned to the cabin, exhausted and cold to the bone, Leni and her mother had to haul in wood to feed the fire. Leni tossed her gloves into the flames. Then she and Mama stood in front of the fire, their trembling hands outstretched to the heat, for how long?

Who knew? Time lost its meaning.

Leni stared numbly down at the floor. There was a bone shard near her foot, another on the coffee table. It would take all night to clean this up and she feared that even if they wiped all his blood away, it would come seeping back, bubbling up from the wood like something out of a horror story. But they had to get started.

"We need to clean up. We'll say he disappeared," Leni said.

Mama frowned, chewed worriedly at her lower lip. "Go get Large Marge. Tell her what I did." Mama looked at Leni. "You hear me? You tell her what *I* did."

Leni nodded and left Mama alone to start cleaning.

Outside, it was snowing lightly again, the world darker, layered with clouds. Leni trudged to the snow machine and climbed aboard. Airy goose-down flakes fell, changed direction with the wind. At Large Marge's property, Leni veered right, plunged into a thicket of trees, drove along a winding path of tire tracks on snow.

At last she came to a clearing: small, oval-shaped, ringed by towering white trees. Large Marge's home was a canvas-and-wood yurt. Like all homesteaders, Large Marge kept everything, so her yard was full of heaps and piles of junk covered in snow.

Leni parked in front of the yurt and got out. She knew she didn't have to yell out a greeting. The headlight and sound of the snow machine had announced her.

Sure enough, a minute later the door to the yurt opened. Large Marge walked out, wearing a woolen blanket like a huge cape around her body. She tented a hand over her eyes to keep out the falling snow. "Leni? Is that you?"

"It's me."

"Come in. Come in," Large Marge said, making a sweeping gesture with her hand.

Leni hurried up the steps and went inside.

The yurt was bigger inside than it looked from the outside, and immaculately clean. Lanterns gave off a buttery light and the woodstove poured out heat and sent its smoke up through a metal pipe that protruded through a carefully constructed opening at the yurt's canvas crown.

The walls were constructed of thin wooden strips in an intricate crisscross pattern, with canvas stretched taut behind them like an elaborate hoop skirt. The domed ceiling was buttressed by beams. The kitchen was full-sized and the bedroom was above, in a loft area that looked down over the living area. Now, in the winter, it was cozy and contained, but in the summer she knew that the canvas windows were unzipped to reveal screens that let in huge blocks of light. Wind thumped on the canvas.

Large Marge took one look at Leni's bruised face and squashed nose, at the dried blood on her cheeks, and said, "Son of a *bitch*." She pulled Leni into a fierce hug, held on to her.

"It was bad tonight," Leni said at last, pulling away. She was shaking. Maybe it was finally sinking in. They'd killed him, broken his bones, dropped him in the water . . .

"Is Cora—"

"He's dead," Leni said quietly.

"Thank God," Large Marge said.

"Mama—"

"Don't tell me anything. Where is he?"

"Gone."

"And Cora?"

"At the cabin. You said you'd help us. I guess we need it now to, you know, clean up. But I don't want to get you in trouble."

"Don't worry about me. Go home. I'll be there in ten minutes."

Large Marge was already changing her clothes when Leni left the yurt.

Back at the cabin, she found Mama standing away from the pool of blood and gore, staring down at it, her face ravaged by tears, chewing on her torn thumbnail.

"Mama?" Leni said, almost afraid to touch her.

"She'll help us?"

Before Leni could answer, she saw a spear of light flash across the window, tarnishing it, casting Mama in brightness. Leni saw her mother's sorrow and regret in sharp relief.

Large Marge pushed open the cabin door, walked inside. Dressed in Carhartt insulated coveralls and her wolverine hat and knee-high mukluks, she took a quick look around, saw the blood and gore and bits of bone.

She went to Mama, touched her gently on the shoulder.

"He went after Leni," Mama said. "I had to shoot him. But . . . I shot him in the back, Marge. Twice. He was unarmed. You know what that means."

Large Marge sighed. "Yeah. They don't give a shit what a man does or how scared you are."

"We weighed him down and dropped him in the lake, but . . . you know how things get found in Alaska. All kinds of things bubble up from the ground during breakup."

Large Marge nodded.

"They'll never find him," Leni said. "We'll say he ran away."

Large Marge said, "Leni, go upstairs and pack a small bag. Just enough for overnight."

"I can help with cleaning," Leni said.

"Go," Large Marge said sternly.

Leni climbed up into the loft. Behind her, she heard Mama and Large Marge talking quietly.

Leni chose the book of Robert Service poetry to take with her for tonight. She also took the photograph album Matthew had given her, full now of her favorite pictures.

She pushed them deep into her pack, alongside her beloved camera, and covered it all with a few clothes and then went downstairs.

Mama was wearing Dad's snow boots, as she walked through the pool of blood, making tracks to the door. At the windowsill, she pressed a bloody hand to the glass.

"What are you doing?" Leni asked.

"Making sure the authorities know your mom and dad were here," Large Marge answered.

Mama took off Dad's boots and changed into her own and made more tracks in the blood. Then Mama took one of her shirts and ripped it and dropped it onto the floor.

"Oh," Leni said.

"This way they'll know it's a crime scene," Large Marge said.

"But we're going to clean it all up," Leni said.

"No, baby girl. We have to disappear," Mama said. "Now. Tonight."

"Wait," Leni said. "What? We're going to say he left us. People will believe it."

Large Marge and Mama exchanged a sad look.

"People go missing in Alaska all the time," Leni said, her voice spiking up.

"I thought you understood," Mama said. "We can't stay in Alaska after this."

"What?"

"We can't stay," Mama said. Gently but firmly. "Large Marge agrees. Even if we could have argued self-defense, we can't now. We covered up the crime."

"Evidence of intent," Large Marge said. "There is no defense for battered women who kill their husbands. There sure as hell should be. You could assert defense of others, and it might fly. You might be acquitted—if the jury thinks deadly force was reasonable—but do you really want to take that chance? The law isn't good to victims of domestic abuse."

Mama nodded. "Marge will leave the truck parked somewhere, with blood smeared across the cab. In a few days, she will report us missing and lead the police to the cabin. They'll conclude—hopefully—that he killed us both and went into hiding. Marge and Tom will tell the police that he was abusive."

"Your mom and dad share the same blood type," Large Marge said. "There's no conclusive test that can identify whose blood this is. At least, I hope there isn't."

"I want to say he ran off," Leni said stubbornly. "I mean it, Mama. *Please.* Matthew is here."

"Even in the bush, they'll investigate a local man who disappears, Leni," Large Marge said. "Remember how everyone came together to look for Geneva Walker? The first place they'll look is the cabin. And what will you say about the shot-out window? I know Curt Ward. He's a by-the-book cop. He might even bring in a dog or call an investigator from Anchorage. No matter how well we clean, there could be evidence here. A human bone fragment. Something to identify your father. If they find it, they'll arrest you both for murder."

Mama went to Leni. "I'm sorry, baby girl, but you wanted this. I was willing to take the blame alone, but you wouldn't let me. We're in it together now."

Leni felt as if she were free-falling. In her naïveté, she'd thought they could do this terrible thing and pay no price beyond the shadowing of their souls, the memories and nightmares.

But it would cost Leni everything she loved. Matthew. Kaneq. Alaska.

"Leni, we don't have a choice now."

"When have we ever had a choice?" Leni said.

Leni wanted to scream and cry and be the child it felt she'd never been, but if her youth and her family had taught her anything, it was how to survive.

Mama was right. There was no way they could clean up this blood. And dogs and police would sniff out the crime. What if Dad had an appointment tomorrow they didn't know about and someone called the police to report him missing before they were ready? What if his body slipped free of the shackles and floated to the shore when the water thawed and a hunter found him?

As always, Leni had to think about the people she loved.

Mama had taken every hit to protect Leni, and she'd shot Dad to save Leni. She couldn't leave Mama alone now, on the run; and Leni couldn't raise her baby alone, either. She felt an overwhelming sadness, a suffocating sense of having run a marathon only to end up in the same place.

At least they would be together, the two of them, like always. And the baby would have a chance at something better.

"Okay." She turned to Large Marge. "What do we do?"

The next hour was spent on final details: they parked the truck on the side of the road, with blood smeared across the door handle. They knocked over furniture and left out an empty whiskey bottle and Large Marge shot twice into the log walls. They left the cabin door open for animals to enter and further ruin any evidence.

"Are you ready?" Mama asked at last.

Leni wanted to say, *No. I'm not ready. I belong here.* But it was too late to salvage Before. She nodded grimly.

Large Marge hugged them both tightly, kissed their wet cheeks, told them to have a good life. "I'll report you missing," she whispered in Leni's ear. "I'll never tell a living soul about this. You can trust me."

By the time Leni and Mama walked down their zigzagged beach steps for the last time, in a blinding snowfall, Leni felt like she was a thousand years old.

She followed her mother down onto the snowy, slushy beach. Wind whipped hair across Mama's eyes, tore the volume from her voice, rattled the pack on her back. Leni could tell Mama was talking to her, but she couldn't hear the words and didn't care. She sloshed through icy waves toward the skiff. Tossing her pack into the boat, she climbed aboard and sat down on the wooden bench seat. On the shore, falling snow would soon erase all evidence of their path; it would be as if they'd never been here at all.

Mama jumped aboard. Without lights to guide them, she motored slowly along the shore, gripping the wheel in gloved hands, her hair flying every which way.

They rounded the bend as a new dawn glimmered and showed them the way.

⤜⟨❀⟩⤚

THEY PULLED UP TO the transient dock in Homer.

"I need to say goodbye to Matthew," Leni said.

Mama tossed Leni a line. "No way. We need to go. And we can't be seen today. You know that."

Leni tied the boat down. "It wasn't a question."

Mama reached down for her pack, hefted it up, slipped it onto her back. Taking care, Leni stepped out of the skiff and onto the icy dock. The lines made a creaking sound.

Mama turned off the engine and stepped off the boat. The two of them stood in the softly falling snow.

Leni pulled a scarf out of her pack and coiled it around her neck, covering the lower half of her face. "No one will see me, Mama, but I'm going."

"Be at the Glass Lake counter in forty minutes," Mama answered. "Not one minute late. Okay?"

"We're going to *fly*? How?"

"Just be there."

Leni nodded. Honestly, she didn't care about details. All she could think about was Matthew. She hefted her backpack and took off, walking as fast as she dared on the icy dock. This early on a cold and snowy November morning, there was no one out here to see her.

She reached the care facility and slowed. Here was where she needed to be careful. She couldn't let anyone see her.

The glass doors whooshed open in front of her.

Inside, she smelled disinfectant and something else, metallic, astringent. At the front desk, a woman was on the phone. She didn't even look up when the doors opened. Leni slipped inside, thinking, *Be invisible* . . . The corridors were quiet this early in the morning, the patients' doors were closed. At Matthew's room she paused, steadied herself, and opened the door.

His room was quiet. Dark. No machines whooshed or thunked. Nothing was keeping him alive except his own huge heart.

They had positioned him so that he was asleep sitting up, his head trapped in the halo thing that was attached to a vest so he couldn't move. His pink-scarred face looked like it had been stitched together with a sewing machine. How could he live this way, stitched up, bolted together, unable to speak or think or touch or be touched? And how could she leave him to do it without her?

She dropped her backpack to the floor, approached the bed, and reached for his hand. His skin, once rough from gutting fish and fixing farm equipment, was now as soft as a girl's. She couldn't help thinking about their school days, holding hands under the desk, passing notes back and forth, thinking the world could be theirs.

"We could have done it, Matthew. We could have gotten married and had a kid too soon and stayed in love." She closed her eyes, imagining it, imagining *them*. They could have stuck it out to the gray years, been a couple of white-haired old people in out-of-date clothes, sitting on a porch under the midnight sun.

Could have.

Useless words. Too late.

"I can't let my mom be alone. And you have your dad and your family and Alaska." Her voice broke on that. "You don't know who I am anyway, do you?"

She bent down closer. Her hand closed tightly around his. Tears landed on his cheek and caught on the raised pink scar tissue.

Samwise Gamgee would never leave Frodo like this. No hero would ever do this. But books were only a reflection of real life, not the thing itself. They didn't tell you about boys who broke their bodies and had their brains sheared down to the stem, who couldn't talk or move or say your name. Or about mothers and daughters who made terrible, irrevocable choices. Or about babies who deserved better than the messed-up lives into which they were born.

She put her hand on her stomach again. The life in there was as small as a frog's egg, too small to feel, and yet she swore she could hear the echo of a second heartbeat running alongside her own. All she really knew was this: she had to be a good mother to this baby and she had to take care of her mother. Period.

"I know how much you wanted kids," Leni said quietly. "And now . . ."

You stand by the people you love.

Matthew's eyes opened. One stared straight ahead. The other rolled wildly in the socket. That one staring green eye was the only part of him she recognized. He struggled, made a terrible moaning sound of pain.

He opened his mouth, screamed, "*Bwaaaa . . .*" He thrashed, bucked up like he was trying to break free. The halo made a clanging sound when it hit the bedrail. Blood started to form at the bolts in his temple. An alarm went off. "*Hermmmm . . .*"

"Don't," she said. "Please . . ."

The door opened behind her. A nurse rushed past Leni and into the room.

Leni stumbled back, shaking, flipped her hood back up. The nurse hadn't seen her face.

He was bellowing in the bed, making guttural animal sounds, thrashing. The nurse injected something in his IV. "It's okay, Matthew. Calm down. Your dad will be here soon."

Leni wanted to say, *I love you*, one last time, out loud, for the world to hear, but she didn't dare.

She needed to leave, now, before the nurse turned around.

But she stood there, eyes glazed with tears, her hand still pressed to her belly. *I'll try to be a good mom and I'll tell the baby about us. About you . . .*

Leni reached down for her pack, grabbed it, and ran.

She left him there, alone with strangers.

A choice she knew he would never have made about her.

⊹⟨❂⟩⊹

HER.

She's here. Is she? *He doesn't know what's real anymore.*

He has words he knows, words he's collected as important, but he doesn't know their meaning. Coma. Brace. Halo. Brain damage. They are there, seen but not seen, like pictures in another room, glimpsed through rippled glass.

Sometimes he knows who he is and where he is. Sometimes, for seconds, he knows he has been in a coma and come out of it; he knows he can't move because they strap him down. He knows he can't move his head because they've drilled screws into his skull and caged him. He knows he sits like this all day, propped up, a monster in a brace, his leg jutting out in front of him, pain constantly chewing on him. He knows that people cry when they see him.

Sometimes he hears things. Sees shapes. People. Voices. Light. He tries to catch them, concentrate, but it's all moths and bramble.

Her.

She's here now, isn't she? Who is she?

The one he waits for.

"Wecouldhavedoneit, Matthew."

Matthew.

He is Matthew, right? Is Her talking to him?

"Youdon'tknowwhoIam . . ."

He tries to turn, to wrench free so he can see Her instead of the ceiling, which seems to roll back and forth above him.

He screams for Her, cries, tries to remember the words he needs, but there's nothing there to be found. Frustration rises up, makes even the pain go away.

He can't move. He's a bread—no, that's not the right thing—tied down, strapped tight. Bound.

Someone else now. A different voice.

He feels it all slipping away. He stills, unable to remember even a minute ago. Her.

What does that mean?

He quits fighting, stares up at the woman in the orange outfit, listens to her soothing voice.

His eyes close. His last thought is Her. Don't leave, *but he doesn't even know what it means.*

He hears footsteps. Running.

It is like the beating of his heart. There and then gone.

TWENTY-FIVE

---•⊶≫⊕⊷⊕⊶≪⊶•---

Falling snow turned Homer into a blurred landscape of muted colors and washed-out skies. The few people out and about were either seeing the world through dirty windshields or looking up at it with tucked-in chins. No one noticed a girl in a huge parka, hood up, scarf wrapped around the lower half of her face, trudging downhill.

Leni's face hurt like hell, her nose throbbed, but none of it was the worst of her pain. At Airport Road, the snow let up a little. She turned and headed to the airfield. At the door to the airfield office, she paused and pulled her turtleneck up over her torn lip.

The office was small and constructed of wood and corrugated metal with a sharply slanted roof. It looked like an oversized chicken coop. Behind it, she saw a small plane out on the airstrip, revving its engine. The sign for Glass Lake Aviation was missing two letters, so the sign read: ASS LAKE AVI-ATION. It had been that way for as long as Leni could remember. The owner said he'd fixed it once and that was plenty. Supposedly schoolkids stole the letters for fun.

Inside, the place looked unfinished, too: a floor made of mismatched peel-and-stick linoleum tiles, a plywood counter, a small display of brochures for tourists, a bathroom behind a broken door. A stack of boxes stood by the back door—supplies recently delivered or soon to be shipped.

Mama sat in a white plastic chair, with a scarf coiled around the lower half of her face and a hat covering her blond hair. Leni sat down beside her in a floral overstuffed recliner that some cat had clawed to ribbons.

In front of them, a Formica coffee table was littered with magazines.

Leni was tired of crying, of feeling this grief that kept opening and closing inside of her, but even so, she felt tears sting her eyes.

Mama put her cigarette out in the empty Coke can on the table in front of her. Smoke sizzled up, wafted into nothingness. She leaned back, sighing.

"How was he?" Mama asked.

"The same." Leni leaned against her mama, needing the solid warmth of her body. She reached into her pocket and felt something sharp.

The present Mr. Walker had given her from Matthew. In all that had happened, she'd forgotten about it. She pulled it out, stared down at the small, thin gift, wrapped in newsprint, upon which Matthew had written: *HAPPY BIRTHDAY LENI!*

Her eighteenth birthday had gone by almost unnoticed this year, but Matthew had been planning for it. Maybe he'd had an idea about how to celebrate it.

She peeled the newsprint back, folded it carefully into something she would save. (He'd touched it while thinking of her.) Inside, she found a slim white box. Inside of that, a piece of yellowed, ripped-edge newsprint carefully folded.

It was a newspaper article and an old black-and-white photograph of two homesteaders, holding hands. They were surrounded by sled dogs, sitting in mismatched chairs in front of a tiny, mossy-roofed cabin. Junk decorated the yard. A towheaded boy sat in the dirt. Leni recognized the yard and the deck: these were Matthew's grandparents.

Across the bottom, Matthew had written, *THIS COULD BE US.*

Leni's eyes stung. She held the photograph to her heart and looked down at the article.

MY ALASKA by Lily Walker
July 4, 1972

You think you know what wild means. It's a word you've used all your life. You use it to describe an animal, your hair, an undisciplined child. In Alaska, you learn what wild really means.

My husband, Eckhart, and I came to this place separately, which may not seem important, but certainly is. We had each decided on our own, and not when we were young, I might add, that civilization was not for us. It was the middle of the Great Depression. I lived in a shack with my parents and six siblings. There was never enough of anything—not time, not money, not food, not love.

What made me think of Alaska? Even now, I don't recall. I was thirty-five years old, on the shelf, they called us spinsters then. My youngest sister died— of a broken heart maybe, or of the despair that came with watching her own babies suffer—and I walked away.

Just like that. I had ten dollars in my pocket and no real skills and I headed West. Of course I went West, for the romance of it. In Seattle, I saw a sign for Alaska. They were looking for women to do laundry for men in the gold fields.

I thought, "I can wash clothes," and I went.

It was hard work, with men catcalling all the time, and my skin hardening until it was like leather. Then I met Eckhart. He was ten years older than me, and not much to look at, if I'm being truthful.

He caught my eye and told me his dream of homesteading the Kenai Peninsula. When he held out his hand, I took it. Did I love him? No. Not then. Not for years, really, although when he died, it was like God had reached in and yanked the heart out of my chest.

Wild. That's how I describe it all. My love. My life. Alaska. Truthfully, it's all the same to me. Alaska doesn't attract many; most are too tame to handle life up here. But when she gets her hooks in you, she digs deep and holds on, and you become hers. Wild. A lover of cruel beauty and splendid isolation. And God help you, you can't live anywhere else.

"What do you have there?" Mama asked, exhaling smoke.

Leni carefully folded the article into quarters. "An article by Matthew's grandma. She died a few years before we came to Alaska." The photograph of Matthew's grandparents—dated 1940—sat on her lap. "How will I stop loving him, Mama? Will I . . . forget?"

Mama sighed. "Ah. That. Love doesn't fade or die, baby girl. People tell you it does, but it doesn't. If you love him now, you'll love him in ten years and in forty. Differently, maybe, a faded version, but he's part of you now. And you are part of him."

Leni didn't know if that was comforting or frightening. If she felt like this forever, as if her heart were an open wound, how would she ever be happy again?

"But love doesn't come just once in your life, either. Not if you're lucky."

"I don't think we Allbrights are lucky," Leni said.

"I don't know. You found him once, in the middle of nowhere. What were the chances that you'd meet him, that he'd love you, that you'd love him? I'd say, lucky you."

"And then we fell down into a crevice, he got brain damaged and you killed Dad to protect me."

"Yeah. Well. The glass can be half empty or half full."

Leni knew the glass was broken. "Where are we going?" she asked.

"Do you really care?"

"No."

"We're going back to Seattle. It's all I could think of. Thanks to Large Marge, we're flying and not hitchhiking."

The door opened, bringing in a rush of ice-cold air. A woman in a brown parka appeared, a Cowichan tuque pulled low on her forehead. "Plane's ready for take-off. Flight to Anchorage."

Mama immediately pulled the scarf up to just beneath her eyes, while Leni flipped up her parka's hood, pulled the strings so it tightened around her face.

"Are you our passengers?" the woman said, looking down at a sheet of paper in her gloved hands. Before Mama could answer, the phone on the desk rang. The woman moved toward it, answering, "Glass Lake Aviation."

Mama and Leni hurried out of the small office toward the airfield, where their airplane waited, propeller whirring. At the plane, Leni tossed her backpack into the aft area, where it fell amid boxes to be delivered somewhere, and followed her mother into the shadowy interior.

She took her seat (there were only two of them behind the pilot) and tightened her seat belt.

The small plane rumbled forward, clattered hard, then lifted, swayed, leveled out. The engine sounded like the cards the kids on her old block used to put in their bicycle spokes.

Leni stared out the window, down into the gloom. From this height, everything looked charcoal-gray and white, a blurring of land and sea and sky. Jagged white mountains, angry white-tipped waves on an ash-gray sea. Cabins and homes clinging stubbornly to a wild shoreline.

Homer slowly disappeared from view.

✢⟨❀⟩✢

Seattle at night in the falling rain.

A snake of yellow headlights in the dark. Neon signs everywhere, reflections cast on wet streets. Traffic lights changing color. Horns honking out staccato warnings.

Music tumbled out of open doors, assaulting the night, unlike any music Leni had heard before. It had a clanging, angry sound and some of the people standing outside of the bars looked like they'd landed from Mars—with safety pins in their cheeks and stiff blue Mohawks and black clothes that appeared to have been cut to ribbons.

"It's okay," Mama said, pulling Leni in close as they walked past a group of homeless-looking people who stood listlessly in a park, passing cigarettes back and forth.

Leni saw the city in bits and pieces through lowered lashes, blurred by the incessant rain. She saw women with babies huddled in doorways and men asleep in sleeping bags beneath the elevated road that looked down on this section of town. Leni couldn't imagine why people would live this way when they could go to Alaska and live off the land and build themselves a home. She couldn't help thinking about all those girls who'd been abducted in 1974 and found dead not far from here. Ted Bundy had been arrested, but did that mean the streets were safe now?

Mama found a pay phone and called a taxi. As they stood there waiting for it to arrive, the rain stopped.

A bright yellow cab pulled up to the dirty curb, splashing water on them. Leni followed her mama into the backseat, which smelled aggressively of pine. From here on, Leni saw the lights of the city through a window. With water everywhere, in drips and puddles, but no rain falling, the place had a jumbled, multicolored, carnival look.

They angled uphill. The old brick and low-rise part of the city—Pioneer Square—was apparently the pit people climbed out of when they got money. Downtown was a canyon of office buildings, skyscrapers, and stores, set on busy streets, with windows that looked like movie sets, inhabited by mannequins dressed in glitzy suits with exaggerated shoulder pads and cinched-in waists. At the top of the hill, the city gave way to a neighborhood of stately homes.

"There it is," Mama said to the cabbie, giving him the last of their borrowed cash.

The house was bigger than Leni remembered. In the dark, it looked vaguely sinister, with its peaked roof pointing high into a black night sky and glowing diamond-paned windows. All of it was surrounded by an iron fence topped with heart-piercing spires.

"You sure?" Leni asked quietly.

Leni knew what this had cost her mother, coming home for help. She saw the impact of it in her mother's eyes, in the slump of her shoulders, in the way her hands curled into fists. Mama felt like a failure coming back here. "It just proves they were right about him all along."

"We could disappear from here, too. Start over by ourselves."

"I might do that for myself, baby girl, but not for you. I was a crappy mother. I am going to be a good grandmother. Please. Don't give me a way out." She took a deep breath. "Let's go."

Leni took hold of Mama's hand; they walked up the stone path together, where spotlights shone on bushes sculpted to look like animals and spiky rosebushes cut back for winter. At the ornate front door they paused. Waited. Then Mama knocked.

Moments later, the door opened and Grandma appeared.

The years had changed her, imprinted and pulled at her face. Her hair had gone gray. Or maybe it had always been gray and she'd stopped dyeing it. "Oh, my God," she whispered, clamping a thin hand to her mouth.

"Hey, Mom," Mama said, her voice unsteady.

Leni heard footsteps.

Grandma stepped aside; Grandpa moved in beside her. He was a big man—fat stomach straining at a blue cashmere sweater, big floppy jowls, white hair that was combed across his shiny head, the strands carefully tended. Baggy black polyester pants, cinched tight with a belt, suggested bird-thin legs underneath. He looked older than his seventy years.

"Hey," Mama said.

Her grandparents stared at them, eyes narrowed, seeing the bruises on Leni's and Mama's faces, the swollen cheeks, the black eyes. "Son of a bitch," Grandpa said.

"We need help," Mama said, squeezing Leni's hand.

"Where is he?" Grandpa wanted to know.

"We've left him," Mama said.

"Thank God," Grandma said.

"Do we need to worry about him coming to look for you, breaking down my door?" Grandpa asked.

Mama shook her head. "No. Never."

Grandpa's eyes narrowed. Did he understand what that meant? What they'd done? "What do you—"

"I'm pregnant," Leni said. They had talked about this, she and Mama, and decided to say nothing about the pregnancy yet, but now that they were here, asking for help—begging—Leni couldn't do it. She had kept enough secrets in her life. She didn't want to live in the shadows of them anymore.

"Apple doesn't fall far from the tree," Mama said, trying to smile.

"We've been here before," Grandpa said. "I seem to recall my advice to you."

"You wanted me to give her up and come home and pretend I could be the girl I was before," Mama said. "And I wanted you to say it was okay, that you loved me anyway."

"What we said," Grandma said softly, "was that there were women in our church who were unable to have children and would have given your baby a good home."

"I'm keeping my baby," Leni said. "If you don't want to help us, it's fine, but I'm keeping the baby."

Mama squeezed her hand.

Silence followed Leni's declaration. In it, Leni glimpsed the largeness of the world for her and Mama now, the ocean of troubles they faced on their own, and it frightened her, but not as much as the idea of the world she would inhabit if she gave up this baby. Some choices you didn't recover from; she was old enough to know that.

Finally, after what felt like forever, Grandma turned to her husband. "Cecil, how many times have we talked about a second chance? This is it."

"You won't run off in the middle of the night again?" he said to Mama. "Your mother . . . barely survived it."

In those few words, carefully chosen, Leni heard sorrow. There was hurt between these people and her mother, hurt and regret and mistrust, but something softer, too.

"No, sir. We won't."

At last, Grandpa smiled. "Welcome home, Coraline. Lenora. Let's get some ice on those bruises. You both should see a doctor."

Leni saw Mama's reluctance to step into the house. She took Mama by the arm, steadied her.

"Don't let go," Mama whispered.

Inside, Leni noticed the smell of flowers. There were several large floral arrangements positioned artfully on gleaming wooden tables and gilt-edged mirrors on the walls.

Leni glanced into rooms and down hallways as they walked. She saw a dining room with a table that accommodated twelve, a library with floor-to-ceiling bookshelves, a living room in which there were two of everything, sofas, chairs, windows, lamps. A staircase with carpet so plush it felt like walking on muskeg in the summer led to an upstairs hallway that was paneled in mahogany and decorated with brass sconces and paintings of dogs and horses in ornate golden frames.

"Here," Grandma said, finally stopping. Grandpa hung back, as if maybe doling out rooms was women's work. "Lenora, you will sleep in Coraline's old room. Cora, come this way."

Leni stepped into her new room.

At first all she saw was lace. Not the cheap eyelet she was used to seeing at Goodwill; this was fine, almost like cobwebs strung together. Ivory lace curtains framed the windows. There was more ivory lace on the bedding and lampshades. On the floor, pale oatmeal-colored carpeting. Furniture that was ivory with gilt edges. A small kidney-shaped desk had an ivory-colored cushioned stool tucked up underneath.

The air felt stifling, unnatural, bathed in a false lavender scent.

She went to the window, lifted the heavy sash, and leaned out. The sweet night welcomed her, calmed her. The rain had stopped, leaving a glittering black night in its wake. Lights were on in all the houses up and down the street.

There was a small patch of wet roof in front of her. Below that, the well-tended yard, with an old maple tree tucked in close, its branches mostly bare, only a few red-gold leaves still hanging on.

Trees. Night air. Quiet.

Leni climbed out onto the shake-covered roof below her room. Although there were lights on in the house, and houses with lights on across the street, she felt safer out here. She smelled trees and greenery and even a distant tang of the sea.

The sky was unfamiliar. Black. In Alaska the night sky in winter was a deep velvet blue and when snow covered the ground and cloaked the trees, ambient light created a magical glow. And then, sometimes, the northern lights danced overhead. Still, she recognized the stars; they weren't in the same place, but they were the same stars. The Big Dipper. Orion's Belt. Constellations Matthew had shown her that night when they'd lain on the beach.

Her fingers closed around the heart necklace at her throat. She could wear it openly now and not worry about her father asking where she'd gotten it. She would never take it off again.

"You want some company?"

"Sure," Leni said, scooting sideways.

Mama climbed through the open window and made her way onto the roof, then sat beside Leni, drawing her knees up to her chest. "I used to climb down that tree and sneak out on Saturday nights in high school to hang out with boys at Dick's Drive-In on Aurora. Everything was about boys." She sighed, dropped her chin into the valley between her knees.

Leni leaned against her mama, stared out at the house across the street. A blaze of wasteful lights. Through the windows, she saw at least three televisions flashing color.

"I'm sorry, Leni. I've made such a mess of your life."

"*We* did it," Leni said. "Together. Now we have to live with it."

"There's something wrong with me," Mama said after a pause.

"No," Leni said firmly. "There was something wrong with him."

⬩⫰⟨❀⟩⫯⬩

"IT'S THERE, believe me. Right there," Mama said five days later, when their bruises had healed enough to be covered with makeup. They had spent almost a week huddled in the house, never venturing outside. They were both going a little stir-crazy.

Now, with Mama's hair cut in a pixie and dyed brown, they finally left the house and took a bus into busy downtown Seattle, where they merged into the eclectic crowd of tourists, shoppers, and punk rockers.

Mama pointed up into the cloudless blue sky.

Leni didn't care about The Mountain (that was what they called Rainier down here—The Mountain—as if it were the only one that mattered in the world) or the other landmarks Mama had pointed out with such pride, as if Leni had never seen them before. The bright neon PUBLIC MARKET sign that looked down on the fish market booth; the Space Needle, which looked like an alien spacecraft placed on pick-up sticks; the new aquarium that jutted defiantly out into the cold waters of Elliott Bay.

Seattle was beautiful on this sunny, warm November day; that was true. As green as she remembered, and bordered by water and covered in asphalt and concrete.

People crawled like ants over all of it. All noise and movement: honking horns, people crossing streets, buses puffing smoke and grinding gears on the hills that propped the city up. How could she ever be at home here, among all these people?

There was no silence in this place. For the last few nights, she'd lain in her new bed (which smelled of fabric softener and store-bought laundry soap), trying to get comfortable. Once an ambulance or police siren had blared all of a sudden, red light snapping on and off through the window, painting the lace bloodred.

Now she and Mama were north of the city. They had taken a cross-town bus, found seats among the sad-looking travelers out this early, and walked through the busy "Ave" and uphill to the sprawling University of Washington.

They stood at the edge of something called Red Square. For as far as Leni could see, the ground had been layered in red brick. A large red obelisk pointed up at the blue sky. More brick buildings created a perimeter.

There were literally hundreds of students moving through the square; they came and went in laughing, chattering waves. Off to her left, a group dressed all in black was holding up protest signs about nuclear power and weapons. Several demanded a shutdown of something called Hanford.

She was reminded of the college kids she'd seen in Homer every summer, clots of young adults in REI rain gear looking up at the jagged, snow-capped peaks as though they heard God calling their names. She would hear whispered conversations about how they were going to chuck it all and move off the grid and live more authentic lives. *Back to the land*, they'd said, as if it were biblical verse. Like the famous John Muir quote—*The mountains are calling and I must go*. People heard those kinds of voices in Alaska, dreamed new dreams. Most would never go, and of the few who did, the vast majority would leave before the end of their first winter, but Leni had always known they would be changed simply by the magnitude of the dream and the possibility they glimpsed in the distance.

Leni drifted through the crowd alongside her mother, clutching the small backpack she'd had since she was twelve years old. Her Alaska backpack. It felt totemic, the last durable remnant of a discarded life. She wished she'd been able to bring her Winnie the Pooh lunch box.

They arrived at their destination: a sugary pink Gothic building with sweeping arches and delicate spires and intricately scrolled windows.

Inside was a library unlike any Leni had ever seen. Row upon row of wooden desks, decorated with green banker's lamps, were positioned beneath an arched ceiling. Gothic chandeliers hung above the desks. And the books! She'd never seen so many. They whispered to her of unexplored worlds and unmet friends and she realized that she wasn't alone in this new world. Her friends were here, spine out, waiting for her as they always had. *If only Matthew could see this . . .*

She walked in step with her mother, their clunky boot heels clattering on the floor. Leni kept expecting people to look up, to point them out as intruders, but the students in the Graduate Reading Room didn't care about strangers in their midst.

Even the librarian didn't seem to make any judgments about them as she listened to their questions and gave them directions to another desk, where another librarian listened to their request.

"Here you go," the second librarian said, handing them a collection of bound newspapers.

Mama said, "Thank you," and sat down. Leni doubted the librarian heard the tremble in Mama's voice, but Leni did.

She sat down on the wooden bench next to Mama, scooted close.

It didn't take much time to find what they were looking for.

KANEQ FAMILY MISSING
FOUL PLAY SUSPECTED

State authorities released information about a missing Kaneq family. Neighbor Marge Birdsall called State Troopers on November 13 to report her neighbor, Cora Allbright, and her daughter, Lenora, missing. "They were supposed to visit me yesterday. They never showed. I worried right off that Ernt had hurt them," said Birdsall.

On November 14, Thomas Walker reported finding an abandoned truck not far from his homestead. The vehicle—registered to Ernt Allbright—was found at Mile Marker 12 on the Kaneq road.

Authorities reported finding blood on the seat and steering wheel, as well as Cora Allbright's purse.

"We are investigating this as both a missing persons and as a potential homicide," said Officer Curt Ward of Homer. Neighbors reported that Ernt Allbright had a history of violence and they fear he killed his wife and daughter and ran off.

No additional information is available for release at this time, as the investigation is ongoing.

Anyone with information on any of the Allbrights is asked to call Officer Ward.

Mama leaned back, sighing quietly.

Leni saw the pain Mama carried and would now always carry—for all of it, for staying when she should have left, for loving him, for killing him. What came of pain like that? Did it slowly dissipate or did it congeal and turn poisonous?

"Dad says they'll declare us dead at some point—but it might take seven years."

"Seven years?"

"We have to go forward, learn to be happy, or what was it all for?"

Happy.

The word had no buoyancy for Leni, no lift. To be honest, she couldn't imagine ever being happy again, not really.

"Yeah," Leni said, trying to smile. "We'll be happy now."

TWENTY-SIX

———✦———

That evening, after dinner, Leni sat on her twin bed, reading. *The Stand* by Stephen King. In the past week, she'd read three books by him and discovered a new passion. Goodbye science fiction and fantasy, hello horror.

She figured it was a reflection of her inner life. She'd rather have nightmares about Randall Flagg or Carrie or Jack Torrance than about her own past.

She was just turning a page when she heard voices, lowered, moving past her room.

Leni glanced at the bedside clock, one of dozens in the house, all ticking in time like the beat of a hidden heart. Almost nine P.M.

Usually her grandparents were in bed by now.

Leni set the book aside, marking her page. She went to the door, cracked it open just enough so she could peer out.

Lights were on downstairs.

Leni slipped out of her room. Her bare feet made no sound on the plush wool carpeting. Her hand gliding down the smooth mahogany banister, she hurried down the steps. At the bottom, the black-and-white marble felt cold beneath her feet.

Mama was in the living room with her parents. Leni carefully edged forward, just enough so she could see:

Mama sitting on the burnt-orange sofa, with her parents sitting across from her in matching paisley wingback chairs. Between them, the maple coffee table was decorated with a forest of ornate china figurines.

"They think he killed us," Mama said. "I read the local paper today."

"He easily might have," Grandma responded. "I warned you, you recall, not to go to Alaska."

"Not to marry him," Grandpa said.

"Do you think I need I-told-you-sos?" Mama said. She sighed heavily. "I loved him."

Leni heard the sorrow and regret that eddied between the three of them. She wouldn't have understood that kind of regret even a year ago. She did now.

"I don't know what to do from here," Mama said. "I've screwed up Leni's life and my own, and now I've dragged you into it."

"Are you kidding?" Grandma said. "Of course you dragged us into it. We're your parents."

Grandpa said, "This is for you."

Leni wanted to peer around but didn't dare. She heard the squeaking of a chair, then heels clicking on hardwood floors (Grandpa always wore dress shoes, from breakfast to bedtime), and finally a crumpling paper sound.

"It's a birth certificate," Mama said after a moment. "For an Evelyn Chesterfield. Born April 4, 1939. Why are you giving it to me?"

Leni heard the squeaking chair again. "And here's a falsified marriage license. You married a man name Chad Grant. With these two documents, you'll be able to go to the DMV and get a license and a new Social Security card. I have a birth certificate for Leni, too. She'll be your daughter, Susan Grant. You two will rent a house not far from here. We will tell everyone you are a relative, or our housekeeper. Something. Anything to keep you safe," Grandpa said, his voice rough with emotion.

"How did you get these?"

"I'm a lawyer. I know people. I paid a client of mine, a man of . . . flexible morals."

"That's not who you are," Mama said quietly.

There was a pause, then: "We are all of us changed," Grandpa said. "We've learned the hard way, haven't we? By making mistakes. We should have listened to you when you were sixteen."

"And I should have listened to you."

The doorbell rang.

The sound was so unexpected at this time of night, that Leni felt a clutch of fear. She heard the sound of footsteps, then the rustle of wooden blinds.

"Police," she heard her grandpa say.

Mama hurried out of the living room and saw Leni.

"Go upstairs," Grandpa said, following Mama out of the living room.

Mama took Leni's hand and led her up the stairs. "This way," Mama said. "Quiet."

They hurried up the stairs and tiptoed down the unlit hallway into the master bedroom—a huge room with mullioned windows and olive green carpet. A four-poster bed was dressed in lace that matched the carpet precisely.

Mama led Leni to a heating vent in the floor. With care, she pulled the vent out and set it aside.

Mama knelt down, motioned for Leni to scoot beside her. "I used to eavesdrop on the nuns when they came to expel me."

Leni heard footsteps echo through the metal vent slats.

Men's voices.

"Detectives Archer Madison and Keller Watt. Seattle PD."

Grandpa: "Is there something amiss in the neighborhood, Officers, at this late hour?"

"We're here [something they couldn't hear] behalf of Alaska state troopers.

[Words that blended together] your daughter, Cora Allbright . . . [something] last seen her . . . Sorry to say . . . presumed dead."

Leni heard her grandma cry out.

"Here, ma'am, let us help you sit."

A pause. Long. Then a scuffling sound, a briefcase being opened, papers withdrawn. "The pickup truck found . . . cabin full of blood, broken window, obvious crime scene but the evidence was destroyed by animals . . . tests inconclusive . . . X-rays that showed a broken arm . . . broken nose. Search being conducted, but . . . this time of year . . . weather. God knows what we'll find when the snow melts . . . keep you informed . . ."

"He killed them," Grandpa said. These words were loud, angry. "Son of a bitch."

"Many reports . . . his violence."

Leni turned to her mama. "So we got away with it?"

"Well . . . there's no statute of limitations on murder. And everything we've done—and will do at the DMV—will be evidence of guilt. He was shot in the back and we disposed of the body and ran. If he is ever found, they'll come looking for us, and now my parents have lied for us. Another crime. So we have to be careful."

"For how long?"

"Forever, baby girl."

Dear Matthew,

I've called the rehab facility every day this week. I pretend I'm your cousin. The answer is always the same: no change. It breaks a little more of my heart every time.

I know I can never send this letter and that even if I did, you couldn't read it or wouldn't understand the words. But I have to write to you, even if the words are lost. I told myself (and have been told repeatedly by others) that I need to move on with my new life. And I'm trying to do that. I am.

But you are inside of me, a part of me, maybe even the best part. I'm not talking only about our baby. I hear your voice in my head. You talk to me in my sleep so much I've gotten used to waking with tears on my cheeks.

I guess my mama was right about love. As screwed up as she is, she understands the durability and lunacy of it. You can't make yourself fall in love, I suppose, and you can't make yourself fall out of it.

I am trying to fit in down here. Trying hard. I mean, Susan Grant is trying to fit in. The streets are jammed with cars and the sidewalks are wall-to-wall people and pretty much no one looks at anyone else or says hello. You were right about the beauty, though. When I let myself see it, it's there. I see it in Mount Rainier, which reminds me of Iliamna and can magically appear and disappear. Down here, it's called The Mountain because really they only have the one. Not like home, where mountains form the exposed spine of our world.

My grandparents care about the weirdest things. How the table is set, what time we eat, how well I tuck the sheets into the bed, how tightly I braid my hair. My grandmother handed me tweezers the other day and told me to pluck my eyebrows.

But we have a nice little rental house not far from them and we can visit if we are careful. I think Mama is surprised to find that she likes to be with her parents. We have plenty to eat and new clothes and when we all sit around the dinner table, we try to knit our lives together, dropped stitches and all.

Maybe that's what love is.

✦⟨❀⟩✦

Dear Matthew,

Christmas here is like an Olympic event. I've never seen so much glitter and food. My grandparents gave me so many gifts it was embarrassing. But afterward, when I was in my own room alone, staring out the window at neighbors we stay away from, looking at houses strung in twinkling lights, I thought of real winter. Of you. Of us.

I looked at the picture of your grandparents and reread your grandmother's newspaper article.

I wonder what it's like for our baby. Does she feel how uncertain I am? Does the song of my broken heart play for her? I want her to be happy. I want her to be the child of our love, of who we were.

I think I felt the baby move today . . .

I'm thinking of her as Lily. After your grandma.

A girl needs to be strong in this world.

Dear Matthew,

I can't believe it's 1979. I called the rehab facility again today and heard the usual. No change.

Unfortunately, my mother overheard my call. She blew her stack and said I was being stupid. Apparently the police can trace the call if they wanted to. So I can't call anymore. I can't put us all at risk, but how can I stop? It's all I have left of you. I know you're not going to get better, but every time I call, I think, maybe this time. That hope is all I have, useless or not.

But that's bad news and that's easy. You want good news. It's a new year.

I am going to the University of Washington. My grandmother pulled some strings and got Susan Grant registered with no evidence of graduation from high school. Life sure is different in the Outside. How much money you have matters.

College isn't what I expected. Some of the girls wear these fuzzy Shetland sweaters and plaid skirts and knee socks. I guess they're sorority girls. They giggle and clump together like sheep and the boys who follow

them around are so loud a bear could hear them coming from a mile
away.

In class, I pretend you're beside me. Once I believed it so much I
almost wrote a note to pass you under my desk.

I miss you. Every day and even more at night. So does Lily. She's
started to kick me awake sometimes. When she does get all squirrelly,
I read her Robert Service poems and tell her about you.

That quiets her right down.

✦⟨❀⟩✦

Dear Matthew,

Spring here is nothing like breakup. No earth falling away, no
house-sized blocks of ice snapping free, no lost things seeping up from
the mud.

It's just color everywhere. I've never seen so many flowering trees;
pink blossoms float through the campus.

My grandfather says the investigation is still open, but no one is
looking for us anymore. They assume we are dead.

In a way, it's true. The Allbrights vanished into nothing.

At night I talk to you and Lily now. Does that mean I'm crazy or just
lonely? I imagine all three of us huddled in bed, with the northern lights
putting on a show outside our window while wind taps on the glass. I tell
our baby to be smart and brave. Brave like her dad. I try to tell her to
protect herself from the terrible choices she might someday face. I worry
that we Allbright women are cursed in love and I hope she will be a boy.
Then I remember you saying that you wanted to teach your son the things
you had learned on the homestead and . . . well, it makes me so sad I crawl
into bed and pull the covers over my head and pretend I'm in Alaska in the
winter. My heartbeat turns into wind pounding on the glass.

A boy needs a father and I am all Lily has.

Poor girl.

"THOSE LAMAZE CLASSES were *bogus*," Leni yelled when the next contraction twisted her insides and made her scream. "I want drugs."

"You wanted natural childbirth. It's too late for drugs now," Mama said.

"I'm eighteen years old. Why would anyone listen to what I want? I know nothing," Leni said.

The contraction ebbed. Pain receded.

Leni panted. Sweat itched and crawled across her forehead.

Mama picked up an ice chip from the plastic cup on the table by the hospital bed and popped it in Leni's mouth.

"Put morphine in it, Mama," Leni begged. "Please. I can't take this. It was a mistake. I'm not ready to be a mother."

Mama smiled. "No one is ever ready."

The pain began building again. Leni gritted her teeth, concentrated on breathing (like *that* helped), and clutched her mother's hand.

She squeezed her eyes shut, panting, until the pain crested. When it began—finally—to subside, she sank back into the bed, spent. She thought: *Matthew should be here*, but she pushed the thought aside.

Another contraction hit seconds later. This time Leni bit her tongue so hard it bled.

"Scream," Mama said.

The door opened and her doctor came in. She was a thin woman wearing blue scrubs and a surgical cap. Her eyebrows were unevenly plucked, which gave her a slightly askew look. "Ms. Grant, how are we feeling?" the doctor asked.

"Get it out of me. Please."

The doctor nodded and put on gloves. "Let's check, shall we?" She opened the stirrups.

Normally Leni would not be relieved when a relative stranger sat between her spread legs, but right now she would have splayed herself at the observation deck of the Space Needle if it would end this pain.

"It looks like we're having a baby," the doctor said evenly.

"No *shit*," Leni shouted at another contraction.

"Okay, Susan. Push. Hard. Harder."

Leni did. She pushed, she screamed, she sweated, she swore.

And then, as quickly as her pain had come, it ended.

Leni collapsed into the bed.

"A baby boy," the doctor said, turning to Mama. "Grandma Eve, do you want to cut the cord?"

As if through mist, Leni watched her mother cut the cord and follow the doctor over to an area where they wrapped the newborn in a pale blue thermal blanket. Leni tried to sit up but she had no strength left.

A boy, Matthew. Your son.

Leni panicked, thought, *He needs you, Matthew. I can't do this . . .*

Mama helped Leni to a sitting position and put the tiny bundle in her arms.

Her *son*. He was the smallest thing she'd ever seen, with a face like a peach and muddy blue eyes that opened and closed and a little rosebud mouth that made sucking motions. A pink fist burst out of the blue blanket and Leni reached down for it.

The baby's minuscule fingers closed around hers.

A searing, cleansing, enveloping love blew her heart into a million tiny pieces and reshaped it. "Oh, my God," she said in awe.

"Yeah," Mama said. "You've been asking what it's like."

"Matthew Denali Walker, Junior," she said quietly. A fourth-generation Alaskan who would never know his father, never feel Matthew's strong arms around him or hear his steadying voice.

"Hey, you," she said.

She knew now why she had run away from their crime. She hadn't known before, hadn't understood, truly, what she had to lose.

This child. Her son.

She would give up her life to protect him. She would do anything and everything to keep him safe. Even if that meant listening to her mother and cutting the last, tender thread to Alaska and Matthew—the calls to the rehab center. She wouldn't call again. The very thought tore her heart, but what else could she do? She was a mother now.

She was crying softly. Maybe Mama heard and knew why and knew there was nothing to say; or maybe all mothers cried right now. "Matthew," she whispered, stroking his velvet cheek. "We'll call you MJ. They called your Daddy Mattie sometimes, but I never did . . . and he knew how to fly . . . he would have loved you so much . . ."

1986

TWENTY-SEVEN

———— ∘∘≫⊹⊙⊹⊰≪∘∘ ————

I don't know how to live with what I've done to her life," Cora said.

"It's been years," her mother said. "Look at her. She's happy. Why must we keep having this conversation?"

Cora wanted to agree. It was what she said to herself on a daily basis. *Look, she's happy.* Sometimes, she was able to almost wholly believe it. And then there were days like today. She didn't know what caused the change. Weather, maybe. Old habits. The kind of corrosive fear that once it moved in, pitted your bones and stayed forever.

Seven years had passed since Cora had dragged Leni away from Alaska and brought her here, to this city poised on the water's edge.

Cora saw how Leni had tried to put down roots into this rich, wet land, tried to flourish. But Seattle was a city of hundreds of thousands; it could never speak the rugged language of Leni's pioneer soul.

Cora lit a cigarette, drew the smoke into her lungs, and let it linger there; instantly she was calmed by the familiar act. She exhaled and lifted her chin, trying to get comfortable on the camp chair. Her lower back ached from a night spent in the pseudo-wilderness sleeping in a tent; her breathing was ragged from a persistent cold.

Not far away, Leni stood at the river's edge with a little boy on one side of her and an old man on the other. She cast her line out in a graceful, practiced arc, the line snapping and dancing in the air before it cascaded into the calm water. Late spring sunlight painted all of it gold; the water, the three mismatched figures, the nearby trees. Even as the sun shone down on them it began to rain, tiny droplets drawn from the damp air.

They were in the Hoh Rain Forest, one of the last refuges of pure wilderness in the populated western half of Washington State. They came here as often as they could and pitched their tents on campsites that offered both electricity and water. Here, away from the crowds, they could be who they really were. They didn't have to worry about being seen together or making up stories or telling lies. It had been years since anyone had mentioned the Allbright family in Alaska or gone looking for any of them, but still, they were always on guard.

Leni said she could breathe in this wilderness, where the trees were as big around as Volkswagens and grew high enough to block out the recalcitrant sun. She said she had things to teach her son that were part of his heritage, lessons that couldn't be taught where the world was paved and lit by streetlamps. Things his father would have taught him.

In the past few years, Cora's father had become an avid fisherman—or maybe he was just an avid grandfather who did anything and everything to make Leni and MJ smile. He'd quit practicing law and had become a putterer around the house.

So they came camping out here as often as they could, regardless of the rain that greeted them ten times out of twelve, even in midsummer. They caught fish for dinner and fried it in cast-iron skillets over an open flame. At night, while they all sat around the campfire, Leni recited poems and told stories set in the wilderness of Alaska.

It wasn't *fun* for Leni. It was something different. Vital. A way to release the pressure that built up all week as she walked among the hordes at the sprawling University of Washington campus, as she sold books to patrons at her part-time job at the giant Shorey's Bookstore on First Avenue and took photography classes at night.

Leni came out here to re-find herself in nature, to recover whatever small piece of her Alaskan soul she could find, to connect her son to the father he didn't know and the life that was his by birthright but not in fact. Alaska, the last frontier, the land that would always and forever be home to Leni. The place where she belonged.

"You can hear him laughing," her mother said.

Cora nodded. It was true; even with the percussive drumbeat of the increasing rain, drops landing on nylon tents and plastic hoods and plate-sized leaves, she could hear her grandson's laughter.

MJ was the happiest of kids—a boy who made friends easily and followed the rules and still held your hand when you walked down the sidewalk toward school. He cared about the usual things for a boy his age—action figures and cartoons and Popsicles in the summer. He was still young enough that he didn't ask a lot of questions about his father, but that would come. They all knew it. Cora knew, too, that when MJ looked at his mother's smile, he saw none of the shadows crouched behind it.

"Do you think she will forgive me someday?" she asked, staring out at Leni.

"Oh, for the love of Pete. For what? Saving her life? That girl loves you, Coraline."

Cora took a long drag on her cigarette, exhaled. "I know she loves me. I have never doubted for a second that she loves me. But I let her grow up in a war zone. I let her see what no child should ever see. I let her know fear of a man who was supposed to love her, and then I killed him in front of her. And I ran and made her live life under an alias. Maybe if I'd been stronger, braver, I could have changed the law like Yvonne Wanrow."

"It took *years* for that woman's case to get to the Supreme Court. And you were in Alaska, not Washington. Who knew the law would finally recognize a battered woman defense? And your dad still says it rarely works. You have to let all of that go. *She* has. Look at her, down there with her son, teaching him how to fish. Your daughter is fine, Cora. Fine. She's forgiven you. You need to forgive yourself."

"She needs to go home."

"Home? To the cabin with no plumbing or electricity? To the brain-damaged boy? To an accessory-after-the-fact charge? There's that new blood test now. Something about DNA. So don't be ridiculous, Cora." She reached out, slid her arm around Cora's shoulder. "Think of all that you've found here. Leni is getting an education and becoming a wonderful photographer. You like your job at the art gallery. Your home is always warm and you have a family you can count on."

What she'd done to her daughter had been forgiven, it was true, and Leni's forgiveness was as real and true as sunlight. But Cora, try as she had for all of these years, couldn't forgive herself. It wasn't the shooting that haunted her; Cora knew she would commit the same crime again in the same circumstances.

She couldn't forgive herself for the years that came before, for what she allowed and accepted, for the definition of love she'd handed down to her daughter like a dark incantation.

Because of Cora, Leni had learned to be happy with half a life, pretending to be someone else, somewhere else.

Because of Cora, Leni could never see the man she loved or go home again. How was Cora supposed to forgive herself for that?

⟶⟩❀⟨⟵

SMILE.

You're happy.

Leni didn't know why she had to remind herself to smile and look happy on this bright day, when they were at the park to celebrate her graduation from college.

She *was* happy.

Really.

Especially today. She was proud of herself. The first female in her family to graduate from college.

(It had taken a long time.)

Still. She was twenty-five years old, and a single mother, with—as of tomorrow—a college degree in visual arts. She had a loving family, the best kid in the world, and a warm place to live. She was never hungry or freezing or afraid for her mother's life. Her only fears now were garden-variety parenting fears. Kids crossing the street alone, falling off swing sets, strangers appearing out of nowhere. She never fell asleep to the sound of screaming or crying and never woke to a floor strewn with broken glass.

She was happy.

It didn't matter that she sometimes had days like today, where the past poked insistently into her view.

Of course she would think of Matthew today, on this day, which was one they'd talked about so often. How many times had a conversation between them begun with: *When we finish college . . . ?*

Instinctively, she lifted her camera and minimized her view of the world. It was how she managed her memories, how she processed the world. In pictures. With a camera, she could crop and reframe her life.

Happy. Smile.

Click, click, click and she was herself again. She could see what mattered.

Unbroken blue sky, not a cloud in sight. People all around.

Sunshine called out to Seattleites in a language they understood, dragged them out of their hillside homes and encouraged them to put on expensive sneakers and enjoy the mountains and lakes and winding forest roads. After which they would stop by their local Thriftway Grocery Store for prepackaged steaks to put on their grills at weekend barbecues.

Life was soft here in Seattle. Safe and contained. Crosswalks and traffic lights and helmets and policemen on horses and bicycles.

As a mother, she appreciated all that protection, and she had tried to settle into this comfortable life. She never told anyone—not even Mama—how much she missed the howling of wolves or a day spent alone on the snow machine or the echoing crack of ice in the spring breakup. She bought her meat instead of hunting it; she turned on the faucet for water and flushed her toilet when she was finished. The salmon she grilled in the summer came already cleaned and filleted and washed, caught like strips of silver and pink silk behind cellophane canopies.

Today, all around her people were laughing, talking. Dogs were barking, jumping up to catch Frisbees. Teenage boys threw footballs back and forth.

"Look!" MJ said, pointing up at the pink *Congratulations Graduate!* balloon bobbing at the end of a yellow streamer. He had a half-eaten cupcake in one hand and wore a goatee of frosting.

Leni knew he was growing up fast (a first-grader now), so she had to snuggle and kiss him while he still allowed it. She scooped him into her arms. He gave her a sweaty, buttercream kiss and hugged her in that way of his, all in, arms thrown around her neck as if he would drown without her. The truth was that she would drown without him.

"Who else is ready for dessert?" Grandma Golliher said from her place by the picnic table. She had just finished setting out Leni's favorite dessert: *akutaq*. Eskimo ice cream made of snow, Crisco, blueberries, and sugar. Mama had saved clumps of winter snow in the freezer, just for this.

MJ sprang free, hands raised triumphantly (both hands, just to be sure he was seen). "Me! I want *akutaq*!"

Grandma came around the picnic table and stood beside Leni. Grandma had changed a lot in the past few years, softened, although she still dressed for the country club even on a picnic.

"I'm so proud of you, Leni," Grandma said.

"I'm proud of me, too."

"My friend Sondra from the club. She says there's an opening for a photographer's assistant at *Sunset* magazine. Should I have her make a call on behalf of Susan Grant?"

"Yeah," Leni said. "I mean, yes, please." She could never quite adjust to the way things were done down here. Life seemed to reward who you knew more than what you could do.

One thing she knew, though: she was loved. Grandma and Grandpa had welcomed them from the beginning. For the past few years, Leni and Mama and MJ had lived in a small rental home in Fremont and visited her grandparents on weekends. At first they'd been on guard constantly, afraid to make friends or talk to strangers, but in time, the Alaska police had stopped looking for them and the threat of discovery had faded into the background of their lives.

MJ made so much noise and had so much energy that the staid house on Queen Anne Hill had become a boisterous place. On their nights together, they gathered around the television to watch shows that made no sense to Leni. (She read, instead; she was on her third consecutive read of *Interview with the Vampire*.) MJ was the wheel; they were the spokes. Love for him united them. As long as MJ was happy, they were happy. And he was a very happy child. People remarked on it all the time.

Leni saw her mother, standing off by herself at the edge of the playground, smoking, a hand splayed across her lower back in a way that looked unnatural.

In profile, Leni could see how sharp her mother's cheekbones were, how colorless her lips, how thin her face was. As usual, she wore no makeup and she was almost translucent. She had stopped dyeing her hair a year ago; now it was a washed out, gray-threaded blond.

"I want *akutaq*!" MJ yelled, tugging on Leni's sleeve. His voice was sluggish from the stuffiness of his latest cold. Ever since he started at the private school near the house, he—and all of them, really—had battled colds.

"And how do we ask for that?" Leni asked.

"Pleeeease," MJ said.

"Okay. Go get Grandma. Tell her to put out the dang cigarette and come to the table."

He was off like a shot, scrawny white legs moving like egg beaters, his blond hair streaming back from his pale, pointed face.

Leni watched him drag Mama back to the picnic table, her face flushed with laughter.

Leni glanced sideways, turning her attention away for just a moment. She saw a man standing near the entrance gate to this public park. Blond hair.

It was him.

He'd found her.

No.

Leni sighed. She hadn't called the rehabilitation center in years. She'd picked up the phone often but never dialed. It didn't matter that the threat of discovery had lessened; it still existed. Besides, when she had called, all those years ago, his condition had always been the same: *No change.*

She knew he'd been irreparably damaged by the fall and that the boy she loved lived only in her dreams. Sometimes, at night, he whispered to her in her sleep, not always, not even often, but enough to sustain her. In her dreams, he was still the smiling boy who'd given her a camera and taught her that not all love was scary.

"Come on," Grandma said, taking Leni by the arm.

"This is great," Leni said. The words felt wooden at first. Perfunctory. But when MJ shot up and started clapping and yelled, "Yay, Mommy!" in that Mickey Mouse voice of his, she couldn't help smiling.

The dark edges fell back again, receded until there was only here, only now. A sunlit day, a celebration, a family. Life was like that, full of quicksilver changes. Joy reappeared as unexpectedly as sunlight.

She was happy.

She *was.*

⊷⤙❁⤚⊶

"TELL ME ABOUT ALASKA, Mommy," MJ said that night as he crawled into his bed and pulled up his comforter.

Leni brushed the fine white curls from her son's forehead, thinking—again—how much he looked like his father. "Shove over," she said.

Leni climbed in beside him. He rested his head on her shoulder.

The room was mostly dark, illuminated only by a small *Star Wars* bedside lamp. Unlike Leni, her son was growing up as a child of commercial America. After the picnic at the park and all the fun they'd had today, she knew that MJ was exhausted, but he wouldn't sleep without a story.

"The girl who loved Alaska . . ."

It was his favorite story. Leni had begun it years ago and expanded it over

time. She'd imagined a society living in the turquoise, glacial-cold waters of
an Alaskan fjord, in buildings that had been downed when the mighty
Mount Aku erupted. These people—the Raven clan—wanted desperately
to rise into the light again, to walk in the sunshine, but a curse made by the
eldest son of the Eagle clan had condemned them to remain in the icy water
forever—until a whisperer could call them back. Katyaaq was the whisper-
ess. A foreign girl of pure heart and quiet strength.

The story had unfolded week by week, with Leni telling just enough each
night to lull her son to sleep. She'd created Katyaaq from the native Alaskan
myths she'd read as a girl, and from the harsh, beautiful land itself. Uki, the
boy Katyaaq loved—the landwalker—had called to her from the shore.

There was no doubt in Leni's mind who the lovers were, or why the story
felt so tragic to her.

"Katyaaq defied the gods and dared to swim to the shore. She shouldn't
have been able to do it, but her love for Uki gave her a special power. She
kicked and kicked and finally broke out of the waves, felt sunlight on her
face.

"Uki plunged into the ice-cold water, calling out her name. She saw his
eyes—as green as the calm waters of the bay which had once been her
people's home, his hair the color of sunlight. 'Kat,' he said, 'take my hand.'"

Leni saw that MJ had fallen asleep. She leaned over to kiss him and eased
out of bed.

The small, single-story house was quiet. Mama was probably in the living room, watching *Dynasty*. Leni walked down the narrow hallway of their
rented house, the walls on either side of her decorated with Leni's photographs and MJ's artwork. The claustrophobia that had once assailed her in
this fake-wood-paneled, dimly lit hallway had disappeared long ago.

She had tamed the wildness within her as determinedly as she'd once
tamed the wilderness itself. She'd learned to navigate in crowds, to live
with walls, to stop for traffic. She'd learned to watch for robins instead of
eagles, to buy her fish at Safeway, and to pay money for new clothes at Fred-
erick & Nelson. She'd learned to blow-dry and condition her layered,

shoulder-length hair and to care that her clothes matched. These days she plucked her eyebrows and shaved her legs and armpits.

Camouflage. She learned to fit in.

She went into her room and flicked on the light. In the years they'd lived here, she'd changed nothing in this room and bought almost nothing to decorate it. She saw no point. It was bare and ordinary, filled with the garage-sale furniture they'd collected over the years. The only real sign of Leni herself was the photography equipment—lenses and cameras and bright yellow rolls of film. Stacks of pictures and collections of photograph albums. A single album was filled with her pictures of Matthew and Alaska. The rest were more current. Tucked into the corner of the vanity mirror was the picture of Matthew's grandparents. *THIS COULD BE US*. Beside it was the first picture she'd taken of him with her Polaroid.

She opened the door that led out onto the small cedar-planked deck that ran the length of the house. In the backyard, Mama had cultivated a large vegetable garden. Leni stepped out onto the deck and sat in one of the two Adirondack chairs that had been here when they moved in. Overhead, the star-spangled sky looked limitless. A solid cedar fence outlined their small lot. She could smell the distant aroma of the first summer barbecues and hear the jangle of kids' bikes being put away for the night. Dogs barked. A crow scolded something in a sharp little *caw-caw-caw*.

She leaned back in the chair, stared up, and tried to lose herself in the vastness of the sky.

"Hey," Mama said from behind her. "You want some company?"

" 'Course."

Mama sat down in the second chair, positioned close enough that they could hold hands as they sat here. It had become their place over the years, a narrow deck that jutted out into some dimension that was neither past nor present. Sometimes, especially this time of year, the air smelled of roses.

"I'd give anything to see the northern lights," Leni said.

"Yeah. Me, too."

Together they stared up at the immense night sky. Neither of them spoke;

they didn't need to. Leni knew they were both thinking of the loves that had once been theirs.

"But we have MJ," Mama said.

Leni held her mother's hand.

MJ. Their joy, their love, their saving grace.

TWENTY-EIGHT

———————— ⊶≫⊱⊕⊰⊕⊱⊷⊰⊰∘⊸ ————————

C ora had pneumonia. It was hardly a surprise. For weeks, she'd caught every illness that moved through MJ's school.

Now she sat in a sterile waiting room; irritated. Impatient to be let go. Waiting.

She appreciated all of the just-to-be-sure tests her mother's doctor had insisted upon, done, but Cora just wanted to get an antibiotics prescription and get out of here. MJ would be home from school soon.

Cora flipped through the latest *People* magazine. ("Ted Danson Leers Again on *Cheers*" was the absurd headline.) She tried the crossword puzzle in the back of the magazine, but she didn't know enough popular culture to make much headway.

More than thirty minutes later, the blue-haired nurse returned to the waiting room and led Cora into a small office, its walls lined with degrees, awards, that sort of thing. Cora was shown to a hard black chair.

She sat down, instinctively crossing her legs at the ankles as she had been taught years ago in her country-club days. It occurred to her suddenly, stupidly, that it was a metaphor for all that had changed for women in her lifetime. No one cared anymore how a woman sat.

"So, Evelyn," the doctor said. She was a stern-looking woman with steel-wool hair and an obvious affection for mascara. She looked like she survived on black coffee and raw vegetables, but who was Cora to judge a woman for being thin? A series of X-rays hung across a Lite-Brite-like screen behind her desk.

"Where's the pneumonia?" Cora asked, lifting her chin toward the images. An octopus devouring something; that was what it looked like.

The doctor started to speak, then paused.

"Doctor?"

Dr. Prasher pointed to one of the images. "You see these large white areas? Here. Here. And here? You see this white curve? The shadow along your spine? It is all highly suggestive of lung cancer. We will need more tests to be sure, but . . ."

Wait. What?

How could this be happening?

Oh, right. She was a smoker. It was lung cancer. For years, Leni had nagged Cora about the habit, warned her of this very scenario. She had laughed and said, "Hell, baby girl, I could die crossing the street."

"The CT scan shows a mass on your liver, which indicates metastasis," Dr. Prasher said, and kept talking.

The words became a tangle in Cora's mind: consonants and vowels, a series of breaths taken and released.

Dr. Prasher went on, using ordinary words in an extraordinary, impossible-to-grasp context. *Bronchoscopy, tumor, aggressive.*

"How long do I have?" Cora asked, realizing belatedly that she'd interrupted the doctor in the middle of something.

"No one can tell you that, Ms. Grant. But your cancer appears to be aggressive. Stage-four lung cancer that has already metastasized. I know that's a hard thing to hear."

"How long do I have?"

"You're a relatively young woman. We will treat it aggressively."

"Uh-huh."

"There's always hope, Ms. Grant."

"Is there?" Cora said. "There's also karma."

"Karma?"

"There was a poison in him," Cora said to herself, "and I drank it up."

Dr. Prasher frowned, leaned forward. "Evelyn, this is a disease, not retribution or payback for sin. Those are Dark Ages thoughts."

"Uh-huh."

"Well." Dr. Prasher stood, frowning. "I want to schedule a bronchoscopy for this afternoon. It should confirm the diagnosis. Is there someone you'd like to call?"

Cora got to her feet, feeling unsteady enough that she had to grasp the back of the chair. The pain at the base of her spine leaped out again, worse now that she knew what it was.

Cancer.

I have cancer.

She couldn't imagine saying it out loud.

She closed her eyes, exhaled. Imagined—remembered—a little girl with wild red hair and chubby little hands and freckles like cinnamon flakes, reaching out for her, saying, *Mama, I love you.*

Cora had gone through so much. Lived when she could have died. She'd imagined her life a hundred different ways, practiced a thousand ways to atone. She'd imagined growing old, growing senile, laughing when she was supposed to cry, using salt instead of sugar. In her dreams, she'd seen Leni fall in love again and get married and have another baby.

Dreams.

In a breathtaking instant, Cora's life crashed into focus, became small. All of her fears and regrets and disappointments fell away. There was just one thing that mattered; how could she not have known it from the beginning? Why had she spent so much time searching for who she was? She should have known. Always. From the very beginning.

She was a mother. A *mother.* And now . . .

My Leni.

How would she ever say goodbye?

✦⟨❀⟩✦

LENI STOOD OUTSIDE the closed door to her mother's hospital room, trying to calm her breathing. She heard noises all around her, up and down the hall, people hurrying on rubber-soled shoes, carts being rolled from room to room, announcements coming over the loudspeakers.

Leni reached for the silver metal door handle, gave it a twist.

She walked into a large room, separated into two smaller spaces by curtains that hung from metal runners on the ceiling.

Mama was sitting up in bed, leaning back into a pile of white pillows. She looked like an antique doll, with eggshell skin stretched too tightly across her delicately crafted face. Her collarbone peered out above the neckline of her oversized hospital gown, the skin on either side hollowed out.

"Hey," Leni said. She leaned down, kissed her mother's soft cheek. "You could have told me you were going to the doctor's. I would have come with you." She pushed the feathery gray-blond hair out of her mother's eyes. "Do you have pneumonia?"

"I have stage-four lung cancer. Only it's a sneaky little shit and has invaded my spine and liver, too. It's in my blood."

Leni literally took a step back. She almost lifted her hands to block her face. "What?"

"I'm sorry, baby girl. It's not good. The doctor was not particularly hopeful."

Leni wanted to scream, *STOP!*

She couldn't breathe.

Cancer.

"A-are you in pain?"

No. That wasn't what she wanted to say. What did she want to say?

"Ah," Mama said with a wave of her veiny hand. "I'm Alaska-tough." She reached past Leni for her cigarettes.

"I'm not sure they allow that in here."

"I'm pretty sure they don't," Mama said, her hand trembling as she lit up. "But soon I'll start chemotherapy." She tried to smile. "So I can look forward to baldness and nausea. I'm sure it will be a good look for me."

Leni moved closer. "You'll fight it, right?" she said, blinking back tears she didn't want her mother to see.

"Of course. I'll kick this bitch's ass."

Leni nodded, wiped her eyes.

"You'll get better. Grandpa will get you the best care in the city. He's got that friend who's on the board at Fred Hutch. You'll be—"

"I'll be fine, Leni."

Mama touched Leni's hand. Leni stood there, connected to her mother by breath and touch and a lifetime of love. She wanted to say just the right thing, but what would that be, and how could a few flimsy words matter in a cancer sea? "I can't lose you," Leni whispered.

"Yeah," Mama said. "I know, baby girl. I know."

❖✦⟨❀⟩✦❖

Dear Matthew,

It's only been a few days since I wrote to you. Funny how much life can change in a week.

Not funny ha-ha. That's for sure.

Last night, as I lay in my comfy bed, in my store-bought pajamas, I found myself with a lot of things I didn't want to think about. And so I found my way to you.

I don't think we talked enough about your mother's death. Maybe that was because we were kids, or maybe it was because you were so traumatized. But we should have talked about it later, when we were older. I should have told you I would listen to your pain forever. I should have asked you for memories.

I see now how grief becomes thin ice. I haven't lost my mom yet, but a single word has pushed her away from me, created a barrier between

us that never existed before. For the first time ever, we are lying to each
other. I can feel it. Lying to protect each other.

But there's no protection, is there?

She has lung cancer.

God. I wish you were here.

Leni put down her pen. This time, the act of writing to Matthew was no comfort at all.

It made her feel worse, in fact. More alone.

How pathetic, that she had no one to talk to about this. That her best friend had no idea who she was.

She folded the letter up and put it in the shoe box with all the others she'd written over the years and never sent.

✦⤙⟨⊛⟩⤚✦

THAT SUMMER, Leni watched cancer erase her mother. First to go was her hair, then her eyebrows. Next was the firm line of her shoulders; they began to droop. Then she lost her posture and her stride. Finally, cancer took away movement altogether.

By late July, after cancer had erased so much, the truth was revealed by her latest CT scan. Nothing they had done had helped.

Leni sat quietly beside her mother, holding her hand when they learned that the treatment had failed. The cancer was everywhere, an enemy on the move, hacking through bones, destroying organs. There was no discussion about trying again or fighting it.

Instead, they moved back into the Golliher house, set up a hospital bed in the sunroom, where light flowed through the windows, and contacted hospice care.

Mama had fought for her life, fought harder than she had fought for anything, but cancer did not care about effort.

Now Mama slowly, slowly angled up in the bed to a slouchy sitting position. An unlit cigarette trembled in her veiny hand. She could no longer smoke, of course, but she liked to hold them. There were a few strands of hair on the pillow, running like gold veins on white cotton. An oxygen tank stood by the bed; clear tubes inserted into Mama's nostrils helped her breathe.

Leni got up from her place beside the bed and put down the book she'd been reading aloud. She poured Mama a drink of water and offered it. Mama reached for the plastic cup. Her hands were shaking so badly Leni placed her own hands over her mother's, helped her hold on to the cup. Mama took a hummingbird sip and coughed. Her bird-thin shoulders shook so hard Leni swore she heard the bones rattling beneath the thin skin.

"I dreamed of Alaska last night," Mama said, slumping back into the pillows. She looked up at Leni. "It wasn't all bad, was it?"

Leni felt a shock at hearing the word mentioned so casually. By tacit agreement, they hadn't spoken about Alaska—or Dad or Matthew—in years, but perhaps it was inevitable that they would circle back to the beginning as the end neared.

"A lot of it was great," Leni said. "I loved Alaska. I loved Matthew. I loved you. I even loved Dad," she admitted quietly.

"There was fun. I want you to remember that. And adventure. When you remember, I know it's easy to pull the bad up. Your dad's violence. The excuses I made. My sad love for him. But there was good love, too. Remember that. Your dad loved you."

This hurt more than Leni could bear, but she saw how much her mama needed to say these words. "I know," Leni said.

"You'll tell MJ all about me, okay? You tell him how I never sang the words to any song right and how I wore hot pants and sandals and I looked good in that shit. You tell him how I learned to be Alaska-tough even though I didn't want to, and how I never let the bad stuff kill me, how I kept going. You tell him I loved his mother from the moment I saw her and that I'm proud of her."

"I love you, too, Mama," Leni said, but it wasn't enough. Not nearly enough, but all they had now was words—too many of them—and too little time.

"You're a good mother, Leni, even as young as you are. I was never as good a mom as you are."

"Mama—"

"No lies, baby girl. I don't have time."

Leni leaned down to smooth the few hairs back from Mama's forehead. They were fine as goose down, wispy. This whittling down of her was unbearable. With every exhalation, it seemed, Mama lost a little more of her life force.

Mama reached slowly for the nightstand. The top drawer glided open with the soundlessness of expensive crafting. With a shaking hand, she pulled out a letter, folded crisply into thirds. "Here."

Leni didn't want to take it.

"Please."

Leni took the letter, unfolded it carefully, and saw what was written on the page, in a scrawling, barely legible handwriting. It read:

> *I, Coraline Margaret Golliher Allbright, shot my husband, Ernt Allbright, when he was beating me.*
>
> *I weighed his dead body down with animal traps and sank it in Glass Lake. I ran away because I feared going to prison, even though I believed then—and now—that I saved my life that night. My husband had been abusive for years. Many Kaneq residents suspected the abuse and tried to help. I didn't allow it.*
>
> *His death is on my hands and on my conscience. Guilt has turned itself into cancer and is killing me. God's justice.*
>
> *I killed him and hid the body. I did it all alone. My daughter had nothing to do with it.*
>
> *Sincerely, Coraline Allbright*

Beneath her mother's shaky signature was her grandfather's signature both as an attorney and as a witness, and a notary seal.

Mama coughed into a ball of tissue. She drew in a phlegmy breath and looked up at Leni. For a terrible, exquisite moment, time stopped between them, the world caught its breath. "It's time, Leni. You've lived my life, baby girl. Time to live your own."

"By calling you a murderer and pretending I'm an innocent? That's how you want me to start a life?"

"By going home. My dad says you can pin it all on me. Say you knew nothing about it. You were a kid. They'll believe you. Tom and Marge will back you up."

Leni shook her head, too overwhelmed by sadness to say anything more than, "I won't leave you."

"Ah, baby girl. How many times have you had to say that in your life?" Mama sighed tiredly, gazed up at Leni through sad, watery eyes. Her breath was wheezing, labored. "But I am going to leave you. It's the thing we can't run from anymore. Please," she whispered. "Do this for me. Be stronger than I ever was."

❖

Two DAYS LATER, Leni stood just outside of the sunroom, listening to Mama's wheezing breaths as she talked to Grandma.

Through the open door, Leni heard the word *sorry* in her grandmother's trembling voice.

A word Leni had come to despise. She knew that in the past few years Mama and Grandma had already said what they needed to say to each other. They'd talked about the past in their bits-and-pieces way. Never all at once, never one big end-up-crying-and-hugging moment, but a constant brushing up of the past, reexamining actions and decisions and beliefs, offering apologies, forgiveness. All of it had brought them closer to who they were, who they'd always been. Mother and daughter. Their essential, immutable bond—fragile enough to snap at a harsh word a long time ago, durable enough to survive death itself.

"Mommy! There you are," MJ said. "I looked *everywhere*."

MJ skidded into place, bumping her hard. He was holding his treasured copy of *Where the Wild Things Are*. "Grammy said she'd read to me."

"I don't know, baby boy—"

"She promised." On that, he pushed past her, moving into the sunroom like John Wayne looking for a fight. "Did you miss me, Grammy?"

Leni heard her mama's quiet laughter. Then she heard the clang and squeak of MJ hitting the oxygen tank.

Moments later, Grandma exited the sunroom, saw Leni, and came to a stop. "She is asking for you," Grandma said quietly. "Cecil has already been in."

They both knew what that meant. Yesterday, Mama had been unresponsive for hours.

Grandma reached out, held Leni's hand tightly, and then let go. With a last, harrowingly sad look, Grandma walked down the hallway and up the stairs to her own bedroom, where Leni imagined she let herself cry for the daughter she was losing. They all tried so hard not to cry in front of Mama.

Through the open sunroom door, Leni heard MJ's high-pitched, "Read to me, Grammy," and Mama's inaudible reply.

Leni glanced down at her watch. Mama couldn't handle much more than a few minutes with him. MJ was a good boy, but he was a boy, which meant bouncing and chatter and nonstop motion.

Mama's thready voice floated on the sunlit air, bringing a flood of memories with it. "*The night Max wore his wolf suit and made mischief of one kind or another . . .*"

Leni was as drawn to her mother's voice as she'd always been, maybe more so now, when every single moment mattered and every breath was a gift. Leni had learned to submerge fear, push it down to a quiet place and cover it with a smile, but it was there always, the thought, *Is that breath the end? Is that the one?*

Here, at the end, it was impossible to believe in a last-minute reprieve. And Mama was in such pain, even hoping for her to survive another day, another hour, felt selfish.

Leni heard her mother say, "The End," and the words carried a sharp double meaning.

"One more story, Grammy."

Leni entered the sunroom.

Mama's hospital bed had been placed to take advantage of the sunlight through the window. It almost looked like a fairy-tale bed in deep woods, lit by the sunlight, surrounded by hothouse flowers.

Mama herself was Sleeping Beauty or Snow White, her lips the only place left to have any color. The rest of her was so small and colorless, she seemed to melt into the white sheets. The clear plastic tubes looped from her nostrils, around her ears, and went on to the tank.

"That's enough, MJ," Leni said. "Grammy needs a nap."

"Aw, crap," he said, his little shoulders dropping.

Mama laughed. It turned into a cough. "Nice language, MJ." Her voice was a whispery sound.

"Grammy's cough is bleeding again," MJ said.

Leni pulled a tissue from the box by her mother's bed and leaned close to dab the blood from her mother's face. "Give Grammy's hand a kiss and go, MJ. Grandpop has a new model airplane for you guys to put together."

Mama's hand fluttered up from the bed. The whole back of her hand was bruised from IVs.

MJ leaned close, banging the bed so hard it jostled her mother, clanging a knee into the oxygen tank. He kissed the bruised hand carefully.

When he was gone, Mama sighed, lay back into the pillows. "The kid is a bull moose. You should get him into ballet or gymnastics." Her voice was almost too quiet to hear. Leni had to lean close.

"Yeah," Leni said. "How are you?"

"I'm tired, baby girl."

"I know."

"I'm so tired, but . . . I can't leave you. I . . . can't. I don't know how. You are it for me, you know. The great love of my life."

"Peas in a pod," Leni whispered.

"Two of a kind." Mama coughed. "The thought of you being alone, without me . . ."

Leni leaned down, kissed her mother's soft forehead. She knew what she had to say now, what her mother needed. One always knew when to be strong for the other. "I'm okay, Mama. I know you'll be with me."

"Always," Mama whispered, her voice barely heard. She reached up, her hand shaking, and touched Leni's cheek. Her skin was cold. The effort it took for that single motion was evident.

"You can go," Leni whispered.

Mama sighed deeply. In the sound, Leni heard how long and how hard her mother had been fighting this moment. Mama's hand fell from Leni's face, thumped to the bed. It opened like a flower, revealing a bloody wad of tissue. "Ah, Leni . . . you're the love of my life . . . I worry . . ."

"I'll be okay," Leni lied. Tears slid down her cheeks. "I love you, Mama."

Don't go, Mama. I can't be in the world without you.

Mama's eyelids fluttered shut. "Loved . . . you . . . my baby girl."

Leni could barely hear those last, whispered words. She felt her mother's last breath as deeply as if she'd drawn it herself.

TWENTY-NINE

—————··❯❯❮❮··—————

S he wanted you to have this."

Grandma stood in the open doorway to Leni's old bedroom, dressed in all black. She managed to make mourning look elegant. It was the kind of thing that Mama would have made fun of long ago—she would have looked down on a woman concerned with appearances. But Leni knew that sometimes you grabbed hold of whatever you could to stay afloat. And maybe all that black was a shield, a way to say to people: *Don't talk to me, don't approach me, don't ask your ordinary, everyday questions when my world has exploded.*

Leni, on the other hand, looked like something washed up by the tide. In the twenty-four hours since her mother's death, she hadn't showered or brushed her teeth or changed her clothes. All she did was sit in her room, behind a closed door. She would make an effort at two, when she had to go pick up MJ from school. In his absence, she swam alone in her loss.

She pushed the covers back. Moving slowly, as if her muscles had changed in the absence of her mother, she crossed the room and took the box from her grandmother, said, "Thank you."

They looked at each other, mirrors of grief. Then, saying nothing more—

what good were words?—Grandma turned and walked down the hall, stiffly upright. If Leni didn't know her, she'd say Grandma was a rock, a woman in perfect control, but Leni did know her. At the stairs, Grandma paused, missed a step; her hand clutched at the banister. Grandpa came out of his office, appearing when she needed him, to offer an arm.

The two of them, heads bowed together, were a portrait of pain.

Leni hated that there was nothing she could do to help. How could three drowning people save each other?

Leni went back to bed. Climbing in, she pulled the rosewood box into her lap. She'd seen it before, of course. Once, it had held their playing cards.

Whoever had made this box had sanded it until the surface felt more like glass than wood. It was a souvenir, maybe from the road trip they'd taken a lifetime ago, when they'd lived in a trailer and driven all the way to Tijuana. Leni was too young to remember the trip—before Vietnam—but she'd heard her parents talk about it.

Leni took a deep breath and opened the lid. Inside, she saw a tangle of things. A cheap silver charm bracelet, a set of keys on a ring that read *Keep On Truckin'*, a pink scallop shell, a beaded suede coin purse, a set of playing cards, a Native tusk carving of an Eskimo holding a spear.

She picked up the items one by one, trying to put them in the context of what she knew of her mother's life. The charm bracelet looked like the gift one girl would give another in high school and reminded Leni of all the missing pieces in her mother's life. Questions Leni had failed to ask; stories Mama hadn't had time to share. All of it lost now. The keys Leni recognized—they were to the house they'd rented on the cul-de-sac outside Seattle all those years ago. The scallop shell showed her mother's love for beachcombing, and the suede purse probably came from one of the reservation gift shops.

There was a *SALTY DAWG* shot glass. A piece of driftwood, into which had been carved *Cora and Ernt, 1973*. Three white agates. A photograph of her parents' wedding day, taken at the courthouse. In it, Mama was smiling brightly, wearing a tea-length white dress with a bell-shaped skirt and holding a single white rose in white-gloved hands; Dad was holding her close, his smile a little stiff, dressed in a black suit and narrow tie. They looked like a couple of kids playing dress-up.

The next photograph was of the VW bus with their boxes and suitcases lashed on top. The door was open and you could see all of their junk piled inside. It had been taken only a few days before they headed north.

The three of them stood beside the bus. Mama was wearing elephant-bell jeans and a midriff-baring top. Her blond hair had been twined into pigtails and a beaded headband encircled her head. Dad wore pale blue polyester pants and a matching shirt with oversized collar points. Leni was in front of her parents, wearing a red dress with a white Peter Pan collar and Keds. Each of her parents had a hand on one of her shoulders.

She was smiling broadly. Happily.

The photograph turned blurry, danced in Leni's unsteady hand.

Something red and blue and gold captured Leni's attention. She put down the picture, wiped her eyes.

A military medal; a red-white-and-blue ribbon with a bronze star affixed to its pointed end. She turned the star over, saw the inscription on the back: *Heroic or meritorious achievement. Ernt A. Allbright.* Beneath it lay a folded-up newspaper article with the headline "Seattle POW Released" and a picture of her dad. He looked like a cadaver, his eyes staring dully ahead. There was almost no similarity to the man in the wedding photo.

I wish you remembered him from before . . . How often had her mother said that over the years?

She pressed the picture and the medal to her chest, as if she could imprint them onto her soul. These were the memories Leni wanted to keep: their love, his heroism, the image of them laughing, the idea of her mother beachcombing.

There were two things left in the box. An envelope and a folded piece of notebook paper.

Leni set the medal and photograph aside and picked up the piece of paper, unfolding it slowly. She saw Mama's fine, private-schoolgirl script.

To my beautiful baby girl,

It's time to undo what I did. You live under a false name because I killed a man. Me.

You may not see it yet, but you have a home and home means something. You have a chance for a different life. You can give your son all that I couldn't give you, but it takes courage. And courage is something you have. All you have to do is go back to Alaska and give the police my confession letter. Tell them I'm a murderer and let the crime finally end as it should have, with you excused from its taint. They'll close the case and you'll be free. Take your name and your life back.

Go home. Scatter my ashes on our beach.

I'll be watching out for you. Always.

You have a child, so you know. You are my heart, baby girl. You are everything I did right. And I want you to know I would do it all again, every wonderful terrible second of it. I would do years and years of it again for one minute with you.

Inside the envelope, she found two one-way tickets to Alaska.

✦✦✦

ALL UP AND DOWN the well-manicured street of Queen Anne Hill, life clattered along on this last Saturday in July. Her grandparents' neighbors were gathered around Weber barbecues grilling store-bought meat, and making designer margaritas in blenders, their kids playing on swing sets that cost as much as a used car. Had any of them noticed the drawn shades in the Golliher house? Could they somehow sense grief emanating through stone and glass? This sorrow couldn't be talked about in public. How could they express grief for the loss of a woman—Evelyn Grant—who had never really existed?

Leni climbed out her bedroom window and sat on the roof, the wooden shakes worn smooth by years of people sitting in this spot. Here more than anywhere else, she felt Mama beside her. Sometimes the feeling was so strong Leni thought she heard her Mama breathing, but it was just the breeze, whispering through the maple leaves on the tree out front.

"I used to catch your mother out here smoking cigarettes when she was thirteen years old," Grandma said quietly. "She thought a closed window and a breath mint could fool me."

Leni couldn't help smiling. Those few words were like an incantation that brought Mama back for a beautiful, exquisite second. A flame of blond hair, a laugh in the wind. Leni glanced behind her, saw her grandmother standing at the upstairs bedroom's open window. A cool evening breeze plucked at her black blouse, ruffled the trim at her throat. Leni had a fleeting, surprising thought that her grandmother would wear black for the rest of her life; maybe she would put on a green dress and regret and loss would eke from her pores and change the fabric to black.

"May I join you?"

"I'll come in." Leni started to back up.

Grandma angled through the open window, her hair crunching on the frame, getting dented. "I know you think that I'm Jurassic, but I can climb out onto a ledge. Jack LaLanne was sixty when he swam from Alcatraz to San Francisco."

Leni scooted sideways.

Grandmother climbed through the opening and sat down, keeping her straight back flush against the house.

Leni backed up to be even with her, carrying the rosewood box with her. She hadn't stopped touching its smooth surface since she'd opened it the day before.

"I don't want you to go."

"I know."

"Your grandfather says it's a bad decision, and he should know." She paused. "Stay here. Don't give them that letter."

"It was her dying wish."

"She's gone."

Leni couldn't help smiling. She loved that her grandmother was a complex mixture of optimism and practicality. The optimism had allowed her to wait almost two decades for her daughter's return; the practicality had allowed her to forget all the pain that had preceded it. Over the years, Leni knew that Mama had more than forgiven her parents; she'd grown to understand them and to regret how harshly she'd treated them. Perhaps it was a road every child ultimately traveled. "Have I ever told you how grateful I am that you took us in, that you love my son?"

"And you."

"And me."

"Make me understand, Leni. I'm afraid."

Leni had thought about this all night. She knew it was crazy and maybe dangerous, but there was hope, too.

She wanted—needed—to be Leni Allbright again. To live her own life. Whatever the cost. "I know you think of Alaska as cold and inhospitable, a place where we were lost. But the truth is, we were found there, too. It's in me, Grandma, that place. I belong there. All these years away have cost me something. And there's MJ. He's not a baby anymore. He's a boy and growing up fast. He needs a dad."

"But his dad is . . ."

"I know. I've spent years telling MJ as much of the truth as I could about his father. He knows about the accident and the rehab center. But its not enough to tell stories. MJ needs to know where he comes from, and it won't be long before he starts asking real questions. He deserves answers." Leni paused. "My mom was wrong about a lot of things, but one thing she had right was about the durability of love. It stays. Against all odds, in the face of hate, it stays. I left the boy I loved when he was broken and sick, and I hate myself for that. Matthew is MJ's dad, whether Matthew can know what that means or not, whether he can hold him or talk to him or not. MJ deserves to know his own family. Tom Walker is his grandfather. Alyeska is his aunt. It is unforgivable that they don't know about MJ. They would love him as much as you do."

"They could try to take him from you. Custody is a tricky thing. You couldn't survive that."

That was a dark corner Leni couldn't look around. "It's not about me," Leni said quietly. "I have to do the right thing. Finally."

"It's a bad idea, Leni. A terrible idea. If you've learned anything from your mother and what happened, it should be this: life—and the law—is hard on women. Sometimes doing the right thing is no help at all."

⊹⟨✻⟩⊹

Summer in Alaska.

Leni had never forgotten the exquisite, breathtaking beauty, and now, in a small plane, flying from Anchorage to Homer, she felt a great opening up of her soul. For the first time in years, she felt fully herself.

They flew over the green marshlands outside of Anchorage and the silvery expanse of Turnagain Arm, low tide revealing the gray sand bottom, where so many unwary fishermen went aground and the magical bore tide rolled in on waves big enough to surf.

And then Cook Inlet, a swath of blue, dotted with fishing boats. The plane banked left toward the snow-clad mountains, and flew over the glacial-blue Harding Icefield. Above Kachemak Bay, the land turned richly green again, a series of emerald humps. Hundreds of boats dotted the water, ribbons of white water fluttering out behind them.

In Homer, they bumped down onto the gravel runway and MJ squealed happily, pointed out the window. When the plane came to a stop, the pilot came around and opened the back door and helped Leni with her rolling suitcase (so Outside, that bag—it didn't even have shoulder straps).

She held on to MJ with one hand and rolled her suitcase along the gravel runway toward the small aviation office. A big clock on the wall told her it was 10:12 A.M.

At the counter, she gained the receptionist's attention.

"Excuse me. I understand there's a new police station in town."

"Well, not that new. It's up past the post office on Heath Street. You want me to call you a cab?"

If Leni hadn't been so nervous, she would have laughed at the idea of catching a cab in Homer. "Uh. Yes. Please. That would be great."

Waiting for the cab, Leni stood in the small aviation office, staring in awe at the entire wall filled with four-color brochures advertising adventures for tourists: the Great Alaska Adventure Lodge in Sterling and Walker Cove Adventure Lodge in Kaneq; fly-out lodges in the Brooks Range, river guides who hired out for the day, hunting trips in Fairbanks. Alaska had apparently become the tourist mecca Tom Walker had imagined it could be. Leni knew that cruise ships pulled into Seward every week in the summer, off-loading thousands of people.

Moments after the cab arrived, she and MJ were at the police station, a long, low-slung, flat-roofed building set on a corner.

Inside, the station was brightly lit, freshly painted. Leni fought with her rolling suitcase, muscling it up over the doorsill. The only person in the place was a uniformed woman sitting at a desk. Leni moved resolutely forward, clutching MJ's hand so tightly he squirmed and whined, tried to wrench free.

"Hello," she said to the woman at the desk. "I'd like to speak to the police chief."

"Why?"

"It's about a . . . killing."

"Of a human?"

Only in Alaska would that question ever be asked. "I have information on a crime."

"Follow me."

The uniformed woman led Leni past an empty jail cell to a closed door with a placard that read: CHIEF CURT WARD.

The woman knocked hard. Twice. At a muffled, "Come in," she opened the door. "Chief, this young woman says she has information on a crime."

The chief of police stood slowly. Leni remembered him from the search for Geneva Walker. His hair was trimmed into a tall crew cut. A bushy red mustache stood out against the auburn stubble that had obviously grown since he shaved this morning. He looked like a once-gung-ho high school hockey player turned small-town cop.

"Lenora Allbright," Leni said in introduction. "My dad was Ernt All-bright. We used to live in Kaneq."

"Holy shit. We thought you were dead. Search and Rescue went out for days looking for you and your mom. What was it, six, seven, years ago? Why didn't you contact the police?"

Leni settled MJ in a comfortable chair and opened a book for him. Her grandfather's advice came back to her: *It's a bad idea, Leni, but if you're going to do it, you have to be careful, smarter than your mother ever was. Say nothing. Just give them the letter. Tell them you didn't even know your dad was dead until your mother gave you this letter. Tell them you were running from his abuse, hiding so that he wouldn't find you. Everything you've done—the changed identities, the new town, the silence—it all fits in with a family hiding from a dangerous man.*

"I wanna go, Mommy," MJ said, bouncing on the seat. "I want to see my daddy."

"Soon, kiddo." She kissed his forehead and then went back to the chief's desk. Between them was a wide swath of gray metal decorated with family photographs, studded with sloppy stacks of pink while-you-were-out mes-sages, and cluttered with fishing magazines. A fishing reel with impossibly tangled line was being used as a paperweight.

She pulled the letter out of her purse. Her hand was shaking as she handed over her mother's confession.

Chief Ward read through the letter. Sat down. Looked up. "You know what this says?"

Leni dragged a chair over and sat down facing him. She was afraid her legs would stop supporting her. "I do."

"So your mother shot your dad and disposed of his body and you two ran away."

"You have the letter."

"And where is your mother?"

"She died last week. She gave the letter to me on her deathbed and asked me to deliver it to the police. It was the first I'd heard of it. The . . . killing, I mean. I thought we were running from my father's abuse. He . . . was violent. Sometimes. He beat her really badly one night and we ran away while he slept."

"I'm sorry about her death."

Chief Ward stared at Leni for a long time, his eyes narrowed. The intensity of his gaze was unsettling. She fought the urge to fidget. Finally he got up, went to a file cabinet in the back of the room, riffled through a drawer, and pulled out a folder. He dropped it on his desk, sat down, and opened it. "So. Your mother, Cora Allbright, was five-foot-six. People described her as slight, fragile, thin. And your dad was nearly six feet tall."

"Yes. That's right."

"But she shot your father, dragged his body out of the house, and, what— strapped him onto a snow machine—and drove up to Glass Lake in the winter and cut a hole in the ice, loaded him with iron traps, and dropped him. Alone. Where were you?"

Leni sat very still, her hands clasped in her lap. "I don't know. I don't know when it happened." She felt the need to add on, layer words to solidify the lie, but Grandpa had told her to say as little as possible.

Chief Ward set his elbows on the desk and steepled his blunt-tipped fingers. "You could have mailed this letter."

"I could have."

"But that's not who you are, is it, Lenora? You're a good girl. An honest person. I have glowing reports about you in this file." He leaned forward. "What happened on the night you ran away? What set him off?"

"I . . . found out I was pregnant," she said.

"Matthew Walker," he said, glancing down at the file. "People said you two kids were in love."

"Uh-huh," Leni said.

"Sad as hell about what happened to him. To both of you. But you got better, and he . . ." Chief Ward let it hang there; Leni felt her shame hang on the hook of the unspoken. "I hear your dad hated the Walkers."

"More than hated them."

"And when your father found out you were pregnant?"

"He went crazy. Started beating me with his fists, with his belt . . ." The memories she'd spent years submerging broke free.

"He was a mean son of a bitch, from what I hear."

"Sometimes." Leni looked away. Out of the corner of her eye she saw MJ reading his book, his mouth moving as he worked to sound out the words. She hoped these spoken words didn't find purchase in some dark corner of his subconscious, able to rise one day.

Chief Ward pushed some papers toward her. Leni saw *Allbright, Coraline* in the corner. "I have sworn statements from Marge Birdsall, Natalie Watkins, Tica Rhodes, Thelma Schill, and Tom Walker. All of them testified to seeing bruises on your mother over the years. There were a lot of tears when I took these statements, I can tell you that, a lot of folks wishing they'd done things different. Thelma said she wished she'd shot your dad herself."

"Mama never let anyone help her," Leni said. "I still don't know why."

"Did she ever tell anyone he beat her?"

"Not that I know of."

"You have to tell the truth if you want real help," Chief Ward said.

Leni stared at him.

"Come on, Leni. You and I both know what happened that night. Your mom didn't do this alone. You were a kid. It wasn't your fault. You did what your mom asked of you, and who wouldn't? There's no one on the planet who wouldn't understand. He was beating her, for God's sake. The law will understand."

He was right. She *had* been a kid. A scared, pregnant eighteen-year-old.

"Let me help you," he said. "You can get rid of this terrible burden."

She knew what her mother and grandparents wanted her to do now: to keep lying, to say Leni hadn't witnessed the murder or the drive to Glass Lake or her father sinking into the icy water.

To say: not me.

She could blame it all on Mama and stick to that story.

And forever be a woman with this dark, terrible secret. A liar.

Mama had wanted Leni to come home, but home was not just a cabin in a deep woods that overlooked a placid cove. Home was a state of mind, the peace that came from being who you were and living an honest life. There was no going halfway home. She couldn't build a new life on the creaky foundation of a lie. Not again. Not for home.

"The truth will set you free, Leni. Isn't that what you want? Why you're here? Tell me what really happened that night."

"He hit me when he found out about the baby, hard enough to fracture my cheek and break my nose. I . . . I don't remember all of it, just him hitting me. Then I heard Mama say, *Not my Leni*, and a gunshot. I . . . saw blood seep across his shirt. She shot him twice in the back. To stop him from killing me."

"And you helped her get rid of his body."

Leni hesitated. The compassion in his eyes made her say quietly, "And I helped her get rid of the body."

Chief Ward sat there a moment, looking down at the records in front of him. He appeared ready to say something, then changed his mind. He opened his desk drawer (it made a scratchy, creaking sound) and pulled out a piece of paper and a pen. "Can you write it all down?"

"I've told you everything."

"I need it on paper. Then we'll be done. Don't lose steam now, Leni. You're so close to the end. You want all of this behind you, right?"

Leni reached for the pen and pulled the paper toward her. At first she just stared down at the blank page. "Maybe I should ask for a lawyer? My grandfather would recommend that. He's a lawyer."

"You can do that," he said. "It's what guilty people do." He reached for the phone. "Shall I call for one?"

"You believe me, right? I didn't kill him and Mama didn't want to. The law knows about battered women now."

"Of course. And besides, you've already told me the truth."

"So I just have to write it down and I'll be done? I can go to Kaneq?"

He nodded.

What difference did it make to write the words? She began slowly, word by word, rebuilding the scene of that terrible night. The fists, the belt, the blood, the gore. The frozen trek to the lake. The last image of her father's face, ivory in the moonlight, sinking into water. The sound of ice slushing over the rim of the hole.

The only omission was about Large Marge's help. She mentioned nothing about her at all. She didn't mention her grandparents, either, or where she and Mama had gone when they left Alaska.

She ended with: *We flew from Homer to Anchorage and then left Alaska.*

She pushed the paper across the desk.

Chief Ward looked down at her confession.

"I'm done reading, Mommy," MJ said. She waved him over.

He slapped the book shut and half charged across the room. He climbed up onto her lap like a monkey. Even though he was too big, she held him, let him stay, his skinny legs hanging as he kicked the metal desk with his sneaker toe. *Bang. Bang. Bang.*

Chief Ward looked at her. "You're under arrest," he said.

Leni felt the world literally drop out from under her. "But . . . you said we'd be done if I wrote it down."

"You and I are done. Now it's up to someone else." He shoved a hand through his hair. "I wish you hadn't come in here."

All the warnings over the years. How had she forgotten? She'd let her need for forgiveness and redemption trump common sense. "What do you mean?"

"This is out of my hands, Leni. It's up to the court now. I am going to have to lock you up, at least until your arraignment. If you can't afford an attorney—"

"Mommy?" MJ said, frowning.

The chief read Leni her Miranda rights from a sheet of paper, then finished up with: "Unless you know someone who can take your son, he's going to have to go to Social Services. They'll take good care of him. I promise."

Leni couldn't believe she'd been so stupid and naïve. How could she not have seen this coming? She'd been *warned.* And still she'd believed the police. She knew how unforgiving the law could be to women.

She wanted to rail and scream and cry and throw furniture, but it was too late for that. She'd made a terrible mistake. There couldn't be another. "Tom Walker," she said.

"Tom?" Chief Ward frowned. "Why would I call him?"

"Just call him. Tell him I need help. He'll come for me."

"What you need is a lawyer."

"Yeah," she said. "Tell him that, too."

THIRTY

P rocessed.

Before today, Leni associated that word with food that had been stretched out of recognition and changed into something bad for you. Like spray cheese.

Now it had a whole new meaning.

Fingerprints. Mug shots. *Turn to the right, please.* Hands patting her down.

"This is fun!" MJ said, banging his hands along the cell bars, running from side to side. "I sound like a helicopter. Listen." He ran again, as fast as he could, his hand hitting the bars.

Leni couldn't manage a smile. She couldn't look at him but she couldn't look away. It had taken endless pleading on her part to get them to let him be in here with her. Thank God she was in Homer, not Anchorage, where she was pretty sure the rules would be more strictly enforced. Apparently there still wasn't much crime in the area. Mostly this cell was used to house drunks on the weekends.

Clang. Clang. Clang.

"MJ," Leni said sharply. It wasn't until she saw his face—the worried green eyes, the gaped mouth—that she realize she'd screamed it.

"Sorry," she said. "Come here, kiddo."

MJ's moods were like the sea; one glance told you all you needed to know. She'd hurt his feelings, maybe even frightened him with her outburst.

Something else to feel bad about.

MJ shuffled across the small cell, purposely scuffling his rubber-soled tennis shoes. "I'm ice-skating," he said.

Leni managed a smile as she patted the empty place beside her on the cement bench. He sat down next to her. The cell was so small the lidless toilet was practically touching his knee. Through the metal bars, Leni could see most of the police station—the front desk, the waiting area. The door to Chief Ward's office.

She had to force herself not to take MJ into her arms and hold him tightly. "I have to talk to you," she said. "You know how we're always talking about your dad?"

"He's brain damaged, but he would love me anyway. That's a gross toilet."

"And he lives in a facility where they take care of people like him. That's why he doesn't visit us."

MJ nodded. "He can't talk anyway. He fell down a hole and broke his head."

"Uh-huh. And he lives up here. In Alaska. Where Mommy grew up."

"I know that, silly. It's why we're here. Can he walk?"

"I don't think so. But . . . you also have a grandfather who lives here. And an aunt named Alyeska."

MJ finally stopped banging his plastic triceratops on the bench and looked at her. "Another grandpa? Jason has three grandpas."

"And you have two now, isn't that cool?"

She heard the station door open. Through it, the sound of a truck rumbling past outside, tires crunching on gravel. A horn honking.

And there was Tom Walker, striding into the police station. He wore faded jeans tucked into boots and a black T-shirt that had a huge, colorful

Walker Cove Adventure Lodge logo on the front. A dirty trucker's hat was pulled low on his broad forehead.

He came to a stop in the center of the station, looked around.

Saw her.

Leni couldn't have remained seated even if she'd tried, which she didn't. She eased away from MJ and got to her feet.

She felt a flutter of energy that was equal parts anxiety and joy. She hadn't realized until right now, this moment, how much she'd missed Mr. Walker. Over the years, she'd romanticized him. She and Mama both had. For Mama, he'd been the chance she should have taken. For Leni, he'd been the ideal of what a dad could be. In the beginning, they'd talked about him often, until it had become too painful for both of them and they'd stopped.

He moved toward her, pulled the hat from his head, crushed it in his hands. He looked different, more weathered than aged. His long blond hair was gray around his face and had been pulled back into a ponytail. He had obviously been working in the woods when Chief Ward called him. Dried leaves and twigs stuck to his flannel shirt. "Leni," he said when there was nothing but a set of jail-cell bars between them. "I didn't believe Curt when he said you were here." He clutched the bars in his big, work-reddened hands. "I thought your dad killed you."

Leni's shame reared up; she felt her face warm. "Mama killed him. When he started in on me. We had to run."

"I would have helped you," he said, lowering his voice, leaning in. "We all would have."

"I know. That's why we didn't ask."

"And . . . Cora?"

"Gone," Leni said in a thick voice. "Lung cancer. She . . . thought of you often."

"Oh, Leni, I'm so sorry. She was . . ."

"Yeah," Leni said softly, trying right then not to think of all the ways her mother was special, or how much her loss hurt. It hadn't been long enough yet; Leni hadn't learned how to talk about her pain. Instead, Leni stepped sideways, so he could see the boy sitting behind her. "MJ—Matthew Junior—this is your Grandpa Tom."

Mr. Walker had always seemed impossibly, superhumanly strong, but now, with one look at the boy who looked so much like his son, she saw how it cracked him open. "Oh, my God . . ."

MJ popped to his feet. He was clutching a red plastic dinosaur in one fist.

Mr. Walker squatted down to be eye to eye with his grandson through the cell bars. "You remind me of another boy with blond hair."

Hold it together.

"I'm MJ!" he said with an oversized smile, jumping up. "You wanna see my dinosaurs?" MJ didn't wait for an answer, started pulling his plastic dinosaurs from his pockets, producing each new one with flourish.

Over the sound of the growling (that's what *T. rex* sounds like, *grrr*), Mr. Walker said, "He looks just like his dad."

"Yeah." The past muscled its way into the present. Leni looked down at her feet, unable to meet Mr. Walker's gaze.

"I'm sorry I didn't tell you," she said. "We had to leave fast and I didn't want to get you into trouble. I didn't want you to have to lie for us, and I couldn't let Mama go to prison . . ."

"Ah, Leni," Mr. Walker said at last, rising to his feet. "You always had too many worries for a girl your age. So why are you in here if your mom killed Ernt? Curt should give you both a freaking medal, not lock you up."

Leni could have crumpled at the kindness she saw in his eyes. How could he not be angry? She'd abandoned his brain-damaged son, lied for years by her absence, and stolen years of his grandson's life from him. And now she had to ask him for another favor. "I helped her after the fact. You know . . . to get rid of the . . . body."

He leaned in. "You admitted that? Why?"

"The chief outsmarted me. Anyway, maybe it's the way it has to be. I needed to tell the truth. I'm tired of pretending to be someone else. I'll figure it all out. My grandfather is a lawyer. I just . . . need to know MJ is safe until I'm . . . out. Will you take him?"

"Of course I will, but—"

"And I know I have no right to ask you this, but please don't tell Matthew about his son. I need to do that myself."

"Matthew won't—"

"I know he won't understand, but I need to be the one to tell him he has a son. It's the right thing to do."

She heard the jangle of keys, footsteps. Chief Ward was coming this way. He eased in past Mr. Walker and unlocked the cell door. "It's time," he said.

Leni bent down to her son. "Okay, baby boy," she said, trying to be strong. "You need to go with your grandpa now. Mommy has . . . things to do." She gave him a little shove, so that he was outside the cell.

"Mommy? I don't wanna go."

Leni looked to Mr. Walker for help. She didn't know how to do this.

Mr. Walker laid his big hand on MJ's little shoulder. "It's a pink year, MJ." His voice was as unsteady as Leni felt. "That means the humpies are clogging the rivers. We could fish the Anchor River today. Chances are good you'll catch the biggest fish of your life."

"Can my mommy and daddy come?" MJ asked. "Oh. Wait. My daddy can't move. I forgot."

"You know about your dad?" Mr. Walker said.

MJ nodded. "Mommy loves him more than the moon and the stars. Like she loves me. But he has a broke head."

"The boy needs to leave now," Chief Ward said.

MJ looked at Leni. "So I'm going fishing with my new grandpa, right? Then we'll play jail more?"

"Uh-huh," Leni said, doing her best not to cry. She had taught her son to trust her, always, and to believe her, and so he did. She reached out and pulled him into a hug, imprinting the feel of him. Of all the courage she had expended so far—coming home, telling the truth, calling for Tom Walker— it took the greatest toll on her to simply let her son go. She managed a shaky smile. " 'Bye, MJ. Be good for Grandpa. Try not to break anything."

" 'Bye, Mommy."

Mr. Walker swept MJ into the air, planted him on his shoulders. MJ's high-pitched giggle rang out.

"Look, Mommy, look! I'm a giant!"

"She doesn't deserve to be here," Mr. Walker said to Chief Ward, who shrugged. "You always were a by-the-book prick."

"Insulting me. Good plan. Tell it to the court, Tom. We'll arraign her quickly. Three o'clock. Judge wants to be out on the river by four."

"I'm sorry, Leni," Mr. Walker said.

She heard the gentleness in his voice and knew that the man was ready to offer comfort. Leni didn't dare reach out. Any kindness now could break what little control she had. "Take care of him, Tom. He's my world."

She stared up at her son on his grandfather's shoulders, and she thought, *Please let this be okay*, and then the cell door clanged shut.

The rest of the day passed slowly, in unfamiliar sights and sounds, in a phone jangling, in doors opening and closing, in lunch orders being taken and delivered, in boots stomping across the station floor.

Leni sat on the hard concrete bench, slumped back against the cold wall. Sunlight streamed through the small cell window, heated everything. She pushed the damp hair out of her eyes. She'd spent the last two hours crying and sweating and muttering curses. Everywhere she could be damp, she was. Her mouth tasted like the inside of an old shoe. She went to the small, lid-less toilet, pulled down her pants, and sat down, praying no one saw her.

How was MJ? She hoped Mr. Walker had found the stuffed orca (inexplicably named Bob) in his suitcase. MJ wouldn't be able to sleep tonight without him. How had Leni forgotten to tell Mr. Walker that?

The station door opened. A man walked in. He had hunched shoulders and hair so tangled it looked like he'd been electrified. He wore hip waders and carried a scuffed green nylon briefcase. "Hey, Marci," he said in a booming voice. Leni returned to her place on the bench.

"Morning, Dem," said the female officer at the front desk.

He glanced sideways. "That her?"

The female officer nodded. "Yep. Allbright, Lenora. Arraignment at three o'clock. John's coming in from Soldotna."

The man headed her way, came to a stop outside the jail cell. With a sigh, he pulled a folder out of his dirty nylon briefcase and started reading. "Pretty detailed confession. Don't you watch television?"

"Who are you?"

"Demby Cowe. Your court-appointed attorney. We're going to zip in, enter a plea of not guilty, and zip out. The pinks are running. Okay? All you have to do is stand up when the court tells you to and say not guilty." He closed the file. "Do you have someone who can pay bail?"

"Don't you want to hear my side of it?"

"I've got your confession. We'll talk later. Plenty, I promise. Brush your hair."

He was gone before Leni could even really process that he'd been there.

⊹⟨✦⟩⊹

THE COURTROOM LOOKED more like a small-town doctor's office than a hallowed hall of justice. There was no shining wood, no pewlike seats, no big desk up front. Just linoleum floors, a bunch of chairs set out in rows, and desks for the prosecutor and the defense. In the front of the room, beneath a framed picture of Ronald Reagan, a long Formica desk awaited the judge; beside it, a plastic chair awaited witnesses.

Leni slid into her chair alongside her attorney, who was sitting close to the desk, studying tide charts. The prosecutor was seated at the desk across the aisle. A skinny man with a bushy beard, wearing a fishing vest and black pants.

The judge walked into the courtroom, followed by the stenographer and the bailiff. The judge wore a long black robe and Xtratuf fishing boots. He took his place behind the desk and glanced at the clock. "Let's be quick, gentlemen."

Leni's lawyer stood. "May it please the court—"

The courtroom door banged open behind them. "Where is she?"

Leni could live to be one hundred and ten and still know that voice. Her heart did a little flip of joy. "Large Marge!"

Large Marge barreled forward, bracelets rattling. Her dark, aging face was speckled with tiny black moles and her hair was a tangle of fuzzy dreadlocks held back from her face by a folded bandanna headband. Her denim shirt was too small—stretched taut across her large breasts—and her pants were stained blue from berry picking and tucked into rubber boots.

She yanked Leni right out of the chair and hugged her. The woman smelled of homemade shampoo and wood smoke. Of Alaska in the summer.

"Damn it to hell," the judge said, banging his gavel. "What's going on here? We are arraigning this young woman on serious criminal charges—"

Large Marge extricated herself from the hug and pushed Leni back down into the chair. "Goddamn it, John, this proceeding is what's criminal." Marge strode up to the judge's bench, her boots squeaking at every step. "This girl is innocent of everything and Whack Job Ward coerced a confession out of her. And for what? Rendering criminal assistance? Accessory after the fact? Good God. She didn't kill her piece-of-shit old man, she just ran when her terrified mother told her to. She was eighteen years old with an abusive dad. Who wouldn't run?"

The judge slammed his mallet on the desk. "Marge, you got a mouth on you like a king salmon. Now shut up. This is my courtroom. And this is just a damned arraignment, not a trial. You can present your evidence when it's time."

Large Marge turned to face the prosecutor. "Drop the damn charges, Adrian. Unless you want to spend the last days of the season in court. Everyone in Kaneq—and probably on the pipeline—knew Ernt Allbright was abusive. I will bring an endless stream of folks to testify on this girl's behalf. Starting with Tom Walker."

"Tom Walker?" the judge said.

Large Marge faced the judge again, crossed her arms in a way that communicated a settling-in, a willingness to stand here all day arguing her point. "That's right."

The judge glanced over at the skinny prosecutor. "Adrian?"

The prosecutor looked down at the papers spread out in front of him. He tapped a pen on the desk. "I don't know, Your Honor . . ."

The courtroom door opened. The woman from the front desk at the police station walked through. She was nervously smoothing her pant leg. "Your Honor?" she said.

"What is it, Marci?" the judge boomed. "We're busy here."

"The governor is on the line. He wants to talk to you. Right now."

⊰⟨✦⟩⊱

ONE MINUTE, Leni was standing beside her lawyer at the desk in the courtroom, and the next thing she knew, she was leaving the police station.

Outside, she saw Large Marge standing beside a pickup truck.

"What happened?" Leni asked.

Large Marge took Leni's suitcase and tossed it into the rusted bed of the pickup. "Alaska isn't so different as everyplace else. It helps to have friends in high places. Tommy called the governor, who got the charges dropped." She touched Leni's shoulder. "It's over, kiddo."

"Only part of it," Leni said. "There's more."

"Yeah. Tom wants you to come to the homestead. He'll take you to see Matthew."

Leni couldn't let herself think about that yet. She walked around to the passenger side of the pickup and climbed up into the blanket-covered bench seat.

Large Marge stepped up into the driver's seat, settling her bulk with a shimmying motion. When she started the engine, the radio came on.

Another little piece of my heart now, baby came growling through the speaker. Leni closed her eyes.

"You look fragile, kiddo," Large Marge said.

"Hard not to be." She thought about asking Large Marge about Matthew, but honestly, Leni felt as if the smallest thing could break her. So she stared out the window instead.

As they drove down to the dock, Leni couldn't help but stare in awe at the magical drizzle of light. The world seemed illuminated from within, fantastical colors bold and gilded, knife peaks of snow and rock, vibrantly green grass, blue sea.

The docks were full of fishing boats and noise. Seabirds cawing; engines growling, puffing black smoke into the air; otters gliding in the water between boats, chattering.

They boarded Large Marge's red fishing boat—the *Fair Chase*—and sped across a calm blue Kachemak Bay, toward the soaring white mountains. Leni had to shield her eyes from the glare of sunlight on the water, but there was no way to shield her heart. Memories came at her from all sides. She remembered seeing these mountains for the first time. Had she known then how Alaska would take hold of her? Shape her? She didn't know, couldn't remember. It all felt like a lifetime ago.

They rounded the tip of Sadie Cove and ducked in between two green, humped islands, their shorelines littered with silvery driftwood and kelp and pebbles. The boat slowed and motored around the rock breakwater.

Leni got her first glimpse of Kaneq Harbor and the town set on stilts above it. They tied down the boat and walked up the gangplank toward the chain-link fence that created the entrance to the harbor from town. She didn't think Large Marge had said anything, but Leni couldn't really be sure. All she could hear was her own body, coming alive again in this place that would always define her—her heart beating, her lungs drawing breath, her footsteps on the gravel of Main Street.

Kaneq had grown in the past years. The clapboard-fronted storefronts were painted bright colors, like pictures she'd seen of fjord-side towns in Scandinavia. The boardwalk that connected everything looked brand-new. Streetlamps stood like sentinels, planters full of geraniums and petunias hung from their iron arms. Off to her left was the General Store, expanded to twice its original size, with a new red door. The street boasted one shop after another: the Snackle Shop, the diner, the yarn shop, souvenir places, ice-cream stands, outfitters, guides, kayak rentals, and the new Malamute Saloon and Geneva Inn, which boasted a giant white rack of antlers above the door.

She remembered their first day here, with Mama in her new hiking boots and a frothy peasant blouse, saying, *I'm a little suspicious of people who use dead animals in their decorating.*

Leni couldn't help smiling. Good Lord, they'd been unprepared.

Tourists mingled with locals (one still easily distinguishable from the other by clothing). Vehicles lined the street in front of the Malamute Saloon: a few ATVs, some dirt bikes, two pickup trucks, and a lime-green Pinto with a duct-taped fender.

Leni climbed into Large Marge's old International Harvester. They drove past the General Store. A newly painted bridge (fishermen with lines in the water on either side) swept them over the crystal-clear river and deposited them on the gravel road that soon turned to dirt.

For the first half mile, there were new signs of civilization: A travel trailer was on blocks in the tall grass; beside it, a tractor was rusted through. A couple of new driveways. A mobile home. An old school bus parked near the ditch had no tires.

Leni noticed that Large Marge had a new sign at her place. It read KAYAK AND CANOE RENTALS HERE!

"I love exclamation marks," Large Marge said.

Leni was going to say something, but then she saw the start of Walker land, where the arch welcomed guests to the adventure lodge and promised FISHING, KAYAKING, BEAR VIEWING, AND SIGHTSEEING FLIGHTS.

Large Marge eased up on the accelerator as they neared the driveway. She glanced at Leni. "You sure you're ready to do this? We could wait."

Leni heard the gentleness in Large Marge's voice and knew that the woman was offering to give Leni time before she saw Matthew again. "I'm ready."

They crossed beneath the Walker arch and rumbled along, the road evened out by gravel. To her left, eight new log cabins had been built among the trees, each one positioned to have a sweeping view of the bay. A twisting, handrailed trail led down to the beach.

Not much farther and they came to the Walker house, now Walker Lodge. Still a crown jewel; two stories of skinned logs, with a huge porch and windows that overlooked the bay and the mountains. There was no junk showing in the yard anymore; no rusting trucks or coils of wire or stacked pallets. Instead, there were wooden partitions here and there, free-standing walls to hide whatever was behind. Adirondack chairs populated the deck. The animal pens had been moved to the distant tree line.

Down at the dock, a float plane was tied up alongside three aluminum fishing boats. There were people walking along paths, fishing on the beach. Employees in brown uniforms and guests in color-coordinated rain gear and brand-new fleece vests. Leni got out of the truck, looked around.

MJ bolted out of the lodge, bounded across the deck, maneuvering around the chairs, and came at her, waving something in his hand.

Leni bent down and scooped him up, holding him so tightly he started to wiggle to get free. She didn't realize until right then how afraid she'd been of losing him.

Tom Walker headed toward her. Beside him was a pretty, broad-shouldered Native woman with hip-length black hair that was going gray in a single wide streak. She wore a faded denim blouse tucked into khaki pants, with a knife sheathed at her belt and a pair of wire cutters sticking out of her breast pocket.

"Hey, Leni," Mr. Walker said, "I'd like you to meet my wife, Atka."

The woman held out her hand and smiled. "I have heard so much about you and your mother." ·

Leni's throat felt tight as she shook Atka's rough hand and said, "It's nice to meet you." She looked at Mr. Walker. "Mama would be happy for you." Leni's voice cracked.

They fell silent after that.

MJ dropped to his knees in the grass, making his blue triceratops fight his red *T. rex*, with growling sound effects.

"I'd like to see him now," Leni said. She knew instinctively that Mr. Walker was waiting for her to tell him she was ready. "Alone, I think. If that's okay with you."

Mr. Walker turned to his wife. "Atka, would you and Marge watch the little one for a minute?"

Atka smiled, swept the long hair to her back. "MJ, do you remember the starfish I told you about? The animal called *Yuit* by my people, the wrestler of the waves? Would you like to see one?"

MJ shot to his feet. "Yes! Yes!"

Leni crossed her arms as she watched Large Marge and Atka and MJ walk toward the beach stairs. MJ's high, chattering voice faded gradually away.

"This isn't going to be easy," Mr. Walker said.

"I wish I could have written," she said. "I wanted to tell you and Matthew about MJ, but . . ." She took a deep breath. "We were afraid they'd arrest us if we came back."

"You could have trusted us to protect you, but we don't need to talk about what happened back then."

"I abandoned him," she said quietly.

"He was in so much pain he didn't know who he was, let alone who you were."

"You think that eases my conscience? That he was in pain?"

"You were in pain, too. More than I knew, I guess. You knew you were pregnant?"

She nodded. "How is he?"

"It's been a rough road."

Leni felt acutely uncomfortable in the quiet that fell between them. Guilty.

"Come with me," he said, and took her by the arm, steadying her. They walked past the lodge's cabins, past where the goat pens used to be, and across a sheared hayfield, into a stand of black spruce.

Mr. Walker stopped. Leni expected to see a truck, but there wasn't one. "Aren't we going to Homer?"

Mr. Walker shook his head. He led her deeper into the trees, until they came to a slatted boardwalk, lined with gnarly branch railings on either side. Just below it, on a lip of land surrounded by trees, was a log cabin that overlooked the bay. Geneva's old cabin. A wide wooden bridge led from the boardwalk to the front door. No, not a bridge. A ramp.

A wheelchair ramp.

Mr. Walker walked on ahead, his boots thudding on the ramplike bridge.

He knocked on the door. Leni heard a muffled voice and Mr. Walker opened the door and led Leni inside. "Go on," he said gently, pushing her inside a small, cozy cabin with a wall of windows overlooking the bay.

The first thing Leni saw was a series of large paintings. One of them—a huge work-in-progress canvas—was propped on an easel. On it, an explosion of color; drops and splatters and streaks that somehow—impossibly—gave Leni the impression of the northern lights, although she couldn't say why. There were strange, misshapen letters in all that color; she could almost make them out but not quite. Maybe it said, HER? The painting made her feel something. Pain first, and then a rising sense of hope.

"I'll leave you two," Mr. Walker said. He left the cabin and closed the door at the same time Leni saw the man in the wheelchair, sitting with his back to her.

He executed a slow turn, his paint-splattered hands agile on the wheelchair, maneuvering himself around.

Matthew.

He looked up. A network of raised pale pink scars ran across his face, gave him an odd, stitched-together look. His nose was flattened, had the splayed look of an old boxer's, and his right eye was tugged just the slightest bit downward by a starburst of scar tissue at the top of his cheekbone.

But his eyes. In them, she saw *him,* her Matthew.

"Matthew? It's me, Leni."

He frowned. She waited for him to say something, anything, but there was nothing, just this aching, drawn-out silence where once there had been an endless stream of words.

She felt tears start. "It's Leni," she said again, softer. He stared at her, just kept staring, like he was dreaming. "You don't know me," she said, wiping her eyes. "I knew you wouldn't. And you won't understand about MJ. I knew that. I *knew* it, it's just . . ." She took a step backward. She couldn't do this now, not yet.

She would try again later. Practice her words. She'd explain it to MJ, prepare him. They had time now, and she wanted to do this right. She turned toward the door.

THIRTY-ONE

"W ait."

Matthew sat in the wheelchair, clutching a sticky paintbrush, his heart racing.

They had told him she was coming, but then he'd forgotten and remembered and forgotten again. It was like that for him sometimes. Things got lost in the confused circuitry of his brain. Less often these days, but it happened.

Or maybe he hadn't believed. Or he'd thought he'd imagined it, that they'd said the words to make him smile, hoping he'd forget.

He still had fog days when nothing made it up from the mist, not words or ideas or sentences. Just pain.

But she was here. He had dreamed of her return for years, played and replayed the possibilities. Imagined and massaged ideas. He had practiced words for it, for her, alone in his room, where stress wouldn't seize control and render him mute, where he could pretend that he was a man worth coming back to.

He tried not to think about his ugly face and his never-quite-right leg. He knew that sometimes he couldn't think well, and words became impos-

sible creatures that ran at his approach. He heard his once-strong voice tripping up, sending out idiot words and he thought, *That can't be me*, but it was.

He dropped the wet paintbrush and clutched the armrests of the wheelchair, forced himself to stand. It hurt so badly he made a grunt of pain, and
it shamed him, that noise, but there was nothing he could do. He gritted his
teeth, repositioned his leg. He'd been sitting for too long, consumed by his
painting, the one he called *Her,* about a night he remembered on her beach,
and he'd forgotten to move.

He shambled forward in a lurching, unsteady gait that probably made her
think he could fall at any moment. He'd fallen a lot, gotten up more.

"Matthew?" She moved toward him, her face tilted up.

Her beauty made him want to cry. He wanted to tell her that when he
painted, he felt her, remembered her, that it had started in rehab as occupa-
tional therapy and now it was his passion. Sometimes when he was painting he could forget all of it, the pain, the memories, the loss, and imagine a
future with Leni, their love like sunshine and warm water. He imagined
them having kids, growing old together. All of it.

He strained to find all those words. It was like suddenly being in a dark
room. You knew there was a door, but you couldn't find it.

Breathe, Matthew. Stress made it worse.

He drew in a breath, released it. He limped over to the bedside table,
picked up the box full of the letters she'd sent him all those years ago, while
he was in the hospital, and the others, the ones she'd sent when he was a
grief-stricken kid in Fairbanks. They were how he'd learned to read again.
He handed it to her, unable to ask the question that had haunted him: Why
did you stop writing to me?

She looked down, saw her letters in the box, and looked up at him. "You
kept them? After I left you?"

"Your letters," he said. He knew the words were elongated; he had to concentrate to create the combinations he wanted. "Were how I. Learned to
read again."

Leni stared up at him.

"I prayed. You'd. Come back," he said.

"I wanted to," she whispered.

He gave her a smile, knowing how it pulled down the skin at his eye, made him look even more freakish.

She put her arms around him and he was amazed at how they still fit together. After all the ways he'd been put back together, restrung and bolted up; they still fit together. She touched his scarred face. "You are so beautiful."

He tightened his hold on her, tried to steady himself, feeling suddenly, inexplicably afraid.

"Are you okay? Are you in pain?"

He didn't know how to say what he was feeling, or he was afraid that if he said it, she'd think less of him. He'd been drowning for all of these years without her, and she was the shore he'd been flailing to find. But surely she would look into his ravaged, stitched-together face and run away, and then he would drift back into the deep, dark waters alone.

He pulled away, limped back over to his wheelchair, and sat down with an *oomph* of pain. He shouldn't have held her, felt her body against his. How would he ever forget the feel of her again? He tried to get back onto an ordinary track, but couldn't find his way. He was trembling. "Where. Have you been?"

"Seattle." She moved toward him. "It's a long story."

At her touch, the world—his world—had cracked open or broke apart. Something. He wanted to revel in the moment, burrow into it like a pile of furs and let it warm him, but none of it felt real or safe. "Tell me."

She shook her head.

"I disappoint. You."

"You aren't the disappointment, Matthew. I am. I always have been. I was the one who left. And when you needed me most. I would understand if you can't forgive me. I can't forgive me. I did it because, well . . . there's someone you need to meet. Afterwards, if you still want to, we can talk."

Matthew frowned. "Someone. Here?"

"Outside with your dad and Atka. Will you come with me to meet him?"

Him.

Disappointment settled deep, all the way to his bolted-together bones. "I don't need to meet. Your *him*."

"You're mad. I get it. You said we always stand by the people we love, but I didn't. I ran."

"Don't talk. Go," he said in a harsh voice. "Please. Just go."

She looked at him, tears in her eyes. She was so beautiful he couldn't breathe. He wanted to cry, to scream. How would he ever let her go? He had been waiting for this moment, for her, for them, for all the years he could remember, through pain so bad he cried in his sleep, but every day he woke and thought, *Her*, and he tried again. He'd imagined a million versions of their future, but he'd never imagined this. Her coming back just to say goodbye.

"You have a son, Matthew."

It happened for him like that sometimes. He heard the wrong words, took in information that wasn't there. His screwed-up brain. Before he could guard against it, use his learned tools, the pain of those words crashed down on him. He wanted to let her know that he'd misunderstood, but all he could do was howl, a deep, rolling growl of pain. Words abandoned him; all he had left was pure emotion. He lurched out of the chair and stumbled backward, away from her, hitting the kitchen counter hard. It was his damaged brain, telling him what he wanted to hear instead of what was actually said.

Leni moved toward him. He could see how hurt she was, how crazed she thought he was, and shame made him want to turn away. "Go. If you're leaving. Go."

"Matthew, please. Stop. I know I've hurt you." She reached out for him. "Matthew, I'm sorry."

"Go away. Please."

"You have a son," she said slowly. "A son. We have a son. Do you understand me?"

He frowned. "A baby?"

"Yes. I brought him to meet you."

At first he felt pure, exquisite joy; then the truth hit him hard. A son. A child of his, of theirs. It made him want to cry for what he'd lost.

"Look at me," he said quietly.

"I'm looking."

"I look like. Someone rebuilt me with. A bad sewing machine. Sometimes it hurts. So much I can't speak. It took me two *years* to stop. Grunting and screaming. And say my first. Real word."

"And?"

He thought of all the things he'd once imagined he would teach a son, and it collapsed around him. He was too broken to hold anyone else together. "I can't pick him up. Can't put him. On my shoulders. He won't want this. For a dad." He knew Leni heard the longing in his voice at that; the universe in a three-letter word.

She touched his face, let her fingers trace the scars that put him back together, stared up into his green eyes. "You know what I see? A man who should have died but wouldn't give up. I see a man who fought to talk and walk and think. Every one of your scars breaks my heart and puts it back together. Your fear is every parent's fear. I see the man I have loved for my whole life. The father of our son."

"Don't. Know how."

"No one knows how. Believe me. Can you hold his hand? Can you teach him to fish? Can you make him a sandwich?"

"I'll embarrass him," he said.

"Kids are durable, and so is their love. Trust me, Matthew, you can do this."

"Not alone."

"Not alone. It's you and me, just like it was always supposed to be. We'll do it together. Okay?"

"Promise?"

"I promise."

She held his face in her hands and rose up onto her toes to kiss him. With that one kiss, so like another kiss from long ago, a lifetime ago, two kids believing in a happy ending, he felt his world come back into alignment.

"Come meet him," she whispered against his lips. "He snores just like you do. And he bumps into every piece of furniture. And he loves Robert Service poems."

She took his hand. Together they walked out of the cabin, him limping slowly, holding her hand tightly, leaning on her, letting her steady him. Wordlessly, they made their way out of the trees and past the house that was now a world-class fishing lodge, toward the new beach stairs.

As always, the shoreline was full of guests, dressed in their new Alaska rain gear, fishing at the water's edge, birds cawing in the air, waiting for scraps.

He held on to Leni with one hand and clutched the handrail with his other and made his slow, halting way down the stairs.

On the beach, off to the right, Large Marge was drinking a beer. Alyeska was out in the bay, giving kayak lessons to guests. Dad and Atka were with a child, a blond boy, who was squatted over a big purple starfish.

Matthew came to a stop.

"Mommy!" the boy said at Leni's appearance. He jumped up, smiling so big it lit his whole face. "Did you know that starfishes have *teeth*? I seen 'em!"

Leni looked up at Matthew. "Our son," she said, and let go of Matthew's hand.

He limped toward the little boy, stopped. Meaning to bend, he crashed down to one knee, grimaced in pain, groaned.

"You sound like a bear. I like bears, so does my new grandpop. Do you?"

"I like bears," Matthew said, unsure.

He looked into his son's face and saw his own past. He suddenly remembered things he'd forgotten—the feel of frogs' eggs in your hand, the way a good laugh sometimes shook your whole body, stories being read by a campfire, playing pirates on the shore, building a fort in the trees. All of that he could teach. Of all the things he'd dreamed of over the years, tried like hell to believe in when his pain was at its worst, this was something he'd never dared to even hope for.

My son. "I'm Matthew."

"Really? I'm Matthew Junior. But everyone calls me MJ."

Matthew felt an emotion unlike anything he'd ever felt before. Matthew Junior. *My son*, he thought again. He found it difficult to smile; realized he was crying. "I'm your dad."

MJ looked at Leni. "Mommy?"

Leni came up beside them, laid a hand on Matthew's shoulder, and nodded. "That's him, MJ. Your dad. He's waited a long time to meet you."

MJ grinned, showed off his two missing front teeth. He threw himself at Matthew, hugged him so ferociously they toppled over. When they came back up, MJ was laughing. "You wanna see a starfish?"

"Sure," Matthew said.

Matthew tried to get up, put his hand on the ground. Bits of shell stuck to his palm as he stumbled, his bad ankle giving way. And then Leni was there, taking his arm, helping him stand up again.

MJ raced down to the water, talking all the way.

Matthew couldn't make his feet move. All he could do was stand there, breathing shallowly, a little afraid that all of this could break like glass at the merest touch. At a breath. The boy who looked like him stood at the shore, blond hair glinting in the sun, the hem of his jeans wet with saltwater. Laughing. In that one image, Matthew saw the whole of his life; past, present, and future. It was one of those moments—an instant of grace in a crazy, sometimes impossibly dangerous world—that changed a man's life.

"You'd better go, Matthew," Leni said. "Our son is not very good at waiting for what he wants."

He looked down at her and thought, *God, I love her,* but his voice was gone, lost in this new world in which everything had changed. In which he was a father.

They had come so far from their beginnings as two damaged kids, he and Leni. Maybe it had all happened the way it needed to, maybe they'd each crossed their own oceans—hers of damaged love and loss, his of pain— to be here again together, where they belonged. "Good thing I am."

He saw what those words meant to her.

"I wanted to stand by you. I wanted—"

"You know what I love most about you, Leni Allbright?"

"What?"

"Everything." He took her in his arms and kissed her with everything that he had and all he hoped to have. When he finally let go, reluctantly, and drew back, they stared at each other, had a whole conversation in breaths taken and expelled. This was a beginning, he thought; a beginning in the middle, something unexpected and beautiful.

"You'd better go," Leni finally said.

Matthew walked carefully across the pebbled beach toward the boy standing at the waterline.

"Hurry up," MJ said, waving Matthew over to the big purple starfish. "It's right here. Look! Look, Daddy."

Daddy.

Matthew saw a flat charcoal-gray stone, small as a new beginning, polished by the sea, and picked it up. The weight of it was perfect, the size exactly what he wanted. He held it out to his son, said, "Here. I'll show you. How to. Skip rocks. It's cool. I taught your mom. The same thing. A long time ago . . ."

❖❖⟨❀⟩❖❖

"He always believed you'd come back," Mr. Walker said, coming up beside Leni. "Said he'd know if you were dead. That he'd feel it. His first word was 'her.' It didn't take us long to know he meant you."

"How do I make up for leaving him?"

"Ah, Leni. It's life. Things don't always go the way you expect." He shrugged. "Matthew knows that, better than any of us."

"How is he, really?"

"He has struggles. Pain sometimes. He has trouble putting his thoughts into words when he gets stressed, but he's also the best guide on the river and the guests love him. He volunteers at the rehab center. And you've seen his paintings. It's almost like God gave him that gift in compensation. His future isn't like everyone else's, maybe, not what you'd imagined when you were both eighteen."

"I have my struggles, too," Leni said quietly. "And we were kids then. We're not now."

Mr. Walker nodded. "There's really only one question. Everything else will follow." He turned to look at her. "Are you staying?"

She did her best to smile. She was pretty sure this was the question he'd come over to ask. As a parent herself, she understood. He didn't want his son hurt again. "I have no idea what this new life of mine will look like, but I'm staying."

He laid a hand on her shoulder.

Down on the beach, MJ leaped into the air. "I did it! I made the rock skip. Mommy, did you see that?"

Matthew looked back and gave Leni a crooked smile. He and his son looked so much alike, both of them smiling at her, standing together against the cornflower-blue sky. Peas in a pod. Two of a kind. The beginning of a whole new world of love.

⋆⊰⟨❀⟩⊹⋆

ALTHOUGH SHE HAD THOUGHT about it often over the years, mythologized it almost, Leni realized that she had forgotten the true magic of a summer night when the darkness didn't fall.

Now she was sitting at one of the picnic tables down on the Walker beach. A lingering scent of roasted marshmallows hung in the air, sweetened the briny tang of the sea washing ceaselessly back and forth. MJ stood at the shore, casting his line into the water, reeling it back in. Mr. Walker stood on one side of him, giving him tips, helping him when the line got tangled or when he snagged something. Alyeska was standing on his other side, casting a line of her own. Leni knew that MJ was going to fall asleep where he stood any minute.

As much as she loved sitting here, soaking in this new image of her life, she knew she was avoiding something that mattered. With each minute that passed, she felt the weight of her avoidance; like a hand on her shoulder, a gentle reminder.

She slid off the seat, got to her feet. She no longer knew how to judge time by the color of the sky—a brilliant amethyst, speckled with stars—so she looked at her watch: 9:25.

"Are you okay?" Matthew said. He held on to her hand until she pulled gently away, then he let go.

"I need to go see my old house."

He rose, winced in pain as he put weight on his bad foot. She knew it had been a long day on his feet for him.

She touched his scarred cheek. "I'll go. I saw a bike up by the lodge. I just want to stand there. I'll be right back."

"But—"

"I can do it alone. I know you're in pain. Stay with MJ. When I get back, we'll put him to bed. I'll show you the stuffed animals he can't sleep without and tell you his favorite story. It's about us."

She knew that Matthew would argue, so she didn't let him. This was her past, her baggage. She turned away from him and went up the beach stairs and climbed to the grassy land above. There were still several guests sitting on the deck at the lodge, talking loudly, laughing. Probably honing the fish stories they would take home with them.

She took a bike from the rack by the lodge and climbed on, pedaling slowly over the spongy muskeg, crossing the main road, turning to the right, toward the end of the road.

There was the wall. Or what was left of it. The planks had been hacked apart, pulled away from the stanchions; the ruined slats lay in heaps, furred with moss and darkened by years of harsh weather.

Large Marge and Tom. Maybe Thelma. She could imagine them gathering here in their grief, holding axes, splintering the wood.

She turned into the driveway, which was knee-high with weeds and grass. Shade siphoned away the light; the world was quiet here in the way of woodlands and abandoned homes. She had to slow down, pedal hard.

At last she turned into the clearing. The cabin sat off to the left, worn by time and the elements, but still standing. Alongside it, empty, sagging animal pens, gates gone, fences broken by predators, probably home to all kinds of rodents. The tall grass, threaded with bright pink fireweed and prickly devil's club, had grown up around the junk they'd left behind; here and there she could see mounds of rusting metal and decaying wood. The old truck had collapsed, bowed forward like an old horse. The smokehouse was a pyramid of silvered, moldy boards, collapsed in on itself. Inexplicably, the clothesline remained, clothespins attached, bouncing in the breeze.

Leni dismounted, carefully set the bike on its side in the grass. Feeling more than a little numb, she headed toward the cabin. Mosquitoes buzzed in a cloud around her. At the door she paused, thought, *You can do it*, and opened the door.

It felt like going back in time, to the first day she'd been in here, with insect carcasses thick on the floor. Everything was as they'd left it, but covered in dust.

Voices and words and images from the past drifted through her mind. The good, the bad, the funny, the horrific. She remembered it all in a blinding, electric flash.

She closed her hand around the heart necklace at her throat, her talisman, felt the sharp bit of bone press into her palm. She drifted through the place, rattled the psychedelic beads that had given her parents the illusion of privacy. In their bedroom, she saw the dusty heap of belongings that revealed who they'd once been. A tangle of furs on the bed. Jackets hanging from hooks. A pair of boots with the toes eaten away.

She found her dad's old bicentennial bandanna and shoved it in her pocket. Her mother's suede headband hung from a hook on the wall. She took it, wound it like a bracelet around her wrist.

Up in her loft, she found her books lying scattered, the pages yellowed and chewed through; many had become a home to mice, as had her mattress. She could smell their scent in the air. A decaying, dirty smell.

The smell of a place forgotten.

She climbed back down the loft ladder, dropped onto the dirty, sticky floor, looked around.

So many memories. She wondered how long it would take her to work through them all. Even now, standing here, she didn't know exactly how she felt about this place, but she knew, she *believed*, she could find a way to remember the good in it. She would never forget the bad, but she would let it go. She had to. *There had been fun, too,* Mama had said, *and adventure.*

Behind her, the door opened. She heard uneven footsteps come up behind her. Matthew stepped in beside her. "Alone is overrated," he said simply. "Do you want. To fix it up? Live here?"

"Maybe. Or maybe we'll burn it down and rebuild. Ashes make great soil."

She didn't know yet. All she knew was that she was back here at last, after all those years away, back with the crazy, durable fringe-dwellers in a state that was like nowhere else, in this majestic place that had shaped her, defined her. Once, a lifetime ago, she had worried about girls, only a few years older than her, who had gone missing. The stories had given her nightmares at thirteen. Now she knew there were a hundred ways to be lost and even more ways to be found.

SUCH A THIN VEIL separated the past from the present; they existed simultaneously in the human heart. Anything could transport you—the smell of the sea at low tide, the screech of a gull, the turquoise of a glacier-fed river. A voice in the wind could be both true and imagined. Especially here.

On this hot summer day, the Kenai Peninsula was vibrant with color. There wasn't a cloud in sight. The mountains were a magical mixture of lavender and green and ice-blue—valleys and cliffs and peaks; there was still snow above the tree line. The bay was sapphire, almost waveless. Dozens of fishing boats puttered alongside kayaks and canoes. Today was a day to be on the water for Alaskans. Leni knew that Bishop's Beach, the straight, sandy stretch below the Russian church in Homer, would be one long line of trucks and empty boat trailers, just as she knew that some clueless tourist would be out on the sand, digging for clams and not paying attention, and get caught by the tide.

Some things never changed.

Now Leni stood in her overgrown yard, with Matthew beside her. Together, they walked over to the grassy rise above the beach, met up with Mr. and Mrs. Walker, Alyeska, and MJ, who were already there, waiting. Alyeska gave Leni a warm, welcoming smile, one that said, *We're in this together now. Family.* They hadn't had much time to talk in the past two days, with the whirlwind of Leni's return to Alaska, but they both knew there would be time for them, time to stitch their lives together. It would be easy; they loved so many people in common.

Leni took her son's hand.

A crowd waited for her on the beach. Leni felt their eyes on her, noticed how they stopped talking at her approach.

"Look, Mommy, a seal! That fish jumped right outta the water! Whoa. Can we go fishing with Daddy today, can we? Aunt Aly says the pinks are still running."

Leni stared out at the friends gathered at the water's edge. Almost everyone from Kaneq was here today, even several of the hermits who were only seen at the saloon and sometimes at the General Store. At her arrival, no one spoke. One by one, they climbed into their boats. She heard the smack of water on hulls, the crunching of shells and pebbles as they pushed off.

Matthew guided her over to a Walker Cove Adventure Lodge skiff. He put a bright yellow life vest on MJ and then settled him on the bench seat in the bow, facing the stern. Leni climbed aboard. They motored out to where the other boats were.

The bay was quiet on this sunny, brilliant early evening. The deep *V* of the fjord looked majestic in this light.

The boats drifted out into the cove and floated together, banged bows. Leni looked around her. Tom and his new wife, Atka Walker; Alyeska and her husband, Darrow, and their twin three-year-old boys; Large Marge,

Natalie Watkins, Tica Rhodes and her husband, Thelma, Moppet, Ted, and all the Harlans. The faces of her childhood. And of her future.

Leni felt them all looking at her. She thought suddenly, sharply, how much this would have meant to Mama, these people coming out to say good-bye. Had Mama known how much they cared?

"Thank you," Leni said. The two inadequate words were lost amid the sound of waves slapping on boat hulls. What should she say? "I don't know how . . ."

"Just talk about her," Mr. Walker said in a gentle voice.

Leni nodded, wiped her eyes. Tried again, her voice as loud as she could manage to make it. "I don't know if any woman ever came to Alaska less prepared for it. She couldn't cook or bake or make jam. Before Alaska, her idea of a necessary survival skill was putting on false eyelashes and walking in heels. She brought purple hot pants up here, for God's sake."

Leni took a breath. "But she came to love it here. We both did. The last thing she said to me before she died was, *Go home.* I knew what she meant. If she saw you guys here for her, she would give one of her bright smiles and ask you why you all were here instead of drinking and dancing. Tom, she'd hand you a guitar, and Thelma, she'd ask you what the hell you've been up to, and Large Marge, she'd hug you till you couldn't breathe." Leni's voice broke. She looked around, remembering. "It would fill her heart to see you all here, to know you'd given up time, with all you have to do, to remember her. To say goodbye. She said to me once that she felt like she'd been nothing, a reflection of other people. She never quite understood her own worth. I hope she's looking down now and knows . . . finally . . . how loved she was."

A murmur of agreement, a few words, and then: quiet. Grief this deep was a silent, lonely thing. From now on, the only time Leni would hear her mother's voice would be in her own mind, thoughts channeled through another woman's consciousness, a continual quest for connection, for meaning. Like all motherless girls, Leni would become an emotional explorer, trying to uncover the lost part of her, the mother who had carried and nurtured and loved her. Leni would become both mother and child; through her, Mama would still grow and age. She would never be gone, not as long as Leni remembered her.

Large Marge threw a bouquet of flowers into the water.

"We'll miss you, Cora," Large Marge said.

Mr. Walker threw a bouquet of fireweed into the water. It floated past Leni, a bright pink splash on the waves.

Matthew met Leni's gaze. He was holding a bouquet of fireweed and lupine that he'd picked this morning with MJ.

Leni reached into a box and pulled out the mason jar full of ashes. For a lovely moment the world blurred and Mama came to her, smiled her bright smile and gave her a hip bump and said, *Dance, baby girl.*

When Leni looked again, the boats were splashes of color against the blue-green world.

She opened the jar, poured the contents slowly into the water. "I love you, Mama," Leni said, feeling loss settle deep, as much a part of her now as love. They'd been more than best friends; they'd been allies. Mama had called Leni the great love of her life and Leni thought maybe that was always true for parents and their children. She remembered something Mama had said to her once. *Love doesn't fade or die, baby girl.* She'd been talking about Matthew and sadness, but it was equally true for mothers and their children.

This love she felt for her mother and her son and Matthew and the people around her was a durable thing, as vast as this landscape, as immutable as the sea. Stronger than time itself.

She leaned over and dropped some bright pink fireweed on a gently rolling wave and watched it float toward the shore. She knew that from now on, she would feel her mother's touch in the breeze, hear her voice on the sound of the rising tide. Sometimes, berry-picking or making bread, or even the smell of coffee would make her cry. For the rest of her life, she would look up into the vast Alaskan sky and say, "Hey, Mama," and remember.

"I will always love you," she whispered to the wind. "Always."

MY ALASKA
July 4, 2009
by Lenora Allbright Walker

If you had told me when I was a kid that someday a newspaper would come to me to talk about Alaska on the fiftieth anniversary of its statehood, I would have laughed. Who would have thought my photographs would mean so much to so many? Or that I would take a picture of the Valdez oil spill that would change my life and make it onto the cover of a magazine?

Really, my husband is the one you should speak to. He's overcome every challenge this state has to offer and is still standing. He's like one of those trees that grow on a sheer granite cliff. In the wind and snow and icy cold, they should fall, but they don't. Stubbornly, they remain. Thrive.

I am just an ordinary Alaskan wife and mother who prides herself primarily on the children she has raised and the life she has managed, somehow, to wrest from this harsh landscape. But like all women's stories, mine has more to it than sometimes appears on the surface.

My husband's family is practically Alaskan royalty. His grandparents carved a life out of the remote wilderness with a hatchet and a dream. The quintessential American pioneers, they homesteaded hundreds of acres and started a town and settled in. My children, MJ, Kenai, and Cora, are the fourth generation to grow up on that land.

My family was different. We came to Alaska in the seventies. It was a turbulent time, full of protests and marches and bombings and kidnappings. Young women were being abducted from college campuses. The Vietnam War had divided the country.

We came to Alaska to run away from that world. Like so many cheechakos before and since, we planned poorly. We didn't have enough food or supplies or money. We had almost no skills. We moved into a cabin in a remote part of the Kenai Peninsula and learned fast that we didn't know enough. Even our car—a VW bus—was a poor choice.

Someone said to me once that Alaska didn't create character; it revealed it.

The sad truth is that the darkness in Alaska revealed the darkness in my father.

He was a Vietnam veteran, a POW. We didn't know then what all that meant. Now, we know. In our enlightened world, we know how to help men like my father. We understand the ways in which war can break the strongest mind. Then, there was no help. Nor was there much help for a woman who was his victim.

Alaska—the darkness and the cold and the isolation—got inside of my father in a terrible way, turned him into one of the many wild animals who populate the state.

But we didn't know that in the beginning; how could we? We dreamed, like so many others, and planned our course and duct-taped our Alaska or Bust banner on our bus and headed north, unprepared.

This state, this place, is like no other. It is beauty and horror; savior and destroyer. Here, where survival is a choice that must be made over and over, in the wildest place in America, on the edge of civilization, where water in all its forms can kill you, you learn who you are. Not who you dream of being, not who you imagined you were, not who you were raised to be. All of that will be torn away in the months of icy darkness, when frost on the windows blurs your view and the world gets very small and you stumble into the truth of your existence. You learn what you will do to survive.

That lesson, that revelation, as my mother once told me about love, is Alaska's great and terrible gift. Those who come for beauty alone, or for some imaginary life, or those who seek safety, will fail.

In the vast expanse of this unpredictable wilderness, you will either become your best self and flourish, or you will run away, screaming, from the dark and the cold and the hardship. There is no middle ground, no safe place; not here, in the Great Alone.

For we few, the sturdy, the strong, the dreamers, Alaska is home, always and forever, the song you hear when the world is still and quiet. You either belong here, wild and untamed yourself, or you don't.

I belong.

ACKNOWLEDGMENTS

I come from a long line of adventurers. My grandfather left Wales at fourteen to become a cowboy in Canada. My father has spent his life in search of the extraordinary, the remote, the unusual. He goes where most people only imagine going.

In 1968, my father thought that California was becoming too crowded. He and my mother decided to do something about it. They loaded all of us (three young kids—and two of our friends—and the family dog) into a VW bus. In the heat of the summer, off we went. We drove around America, through more than a dozen states, looking for a place to belong. We found it in the green and blue beauty of the Pacific Northwest.

Years later, my dad went in search of adventure again. He found it in Alaska, on the shores of the magnificent Kenai River. There, my parents met homesteaders Laura and Kathy Pedersen, a mother and daughter, who had operated a resort on that incomparable stretch of riverfront for years. In the early eighties, these two pioneering families came together and began a company that would come to be known as the Great Alaska Adventure Lodge. Three generations of my family have worked at the lodge. All of us have fallen in love with the Last Frontier.

I'd like to thank the Johns—Laurence, Sharon, Debbie, Kent, and Julie—and Kathy Pedersen Haley, for their boundless enthusiasm and vision in creating such a magical place.

I'd also like to thank Kathy Pedersen Haley and Anita Merkes for their expertise and editorial help in re-creating the homesteading world of Alaska and Kachemak Bay in the seventies and eighties. Your insight and support for this project meant so much to me. Any remaining mistakes are, of course, mine.

Also, to my brother, Kent—another adventurer—who answered an endless stream of bizarre questions about Alaska for me. You are, as always, a rock star.

Thanks to Carl and Kirsten Dixon and the fabulous team at the Tutka Bay Lodge on Kachemak Bay for welcoming me to their lovely corner of the world.

I'd also like to thank a few very special people who helped immeasurably on this novel, especially in the hardest of times, when I felt ready to give up. My brilliant editor, Jennifer Enderlin, who waited patiently, gave advice when asked, and then waited patiently some more. I am so grateful for the extra time and your support. Thanks to Jill Marie Landis and Jill Barnett, who encouraged me when I needed it most; to Ann Patty, who taught me to trust myself; to Andrea Cirillo and Megan Chance, who are always there for me; and to Kim Fisk, who believed in this story and the Alaskan setting from the get-go and was never afraid to say so.

Thanks to Tucker, Sara, Kaylee, and Braden. You have expanded the boundaries of love for me and given me a new world in the middle of my life.

And finally, to my husband of thirty years, Benjamin. We have been partners in this writing thing from the beginning, and none of it would be possible without your love and support. Falling in love with you was the best thing I ever did.